PRAISE F
SHADOWS IN T

From Kim Stanley Robinson, New York Times bestselling author:

"Jack Dann returns to the Italian Renaissance, a very fertile story zone for him, to weave an absorbing novel that presents historical elements of the Renaissance as aspects of an immense cosmic battle of spirits. Somewhat like Susanna Clarke's *Jonathan Strange and Mr. Norrell's* treatment of the English Regency period as being a space filled with spirits, Dann's *Shadows In the Stone* creates such a complete world that Italian history no longer seems comprehensible without his cosmic battle of spiritual entities behind and within every historical actor and event.

"This then serves to suggest that Dann's complex network of spiritual entities are also allegories for the various urges and forces that have driven humanity throughout its history, inspiring us to do what we've done. That aspect of his novel creates a kind of X-ray vision through to the underlying realities of human experience which is quite exhilarating, and all this in a novel with all the more usual pleasures of sharply observed place and character and plot.

"*Shadows in the Stone* joins Dann's *The Memory Cathedral*, *The Rebel*, and *Promised Land*, as one of his deep plunges into historical characters we thought we knew, but whose true natures have never before been seen so clearly and dramatically. It's an amazing gift Jack has."

From Chelsea Quinn Yarbro, Bram Stoker Grandmaster and World Fantasy Lifetime Achievement Award-winning author:

"Jack Dann has gone beyond alternate world to alternate universe in this stunning take on the Renaissance. His language is eloquent, his characters wholly engaging—this is a book to lose yourself in. You'll be the richer for it."

Jack Dann has written or edited over seventy-five books, including the international bestsellers *The Memory Cathedral*, *The Rebel*, *The Silent*, *Bad Medicine*, and *The Man Who Melted*. His work has been compared to Jorge Luis Borges, Roald Dahl, Lewis Carroll, Castaneda, Ray Bradbury, J. G. Ballard, Mark Twain, and Philip K. Dick. *Library Journal* called Dann "…a true poet who can create pictures with a few perfect words," *Best Sellers* said that "Jack Dann is a mind-warlock whose magicks will confound, disorient, shock, and delight," and bestselling author Morgan Llwelyn called his novel *The Memory Cathedral* "a book to cherish, a validation of the novelist's art and fully worthy of its extraordinary subject. I can only say Bravo!"

Jack is a recipient of the Nebula Award, the World Fantasy Award (twice), the Australian Aurealis Award (three times), the Chronos Award, the Darrell Award for Best Mid-South Novel, the Ditmar Award (five times), the Peter McNamara Achievement Award and also the Peter McNamara Convenors' Award for Excellence, the Shirley Jackson Award, and the *Premios Gilgames de Narrativa Fantastica* award. He has also been honored by the Mark Twain Society (Esteemed Knight). He is the co-editor, with Janeen Webb, of *Dreaming Down-Under*, which won the World Fantasy Award, and the editor of the sequel *Dreaming Again*. He is the managing director of PS Australia, and his latest anthology *Dreaming in the Dark* is the first volume in the new line: it won the World Fantasy Award in 2017. Dr. Dann is also an Adjunct Senior Research Fellow in the School of Communication and Arts at the University of Queensland.

Jack lives in Australia on a farm overlooking the sea. You can visit his website at www.jackdann.com and follow him on Twitter @jackmdann.

A FANTASY MASTERS
TITLE BY
IFWG PUBLISHING

SHADOWS IN THE STONE

THE STONE

A Book of Transformations

by
JACK DANN

Shadows in the Stone

All Rights Reserved

ISBN-13: 978-1-925956-25-2

Printed in Times and ITC Isadora Std font types

All images sourced from the British Library, released to the Public Domain (The Paradise Lost of Milton, with illustrations designed and engraved by John Martin, 1827)

IFWG Publishing International
Melbourne

www.ifwgpublishing.com

ACKNOWLEDGEMENT

The author would like to thank the following people for their support, aid, and inspiration:

Kevin Anslow, Jenny Blackford, Leigh Blackmore, Paul Brandon, Sarah Calderwood, Lorne Dann, Gardner Dozois, Peter and Nicky Crowther, Andrew Enstice, Keith Ferrell, Linda Funnell, Rob Gerrand, Stuart Glover, Richard Harland (angelologist par excellence!), Gerry Huntman (my perspicacious publisher), Merrilee Heifetz, Van Ikin, Charles and Betty Ann Kochis, Joe Lindsley, Patsy LoBrutto and Mary Greene (who know why), Barry N. Malzberg, Helen Marshall, David McDonald, Steve Paulsen, Gillian Polock, Pamela Sargent, Mark Shirrefs, Stephanie Smith (professional muse!), Jonathan Strahan, Angela Tuohy, Kim Wilkins, George Zebrowski, and, as always, my partner Janeen...for love, constancy, and patience that continues to astonish.

For Caren Bohrman and Lulu—Lucius Shepard.

Rest in peace, my dear pals.

Know this, you who would cling to the Truth and avert annihilation. Remember this, Children of Light, for it is your sole ember of hope:

Remember that the incarnation and embodiment of both fire and light is the two-winged angel Gabriel. Know that he is the First of the seraphs.

Know that his place is beside the diamond throne of the Invisible One, the True God. Remember that his element and substance is sapphire, which is his seal, key, and sigil.

Remember that he burns with the fire of charity and is brother and sister to the serpent and the lion. Know that even now he searches for those saviors who will be his companions in the coming struggle with darkness...the final struggle against the demiurge you call Jehovah.

Know that he may select you [repeated for emphasis] to receive the serpent... [Remember that he may select you] to receive his sapphire seal, key, and sigil, which will burn and blister your flesh.

Know also that his miraculous gifts accompany the companion's stigmata

Remember that even you may become one of the Powers... [one] of the shadows in the stone.

—*charred fragment translated from the Ethiopic; thought to be a lost scroll from The Gospel of the Damned*

CONTENTS

ANGELS, DEMONS, AND PEOPLE IN THE STORY

Adversary:
See Satan.

Aeons:
High order angels...extensions of the highest source of being. Upper aeons are emanations or creations of the true creator known as the Invisible Spirit. Lower aeons are emanations or creations of the demiurge Yaldabaoth (also known as Jehovah), who is himself a lower aeon.

Giambattista Ammirato:
Scion of a powerful Venetian merchant and shipping dynasty, and a senior officer on the papal airship *Ascensione*.

Vincenzo Antellesi:
A Dominican soldier-priest.

Athoth:
A powerful lower aeon who can assume other identities. He is also known as the Whirlwind and the Reaper, and some scriptures represent him (mistakenly) as the dark aeon Belias.

Azâzêl:
A fire demon.

Agnolo Baldassare:
A high-ranking and secretive Dominican soldier-priest and Pico Della Mirandola's skryer and protector.

Belias:
The angel Gabriel's dark twin known as the dark aeon. Favorite of the demiurge and the most powerful of his aeons. Sometimes referred to as the Destroyer, Punisher, Betrayer, or Swallower of Souls, he rules

the aetheric darkness and brings destruction at the behest of the demiurge. Believers often mistakenly confuse him with the rebellious aeon Satan whom he, Belias, holds captive in his realm of ice and darkness.

Lucian ben-Hananiah: A servant and apprentice in the household of Pico Della Mirandola

Hananiah ben-Yohanan: *Maskil* (leader) of the *Khirbet Qumran* community in Palestine and father of Lucian ben-Hananiah.

Achille Bentivogli: Dwarf and house-carl to Guidobaldo di Montefeltro, the ducal ruler of the city-state of Urbino.

Cesare Valentinus Borgia: *Condottiere* known as Valentine or Valentino. He is the bastard son of Pope Alexander VI and his titles include Duke of Valentinois and Cardinal of Valencia.

Roderigo Borgia: Alexander VI, pope of Venice and father of Cesare Valentinus Borgia

Paolo Caraffa: Cardinal and commander of the hated and feared Dominican Companions of the Night.

Domenico Casola: Mendicant priest and agent for the prioress of Santa Sophia dei Miracoli.

Jack Day: See Gian Dei.

Gian Dei: Also known as John (or Jack) Day, infamous sorcerer and alchemist and former advisor to the Angevin king, Richard III. Sentenced to death for treason, apostasy, and practicing demonology, he fled his native land and was granted the protection of Pope Alexander VI.

Demiurge: Foremost of the lower aeons and creator of Heaven and Earth. Mistakenly believed by Christians to be the Supreme Being. See Yaldabaoth.

Arcangela Dolabella: Prioress of the convent of San Zaccaria.

Lawrence Dunean:	An aeronaut and commissioned officer in the Army of the Confederate States of America.
Bartolomeo Falce:	Grand Master inquisitor of the Knights Templar of the Crimson Cross. He is more than he appears to be.
Gabriel:	Upper aeon and archangel of the supreme being, the great Invisible Spirit whose name cannot be named; also known as the angel of mercy, vengeance, death, and revelation.
Antonio Gianmaria:	Soldier priest and one of Agnolo Baldassare's most trusted guards.
Invisible Spirit:	The True Creator, the First Principle…as opposed to the Demiurge Yaldabaoth, who is a lesser being: the lower aeon known as Yaldabaoth (and Jehovah).
Allesandra Lorenzetti:	Prioress of the convent Santa Sophia dei Miracoli.
Guiliano de Medici:	First citizen and ruler of Florence; also known as Guiliano Magnifico.
Pico Della Mirandola:	Famous and well-connected Florentine theurgist, physician, and scholar.
Guidobaldo da Montefeltre:	Ducal ruler-king of the Duchy of Urbino.
Elisabetta da Montefeltre:	Duchess of Urbino, wife and consort to Guidobaldo.
Louisa Mary Morgan:	A sixteen year old incarnation of Sophia: the snake goddess and mother of the demiurge Yaldabaoth. See Sophia.
Pietro Neroni:	Pico Della Mirandola's first apprentice, also known as Remembrancer.
Lucca Parenti:	One of Agnolo Baldassare's field lieutenants.
Jacopo di Pecori:	Agnolo Baldassare's second-in-command, a veteran soldier, and aristocrat.
Gentile della Penna:	A Dominican priest.
Marin Priuli:	Theurgist, physician, and skryer to the prioress Allesandra Lorenzetti.

Maria Theresa da Rieti:	Young nun and agent for the prioress of Santa Sophia dei Miracoli.
Isabella Sabatini:	Cousin and ward of Pico Della Mirandola.
Francesco Salviati:	Archbishop of Florence and a magus.
Matteo Sassetta:	One of Jacopo di Pecori's field lieutenants.
Satan:	A lower aeon who seduced others to rebel against the demiurge. Also known as the Adversary, Mastema, and Lucifer. Sometimes confused with the lower aeon Belias, who holds him and his fallen angels in captivity.
Gentile Serafino:	Captain of the papal airship *Ascensione*.
Sophia:	An upper aeon of the highest celestial rank. The most beloved luminary of the Invisible Spirit. Known as Queen of the Angels. But she tried to bring forth a luminary in the image of herself without the approval of the Invisible Spirit and gave birth to an imperfect creature: the demiurge.
Rudolfo Tagliare:	Personal eunuch guard to Gentile Serafino.
Yaldabaoth:	Conceived in shame by the upper Aeon Sophia, Yaldabaoth is the source and creator of all the lower aeons and (lower) angels. He is considered by Christians and the Church to be the Supreme Being and is known by many names including Yahweh and Jehovah. He is known to the Gnostics as the Demiurge. (See Aeons)

EXORDIUM

Before the Cataclysm

'Trismegistus, who will the angel Gabriel choose to be his companions?'

'The angel selects many companions to do God's will, Rheginus.'

'Listen to me, Trismegistus. I mean who will he choose to walk beside him in the final struggle against the demiurge and his aeons?'

'Ah, Rheginus, that is different, for then he must choose dark companions to protect the one who will return from eternity to struggle with the demiurge.'

'Trismegistus, is the one who will return known as the daughter of light?'

'Yes, Rheginus.'

'But why, Trismegistus, do you refer to these companions who are to protect the daughter of light as dark?'

'Because of the great darkness that will engulf and violate them.'

—Excerpt from the Preliminary Discourse 22,17-11

ONE

Basilisk

As we have two eyes and two ears, so we have two minds:
one to see and hear that which is born of the world, and
one to see and hear the gods themselves.

—*The Partite Vision of Julian 45.15*

And Sophia, an aeon called the Wisdom of Insight, named
her terrible offspring Yaldabaoth, the demiurge known to
you as Jehovah.

—*The Apocryphon of John 9.25*

Yesterday, when Lucian ben Hananiah had climbed the sheer precipice that
overlooked the yellow, sulfurous expanse of the Dead Sea, he was a boy
of twelve. Today he was a man who had reached his majority. Today he was
allowed the singular privilege of praying and studying inside the innermost
sanctuary of *Merh Fl'awr*, the Cave of Light, the highest and most sacred
repository in all the fortified settlement of *Khirbet Qumran*. But as he sat
before a natural outcrop that had been used for centuries as a reading plinth, his
back against a wall of smooth, worn stone, he did not feel the joy of privilege.
He felt trapped, alone, and humiliated, for other boys were not allowed to take
the oath of the Covenant until they had reached their eighteenth year and were
considered learned enough in the *Book of Meditation* to be recognized by the
Council and the twelve priests as a 'son of light'. And only the *maskil* and his
chosen priests were allowed to enter the Cave of Light.

However, other boys weren't the firstborn son of Hananiah ben-Yohanan
the Zadokite, the hereditary leader of the community. Other boys couldn't
trace their lineage back to God's chosen *maskil*: the first master and guardian

of the sacred scrolls. Other boys had to *earn* the privileges of entering the Covenant.

Lucian had felt the force of their hatred and disdain—and the hatred and disdain of their white robed fathers as they accompanied him to the foot of the cliff face; and even after his father and the twelve priests blessed him, even after his father blessed and thanked the standing congregation—none of them remained to watch the newest member of the Covenant navigate the dangerously stepped handholds and footholds called the stairs. Only his father remained to guard, fast, and pray on the heat-shimmering stones and marl below.

Lucian gazed out at the dusty light of the cave's narrow twilight zone, shook his head as if to clear it of unworthy thoughts, and then looked back down at the copper scroll before him. It shone like burnished gold in the flickering light of the oil lamps. His father called it the golden scroll and swore Lucian to secrecy before speaking of it in tones of awe. Older than the mountains, as old as the moon, it was God's terrible and puzzling warning to the chosen. No one else in the community, not even the twelve priests, knew of its existence or whereabouts. But the future *maskil* needed to know; and now, until the waxen moon rose full above the cliffs and crown of the settlement, Lucian would have the priceless artifact to himself.

The scroll was pitted, creased, and wrinkled. A section at the end had been cut or torn away, and some of the ancient proto-Hebrew script was impossible to read: words and entire lines looked like they had been scratched or pounded out. He touched the indented script and filled in the missing or indecipherable words as best he could:

> *Listen to me now, sweet, vulnerable children of light, listen to me, you who are worthy but will not see until the shadows of the tree of death are upon you. Until its twisted vines are already emptying your souls into the darkness. Yea, even as they devour the aeons and angels sent by the Lord of Hosts to protect and nourish you.*

He memorized as he read, as he would be expected to discuss the scroll in detail with his father, for it was unlikely that he would be allowed to return to this place until he reached his physical majority in another seven years.

> *The demiurge who is the shadow of a shadow that your fathers and mothers and brothers and sisters mistakenly worship and offer sacrifice to as the true Lord of Hosts awakens with intention. He will make certain that the aeons he created with his own seed are not disturbed or*

turned by the creatures of light. And his faithful servant
Belias who rules the darkness will make certain that his
intention is their intention.

Blasphemy, he thought. But, no, that could not be. It *must* be God's truth or
his father—and all the *maskils* who guarded and kept the scroll secret before
him—would not revere it so. He continued reading; but try as he might, he
could not make out the words that were partially scratched away.

And what is the intention of the demiurge, the one I will
call Yaldabaoth, vulnerable children? It is to end the age
of life, destroy your souls and mine, and humiliate and
destroy the True Father of us all in His heaven above all
aeons and thrones. It is written that such calamity shall
come to pass unless you can find the last maskil and
possess the

And there the scroll ended.
Feeling perplexed—and somehow soiled—he searched for answers:
Possess what?
And who is to end the age of life?
The Lord of Hosts?
No, the Lord God in Heaven, Holy be His Name, could not be the Adversary.
Satan is the Adversary.
But Father will know, he consoled himself. *Father always knows.*

The cave's depths seemed to be closing in on him, as if the dusty darkness
had weight. He felt the need for light and air, for the bright sunlight that baked
even the sea to salt and the air that was as soft as hair. As Lucian began to
pull himself away from the scroll—it was a tight squeeze between the plinth
and sitting stone: there were no fat scholars in *Khirbet Qumran*—he heard a
rasping noise that sounded like wind blowing. But it was not the wind. As he
leaped away from the sound, he felt something strike his bare foot; then felt a
searing, burning pain like the touch of red hot iron. And he saw a rock snake
side-slip across the floor, its smooth scales glittering like cut sapphires in
the flickering lamplight. Its rasping coils sounded like wind pushing through
stone chimneys.

fh-fh-fhh-fff fh-fh-fhh-fff fh-fh-fhh-fff.

Fh: the Egyptian name for viper.

It slowly side-slipped back and forth toward Lucian as if it were now
stalking him, or herding him. Lucian backed away and would have cried out
in terror, but for the burning numbness that struck him like icy-sharp shards

11

of hail. Then the snake dartled into a fissure in the cave wall a handbreadth's away from him. But the wall was smooth, rippled stone. There was no fissure. The snake had just…disappeared.

Lucian felt dizzy, lightheaded. He shook his head to clear it.

It's the venom, the poison.

Then turned to stagger toward the mouth of the cave. But venom was coursing through his arteries like Greek fire. Both legs were burning. Both legs were numb. Soon they would be useless.

If I can just get far enough to call down to Father keeping vigil below. If I can just…

His labored breathing sounded like the rasping coils of the sapphire snake. His vision blurred; and as he fell he heard the droughty, fricative *fh-fh-fhh-fff.* But it was not the hollow sound of his own breathing echoing in his ears. He turned his head toward the rasping…and saw an angel hovering before him.

It was bathed in pure white light, and its great feathered wings were partly furled, as the cave walls were too narrow to contain them. The beautiful apparition seemed to shift in and out of sight.

Lucian took a deep, dying breath.

fh-fh-fhh-fff fh-fh-fhh-fff fh-fh-fhh-fff.

And the sweet uplifting scent of cinnamon perfumed the air.

"**A**m I dead?" Lucian asked the angel, blinking.

The angel smiled at the skinny, gangly, and frightened thirteen-year old and settled to the ground. He wore purple robes and a white circlet around his head. His features were sharp as etched glass. Handsome and beautiful he was, heroically masculine, yet gracefully feminine…he was translucent as vapor, and as substantial as the cave itself.

"No, young maskil, *you will not die this day. Today is a day of learning and forgetting. Your tomorrows will be for remembering."*

"The snake that bit me—?"

"Yes?"

"Is it…real?"

"Do you still feel the pain of its bite?"

"Yes," Lucian said. He propped himself against the cave wall and looked at his leg, which was red and swollen.

"But you mean to ask if I *am real or a vision, a phantasm."*

"Yes," Lucian said again. His head seemed to clear, the pain suddenly abated, and he felt comforted by the soft brume of warmth and light that radiated from the angel. "Who are you, and why have you come to me here… and now? And…"

"What else would you have?"

Lucian felt the angel's laughter, although he could not hear it. "If you are an angel, as you seem to appear, can you not draw away the poison that sickens me?"

"A poultice of physalis somnifera *and onion would serve as well."*

"But as you can see, angel," he said impatiently, "I don't have such a poultice."

"Would you speak in such a manner to your father?"

Searing, pulsing pain and dizziness returned.

Lucian groaned and said, "No, I would not. Please forgive me, Holy One."

Now Lucian felt the angel's amusement.

"You may call me Gabriel, and I am both real and a phantasm. Like the snake that bit you. But even when you forget, as you surely will, you must try to remember that although both the snake and the vine will seek you out, only the snake will sustain you."

"But how can I both remember and forget?"

"Your heart will remember, and your heart is yoked to your soul."

"Why must I forget?"

"So that you may grow into your great soul and discover how to fulfill your destiny."

"Can you not just tell me…or show me?"

The angel laughed, a swirling lightness of cinnamon and joy, and said, *"I could easier teach you to fly. And if I did—if I could and would—you would become as loathsome as the twisting shadows that seek you out."*

"What shadows? What you said before: the vines? Or the snake? Why would such things seek *me* out?"

"The snakes are my own. The vines are the creatures of another: they belong to Belias, the dark aeon described in the scripture your father sent you here to study. Belias is bound to Yaldabaoth, the demiurge you call Jehovah. It is he who created you and all your kind. And now he is ready to destroy all creation, all that has been, is, and will be."

"But why would the Lord of Hosts wish to—?"

"The demiurge is not *the Lord of Hosts…any more than I am. He is an aeon, who was created by the Lord's most beloved aeon Sophia, Queen of Angels."*

Lucian could feel the angel's controlled wrath; and for an instant his chest froze, and he couldn't breathe. Then, with a gasp, he inhaled the cloying smell of cinnamon sweetness and tasted the tongue-searing bitterness of ash.

"Sophia wanted to bring forth another luminary like herself," Gabriel

continued, *"but she did so without the consent of her creator; and her miscreant desire produced an imperfect, misshapen thing. When she tried to hide her shame from the Lord of Hosts, the demiurge overwhelmed her, stole her power, and created his own realm of aeons and authorities and seraphim. In his arrogance, the demiurge exults himself over all. He cannot admit to being consequent, to being other than the One. And his intention, young maskil, is to destroy the Lord of Hosts."*

Lucian was still shivering; whether from abyssal fear or the snake's flesh-swelling poison, he could not know.

"Now you understand the warning of the scroll," the angel said, reading him like writing on parchment. His voice was soft and lyrical, a tangible manifestation of a profound, sympathetic sadness. *"If the demiurge is to prevail, he must destroy everything, including himself and his minions. His very success depends upon his own annihilation."*

"But how can he become the One if he destroys the world and the heavens and himself? And surely no one—or no thing—can prevail over the Lord of Hosts."

"By possessing and destroying every single soul, he denies—and destroys— the Lord of Hosts. And all that would remain is—"

"Himself," Lucian said, overwhelmed by the angel's radiating grief.

"Yes, child, for one eternal instant the demiurge would become the One, the only one."

Lucian shook his head, as if he could deny by force of will what the angel had just told him. The angel gentled the boy's hair, soothing him as if he was a startled animal and then said softly, *"Even now one of Yaldabaoth's servants approaches...even now you are in danger."*

"But why? I am nothing, I—"

"He seeks you because of what I will give you...and because of what you have the potential to become."

"And what would that be?"

"Perhaps the last maskil," the angel said, looking sadly at the boy.

TWO

The Hanging

That Judas perished by hanging, there is no certainty in
Scripture...

—Thomas Browne, *Religio Medici*

"If the Lord of Hosts awakens his angels to destroy us, what can *I* do?"
he asked the angel. "You should be speaking to my father, not to me. He
knows...he knows..."

"I'm right here, Lucian."

Lucian stared hard at the angel, whose robes were no longer purple, but
were striped black and white linen. "Father...?" he asked earnestly, grasping
his father's linen sleeve in recognition and twisting his hand inside the fold as
he did when he was a child. "I'm very glad to see you. But why did you come
to find me? Is everything all right?"

His father nodded, touching Lucian's forehead gently with his free hand.

"When you did not come down from the cave at sunset, I became worried.
I found you in high fever and dared not move you until you awakened. It will
soon be light...and thanks be to God who delivers us from all distress, your
fever has broken."

Lucian shivered and looked around the cave. The oil lamp on the opposite
wall was guttering, and there was no twilight zone around the cave opening.
"Did you find the snake?"

His father looked at him quizzically.

"The snake that bit me."

"No snake has ever been found up here," his father said. His eyes looked
deep and shadowed in the flickering lamplight. "I fear that my rashness
has made you ill. I have asked too much of you too soon, worked you to
exhaustion, but—"

Lucian examined his leg, but could find no swelling or puncture marks. There had been no need of a poultice. There had been no snake. No angel. Just fevered imaginings brought on by a sudden ague. Relieved, he drank deeply from the water skin his father proffered. He wiped his mouth, which felt cottony and swollen, and asked, "But what, Father?"

"You have accomplished the tasks I set before you, and you have made me proud," the older man said softly. He stared into the cave entrance, stared at the halo of dawn's first light as if he were trying to see through time itself. "Did you commit the words of the Golden Scroll to memory?"

"Yes, Father."

"Every one of them? Even the excision marks?"

"Yes, Father. Do you wish to test me?"

He turned to Lucian and embraced him. "No, my son. You have already been burned deeply enough by God's words. Your fever was proof enough." His father still held him close.

"Are you cold, Father?"

The *maskil* released his son and said, "No, I am perfectly fine."

"But you're trembling."

His father smiled indulgently. "I am old. Old men tremble. Now ask me the questions that must be still burning inside you, and then we will climb down the stairs together. Surely you must be hungry, and I promise not to exhaust you with study again. Your mother will take a long time forgiving me."

"Does she know why you readied me to take the oath and enter the sanctuary?"

"She knows that you are the future *maskil*."

"You are the *maskil*, father. My time is many years away."

His father looked at him, touched his forehead again, and nodded.

"But you are worried that something bad is going to happen, aren't you?" He leaned closer to his father. "That something will happen to you."

"I just need you to be ready. If you read the tablet with understanding, you know that the age of life might come to an end at any moment."

Lucian nodded.

"Are you strong enough to climb down the stairs?" his father asked, meaning the footholds and handholds that were cut into the cliff face.

"Yes, father, I will try."

"Try? No, you rest here. I will—"

The piercing trills of distant rams' horns echoed across the Dead Sea, which magnified sound like a crystal focusing heat.

"Father...?"

Lucian's father sighed and said, "They have found their way to us sooner than I expected."

"Who, Father?"

"The Christian Knights of the Temple. Their grand master inquisitor leads them. They've made no secret that they seek our scrolls." He smiled ruefully. "To protect them, of course, as they do all holy relics."

"We must not let them—"

"No, we must welcome them, as we would any other honored guest." Lucian's father caressed his son's hand. "We might succeed with brigands, but our swords and numbers are no match for these sons of Cain." He tapped his forehead and his chest, indicating wisdom and guile, and said, "But we are not entirely without resources." Then he stood up and adjusted his robes for climbing. "Now I must go down and oversee what must be done. Are you strong enough to climb?"

"Yes, Father, but what can we do?"

"We will do what we have always done: We will pay Caesar his tribute… but we will give him brass instead of silver." He nodded, as if trying to convince himself. "You will see, my son, I promise, you will see."

Hidden atop an ancient *birkeh* tower that was no longer used for smelting, Lucian watched the company of armored, black-tunicked riders approach the main gate of the settlement on their sweat-steaming warhorses. Then he flicked his gaze down to the delegation of elders and priests waiting to greet the Christian knights in the cooling shade of the stately palm trees that lined the public *mikveh*. The immersion pool was fed by an aqueduct that was as old as the settlement's square watchtowers and tumbledown fortification walls… and by God's own miracle, it magnified sounds toward the heavens. His father, dressed in his finest white, turned away from the priests and his fellow elders and looked up in Lucian's direction. Only for in instant, and then he stepped ahead of the others to greet the Grand Master *inquisitore*, who alone wore a white surcoat emblazoned with a crimson cross. The inquisitor dismounted and then signaled his guard of brown-mantled knights to do the same. The rest of the soldiers—hard-faced lancers, alert and a hundred strong—remained in saddle. He bowed to Lucian's father who said, "*Salam*. May peace be upon you and all those in your favor."

Lucian could hear his father's voice clearly, and he could make out the features of the inquisitor who had soft, kindly eyes and an aquiline nose that did not seem to be in harmony with his full, generous mouth and slight double chin.

"Please, refresh yourself," Lucian's father said, gesturing toward the immersion pool and long tables covered in linen and set with earthenware bowls, cups, and plates. Slaves appeared, bustling back and forth from nearby pantries and kitchens with pitchers of sour milk, loaves of freshly baked bread, terrines of soup, platters of meat and wild greens, pitchers of wine and green olive oil, dipping dishes, and pomegranates, olives, dates, honeycombs, grapes, cucumbers, and cakes of pressed figs. One of the slaves was Lucian's childhood playmate and only friend: dark-skinned Orpha, the daughter of Jerobaal who removed ash from the ovens. She was two years older than Lucian and already a woman.

The inquisitor washed his hands and face perfunctorily in the pool, then after handing back the towel proffered by young Orpha, he politely took a date and said, "My officers and I eat what the Lord provides. Thank you, but we are sufficient." The men in saddle did not even look at the pool or the food; but for the horses that had to be kept under tight rein, these soldiers of the cross might have been sculpted out of stone.

Lucian's father nodded and said, "Then how may we be of service to the Knights of the Temple?"

His father's back was turned to the *birkeh*, so Lucian could not see his face; but he could see the inquisitor smile indulgently.

"You very well know what we've come for, *maskil*. Although we've not met before, I know you well. My...predecessor told me that he had visited you some time ago. In vain."

"I hardly think it was in vain," said Josephus, the high priest. He was a tall, imposing man, his hair black as a youth's; only his beard was flecked with gray. "Your crossed knights pillaged our sacred scrolls and—"

Lucian's father stepped forward, cutting off the impetuous high priest; and the inquisitor smiled and said, "I do not expect to impose on the generosity of your community for very long, *maskil*." He smiled again and bowed: one man of knowledge and power addressing another. "I am Bartolomeo Falce... Bartolomeo. And you are Hananiah ben-Yohanan."

Lucian's father bowed, but said nothing.

"We are all sons of Abraham," continued the inquisitor.

"No, *we* are not," said the high priest, shouldering past the *maskil*. "*You* are the seed of—"

Without hesitation, the inquisitor snapped a blade out of his sleeve and slit the high priest's throat. In a trice his guards were all around him, swords unsheathed, and leveled at the priests and elders. A few of the slaves and servants tending the tables and the pool panicked and ran off; but the rest kept to their places, their heads bowed.

Lucian watched in shock as his father and one of the elders caught the dying priest and gently laid him to rest on the ground. Although he was terrified for his father at the hands of this executioner with the kindly face; there was nothing he could do, except obey his father's orders to remain hidden on the tower roof.

This certainly wasn't what Father had in mind. This—

After Lucian's father blessed the dead priest and stood up, the inquisitor continued as if nothing had happened. "As I was saying, Hananiah ben-Yohanan, we are *all* sons of Abraham. We both wish to protect God's word and holy relics. We both seek the knowledge hidden in the sacred scrolls. You and your community have born the burden of caring for God's words"—with that he nodded to the other priests and elders, who stood stock-still in fear—"and for that we honor you."

"By killing our leader?" Lucian's father asked.

"*You* are their leader," the inquisitor said, "and I seek but two sacred artifacts. Return what belongs by divine right to the church, good *maskil* Hananiah, and we will leave your community in peace forever more. On that you have my word."

None of the other priests or elders responded.

"You have little to lose, and everything to gain," he continued. "Surely you have memorized the contents of at least one of the relics we seek."

"What artifacts might that be?" asked Lucian's father.

"The golden scroll, as you call it, and…the sapphire tablet." The inquisitor looked at the maskil benevolently.

"I am not aware of these artifacts," Lucian's father said.

What is the sapphire tablet?" Lucian wondered as he watched from behind the rubble on the roof. *Father never mentioned it.*

"I don't believe you," said the inquisitor. "But I can see you are a man of honor and would not carelessly reveal what you know…even if I executed every one of these holy and learned men who stand beside you. Is that not so?"

The *maskil* was silent.

The inquisitor looked past the maskil as if he were surveying the brick and stone buildings and the cliffs beyond. Lucian felt something wet and cold spray inside his chest: for an instant, he felt that the inquisitor was looking directly at *him*.

"My spies tell me that you have sent your women, children, and most of your able-bodied men away."

"Your spies?" asked the *maskil*.

"Oh, don't be so surprised, *maskil* Hananiah. We all must do what we can to gain knowledge and power, is that not so?"

The maskil said something, but in a voice so low that Lucian could not hear it.

"Sending the flower of your community away was a wise strategy," the inquisitor continued. He gazed at the priests and then nodded approvingly to the *maskil*. "And I see that your most learned mnemonists are not here to greet us—I must congratulate you: you've certainly done your best to ensure that your community and its precious knowledge survive. But I, too, have prepared, *maskil* Hananiah. Turn around and look there."

The inquisitor pointed to the *birkeh* tower...

"Look up at the roof."

L ucian heard soft rustling behind him, but too late. Before he could even turn, he was overpowered by three men wearing the rough, white bleached robes of the sectaries. Lucian struggled as they tied and gagged him. He heard his father's scream, followed by the inquisitor's modulated voice: "Hiding that which you love in open sight. Another good strategy. However, a better strategy would have been to expunge those who are dissatisfied with your society..."

As the men carried him down the cracked and crumbling inside stairwell— they seemed to be familiar with every crevasse and loose stone—all outside sounds became muted. There was only the guttural rasp of breath, the rustle of fabric, the plash of leather on gravel...and later, after all the horrors of the day were past, he would still smell the thickening stink of their sweat.

T he inquisitor's lancers had insinuated themselves into the town and the surrounding arid countryside. They gathered the wives and children of the sectaries of importance—the elders, intermediates, priests, councilors, judges, and scholars—and marched them to a plain that overlooked *Reĉhes Shell N'eshah*.

The Ridge of Punishment.

There, up close, on high, and under close guard, they could watch the proceedings.

"You must not do this," Lucian begged the inquisitor. He strained against the two burly guards who held him fast. They were deep in a glen at the bottom of *Reĉhes Shell N'eshah*. No vegetation grew here, not even scrub. Above were cracked towers of stone and broken mountains of yellow marl. Beside him, cowed and ashen-faced, stood the community's elders and priests...blades at their throats. A few yards away from him were his mother and father. They stood upon makeshift platforms beneath a stone overhang. Their hands were tied behind their backs, and rough-fibered ropes pulled tightly around their necks: the inquisitor's knights had used the stone outcrop above as a gibbet.

"Look away from us, Lucian," his father said. "You must not—"

The inquisitor turned away from Lucian, frowned at the *maskil*, and then slapped Lucian's mother hard in the face. "Silence, *maskil* Hananiah, or I will give her—and your son—to pleasure my men." Then he turned back to Lucian and said, "You are soft enough to be a woman, are you not?"

Lucian's mother groaned.

With a nod from the inquisitor, one of the knights stepped onto the platform, ripped apart her linen gown, slapped her stomach, and squeezed her breast. Exposed and humiliated, she bit her lip so hard that blood dribbled down her chin. But she did not scream.

"Well, young *maskil*-to-be," said the inquisitor, "tell me—"

It was Lucian who screamed; and in that red-limned instant of fear and wrath, in that instant of adrenal strength, he managed a wild kick at one of his captors, unintentionally breaking the guard's shin, and pulled himself away from the sweaty grip of the other astonished knight. As he leaped toward his mother, the inquisitor barked "*Goccia di lei!*"

Drop her!

Before Lucian could reach her, the guard who had torn his mother's dress stepped back and kicked the platform out from under her feet…and he heard his mother's neck snap heard his father scream heard groaning and shrieking from those watching from the plain above and he smelled feces and death and heard thunder inside his head and then he was back in the custody of the inquisitor's guards. He called out to his father, even as one of the guards was gagging the *maskil*. He could *see* the desperate warning in his eyes. As if the igneous rays of sight could be transformed into words.

Remember the covenant. Tell them nothing.

Then the inquisitor was upon him. His face was so close to his that he could taste his breath as if it were uncooked liver. Lucian tried to turn his head, tried to look toward his father, but the inquisitor held him close. His small, pudgy hands were like cold iron clamps clasping his face. His sad, brown eyes were like tunnels; and Lucian suddenly felt dizzy, as if he were falling, spinning into a pit.

"Tell me what I need to know now, or your father is next to drop. And then every single one of your priests and elders will hang."

Lucian heard one of the priests or elders gasp, but no one spoke.

"I have only reached majority," Lucian said, sobbing, unable to catch his breath, choking on the bitter bile of fear and hatred. "How…how would I know where the holiest of holies are kept?"

The inquisitor sighed and released Lucian. After gently patting the boy's face he said, "I will count to three, young maskil. Your rash actions have cost your mother her life. Now you must decide whether you will also murder your father."

"It is not I who—" Lucian caught himself. *Yes, it was my fault. Mother is dead because of me, because…*he wanted to look to his father, needed help from his father; but he couldn't raise his head. How could he look again in the direction of his mother? Not after what he did. How could he reveal the secrets the community promised to protect? Death and torture were far preferable to apostasy.

"One…

"Two…"

"I—I only know—"

One of the priest's beside him tried to speak, but was cut off with a gasp. Lucian dared not look, lest he falter and kill his father as he had his mother.

He intoned the Psalm of Forgiveness—

> *Blessed art Thou, oh Lord,*
> *Who pardons rebellion and unfaithfulness,*
> *Who forgives transgression and iniquity,*
> *Who casts away our sin and purifies our hearts*
> *That we may inherit the glory of Adam.*

—and then said, "I speak the truth to save my father. The golden scroll is…it is in the Cave of Light. But I know nothing about a tablet."

The priests beside him wailed and tore their tunics, then chanted the prayer for the dead, which was echoed by those standing on the plain that overlooked the Ridge of Punishment. "*Yis'gadal v'yis'kadash sh'mei raba…*"

But they were not praying for the soul of his mother…they were pronouncing *him*—Lucian—dead. Excluding him. Excising him. Humiliating him. He looked to his father, pleading, but the *maskil* turned away from his son.

"He will forgive you…in time," the inquisitor said; but Lucian knew that was a lie. "Now, young *maskil*, save your father and your people and tell me exactly where the scroll can be found in this cave of yours.

"I am not the *maskil*!" Lucian said angrily. "My father is the chosen one."

"Be that as it may, if you wish to save his life, you must tell me what I need to know."

Lucian gave him the exact location, and the inquisitor sent a contingent of his guards to retrieve it. When they returned with the scroll—and after he examined it carefully—the inquisitor said, "Very good, young *maskil*. Now… you only need to tell me where I can find the tablet that the angel gave you."

"How did you know about—?" Lucian recovered himself…too late.

"Tell me the name of the angel."

"I—"

Once again the inquisitor clasped Lucian's face in his hands. "Tell me!"

Lucian slurred the word "Gabriel."

The inquisitor released him. "Very good. Now tell me where you hid his gift. The tablet of living sapphire."

Lucian looked toward his father and said, "There was no gift. I don't know anything about a tablet. I swear." But his father gazed right through him: the *maskil*'s son was dead, no matter how many times he might draw breath. As Lucian turned back to the inquisitor to plead for his father, he heard thunder behind his temples and his eyes blurred with tears. "I've told you everything I know. Now please—"

The inquisitor lifted his arm, and before Lucian could even take a breath, he heard the scraping of the platform being kicked out from under his father's feet. Saw his father drop. Heard the cracking of bone, the twang of the rope. Smelled ordure. Screamed and kicked and...

Found himself standing on a platform in his father's place.

He remembered being struck by the inquisitor. His head ached; an angry, purple bruise had spread over the right side of his face. He was weak and nauseated. He could barely swallow, for the noose around his neck was tight. His hands were tied behind his back. His arms throbbed. He looked around wildly, trying to shake away the pain that blurred his vision; but the inquisitor and his men were gone, as were his father and mother and the priests and elders and all those who had been watching from the plain above. He tried to swallow, tried to breathe and felt hands around his neck adjusting the noose.

"I have been selected by the priests because I am...unclean," said a hairless slave whose upper lip was curled into a perpetual smile by a scar that extended to what had once been his right eye.

Lucian took a deep, wheezing breath.

Although he had never spoken to this slave, he knew he had been brought to the *Khirbet Qumran* community only last year. Lucian had once caught him embracing Jerobaal, the mother of his playmate Orpha, in the storage cave behind the ovens. But he never spoke of that with anyone, especially Orpha, lest they be stoned for fornicating.

"No one is allowed to look upon you, except for the new high priest and *maskil*," the slave continued.

"You must be born into the lineage," Lucian said, his voice thick. "You cannot be elected. It is not like the priesthood." He could hear himself speak, but it was as if he were somewhere else, somewhere far away, somewhere past the eternal darkness that surrounds the heavens, a small, secret place where time and event are not allowed.

"Well, the one who betrayed the community is now priest and maskil, and he watches. So I must get on with this."

"But who—?"

The slave adjusted the noose again.

"Do not shake so, young maskil," I have experience with this, for I was once a torturer. You will feel but an instant of pain; and when you awaken, you will see the fine grave I have dug for you." The torturer stood in front of Lucian, perhaps to hide him from the eyes of the new rabbi's spies, and pushed a bitter-tasting herb into his mouth. "Do not spit it out! It will ease your way."

Then the slave stepped off the platform and kicked it out from under Lucian's feet.

Lucian awakened from a drugged coma to the claustrophobic weight of earthen walls, the acrid smell of dirt and sweat and sulfur. He could see an angry, cloud-covered moonlit sky above him and feel a burning circlet around his neck. He tried to sit up. He grasped at the walls, which were friable; clots of dirt and sand dropped onto him. He tried to scream, but couldn't breathe. A hand covered his mouth. Another cradled his neck. He moaned in pain and tried to make out the slight but strong figure leaning over him.

"It's all right, Lucian," whispered a familiar voice from above—from the edge of the grave pit—"but we must be quiet, lest someone in the refectory hear us. You know how sound can travel. Now rest a moment, gain your bearings, and I will help you out of—"

"Uhfffrrhahh?" Lucian asked, his voice almost completely muffled.

"Yes, dear Lucian, it's me," Orpha said, releasing one hand from his mouth, but still cradling the back of his neck with the other.

"This...is *this* my grave? Are you, are you dead, too?"

The girl smiled. "No, you are not dead and neither am I." With her help, Lucian sat up. Chilled and suddenly overwhelmed with the horror of memory, he panicked.

"I have to get out of here, I—"

Orpha pulled him out of the shallow grave, and breathing heavily, as if sobbing, he lay on the cool, stony marl and thought of his mother. He called to her, as he did as a child, and then caught himself, embarrassed. Orpha held on to him, as if it were she who had suffered the loss. She stroked him and whispered to him in the baby-talk language they had used since they were children. He touched the linen bandage that was wrapped around his neck. He could feel the damp of blood still oozing. "Leave it be," Orpha said. "Mother said not to remove it for three days. She has soaked it in healing salves."

"Mother?"

"Yes, she sneaked away to tend you. She was a healer before…"

"You never said."

"She smiled sadly, her scarred face beautiful in the moonlight. "I am a slave, you are a—"

"I am nothing now." Lucian felt suddenly calm. It was over. Everything was over. He raised himself on his arm and gazed across the stony terrace with its rows of graves…a thousand graves. Graveyard's end was a deep cliff; and beyond that were more limestone cliffs, more crowns of stone and hidden caves, dry stream beds, and the ghostly expanse of the Dead Sea reflecting the silver of the moon. Behind him, blocking easy views from the settlement, were the remains of what had once been a fortified wall. The large stones were corpse white and shadowed in the moonlight.

"My father says—"

"Your father?" Lucian asked.

"Yes, my father, Lucian. Your mother and mine schemed to have him brought here, but they could not acknowledge that he was her husband and my father. That would not be allowed. It was my father who hanged you and saved your life. My father who brought you here. He dug these graves…"

Lucian saw seven graves neatly dug in a row, the excavated dirt piled beside them, ready to be shoveled over the corpses. Beside him was a grave, freshly filled and smoothed; but there were no stones piled atop the dirt.

"That grave," Orpha continued, motioning, "is empty. It's supposed to be yours. The other graves await your mother and father and the priests and elders killed by the Knights of Cain." She spat, then murmured a prayer. "They will all be buried according to ceremony."

"But I was to be buried as…an animal."

"No, Lucian, they have to bury you on hallowed ground. You are a *maskil*.

Lucian smiled cruelly. "Yes, the angel was right: the last *maskil*."

Orpha retrieved a sac she had secreted under two stones that might have been an ancient dolmen. "Clothes, water, and food, a few *dirhams* and—" she pulled out a curved knife—"this. It belonged to one of the traitors. If you can make it to Jerusalem and avoid slavers, you should be…you will be safe. But you must leave. Now."

Lucian took the gifts and asked, "What about you? Will you be safe?"

"I will stay outside until it is safe to return." Then she embraced Lucian and said, "I'm so sorry." Although he wanted to cry, he felt suddenly and embarrassingly excited. They had never embraced before, not like this. He tried to pull away, but she held him close. "My father believes that one day you will return. An angel told him that you would die and then live. He said you will be the last—and the first—*maskil*."

"An angel told him that?"

"That is what he dreamed," Orpha said, reluctantly releasing him. "I pray for your safety...and your return. And I—" Choking back whatever she wanted to say, she quickly turned away from him and hurried west through the graveyard.

Lucian wanted to call to her, but all he could do was watch her until she disappeared behind a still-standing section of a ruined fortification wall. Then he, too, turned and made his way into the moon-bleached desert: he would have plenty of time to think of angels, death, love, and betrayal over the next eight years of exile in Palestine, Alexandria, Constantinople, Milan, and... Florence.

PARTITION ONE

Soul Stealers

'Trismegistus, who is the favorite of the demiurge known as Jehovah?'

'It has always been Belias, the aeon of ice and darkness.'

'But Trismegistus, is he not also called the betrayer, the adversary? Is he not also known as Satan?'

'Rheginus, do you question your Catechism?'

'I swear to you, I do not. But many confuse Belias with the one they call Satan.'

Rheginus, listen to me. Of course, the ignorant confuse Belias with the one they call Satan.'

'Why, Trismegistus?'

'Because Belias is the one whom the demiurge dispatches to obstruct human activities and desires.'

—*Excerpt from the First Discourse 47,27-53.14*

'Tell me, Trismegistus. Is the one called Satan an angel or aeon in his own right?'

'I should not laugh at what you say, Rheginus. Yes, Satan is an aeon in his own right.'

'Is he, then, the demiurge's adversary?'

'Would you consider your conquered enemy an adversary, Rheginus?

'No, Trismegistus, not after I had taken his sword and shield.'

'And would you not then cast him down and castrate him so that he and his kind could not threaten you again?'

'Yes, of course, Trismegistus.'

'Just so, Rheginus, did the demiurge cast down Satan and give him to his favorite aeon Belias to be entombed in his dark, frozen wastes. So now there is only one adversary.'

'Who would that be?'

'The adversary of the Invisible One. The adversary of the True God.'

'Now I understand, Trismegistus. The adversary of the True God is the demiurge Jehovah.'

—*Excerpt from the First Discourse 48,12-53.14*

THREE

The Boy Who Could See Angels

There is here a great Globe of fire hanging in the top of the Stone; and in the Globe a man standing with a purple Robe like Christ, I cannot well perceive his face.

—Edward Kelley

Now twenty-one years old and house servant to the greatest magus in Florence, Lucian ben-Hananiah peered through the spy hole in the floor at the angels that appeared and disappeared in the roiling mist of the large crystal gazing-globe below.

His eyes burned from the solvents and chemicals that had been spilled in this room during his master's studies on the affinities of certain jewels with black bile and the melancholy humours. He kept very quiet, lest any shifting of weight cause the floorboards to creak and he be found out. He could see only part of his master's secret skrying room below: two ornately carved tables were scattered with alchemical flasks; ancient texts discolored and brittle; new leather-bound folios; polished wafers of sapphire, ruby, amethyst, and beryl; and hermetically sealed jars and round glasses of the precious miracle solvents *aurum potabile* and *spiritus mundi*. Between the tables, and directly below Lucian, stood his master Count Pico Della Mirandola. His skryer, the secretive Dominican soldier-priest Baldassare, was beside him. Although they both leaned toward the gazing-globe that was placed in the center of a huge black obsidian mirror supported by wax tablets, only Baldassare was able to see—and speak to—the angels.

Lucian's master might be the only magician ever to unlock the secrets of the Jews' Cabbala, catalogue the 4,086 supraterrestrial beings, and discover the single great secret of demons; but he had never seen or heard an angel.

Never seen or heard a demon.

And he could only talk to these ghosts of light and shadow through intermediaries such as Baldassare, who often claimed to see and hear angels that might—or might not—be present in the glass.

"What angels do you see?" Mirandola asked. The young magician and scholar was handsome and muscular, with pale skin, golden-flecked grey eyes, and long reddish-blond hair, which he habitually pulled away from his face. "Has purple-robed Gabriel appeared? He promised to construct the remembrancer and teach us how to master its powers. He promised to reveal the plague that will soon descend upon the earth. He—"

"All is in a cloud, as if there is a storm in the gazing globe," Baldassare said. "Wait. It clears. There, I can see Gabriel. He stands alone. No other angels accompany him. Even the surrounding air is clear of them. Now he spreads the air, or it opens before him. And there appears a square table..."

Lucian, lying above, gazed down at the globe through the peephole. He could see the archangel Gabriel dressed in a purple robe with a white circlet around his head; and he could see the angel and the table in correct position, as if he were looking directly at Gabriel rather than looking down upon the angel's head from above. Something turned uncomfortably in Lucian's mind, something important that he could not quite remember; and he had the strong uneasy feeling that it was somehow connected with his life in *Khirbet Qumran*...and with the angel shimmering in the globe below.

"The table has four feet," Baldassare continued, "of which two touch the ground and two do not. The table appears to be made of potter's clay, raw earth. I hear a great voice rumbling and thrumming in the globe. It hurts my ears..."

I don't hear anything, Lucian thought sourly, turning his thoughts away from what was probably a distant or perhaps nonexistent dream. *The priest is faking again.*

"Wait," Baldassare said, stepping backward with great show; then, nodding and genuflecting, he returned to his position before the globe. "The voice tells us not to move, for now this place is holy, and becomes holy. It is the voice of a power I cannot see, and it pains me to stand here. It tells me that there are three other angels with Gabriel, but I see only—"

"What...what do you see? Mirandola asked impatiently.

"It hurts me, I cannot stand here," Baldassare said, seemingly struggling; and then he staggered backward. This time he was not faking, for Lucian could see what Baldassare could not...he could see something quick and bright pass from Baldassare into the gazing globe. He imagined it was a shiny, silvery worm, covered in swirling wisps of something almost fleshy, something roiling and coiling back upon itself, trying to escape the confines of the globe and return to the priest. Baldassare slumped forward, and the flesh of his tonsured head looked grayish-white, lifeless.

"This is for *you* to see," the angel Gabriel said, but he was speaking to Lucian, not Baldassare. The angel looked translucent, and every feature appeared to be beautiful, perfect, without blemish; yet it seemed that the angel was forming himself—creating himself—as Lucian looked at him.

The angel raised both hands, which held a writhing sapphire-scaled snake. The snake coiled like a whip in Gabriel's left hand and extended itself towards the heaven that was now the convexity of the gazing globe. Then it opened its hinged jaws and swallowed the shiny, silvery worm. Gabriel did not need to tell Lucian that the worm was Baldassare's immortal soul; Lucian understood. The snake coiled and twisted, writhed and pulled to escape the angel's grasp. Gabriel held it for a few heartbeats; and then, with a snap of his wrist, threw the serpent upwards, directly at Lucian...who had a developed a terrible fear of snakes since he had escaped from *Khirbet Qumran.*

Lucian yelped and pushed himself away from the peephole; but the snake, which looked like a python with jeweled eyes and glittering, cyanic scales, was on the floor beside him. It raised itself, curving backward, as if it was going to strike...as if it was going to snap up Lucian's soul as it had Baldassare's.

Lucian backed away from the angel's abominable familiar, or whatever it was, and started for the door. But Gabriel—Gabriel, shining, translucent Gabriel—appeared in the room like a bright reflection in a mirror. The angel stood in front of the door, unfurled wings like sails, and blocked the boy's way. Lucian smelled a strangely familiar odor: cinnamon mixed with the sharp odor of air before a storm. "What do you want with me? Why are you here?"

The angel smiled; Lucian could feel the angel's moods like variations of temperature. "I was summoned," Gabriel said.

"Not by me."

"Ah, yes, especially by you, young Lucian...as well as by your master Mirandola and his skryer Brother Baldassare." Gabriel radiated a heat that softened Lucian's fear.

"Then you should be down there in the gazing globe."

"Who says I'm not," Gabriel said softly, a smile passing across his shifting face.

"Because *I'm* here, in this room."

"Yes, but *here* is not always where you think"; and with Gabriel's guidance, Lucian could suddenly see the room below as if he hadn't moved, as if he was still peering through the peephole in the floor. He saw the carved tables covered with their alchemical flasks and folios and incantatory jewels, his master Mirandola, the priest Baldassare (who had fallen to his knees, as if in prayer), the obsidian mirror, the gazing globe with its earthen table.

And yet Gabriel was still standing in front of the door before him.

"Are you going to return Baldassare's soul to him?" Gabriel asked.

"Me? I didn't take it...*you* did."

"Only to help you."

"Me...?"

"You really *must* stop referring to yourself, young master," Gabriel said, still warming him. "Yes, I took it as a lesson for you."

"Why?"

Ignoring his question, the angel said, "Return the soul now. It resides there in the rod. Pick it up."

"It moves...it's a snake."

"And you still fear snakes, don't you? But it is yours, Lucian. A gift...as once I promised you."

"Promised *me*?"

"And soon—if you do not betray yourself—you might have to accept another gift," the angel said, radiating a poignant sadness.

"No, let me go," Lucian said, horrified. "My master will be here. No doubt he has heard us."

"You can see that he hasn't...yet. However, if it is your wish, just look away, and I will be gone." But it was as if the angel had already disappeared, for Lucian felt suddenly empty, bereft, as if his own soul had been swallowed by the snake writhing on the floor. "No, wait, please," Lucian said. "Why have you come to me?"

"Because the time has come for you to remember and find your destiny. Now...accept the gift or take your leave," and with that the angel stepped aside. Or simply ceased to be. Lucian started for the door—he could not pick up the thing on the floor—and then, as if this could be done only by impulse, turned, and grasped the snake. It felt smooth and impossibly warm, blood warm, and he shuddered with fear and revulsion; but he could also feel Baldassare's soul, as if something shuddery and feathery had touched his heart. For a wild, heart-churning, ecstatic instant he could feel, smell, taste, experience all of Baldassare's thoughts and memories...experience his fears, desires, faith, love, and greed; and Lucian was simultaneously enticed, excited, habituated, and sickened. The snake twisted to escape from his grasp. Remembering how the angel had raised his hands, Lucian turned his gaze to see as Gabriel had shown him; and, as if he were looking through the peephole, he saw his master attending the ailing Baldassare.

He threw the snake at Baldassare, restoring his stolen soul.

It found its mark, as if it was a straight arrow shot from a bow, and disappeared whole and entire into Baldassare's chest.

Lucian felt bereft at the loss of the priest's soul. But an instant later he gasped and reeled backwards as the snake returned to him. It snapped back like a cat-o'-nine-tails, passed through him like scalding vitriol, and curled itself around his frantically beating heart.

He felt as if he was on fire, burning into oblivion; and then—

He woke up coughing and gasping.

Mirandola was leaning over him, holding Lucian's head up from the floor with one hand and administering a foul smelling alchemical salt with the other.

"Here it is," Baldassare said. He looked to be fully recovered. "I've found it." He was kneeling, and peering through Lucian's spy hole. His brocaded black cloak and long hood covered the floor around him like a tent. "I told you your young foreign Jew thug was spying on you. Well, here is the proof. He's drilled a tiny hole into the floor. Very neatly done, too. What have you to say to that?"

Lucian tried to get up, his only thought to escape; but his master was strong and held him in place with one hand. "Remain, Lucian," Mirandola said. "You will not be given more punishment than you can bear."

"What?" asked Baldassare, standing up to his full height, as if he could intimidate Mirandola, who needed him if he was to pursue his questioning of Heaven's angels. "The child has heard everything we've said, has probably recorded everything in that garbage dialect he writes in his notebook." The priest drew a knife from under his robes. "Step away, master, the church will take care of this matter."

Mirandola reacted immediately. He stood up, pulling Lucian with him. But Lucian was dizzy, lightheaded, and though he thought to make for the door, he could only grasp his master for balance.

"So now this is church business, is it?" Mirandola said.

"It must be done or the church will have us both for apostasy," Baldassare said. "Stand aside; I'll be quick and merciful." Mirandola would be no match for Baldassare, who was a veteran of many wars and murders…and Mirandola was unarmed. Nevertheless, the magician stood his ground.

"I will not kill you, Master Mirandola," Baldassare continued, "but if you stand in my way, you *will* be hurt." The priest stepped forward, and Lucian reflexively raised both arms, as if to defend himself and his master. Blistering heat coursed through his right arm; and he remembered the delicious exhilaration of capturing and *owning* Baldassare's soul, felt the gnawing emptiness of its loss accompanied by a sudden overwhelming need. He could not help himself: he reached into the priest's chest and tore out his soul, not with his hands, but with Gabriel's terrible gift: the sapphire snake. He took back the soul he had once returned, and his master Mirandola saw absolutely nothing.

Baldassare groaned, dropped his knife, and stepped backwards; then, pressing his hands against his solar plexus as if he had been wounded, he collapsed.

"Fra Baldassare," Mirandola called. "What is the matter?" He rushed over to the friar. Kneeling beside him, he placed one hand on Baldassare's forehead and pressed the friar's wrist for a pulse with his other hand. "Is this like the fit you had looking into the gazing globe?" Baldassare blinked, then tried to stand up. Mirandola tried to help him up, but was straining. He called to Lucian.

"Help me get the friar to a chair. He's heavy as lead."

But Lucian was in his own world of pain and frenzy. When he had first picked up Gabriel's sapphire snake to release the friar's soul, he had felt Baldassare's thoughts, memories, and yearnings. It was different now...now that the snake had burrowed into Lucian's flesh and blood and pneuma...now that it had become part of him, a second self, a familiar that was coiled around his heart but always ready to be released. It had just eaten the soldier-priest's soul, and now Lucian knew *everything* that the priest knew. The priest's soul was Lucian's. The priest's mind and thoughts were Lucian's. He could not bear to give up all those dark, thick layers of experience, faith, and knowledge; but Baldassare's soul was also a poison flowing through him. He felt defiled, stained, ill. He was more than himself...but he was no longer himself. The priest was a liar, a cheat, a deceiver and prestidigitator. Yet he was a skryer; he could see a little through the aether, could summon angels and demons; and he knew so much more than Lucian. No, Lucian could not give up Baldassare's soul. Not yet. Not just yet.

"Lucian, come here and help me!"

But Lucian was fighting for control.

He felt Baldassare's greed—or was it his own anger and insistent need?—and then he suddenly longed for the warmth and cleansing purity of his master's soul. He desperately needed his master's wisdom, knowledge, and power. Responding, the snake released its tight grip on his heart and coursed like a hot needle through his blood. In that instant Lucian *knew* it would take Mirandola's innocent soul; and even as the snake appeared in his hands, even as he grasped it tight, he shouted, "No, I'm not a thief!" and ran out of the room.

He ran past Mirandola's apprentice Pietro Neroni, who had no business loitering in the hallway, and then down the worn, creaking back stairs of the bottega to the second landing, which led to high-ceilinged kitchens, studios, workrooms, and Mirandola's private library. He paused there, wrestling with the snake...wrestling with himself.

He clutched the writhing snake and throttled it, trying to kill it before he succumbed to it. He would not steal again. He would not steal his master's soul. It was enough that he had taken Baldassare's.

But that…that was self defense.

The snake retreated back into his hand, as if into a burrow. Lucian felt it burning inside him and gasped as it coiled like a white-hot filament around his heart. Dizzy and weakened, he made his way to a back door. He unlatched the heavy bolt, forced open the thick oaken door—which groaned, as if in pain— and escaped into the darkening, refuse-strewn streets of Florence. It was late afternoon, and the crowded lanes, avenues, and alleys were overshadowed by the arches and high walls of warehouses, villas, workshops, tenements, and towers. The air was damp and clotted with the smells of horses, feces, urine, moss, smoke, roasting meat, lilies, candle wax, fish, figs, sweat, and sickly-sweet perfume. Vendors stood beside their stalls and shouted at burghers and servants hurrying to complete their chores and return to their homes before the sunset curfew. Whores shouted from windows that were partially covered with red vellum. Cutpurses brushed past fashionably dressed young men and women and magicked away gold florins from satin pouches and polished pearls sewn onto puffed silk sleeves. Ragamuffins in bare feet scampered through the crowds and begged for food. An old man with no arms or legs called for alms and nodded to his begging bowl, as if it was a favored companion.

Lucian hurried along the cobbled Via de Pecore, past the ghetto of the Jews—a part of the city he knew well—past the three and four story tenements that radiated from the magnificent Cathedral of Saint Maria del Fiore, which was called the Duomo. Its blazing copper dome and arcades rose above the city, as if to pierce the cloudless sky. He felt Baldassare's soul heavy within him, and he considered casting it away, letting it fly wherever it might, even if it would never find its true home in the soldier priest's breast. His thoughts were being invaded by Baldassare's soul, by its thoughts and desires… and Lucian felt compelled to return to his master's bottega, return the soul burden, and accept whatever the consequences might be. The soul-shadow of Baldassare—vital, alive, pure spirit—was trying to master the boy. But Lucian looked into his doubled soul and whispered, "*No, I'm a man now. And I've mastered you…*"

"*Hubris,*" whispered a voice inside his head. "*Prideful fool…*"

It sounded like the sweet voice of the angel Gabriel, and Lucian felt himself being pulled toward the great spired cathedral, as if he was nothing more than an iron filing being drawn to a magnet the size of a mountain. He imagined the whisperings to be nothing more than his own thoughts; and as he listened to Baldassare's soul, thought Baldassare's thoughts, dreamed Baldassare's dreams, and absorbed Baldassare's wisdom, he experienced the priest's life as a drowning man might relive his three-score and ten years in a few seconds.

He pushed through the hurrying crowds as the long rays of the sun stained the sky with blood and smoke. He made his way down the narrow Via dei Servi. The great marbled mass of the cathedral blocked out the sky.

"*Come to the high altar*," commanded the voice in his head.

Lucian wanted to run back to his master, but he couldn't trust himself, couldn't trust the sapphire-scaled, soul-swallowing snake that was wrapped around his heart. Gabriel's abominable gift had turned him into a thief, and now the angel was waiting for him, waiting to exact his own form of restitution.

He climbed the stairs and entered the cathedral, which was empty. He walked across the pink and green and white mosaic floor to the high altar flanked by sacristy doors adorned with blue terracottas of the Resurrection and Ascension. A hundred yards above him was Brunelleschi's great dome. Dusty, rainbow-hued light passed through the Duomo's round stained-glass windows. The immense cathedral seemed to exist in an eternal twilight. On the far side of the nave long tables were covered with hundreds of votive candles, which illuminated frescos of Heaven, Hell, and Purgatory into flickering movement.

Lucian looked around knowingly, tasting Baldassare's deep knowledge of the church, its sacred geometry and hidden symbols. Two old priests walked through the aisles and explained in hushed voices the schedules for digging graves and ringing the cathedral bells to a bemused young sexton. One of the priests directed himself to Lucian. "Boy, do you have permission to be here at this hour? Curfew is upon us. What is your name and your business, and—"

The priest suddenly turned away, shook his head, and nodded to his companion, who resumed lecturing the sexton. It was as if they had all suddenly forgotten that they had seen Lucian...forgotten that he was even there. Their low voices became a distant murmuring and growling that seemed to emanate from the stone walls, and then all was silence and shadow again.

Lucian was afraid.

He could smell cinnamon and the acrid odor of an impending storm. He looked around the aisles, frescoed walls, and distant pillars, then raised his gaze along the vaulting arches to the great dome above; and there, standing like a gargoyle on a marble niche below one of the stained glass windows, was Gabriel. His purple robe looked black in the dusty, colored light; his great feathered wings were outstretched and moving rhythmically, as if for balance. The angel drifted down to the altar; or, rather, he appeared and reappeared in something resembling a descent. He stood upon the altar before Lucian and said, "You could not resist taking the priest's soul, could you?"

"He tried to kill me. I was defending myself."

"And now?"

"Take back your gift," Lucian said angrily, "and you can have Baldassare's soul, too."

The angel shook his head. "No, you must willingly return it. The sapphire serpent gives you pain, but it also gives you power…and the soul of the priest."

"Who tried to kill me."

Gabriel nodded and said, "Yes, who tried to kill you. "But you're not yet ready to give up the priest, are you? You have much more to learn, don't you? Isn't that what you've told yourself?"

Lucian averted his eyes, shamed; and for an instant, he felt the angel's compassion as a tingling warmth. "It is true what I told you. Baldassare said he would kill me and hurt my master if he got in the way, but…"

"Yes…?"

"It just happened so fast. I didn't realize I'd taken the soul until I'd done it; and then it was too late."

"Why too late? You could have returned the priest's soul to him. The danger was over in a moment."

So you *were* there…you were watching," Lucian said.

"How could I?" Gabriel asked wryly. "I was in the gazing globe, remember?"

"I wanted to swallow my master's soul, too," Lucian said; he blurted it out, thinking that if he didn't tell someone now, it would be too late.

"Ah, so you would swallow up the world."

"Whatever you say," Lucian said, humiliated.

"You spoke what was in your heart. I commend you, but what are you going to do?"

"I don't know."

"Keep the priest's soul?"

"I don't know."

"Keep the gift you imagine is a snake?"

"I asked you to take it back…and the soul, too," Lucian said; but even as he spoke, he felt the snake nestled inside him; and Baldassare's soul gave him strength and wisdom and distance. He had mastered it. He could control it. Use it. He was not yet ready to return Baldassare's soul, or the angel's gift. He could learn to control the snake, could learn to free himself of its painful presence, even as he allowed it to dwell within him.

"Well, I see you've made your decision," said the angel.

"What do you mean?"

"That was your chance. I leave you now."

"Wait…please," Lucian begged. "Do you read my mind?"

"It doesn't take an angel to read the expressions that cross your face."

"I need to keep the priest's soul," Lucian said. "I…want to keep the priest's soul. It allows me to see as I've never been able to before. It gives me wisdom, knowledge, even now."

"And what wisdom does Baldassare's soul impart to you even now, young thief?" Gabriel asked.

Lucian looked around at the cathedral's seemingly endless pillars, arcades, rib-vaulted aisles, chancels, balustrades, arches, galleries, and naves; and he understood that the master builders had been divinely inspired to express the infinite mind and eternal realm of God in the coarse corruptible, improbable *materia* of earth's stone.

"Yes, young thief, I see what you see and understand what you know; but since you now know how this cathedral has come to be, you also know something more."

"And what is that?" Lucian asked. But even as he questioned the angel, he *knew*. He remembered his dream-meeting with the angel in the Cave of Light, remembered what the angel had told him. He knew that one who swallowed souls would be corrupted, co-opted, and enslaved by the unseen shadow: the demiurge created by the imperfect thought of the aeon Sophia, one of God's first luminaries.

Lucian shuddered, overwhelmed, for now he could also feel and understand Baldassare's fear and despair. Baldassare had been chosen for enlightenment. He had been given the burden of truth: to know what his church denied: that this world and its firmament of heavenly spheres were not created by the true God known to the initiated as the Invisible Spirit, but by a demiurge called Yaldabaoth who had blinded himself to the truth that he was a subordinate deity and called himself *Jehovah Yahweh He-Who-Cannot-Be-Named*. Baldassare knew that *Jehovah* created his own pantheon of aeons, angels, and demons; that *Yahweh* fashioned the spark of his mother Sophia's reflected love into the *materia* of earth, air, and flesh; and that *He-Who-Cannot-Be-Named* yearns to destroy all he created.

And now Lucian had *all* of Baldassare's terrible knowledge; and Baldassare's soul was drowning him, suffocating him with the names and powers of those spawned by the demiurge:

The first is Athoth, the one generations call the whirlwind, or the reaper.
The second is Harmas, the jealous eye.
The third is Kalila-Oumbri.
The fourth is Yabel.
The fifth is Adonaios, also known as Sabaoth.
But only one authority comes to redeem you; and he is known as Belias, beloved of Yaldabaoth: He gathers and makes the darkness shine, yet he is neither light nor darkness. He is the true vine of redemption...

"Redeem?" Lucian asked aloud, shivering. He felt grief and an all-encompassing emptiness, the emptiness that was at the core of everything, the emptiness that swallowed everything into itself. The emptiness that was the demiurge—Yaldabaoth, the Lord God Jehovah—and all of his minions.

"So now you know your redeemer," Gabriel said: "the demiurge's aeon Belias. And you've also tasted Baldassare's black fear and grief. Welcome them, young thief, for they will be your constant companions. According to Belias and his master—whom you believe to be your God—you *have* been redeemed. Welcome to manhood."

The angel began to fade and flicker.

"Help me!" Lucian cried. "Please...don't leave me."

But the angel had disappeared, soft as smoke.

FOUR
The Obsidian Mirror

The demiurge Yaldabaoth is the one who seized great power from his mother and left the place where he was born. With bright fire which still exists he took control and created new aeons for his need. Amazed in the mindlessness which dwelled deep within him, he created authorities for himself.

—*John 10.19*

Some, too, believe that each star may also be called a world, and regard this earth as a dark star over which the least of the gods presides.

—Palingenius

By what condition, nature, or fell chance,
In living death, dead life I live?

—Giordano Bruno, *Gli Eroici Furori*

Pico Della Mirandola attended the ailing Baldassare in the visitor's room. The priest shuddered and shivered in the raised, curtained bed; he was weak and pale as the dead, yet still he raved. He reached out to the night-blue bed canopy above him as if it was a holy presence and begged, "Return to me before it is too late. Return to me…"

"To whom do you speak?" Mirandola asked. "If you don't tell me, I cannot help you." But Baldassare didn't seem to be aware that there was anyone else in the room. He arched his back and whispered, "Lest I be lost completely.

Lest I be well..." He made a mirthless noise. "An empty well... Please, return now or—"

Baldassare began to convulse, and Mirandola called his first apprentice Pietro to help him constrain the priest who was thrashing wildly.

"How can this be?" asked Pietro when the convulsions subsided. "We medicated him with *Cannabis indica* and *Solanum nigrum*. Perhaps we should have purged him with amethyst." Pietro was the scion of an important Venetian family and well educated. He was only a few years younger than his master, and some said he would eclipse Mirandola. But the beautiful and talented twenty-two year old with his pale blue eyes, luxuriant black hair, and unfortunate club-foot, was no match for Mirandola's abilities as a natural magus.

"No, chains and lures will not work," Mirandola said, looking into the priest's eyes, searching... "I don't think his spiritual or earthy body has been poisoned, yet he is somehow dead within himself. I had thought he suffered from some attack of cold melancholy, for he was taken by trance; yet he called to someone—or something—as if awake, and the convulsions would indicate heat. Nor do I think that demonic presences attacked him; and if they did, they do not dwell in him now. The drought we administered would prevent his spirit from binding to anything foreign. His own dreams and visions should have awakened him."

"I am awake, if that's what you can call it," Baldassare said matter-of-factly, and he shook his head as if to clear it; but his words and movements somehow didn't seem to be his own. He sat up in bed, then stood up and slowly and carefully headed for the door. It was as if he was testing his legs... testing his very memory of walking.

"Shall I stop him, master?" Pietro whispered.

"That might not be wise," Mirandola said. "Fra Baldassare," he asked, "where are you going?"

"Where I am called."

"Who calls you?"

"The thief who stole my—"

But as the priest reached for the door latch, the door opened; and standing before him, looking wild-eyed and disheveled and out of breath, was Lucian.

Baldassare stepped backward like a puppet yanked by strings and mumbled, "The commander comes to the one he commands...?"

"I'm sorry," Lucian said, "but you were going to kill me"; and then he pressed his hands against the priest's chest. He felt the snake release itself from around his heart, felt it coursing like heat through his arms and hands. It bit into the priest and released the soul that Lucian had taken; and as the roiling, silvery soul passed from Lucian to Baldassare, Lucian experienced great pain and emptiness. It was as if he was once again reliving the brutal death of his family in the arid wastes of Judea. Reflexively, he called for his mother, then his father, and collapsed to the floor.

As if mimicking him, the priest fell, too.

And neither Mirandola nor Pietro could wake them.

"Master, are they dead?" Pietro asked. He kneeled before Lucian. He had been pressing his mouth against Lucian's to force air into the lungs and pushing upon the boy's chest to force the air out.

"Fra Baldassare has no breath...no pulse either," Mirandola said. "Yes, I fear that—"

Simultaneously Lucian and the priest gasped, choking, gagging, and noisily fighting their way back to life. Frightened, Pietro pushed himself away from Lucian and looked to his master Mirandola, who shrugged and anxiously pulled a lock of hair away from his face. The priest raised himself from the floor to stare at Lucian, who was beside him. "Why did you return?"

Lucian looked cowed and would not meet Baldassare's gaze.

"Tell me," Baldassare insisted.

"I think both of you had better tell *me* what has just happened," Mirandola said; but it was as if neither Lucian nor the priest heard him.

"To restore you, as you know."

"Yes," Baldassare said softly. "To restore me... A keeper of souls—no, stealer of souls—wants to restore me."

"I am not what you said."

"Then what are you?"

"You mean you don't know?" Lucian asked, for he could still see into the priest, feel his emotions and the friction of his thoughts. There was still a connection between them, albeit a shadowy one.

"I know what you stole. I just don't know why you've returned it, although I must confess I am thankful." He grimaced and laughed, which sounded like he was clearing his throat. "Perhaps even in your debt."

"Then you *can* see into me."

"A little," Baldassare said, "but not, I fear, as you can look into me...or have looked into me. But—"

"Yes...?"

"The dark aeon Belias steals souls; that I know. But I did not know that those who are not in thrall to the demiurge could have such a power. How... how could *you* come by it?"

"Gabriel," Lucian said in no more than a whisper.

"Gabriel? Impossible. The snakes and vines that steal souls belong to

Belias: they are at his command, and that of his Lord's."

"No, the vines belong to Belias. The snakes...they belong to Gabriel and the true God."

Mirandola tried to interrupt, but Lucian continued, as if only he and Baldassare were in the room. "I didn't mean to steal—"

Baldassare stared intently at Lucian, probing, trying to search the boy's mind, spirit, and soul. Then he nodded and said, "I know." He leaned closer to Lucian, shivered, and his eyes opened wide with comprehension. For an instant his entire demeanor changed, as if all his protective walls and defenses had suddenly vanished. "Yes, you are right, young thief: the connection travels in both directions. I can sense the snake that now resides within you, coiled around your heart; and I know now what you saw of me and what you saw in the gazing globe. I know what Gabriel said to you...and I know that the angel chose to give his seal to you."

"What?" Lucian asked, but a sudden burst of derisive laughter broke the connection. Pietro glanced embarrassedly at Mirandola; who shook his head and said, "Enough!" Let us help you from the floor. You both need rest and refreshment, and I need to know what in the name of the Invisible Spirit has just happened."

The priest gave Mirandola a sour look for using the Lord's true name with profane familiarly; but he allowed Mirandola to help him back to the bed where he sat stiffly beside Lucian as if no connection had ever existed between them.

"Bring a restorative for our two patients," Mirandola said to Pietro. "And then there are a few errands I need you to attend to."

"I will call for Isabella," Pietro said. "She can bring the restorative and will attend to whatever we request."

Surprised, Mirandola said, "If I wanted Isabella, I would have called for her. Now please do as I ask. Or do you disobey to embarrass me?"

"Please forgive my disobedience, master, but right now my place must be here."

"Your place is where I tell you it is!"

Pietro lowered his eyes in submission, but wouldn't leave the room. "I know that you and Father Baldassare have been calling the angels to appear in your gazing globe."

"So it seems that *all* my servants are spies," Mirandola said. He turned to the priest. "Gentle Father, I fear you would have had to execute everyone in my bottega to keep our secret safe."

"Whatever secrets you have," Pietro said, "they are safe. I am here to learn from you, my master. I would never betray you."

"But you *are* jealous of the boy, are you not?" Baldassare asked Pietro.

Lucian leaned closer to the priest. He could hear *something*. Baldassare seemed to have suddenly recovered his composure, and Lucian glimpsed how the priest willed his frantic fears and doubts into another room in his mind. Lucian did the same, imagining a prison where the fears and dark things that coursed through his mind, heart, and soul could be contained...for a little while.

Pietro was taken aback. "Yes, Father, I suppose I am jealous of Lucian." He looked at Mirandola and said, "Forgive me, master, but my jealousy—if that is what it is—is only natural, for you favor the little Jew over me." But he said nothing of Lucian being the chosen one.

"I will not entertain such nonsense," Mirandola said. "Lucian is a servant in this bottega. You are first apprentice; although if you continue to disobey me, you will be returned to your family."

"You spend as much time teaching him as you do me."

"He has things to teach *me*. Have *you* studied occult philosophy and hermeneutics in Constantinople and lived as a beggar in the streets of Milan? Have *you* been sold into slavery, or watched your parents—"

"And is that why you allow him to spy on you?" Pietro asked. He was obviously nervous and his voice rose in pitch and cracked.

After a long pause, Mirandola said, "Yes, Pietro, that is why I allow him to learn."

"Why didn't you tell me you wanted to include the boy?" Baldassare asked, his anger and astonishment iced with calm.

"Because I feared he would mysteriously disappear. That you would murder him … just as you tried to do."

The priest nodded, then fixed his gaze on Pietro. "And you...how did *you* know our business?"

"Because I am first apprentice," Pietro said.

"Answer Fra Baldassare's question properly," Mirandola said.

"I cannot always see the angels in the gazing globe as you and Lucian do, Father, but I saw the angel's gift that appears like a snake in Lucian's hands when he ran away through the hall. And I know he was fighting it, fighting himself, so no harm would come to you, Master." He turned to Mirandola, then to Lucian.

"Tell us what else you can see," Baldassare asked Pietro.

Pietro stared down at his cloth shoes and wouldn't speak.

"All is in the open now," Mirandola said. "You can speak the truth. I give you my word you will not be punished or harmed."

"And you, Father, do I have your word, too?" Pietro asked.

"Ask the Jew. He knows the secrets of my soul."

Pietro turned to Lucian.

47

"Yes, you can trust his word; but you must ask him to promise before the angels in the gazing-globe."

"Angels will not respond to petulance and selfishness," Baldassare said, walling himself away from Lucian's angel-gifted glamour.

"Perhaps they will…this time," Pietro said.

The priest and the master Mirandola invoked the angels to appear in the gazing globe that rested upon the mirror-topped table.

"It remains clouded," Baldassare said. He turned his sour gaze upon Pietro.

"Concentrate," Mirandola asked, touching the priest's sleeve. "Look again."

Baldassare stared into the globe.

"I see nothing but angry dark clouds swirling."

"Perhaps in time Gabriel will part them and appear to us," Mirandola said.

Baldassare sighed and stepped away from the globe.

"You are too quick to leave their presence."

"There *is* no presence, Ser Mirandola. You cannot use angels as you would demons. You cannot force them to appear at your whim. Perhaps we can try again later."

"No, we cannot leave this room," Mirandola said.

"I have given you my word that no harm will come to your apprentices by my hand," Baldassare said. "That should suffice."

Not by your *hand*, Mirandola thought. After some consideration—he was afraid of losing the priest and his considerable skrying talents—he turned to Lucian and said, "Tell me what *you* see in the globe."

"Me?" Lucian asked, surprised. He could feel the priest's anger. He looked at Baldassare, as if for confirmation; but the priest looked away, then said, "Tell him what you see."

Lucian looked into the globe. Clouds, dark roiling clouds…that's all he could see in the gazing globe. But there was something else, something reflected in the crystal.

"Well?" asked Mirandola.

"I see only what Fra Baldassare described to you." Lucian bent closer to the globe.

"Then we will wait until the clouds part," Mirandola said.

"There is no need," Pietro said, gesturing toward the immaculately clean and polished obsidian mirror that covered the skrying table. "What you seek is not in the crystal, but in the *mirror*."

"I see nothing in the mirror," Baldassare said. "And you?" he asked Lucian.

Lucian turned to Pietro, who met his eyes with taunting anger. He turned back to the mirror, but saw only a mist of swirling grayness in the black obsidian.

"Pietro, tell them what you see," Mirandola said impatiently.

"If you look into the mist, you will see it," Pietro said to Lucian; and as Lucian stared into the swirling storm that silently raged in the mirror, he began to make out a dark geography: high cliffs sharp as steel and smooth as the mirror; adamantine desert bereft of life; descending valleys, each plain a great irregular circle falling into deeper darkness and mystery and movement; the flitting shadows of spirits, ghosts, or demons too quick to be recognized; and above the ebon stone and gunmetal crust was a clear sky cut with bright yet unfamiliar constellations. But there was something in the unearthly air, something out of focus, something there yet not-quite-there and yet...

"Well?" Pietro asked impatiently. "What do you see?"

"I see...Hell."

Pietro nodded. "And there?" Pietro stepped close to the mirror and dipped his finger into what Lucian now saw as Hell's clear dark firmament.

"I see an angel in a magical contraption, flying...floating."

Pietro nodded and pressed Lucian's hand, a signal of respect.

"Perhaps it isn't an angel," Lucian said, gazing at the oddly robed boy? man? creature? standing in a basket that floated through the darkness like a puffball carried by the wind. Above the basket was something large and spherical. "It's falling..."

"Or landing,' Pietro said.

"I cannot see it," Baldassare said, stepping beside Lucian, so close as to almost push him away, "but I can sense it...through you."

Lucian felt his face and his ears burn, and he tried to close his thoughts from the priest.

"Lucian..."

Lucian reflexively moved away from the priest, but it was not the priest who called him. The voice seemed to emanate from the gazing globe, which was now transparent, free of the angry clouds that spun inside it like smoke; and there, standing upon the dark rocks of the same world reflected in the obsidian mirror, was the angel Gabriel.

"Lucian..."

"Yes, angel?" Lucian said softly, tentatively.

Everyone turned to Lucian, then Baldassare and Pietro looked into the gazing globe.

"What do you see?" Mirandola asked.

When Lucian didn't answer, Pietro said, "Nothing. Just clouds roiling, as before." Baldassare, who was staring at Lucian, nodded in agreement.

Lucian could sense the priest's surprise...and consternation.

"Tell us who speaks to you in the crystal," Mirandola demanded.

"Do you want to stay with them, or come with me and expiate yourself?" Gabriel asked.

Lucian felt enveloped by the angel, protected, isolated. Once again he smelled cinnamon and for one delicious instant he thought of sweets and Judea. "Why should I go with you?"

"To save the girl's soul."

"What girl?"

"The one you just saw floating in the dark firmament…"

Baldassare shouted to Lucian, but too late.

Mirandola saw his apprentice seem to somehow soften, as if the light had changed. Then, suddenly, the air snapped, as if sucked into a vacuum; and Lucian disappeared into the gazing globe. The magician imagined that something insubstantial—yet bright as sunlight in a mirror—arced into the skrying crystal.

And he also imagined that he could smell the faint odor of cinnamon…

FIVE

The Desecrated Cathedral

Surely the days of grief are upon us, and when nature
approaches destruction, darkness will come upon the
earth. The numbers of the elect will be few, and the
church will pass into the shadow. Yet a slender strand of
hope comes forth, and her name will be called...

—*The Knowledge of Shem 36.25*

Seek not his dark boles that lead to cold heavens

—Giordano Bruno, *Gli Eroici Furori*

Lucian found himself lying in the Duomo before the altar; but although it was
mid-afternoon, no light poured through the round stained glass windows of
the painted dome high above. It took time for his eyes to adjust to the candle-lit,
flickering gloom. It was unnaturally cold and difficult to breathe—a palpable
miasma filled the cathedral, odors of decomposition and winter forest, the
wild stink of sweat and storm and semen—and he felt weak and dislocated.
He imagined he was somehow still in his master's skrying room, still staring
into the gazing globe; Baldassare was beside him, robes smelling of camphor
and incense; Pietro was touching his hand; and then something was pulled out
of him and he fell and he—

Rose from the cold, glass-smooth parquet floor to greet the angel who
appeared before him. The angel fluoresced into being like a firefly in a candle-
lit garden; but this time Gabriel, beautiful light-cloaked Gabriel seemed vital,
solid, absolute, as if he was really here and not part of the ghostly stuff of air
and evanescence. His great wings shivered, shaking feathers into the clotted
darkness. His scent of cinnamon was strong; in fact, it reeked like fear.

"Now I am here, and *you* are...attenuated," Gabriel said.

"I feel ill, as if something is pulling at me."

The angel nodded. "You'll get used to it, as I have."

"But—"

"I am here entire so I may perhaps protect you with greater strength," Gabriel said. "And should things go awry, well, perhaps you'll have the chance to return."

"Return where?" Lucian asked.

"To your master's bottega, where you still remain."

"Then I am not here? I am dreaming this?"

The angel smiled. "No, you are here. You are not dreaming. Your soul is here...and there, and your material soul is here...and there, but mostly there. Here is where you face your danger, perhaps your death and the loss of your immortal soul. Do you wish to return to your master Mirandola, now that you know how to return to yourself entire? If so, you must leave immediately or it will be too late."

"I do not know how to—"

"*You* lifted yourself here," Gabriel said. "I only beckoned you, showed you what to expect."

"No, you were not *here*," Lucian insisted. "You were not in the cathedral. You were in...Hell."

"I was here, young magus. This cathedral has been harrowed and seized by Belias, and don't even presume that you can imagine Hell..." But Gabriel's words suddenly seemed to be swallowed by the dark, noxious miasma that filled and defiled the cathedral.

"What happened?" Lucian asked.

"Your redeemer has returned."

"You mean...?"

Gabriel smiled sadly and said, "No, I mean your god's beloved aeon, the demon Belias. Now you will know whenever he is present."

"I—"

"Listen..."

And Lucian felt the thick, cold silence. He wanted to shout, talk, gabble, anything to push back the aching emptiness that had found its way into the cathedral. He wanted to close his eyes, close everything out and will himself back to the safety of his master Mirandola's skrying room.

"Now look and you will see the work of the demiurge's servant," the angel said.

"I see only the cathedral," but even as Lucian spoke, he thought he could see ghostly vines snaking slowly through the arched stained-glass windows high above him. The vines twisted around what looked to be translucent columns that had penetrated the cathedral's huge ceilings and domes from altar to narthex to altar.

The entire cathedral was filled with these inverted boles, which did not rest on the cathedral floor, but left enough room for the tallest man to walk under them. Their glittering striated surfaces looked suspiciously like bark, and they seemed to blink in and out of sight. Lucian remembered the first time he saw Gabriel, who had also seemed to shift in and out of sight, as if he were constantly creating and recreating himself. Perhaps these boles and vines that were here — and not here — were made of the same stuff as angels. But, here, now, in this cathedral, it was Gabriel who was solid, tangible, present.

Lucian heard muffled noises and turned to see a woman in mourning clothes with a boy, presumably her son, who was about Lucian's age. Unable to see or sense the ghostly vines and boles above them, they lit votive candles in the narthex; and as they prayed, two translucent vines uncoiled from a bole and attacked them. Writhing like worms, the vines drew the roiling swirling wisps of soul-flesh from the breast of the mother and then the son. Both clutched their chests, uttered small cries of despair, and fell to the floor while their souls, twisting like creatures made of smoke and flesh, were pulled into one of the glittering, striated, inverted boles.

Lucian felt the jeweled snake — the angel's gift — reflexively uncoil from his heart and course down his arm. The snake vibrated in Lucian's hand, and he felt the familiar warmth radiate through his fingers…felt the boiling heat running through his blood. As if it had its own mind and thoughts, the snake stretched away from Lucian's hand without snapping, without separating, and arced upward into the hollow bole above the mother and her son.

"No," Gabriel shouted. "Do not allow the serpent its will. Release it."

But his shout was damped to a whisper by the dead emptiness that permeated the cathedral.

The angel clutched Lucian's shoulders — his hands were as strong and palpable as any man's born of flesh and blood — but it was not enough.

Lucian felt himself jolted away from the angel, pulled through the dark miasma of the cathedral and lifted into the freezing silver-limned darkness of the hollow bole by the snake that would no longer be separated from its host.

He called to Gabriel, but to no avail; and although Lucian tried to obey the angel's last command and release the snake, he could not. The serpent would not be controlled. It attacked the vines that had aspirated the souls of the mother and son. It tore the stolen souls from them, and then greedily stole their aetheric life — if, indeed, the ghostly, writhing things could be called alive — and as it slashed and strangled the vines, Lucian understood with fear and loathing that now *he* was the snake, which was mind, will, and newborn power…*he* was now the servant of the angel Gabriel, enemy of the demiurge

Jehovah and all its demon aeons.

He tasted the thoughts, memories, grief, and skull-freezing fear of the mother and son whose souls now co-existed with his own. He tried to release them, but was wrenched cruelly upward, ever upward, at a dizzying rate. The interior of the bole was a swirling miasma of glittering, reflected darkness and shadow. Then the bole ejected him; and with a sickening thud, he found himself sliding along what seemed to be ice or wet glass. At first, he couldn't see; but his eyes slowly adjusted to the utter darkness, which wasn't really darkness at all, but an absence that resolved into a dark geography defined by silvery perspective lines. It was as if he were looking at a silverpoint etching, only the silverpoint was silvery darkness superposed over a deeper darkness. But there was depth created by the lines and edges, and Lucian grasped that he was staring into negative spaces. Here were the high cliffs, descending valleys, adamantine desert, and unfamiliar night sky he had glimpsed in his master Mirandola's obsidian mirror.

Here was where Gabriel had stood when he summoned Lucian.

Here was the dark heaven of the aeon Belias.

And the angel summoned him once again...but, no, this could not be Gabriel; this was something—or someone—else, and he felt a cold, cruel intelligence speaking to him, whispering though his blood, whispering in rhythm to the thub-a-drub of his heart. He tried to resist, tried to stand; but the agonizingly cold surface beneath him had leached away his will, energy, and pneuma, the stuff that nourished and protected his soul. His serpent floated and curled ominously above him, luminescent, weightless, and silver-limned, as if it had become one of vines it had attacked and now belonged to Belias.

The ground shivered gently; and this cold world whispered to Lucian, who could now understand that the world the presence the invading silvery darkness—and the whispers that were swallowing and choking him—were but manifestations of Belias, who could be person, place, or thought itself.

And as Belias the god the world the aeon spoke to him, so did Lucian's serpent insinuate itself around his throat and wind around his chest. It began to choke him, stealing his warmth and breath and pneuma and soul.

"Lucian, release the snake!"

The voice was Gabriel's.

"Help me," Lucian tried to say, but he could only gasp, *"Where are you?"*

"I have followed you," the angel answered, his voice not heard but sensed. *"I'm inside the beast...near you. But I cannot hold back the creatures of Belias much longer. They slay me even now. You must warm yourself and release the snake. Do so quickly!"*

"I do not understand, I—"

"Find the mother and child."

Although Lucian could feel the snake's insatiable hunger, which was his own hunger; he sought out the souls of the mother and son he had tried to save. But he could no longer hear their thoughts nor taste their emotions. He imagined that the snake had already sucked away their lives. Nevertheless, he tried to feel their presence within him, even as the snake was stealing his life, too, sucking it away into Belias' cold vastness. He searched until he could sense their two souls as warm sparrow-flutterings in his aching chest. Even as the snake tried to draw them away, Lucian focused his entire being on the silent, exhausted, dying souls of mother and son. He gasped, fighting the serpent's will, and pulled them back deeper into himself. And with every ragged, choking breath, he concentrated their attenuated souls into small white-hot knots; only then did he release them. They burned through him like hot coals through parchment and arced skyward. Snapping reflexively, the serpent tried to catch them; and as it did so, it loosened its constricting hold on Lucian for an instant.

But that was enough.

Lucian could remember now how he had transported himself from his master Mirandola's skrying room to the fouled and demon-desecrated cathedral…and he *released* himself from the serpent, which disappeared into the darkness as if it had never been. With a swallowed cry of agony and remorse, Lucian tried to call it back.

He felt suddenly bereft, empty, his essence lost. What had been his blood, bone, and soul was now gnawing nagging grief.

"Help me," Lucian cried, and he heard the angel.

"Leave here if you can. The girl cannot be saved by me. It is too late. You must save yourself."

"What about you…?"

The angel didn't answer, but Lucian felt his presence in his mind.

"Where are you?"

Again, no response.

"Gabriel…?"

The boy was heavy with the burden of pure spiritual emptiness, which, mercifully, left no room for fear. How could nothingness weigh more than lead and fill his entire being with its miasma? It was beyond his comprehension. He had not even felt such loss when he had witnessed the murder of his family… only grief, guilt, fear, and anger. Cursed he might be, but he was resolved. He would not leave—or try to leave—without the angel.

Lucian searched for him, treading carefully, as this frigid, silent, slippery land was beset with deep pits and cracks, which could only lead to eternities of darkness. He walked carefully around a series of craters, which were darker than the silvery darkness around him. Unable to help himself, he stopped and leaned over the glassy edge of a crater and looked down into the darkness…into the darkness of one of the aeon's boles, and there, in the tunneled distance, he imagined he could see the cathedral's altar. But he would not try to fall through the opening, nor would he try to transport himself back to Mirandola's *bottega*. He resumed his search for the angel, and as he drew closer, he inhaled a scent of cinnamon combined with that of rot, of corruption. He saw something move and flicker ahead, something whipping and snapping like serpents or the flickering vines; and as he squinted to see better, the glimpse of movement, the squirming and whipping, resolved itself into a figure, tall and still as a statue with great wings curled tightly against its back. It was surrounded by thousands of shimmering coiling vines. As Lucian stepped closer, he realized that the writhing vines were trying to escape the angel's invisible hold on them.

"*Gabriel.*"

"*Stay away from here. Obey me…leave now. My strength wanes, and I cannot hold them much longer.*"

"*I won't leave without you, angel.*"

Lucian imagined he heard weary laughter. As he moved closer to the angel, he could see the vines clearly; if, indeed, Gabriel was by some force preventing the vines from escaping, from attacking Lucian, the vines were sucking the strength and life out of the angel, or, perhaps, he was absorbing their poisonous vital energies. Whichever it was, Gabriel looked wasted under the crawling, snapping nest of feeders.

"*Stay back, boy. I cannot hold them. They finish me…and they will have you.*"

"*Let us leave together,*" Lucian said, "*or wait for the girl.*"

"*Belligerent fool,*" said the angel, "*I told you it was too late for her, too late for you, too late for…*" The vines, translucent as glass, began to uncoil and pull free of their weakened captor; and they whipped toward Lucian, as insects to light.

Without thinking, Lucian summoned his serpent to fend them off.

But there was no serpent, only emptiness, silver darkness, ever-present cold, and the soul-seeking stings of the tendrils of the aeon that ruled this world…that was this world. The vines clung to him, passed into him. They drained his pneuma, then his soul.

"*Gabriel, help me.*"

As Lucian collapsed lifeless onto the glassy ground, he glimpsed a huge floating, multi-colored envelope falling out of the starry heaven. The bottom of the pear-shaped envelope looked like the trunk of an elephant; and below that—suspended by vines, or netting—was a girl in a wildly swinging basket.

She hung on to the netting for dear life and slashed at transparent vines that were either attacking her…or caressing her.

He heard her screams as whispers.

The balloon fell, and still the empty shell that had been Lucian whispered, *"Gabriel…"*

PARTITION TWO
The Daughter of Light

'Trismegistus, who is the daughter of light?'

'Rheginus, you know her as the aeon Sophia, Queen of Angels. She who is above has also always been below.'

'Of course, Trismegistus. Aeons are synchronous.'

'Listen to me, I mean the fulfillment of her soul reincarnated into earthy flesh. But you are fortunate, Rheginus, for you will not witness that perfection.'

'Fortunate, Trismegistus?'

'Yes, Rheginus, fortunate, for she will return during the Days of Grief.'

'Why, Trismegistus?'

'Because she must defeat her offspring produced in ignorance and sin.'

'Trismegistus, do you refer to the demiurge Jehovah?'

'Yes, Rheginus.'

'And might she fail, Trismegistus?'

'Yes, Rheginus, most certainly. And if she does, then all that is will never be.'

—*Excerpt from the Second Discourse 87,31-34*

SIX

The Crack in the Sky

A genius arose for the occasion and suggested that we send out and gather all the silk dresses in the Confederacy and make a balloon. It was done; and soon we had a great patchwork ship of many and varied hues...

—General James Longstreet, Army of
   Northern Virginia, 1862

Now I have returned, this time in the likeness of a female... I shall tell them of the coming end of this age, and teach them about the beginning of the age to come...

—*Three Forms of First Thought*

And once again the ancient vines have been called forth to devour the innocent.

—John Dee, *Mysteriorum Liber Secundus*

Louisa Mary Morgan saw the crack in the sky only seconds before a shell exploded on the promenade deck of her father's steamer *Teaser*.

The Confederate commandeered ship's 24-pounder howitzer was hit and, dislodged, ripped into the wooden side wheel. As another shell struck the forward mast, the 32-pounder on pivot fired at the Union's river-bank field battery...and found its mark. But the *Teaser*—now dead in the water—was no match for the Union's arrayed fire power; and the captain, a veteran who had bravely commanded the ram *Manassas*, blew the steam whistle twice and ordered the red and blue Confederate flag to be hauled down. A crewman hoisted a white flag in its place.

"It will be all right, child," said Major Dunean. The young aeronaut, handsome in his yellow-gray uniform with blue silk shoulder straps, put his arm protectively around Louisa's shoulder. "The Yanks will stop shooting now," he said sourly as he looked across the muddy water of the James River. "It's all over."

Louisa and the major stood behind the protection of a pulley block assembly on the barge towed by Louisa's father's ship. The *Teaser* had been commissioned to transfer the barge—and the fully-inflated twenty-four foot diameter hydrogen balloon tethered to its deck—from the Richmond Gas Works to General Langdon at Chuffin's Bluff.

"Are they going to take us prisoner?" Louisa asked.

The major smiled. "You will come to no harm. The Northern Aggressors would never harm the balloon. Too valuable a spoil of war. Your daddy knows that. He's a very smart man."

"But they'll take him prisoner and—"

"No, little one, he'll be fine. I assure you. He will be considered a civilian."

"What about you?"

"Ah, now that's something else again."

"You can't just let them have the balloon."

"I don't think we have much choice," he said, signaling to his corpsmen positioned around the reconnaissance balloon. They stood ready with rope and guide wire.

Then, impossibly, a shell hit the wheelhouse of the *Teaser*.

How could the Union battery fire on a ship hoisting a white flag?

Louisa shouted for her father, who would have been in the wheelhouse with the captain. The boiler exploded, spraying shards of twisted metal across what was left of the deck, killing crewmen and passengers alike, and the smokestack collapsed. Louisa screamed again; her father was most certainly dead.

Gun fire sprayed the barge and ricocheted off the pulley assembly, striking a corpsman in the chest. A shell exploded, felling all but one of the corpsmen and tearing the varnished silk covering of the balloon. Deadly hydrogen escaped in a constant hiss. Luckily, it wasn't a huge tear.

Two more shells exploded in the water behind Louisa's father's steamer before one found its mark.

The steamer began to sink.

Major Dunean picked up Louisa and dropped her into the balloon car as if she were no more than a small sandbag. A shell fragment passed through the cordage that encircled the balloon's envelope, but did not dislodge the loop from which the wicker balloon car was suspended...nor did it make another tear in the reinforced fabric. The major shouted to the remaining corpsman to cut the tethers and get into the car. Then he cut a tether and swung himself into the car. It could only be seconds before a shell tore right through the balloon's envelope and ignited the hydrogen gas. Another shell fragment destroyed more of the cordage, and damaged the car. Louisa—who was standing up in the car instead of cowering behind what little protection there was to be had— was unharmed. She heard the rat-tat-tat of bullets and saw Major Dunean's corpsman fall as he tried to climb into the car. He was so young and looked so surprised, as if someone had tapped him in the dark during a game of hide and seek.

The balloon jerked upward and snapped back, almost upending Louisa.

The clear blue sky seemed to be twisting like a top.

Major Dunean cut the last tether and Louisa screamed as a volley of grape-shot struck him in the face, knocking him bloody against the damaged section of the car. As the balloon jerked upward again, he fell through the torn wicker; and Louisa was alone, her stomach churning as the balloon ascended, its cut-away ropes hanging like tentacles on a squid. She heard howling wind and torn cloth flapping. An explosion shook the balloon. She closed her eyes, expecting the hydrogen to catch; and then she was standing up, shivering as if freezing cold, balancing against the unbroken wicker edge of the car, and throwing the small but heavy sandbags over the side. Up and up, five hundred feet, a thousand feet, two thousand feet, and *oh, God, Poppa's dead, and now there's nobody, not after not after what they did to Mother...*she couldn't bear to think about that, wouldn't think about that, and, anyway, she was going to die, and even Major Dunean who was so handsome and kind and showed her everything about balloons, who had even taken her up with him once to spy on the Yankees, was dead, so now it was her turn, just like in her dreams.

Louisa always dreamed. Her father told her that dreams came from unclean spirits to shake our minds and poison our souls and that if she wanted to get back to being as pure as when she was baptized, she would have to pray and ask God to protect her from the devil and his minions. She didn't know what minions meant, but sometimes it was only dreams that were good, dreams that were filled with light, dreams that kept her going after Momma died.

She wasn't going to think about that; and, anyway, the dream that kept coming back to her night after night wasn't a good one. It was dark and full of ice and snaking vines and trees that were upside down and made of glass and alive and could move like the fingers on her hands; and the people—and the devil monsters and spirits—spoke languages that she could only understand a little in her dream, ancient languages full of gutturals and hissings and lilting languages full of heat and emotion.

Louisa figured her father was right; that the dream came from the devil and was a portent that she was going to die. She deserved to die for having dreams that came from sin and damnation, and now, just as her father had told her over and over again, she would suffer Hell's punishments. Hell would swallow her up entire. In fact, she had seen the dire portent...she had seen the ugly-black, deeper-than-night crack in the sky.

But as she looked around, she couldn't find anything but gauzy streamers of cloud floating in the cold and windy blue heavens; and below, far below, she could see the hot reddish ground, the tiny irregular fields, hills, the deep green and black woods, the twists of the great James River, and the spidery roads and branching creeks. Wind buffeted the swinging basket, and Louisa held tight to the wicker and rope supports and prayed—prayed to the very god who would punish her—that she would not be tipped out of the car and thrown onto the spear-tipped trees below.

And as if directed by the punishing hand of God, the only true God who showed no mercy for sinful children and Anabaptists, the balloon descended.

Louisa thought to throw more ballast overboard, but she dared not let go of the rope. The winds carried her east, landmarks below shifting and changing like page numbers on shuffled pages; and she heard a distant rumbling, thundering; heard cannon and musket as the balloon swept her over the brown snake of the Chickahominy River and headed toward thick woods and a bloody field of battle where fifty-five thousand rebels smashed into a line of thirty-five thousand union corps. Smoke and dust obscured the scene of men shooting each other at close range, grappling with bayoneted rifles. Cavalry charged. Men in blue were giving way to men in gray, and Louisa could feel the heat and humidity of this windy, hot, June day; could feel the insane hate and rage and fear wafting upward with the screams and smoke and dust; could taste the blood and carnage as iron filings gritty in her mouth.

The balloon hovered over the battlefield, the air suddenly dead-still.

As the soldiers slaughtered each other, Louisa thought she saw odd things in the smoke...but not only in the smoke. She glimpsed strange things flickering around her, translucent columns that reminded her of tree trunks disappeared into the sky above, yet floated over the battle as if some bloodthirsty deity above was watching the indiscriminate, promiscuous killing below...and she imagined she saw things that looked like vines twisting around the columns. They reminded her of snakes. She didn't usually mind snakes, but these ghostly, transparent, twisting things made her feel sick with fear. They had somehow escaped from the sinful darkness of her dreams into the bright light of the undeniable here-and-now. She prayed—

OhGodhavemercynowIlaymedowntosleepIpraytheLordmysoultokeep

—she wouldn't collide with one of them. She just wanted to curl up in the basket with her eyes squeezed shut and wake up in her bunk in Poppa's steamer. She just wanted all this to disappear, but she kept watching the vines twisting among the men below. The vines were taking something from them, of that she was sure. Something precious. But she couldn't see what. She was too high above to see, but she knew that somehow the vines were...feeding. She threw sandbags over the side, and the balloon began to lift. Perhaps there would be some air movement above, enough to carry her away from here before—

The vines sensed her presence, and in one sweeping, swirling motion, they arced toward her. They wrapped themselves around the bright silk envelope and its cordage, then dropped into the basket as the balloon lifted. Louisa tried to keep away from the coiling and twisting things. She looked for something, anything, to stave them off. She tried to turn back to God again and pray for forgiveness and salvation, but her rote bedtime supplication was transformed into throat-tearing howls...the gnashing guttural dream-words of dream-prayers.

> *Mikma*
> *Lu cif ti as gsíf*
> *Kisˠ A do ĩ a*
> *Sa ba o o áo na*
> *Te lóc vo v im*
> *A do ĩ an Chris*
> *A do ĩ an Chis Gal-zŭn*
> *Mad i á od Bliórb gsíf*
> *Yax má drī iax*
> *Tab jes A do ĩ an*
> *Pe ríp sol*
> *Ad na vah A do ĩ an*

Although she couldn't know what god or demon or aeon was speaking to her, she understood those words from the language-before-languages.

> *Behold*
> *the messenger*
> *of your God*
> *and be wrapped*
> *in servitude to*
> *Him*
> *Holy-be-He*
> *in whose eyes*
> *you born of light*
> *are*
> *nothing but a mote*

> *in the brightness*
> *of His heavens.*

And then an updraft—or the snaking vines—lifted the balloon higher into the heavens, forcing it upward as if it were a midge caught in a squall. Louisa found a tether hook attached to a two foot length of rope. The rope was frayed where it had been torn. Hanging onto the edge of the basket with one hand, she swung the rope at the vines with her other hand. She swung the weighted rope in an oblique circle around her, as if it was itself a vine…as if the hook could bite and cut into the aetheric stuff of the snapping vines. Once again, she tried to pray…and once again dream-words, the demon's words, came spitting and coughing from her mouth.

> *Kũn mre*
> *lŏc vo kis⟨*
> *Sa ba vo kis⟨*
> *Gsner noz kis⟨*
> *Ķir sis sis noz kis⟨*
> *A do ĩ an Chis Gal-zũn*

> *These vines mine*
> *that enrapt you*
> *Capture you*
> *Will deliver you*
> *Sacrifice you*
> *To the Lord thy God*

As she flailed away at the writhing shoots, she imagined that the weighted rope was the snake, that the snake was but an extension of her arm, that *she* was the snake; and in that revelatory moment, the brightly colored balloon slipped from daylight into darkness. Louisa glimpsed the crack that separated this world or this place from another. It was ebon black; yet as she was whisked through it, as she felt a sudden, deep chill permeate her flesh and bones, she could *see* into the darkness. It had its own brightness. Its air was thin and difficult to breathe, and the balloon descended, fell as if hydrogen could hold no lift in this place. Louisa heard a cacophony of voices all around her, as if the vines she was keeping at bay each had a throat and a voice; and she heard the crystalline voice of the aeon Belias, his voice inside her as chilling as the frost-sharp air of this place. Above her, stars, triangulating constellations she had never seen…nor ever would where she had come from. Around her, in the snapping air, Belias' soul-stealing feeders attacked. Below, the purple-shaded, glittering, cratered land seemed to be rushing, spiraling toward her.

His voice was a slicing blade; and she knew the aeon as a god a demon, could see him shining in the surrounding darkness, for he was the darkness, the planet, the very air of this place…and yet he was a creature wearing his spirit like flesh and appearing like a blindingly dark and beautiful angel in her thoughts and memory, as if she had known him, as if she had always known him.

Louisa continued to slash furiously at the vines with her weighted rope, but they found their way around her legs, waist, neck, and—revoltingly— her crotch. They had wrapped themselves around the cordage that enveloped the balloon and had slithered vaporously through the wicker material of the car, which was swinging wildly as it fell. The car landed hard, bounced, and overturned, and Louisa was tossed, sprawling, onto the glassy slippery land. She slid down an incline and came to rest against the lip of a purple-shadowed crater. Her flesh was numbed and bruised by the pitted and cracked ground. The balloon collapsed behind her, and the vines thickened into a huge mass twisting and curling around her as if she was the light that all the dark things in this world sought.

But as the thousands of twisting, aggregating vines fed upon her, probed her, whispered the sacred words and thoughts of the almighty god their aeon to her, Louisa pushed herself against the lip of the crater. She tried to raise herself, certain that if she was prone, the parasite vines would devour her and leave her nothing, not even a thought of her own. She felt cold, dark bliss came over her, poisoning her, numbing her; and she imagined the aeon was giving her power: her inherited power, the power for which she was born.

I am the servant of the lord thy god Jehovah, and thou shalt not take any other gods before Him.

She heard—she *felt*—the strangling, viney voices of the lord's heavenly choir.

Ergo sum qui in re.

And I *am the one who is within you.*

No, she wasn't going to let them have her.

She was not going to let *him* have her.

But he *did* have her. His arms, his vines embraced her, caressed her; and she felt his divine darkness pouring into her like light. She felt wet and cold and invaded. She felt the bliss of revelation and Holy Communion, just as she understood the formal sounds of Latin as if they were her own tongue.

> *Lux manet in tenebris.*
> *Omnia pereunt a facie Dei.*
> *Pro ego sum vine. Ego sum lux lucis.*
> *Light resides in darkness.*

Everyone perishes before me.
For I am the vine. I am the light.

As the Aeon devoured her—as his icy ghost-vines drained her pneuma and her soul just as they had devoured the boy Lucian and his angel Gabriel—Louisa found the strength to respond. It was not the strength of a child, but the strength and understanding gained from recurrence...the strength and understanding gained from a thousand incarnations of her soul...a thousand reincarnations of self brought to sudden realization.

And Louisa whispered, *"Serpens sum, et deuoraui arbustum."*

I am a serpent, and I devour the vine.

She crawled up the glassy, granular crest until she could look over the edge of the crater. The vines ravaged her. They were a swirling cloud.

She cried and thought, *Better to die like Papa than like this.* She was just sixteen; and although she had seen death, smelled death, feared death, she somehow couldn't really believe in death. Even though she had watched her mother die at the hands of men whose lusts were as hot and as tortured as Belias' were cold and ciphered, she couldn't she wouldn't believe it.

Momma was gone.

Poppa was gone.

Handsome Major Dunean was gone.

And Louisa was going to find out where they went.

She threw herself into the darkness of the crater...and as she fell, she thought she saw something grand and crafted: the illuminated altar of a cathedral.

SEVEN

The Boughs of Heaven

Who then would not look with awe and wonder upon such a perfect sapphire, a spiritual mirror which has the appearance of a crystal gazing globe? It is, in fact, the aetheric soul plasm of the angel Gabriel who commands serpents and is also known as the magical stone.

—Pico Della Mirandola, *Emanations of Wisdom and the Celestial Pneuma 24.19*

The root of the tree of Belias is bitter, its branches are death, its shadow is hatred, a trap is in its leaves, its blossom is bad ointment, its fruit is death, desire is its seed, and it blossoms in darkness. The dwelling place of those who taste of it is the underworld, and darkness is their resting place.

—*The Apocryphon of John 20.28*

"What are *you* doing here?"

Pietro Neroni turned away from the gazing-globe to see Isabella, who had opened the door far enough to lean into the room. Her face was heart-shaped and freckled, her long curly hair thick and dark, and her startling blue eyes were the color of lapis lazuli.

"Master Mirandola forbids anyone to enter this room...especially you."

"Quickly, close the door," Pietro said. The images inside the globe swirled into an angry storm before dissipating into flat crystal grayness.

"There's no one else here," Isabella said.

"Close the door anyway. It is not a time for trust and carelessness."

Isabella laughed softly and shut the door quietly behind her. Then she stood beside him and leaned over the gazing-globe, as if she too could read what he saw in its crystal depths. "Don't you trust me?" she asked slyly.

Pietro felt awkward and disconcerted, as he always did in her presence. Although she inhabited his dreams, he would not admit that he was in love with her.

"You should be at the church celebrating the Eastertide miracle with your master and the rest of Florence," Isabella said.

"And you should be minding your business and cleaning his house or emptying the stink; not spying on me," Pietro said.

Stung, she said, "I'm his cousin, Pietro, not his drudge."

He immediately regretted what he said, but it was her own fault. She shouldn't have been spying on him. She shouldn't even be at the *bottega* today. "Why aren't you with the master? I checked the *bottega*. There was no one here. Did he send you back?"

"To spy on you?"

Pietro waited for her to answer, then asked, "Well...?"

"No," Isabella said, "I got separated from him and Fra Baldassare before we reached the Duomo. The crowds were enormous and angry because the guards weren't letting anyone in, and the cutpurses and—"

But Pietro wasn't listening. The gazing-globe seemed suddenly to come alive with phantasms. It was like looking into a window and seeing directly into the Duomo. Through curtains of swirling mist, Pietro could see into the vast interior of the cathedral...could see the miracle, huge and incontrovertible, that stood before the high altar: the impossibly upside-down ash tree that had appeared a fortnight ago in the cathedral on Easter Sunday. It had descended through Brunelleschi's great dome, seemingly without damaging it, and disappeared into the undamaged mosaic floor of the cathedral. The tree wavered and flickered like any creature of the air and spirit; yet it was substantial as stone. Its bark was greenish-gray, covered with skin-colored knots, and cold as snow. Its branches, which reached and curled upwards as if defying gravity, were devoid of leaves. Burghers, wage laborers, petty merchants, and peasants pushed and squeezed, trying to get closer to the tree, which was guarded by a throng of burly, well armed soldier-priests. The priests kept them away from the seated aristocratic families whose importance determined their proximity to the tree...away from the altar of Our Lady where Francesco Salviati, the archbishop of Florence, recited the Paternoster. And as Pietro gazed into the globe, he could not help but notice those in the crowd who were eerily silent and still: gray-faced burghers and peasants who looked vacant, soulless, and somehow threatening.

Standing beside the archbishop were Guiliano de Medici, First Citizen and ruler of Florence, and Cardinal Caraffa, the pox-faced commander of the hated and feared Dominican Companions of the Night.

Pietro saw his master Pico Della Mirandola standing behind the ruler's brother, wife, and four daughters. But where was Baldassare?

The archbishop raised his arms to the tree, as if it were the holy Christ itself, and said, "*Unus est Deus noster, Deus Deus noster.*" The crowd responded with "*Adeste, adeste, amen,*" and then everyone, peasant and patrician alike, kneeled. The archbishop glanced knowingly at the cardinal and shouted, "*Adeste, filiola lucis.*"

The congregation became unsettled.

"He's become a heathen," Pietro mumbled as he gazed into the globe. "Heresy…"

"Who's become a heathen?" Isabella asked. She leaned in front of him, as if by getting closer to the globe, she could see what he saw. Frustrated, she pulled back and said, "Tell me what you see."

"Out of the way," Pietro whispered. "There, he's repeated it again."

"What?"

"The archbishop…in the Duomo…he's reciting the *Laudate Dominum.*"

"So?"

"He keeps calling for the daughter of light."

"There is no daughter of light," Isabella said, crossing herself. "Come away from that globe. It will witch you."

"*Deus,*" he whispered, "I think it already has." Pietro watched as a section of the tree's bole opened like a lipless mouth and expelled an outlandishly dressed young woman, who fell, screaming. She grabbed hold of an upturned branch, hung on for an instant; but her hands slipped, and she dropped onto the stained mosaic floor of the cathedral. She seemed unharmed; the branch had broken her fall. The young woman stood up unsteadily and, terrified, looked around at the stinking, seething crowd and guards that surrounded her. She murmured, "Oh, Lord, am I to be judged by monsters?" and then looked up at the altar, as if Saint Peter himself was standing above the hellish throng. The archbishop looked down upon her with a penitent smile. The cardinal, who stood on the right side of the archbishop, looked impassively toward the lieutenant of his guards. Of the three, only Giuliano de Medici, who stood to the left of the archbishop, seemed truly surprised to witness the miraculous appearance. The archbishop raised his hands to calm those in the crowd who screamed in shock and terror.

"Numerus tuus est benedictus"

The crowd, electrified, pushed toward the miraculous girl who had fallen from the tree: miracle upon miracle.

"Gloria Laus et honor Deo patri et filio et Spritui Santo," intoned the archbishop. But the cardinal silenced him and spoke directly to a large group of

silent, empty-faced congregants that had formed around the patrician, high-born families: they gazed at him fixedly, as if waiting for a signal, a divine pronouncement.

"Arise, now, oh servants of God. Arise and cleanse. Destroy the wickedness of our enemies. The name of God is eternal."

"Purifica Domine sanctum tuum, et dele iniquitatem inimicorum nostro-rum."

Then the cardinal nodded to his lieutenant, drew a knife from inside his carmine robes and with a swift turn, drove it directly into the heart of Guiliano de Medici, the First Citizen.

Two of the cardinal's guards grabbed the girl who had fallen from the tree while soldier-priests and the contingent of silent congregants attacked the highborn families. Knives were drawn and clubs pulled out of hidden belts and pockets. The patricians tried to run, but they were surrounded. The soulless, slack-faced congregants knifed them, beat them, clubbed them, and tore them limb from limb with blind, almost casual efficiency. The rest of the congregation—the stunned and terrified worshipers, the ordinary citizens—clamored to escape the carnage.

All that seen in the crystal...seen in an instant.

Pietro stepped back from the gazing-globe. "Oh, God..."

"What is it?" Isabella asked, insistent. "Tell me."

"I couldn't see our master," Pietro said. "He was there, I saw him, and then I didn't, so he must be...he must be..."

"Pietro..."

Pietro leaned toward the gazing-globe once again. His face felt hot, and his heart seemed to leap into his throat, there to pound so hard that he could feel it in his jaw. The globe was clouded, but he could see into the cathedral, which was now silent and littered with corpses. The stained-glass window behind the altar was dark, as were the three above it...but it wasn't dark outside. Light poured in through the high and narrow windows of Mirandola's skrying room.

Was the globe allowing him to look into time itself?

He blinked, and another phantasm appeared: Cardinal Caraffa's wolves of the church—the Police of Public Morals, the Officers of the Night and of the Monasteries—hurried through tangled, familiar streets toward Mirandola's bottega. Were they coming for his master? No, the cardinal would know he would be at the cathedral. Unless it was early...before the slaughter took place. Perhaps the cardinal wasn't taking any chances. Perhaps he was after the master's secret volumes and objects...the globe, the...

The phantasm in the globe disappeared, to be replaced by erupting flames; and once again Pietro stepped back from the globe.

He could feel the heat of the fire.

The bottega was burning...or would be burning soon.

"Quickly, we must leave here now."

Isabella insisted that he explain what he had seen.

"I will, I promise," Pietro said. "Once we're out of the building. Once we're safe." He couldn't help but make a face when he said that, for he knew there would be little safety anywhere now. "Please... We will be killed if we don't leave immediately. The bottega is to be burned."

Isabella looked at him quizzically, then seeing how upset he was, nodded.

"We can't take very much. He put two of his master's precious leather-bound notebooks into a satchel, and looked around for Albertus Magnus's *Speculum Alchimus*, which Mirandola had kept hidden. "Take the jewels and solvents," he said to Isabella, "but be especially careful with the *aurum potabile* and *spiritus mundi*. Do you know where the master hid his volume of —"

"It's wrapped in a cloth inside the buckler on the wall," Isabella said.

"Do you read minds...did you learn that from the master."

"No, Pietro," she said with an anxious smile, "I only read *your* mind."

Pietro blushed, retrieved the *Speculum Alchimus*, and settled a velvet pouch on top of the obsidian mirror. He wanted to take the mirror, but it was far too large. It would be enough to take the gazing-globe. If his master survived the treachery in the cathedral, he would have great need for the globe...and for a skryer.

At that instant he thought of the traitorous murderer Baldassare and felt rage and fear burning hot in his chest. He thought of his master's servant Lucian, who had disappeared into the globe the day before the feast of the Purification of the Virgin. Baldassare had claimed that he was taken by the angel Gabriel. Pietro wondered where Lucian was and whether he was still alive.

He carefully lifted the gazing-globe from its wax supports, but it felt so hot that he almost dropped it. He yelped, but would not—could not—let it go. Isabella turned to him and saw the globe shimmer, then burst like a soap bubble. She smelled the acrid odor of burning flesh.

Pietro screamed in pain and fell to his knees.

Isabella rushed to help him. The globe was smoke roiling between his hands. "Pietro, release it!"

"I can't."

"Yes, you can," she said, reaching through the lingering vapors and gently prying open his fingers. "My God," she whispered. A small bone-white stone, roughly shaped like a key, had burned and buried itself into his palm. It was smooth as flesh, except for a bruised-blue striation that looked like a coiled snake.

"I have destroyed the globe, or it has destroyed me."

"No, it's a sign," Isabella said, awed. "A miracle. A gift." She dipped a cloth in one of Mirandola's unguents and bandaged Pietro's hand.

Then came the inevitable pounding at the front door.

"It's too late," Pietro said, still dazed. He looked at his bandaged hand as if it belonged to someone else.

"No...it's not too late. Can you get up?"

"Of course I can," he said, forcing himself...willing himself to recover. "But I'm certain that Baldassare's men will cover every exit." Then a quizzical expression crossed his face, and he shook his head, as if suddenly ashamed of himself.

Isabella started to ask him what he had just seen, but there was no time.

"We must get down to the basement before they break in. I know a way out."

She helped Pietro to his feet, and they hurried down the stairs, taking care to be as quiet as possible.

"I know every inch of this bottega," Pietro whispered. "How is it that you know a secret exit?"

"You are first apprentice. I am family, if only a cousin." Isabella took Pietro's hand and led him through the pitch-dark basement, feeling her way like a blind child who could remember the feel and touch of every stone and corner. Above, the Police of Public Morals smashed in the door and stormed through the bottega.

"It is here," she said, grunting as she pushed against a disused door. Pietro helped her. The door creaked, then gave way. Before them were stone steps that descended into a single, thin shaft of light. The light seemed tangible as metal, golden and dust-laden. They closed the door, and it took both of them to fix a heavy piece of lumber into the curved iron jamb fittings on either side of the entrance. The black guards would need a ram to break into the tunnel. Pietro followed Isabella down the stairs into a stone chapel. The shaft of light illuminated a Psalter open on a rough-hewn altar table. Isabella removed a torch from an iron lantern on the wall, found flint and straw stored in an alcove behind the altar, and, as Pietro held the torch, struck a kindling flame. The torch illuminated the chapel, and the ornately carved cross above the archway that led into darkness.

Isabella's hands were shaking, and she dropped the glowing kindle.

"This place...did the master come here to pray often?" Pietro asked gently, ignoring the pulsing ache in his wounded hand.

"He said the chapel was holy ground, that a saint had once hidden here, and that all who prayed here would be blessed."

"Then you'd better say a prayer."

"I have…and so should you. Now you must tell me what you saw in the gazing-globe."

"When we are safe from the black guards."

She was resolute. "No, Pietro, now!"

Pietro nodded and told her everything he could remember. But the images in the gazing globe that had been so sharp and tangible moments ago were now distant and dreamlike; and Pietro wondered if, indeed, he had really seen those phantasms.

"…tell me if my cousin is dead."

"I don't know."

"You *do*. You saw *something*.

"It's as I told you. I saw the cathedral. I saw the cardinal murder the first citizen. I saw the Easter tree spit out the girl. I saw the crowds murdering everyone of rank. I saw—"

"You said you saw the master," Isabella said, insistent.

"Yes. But I didn't see what happened to him."

"You saw the black monks coming here. Perhaps what you saw in the cathedral hasn't happened yet. Perhaps the first citizen still lives. If we could warn him, we could—"

"Did the master tell you where this artery leads?" Pietro asked, looking through the archway.

"No," Isabella said, "and he made me swear never to come here unless I was in fear for my life. He said if I prayed in the chapel, the saint would protect me."

"Did he tell you the name of the saint?"

"No, he said the name of the saint was his alone to know. But he once told me that the bottega was once under the rule of Saint Dominic."

"Ah…"

"What does that mean?" Isabella asked.

"The Duomo was also once under the rule of the Dominicans. Perhaps there is a passage that opens near the cathedral."

She nodded and followed him into the massed darkness of the catacomb.

There was the smell of death in this corridor, dry and ancient. The torchlight revealed stone effigies of saints and demons and human skulls that stared blindly out from their shelves, niches, and open tombs rough-cut into the walls. Isabella gasped when she saw them, then prayed. The pain in Pietro's wounded palm became worse as they made their way deeper into the catacomb, and he had to shift the heavy torch from hand to hand.

"Give me the torch," Isabella said. "I can carry it."

"No, it is all right." But Pietro was coughing.

"Give me the torch! I am stronger than you think."

He handed it over to her, and she led the way, holding the torch high to keep some of the tarry, gagging smoke out of their eyes. There was a cold breeze in the catacomb, which swirled the smoke back into their faces.

"I know there's more you're not telling me," Isabella said.

"I've told you everything."

"No, I saw the look on your face when the black guards broke into the bottega. You were certain they were coming, but something else surprised you. You shook your head and looked away from me. That stone in your hand told you something about my cousin, didn't it... Didn't it."

Her question was a statement.

"No...but I think it told me something about Baldassare."

"Well?"

"He isn't part of the conspiracy," Pietro said. "I was thinking ill thoughts about him, and then..."

"And then?"

"And then I felt sick for thinking like that. I felt...wrong."

"It could be that you wished him to be better than he might be," Isabella said, and swore as the torch flickered and finally died. Purple and red retinal afterimages became more ghostly with every blink, and Pietro and Isabella were left blind in total darkness. "It's my fault," Isabella whispered, as if without light, their chatter and thoughts might be heard by night creatures such as wight-ghosts and cacodemons. "My cousin told me always to refresh the pitch whenever I use a torch. I just forgot."

"Take my hand," Pietro said. "I will keep touch with one wall, and if you can reach to touch the other, we can feel our way. When we come to an opening on either side, we will find it." He didn't feel at all that confident; but as he walked and held her hand, he felt that he must pretend all would be well. Isabella shuddered as her fingers slid along the rough, dry wall. She imagined wet, venomous spiders hiding in bare skulls whenever she touched a shelf or depression in the wall. She forced herself to breath regularly and murmured her bedtime protective prayer over and over. "*Unus est Deus noster, Deus Deus noster.*"

"Tell me about the girl in the Easter tree," she said, squeezing Pietro's hand.

"I don't think we should call it that, and it might be best if we are as quiet as possible."

"Are you frightened?" Isabella asked.

After a pause, Pietro said, "I'm fine. We'll be fine. I would estimate that we've walked half the distance to the Duomo." But the darkness seemed to swirl around Isabella, or so she thought. She imagined that there were things in the darkness that were darker than dark, and a song from her childhood came to mind. She couldn't help herself; she had to do *something* to break the darkness. Being quiet didn't help; in fact, it seemed to make it worse. She sang softly, barely above a whisper, translating the gutturals of her mother's tongue into soft Florentine dialect.

Wounded and grieving
I hung onto that gnarly tree

For nine days and nine nights
I hung onto that gnarly tree

That gnarly tree called night
That tree that pierces all nine realms

That tree 'round which all revolves
And no one knows its roots

And no one gave me food
And no one gave me drink

So into the black abyss I stared
I stared 'till I could spy a light

And then I fell, a-howling
Screaming in despair

Surprised, Pietro asked, "What heretical song is that?"

"It could be about the girl who fell from the tree."

"But it's not, is it."

"I don't know whether it's about a girl or a god or a man. My mother sang it to me before I was taken away."

"Taken away?" Pietro asked.

"Before I came south, away from Midgard...the place my cousin calls the Yellow Country."

"You don't have blond hair."

Under different circumstances she would have laughed; but she felt suddenly cold, weak, and claustrophobic. "Only my mother was from the north," she said softly.

"And the master Mirandola?"

"No, he has only the rich blood of the south. Like you," she teased.

"Wait," Pietro said. "Stay still."

When he let go of her hand, she gasped. For an instant she thought she was falling into a vast darkness below...the abyss of her song. "What is it?" she asked, reaching for him.

"I don't know. Something...*wrong*."

"I don't see anything," Isabella said. "I can't hear anything—"

"Except yourself!"

Stung, Isabella stared into the darkness ahead. She held her arms against her chest, as if to protect herself.

"There, can you hear that?" Pietro asked in a whisper. "Someone's coming."

Isabella thought she heard *something*, soft echoes perhaps. "I don't know... maybe you're right...someone running?"

"Take my hand," Pietro whispered. "We've got to hide. Perhaps one of the tomb shelves would do? We might not to be noticed."

Isabella shuddered, thinking of skulls and spiders. "We can go back to the bottega."

"No, the bottega is ablaze. Can't you feel it?"

Indeed, she felt the new warmth in the air...and heard footsteps.

Ahead in the tunneled distance was a glowing redness; and then a hooded figure carrying a blazing torch appeared, as if from around a corner or from another artery that fed into the catacomb.

Pietro drew his dagger. His hand throbbed in pain, which seemed to increase with every breath he took; the stone was scalding him, just as the gazing-globe had done. "Move back toward the bottega as quietly as you can," he whispered into Isabella's ear, "and pray God he is alone." He could smell her hair and perfumed sweat.

Quietly, he edged forward.

Club-footed he might be, but he was strong and had been trained as a *condottiere* by the ruthless Vitellozzo Vitelli himself.

He was also wrong, for two torches appeared behind the first. Their angry, distraught bearers were arguing. The catacomb made it difficult to judge distance; their voices sounded as if they were coming through the walls beside him. If Pietro could kill the leader with a quick thrust to the heart, then he might have some chance of overcoming the other two who wore the dark-colored hoods and wide-sleeved gowns of monks. But were the men coming toward him Cardinal Caraffa's wolves of the church or friends of his master? The Holy Church was broken, divided: there were those such as Baldassare, cruel and cunning as he might be, who were open to truth; and there were those like Caraffa who did the bidding of the dark aeon Belias and slavishly proclaimed the demiurge Jehovah to be the one true god...

"*They are all traitors.*"

"*You don't know who might be a traitor and who might not.*"

"*We will find out soon, and then—*"

"*We are not dealing with ordinary men, Antonio. Those doing the killing were in thrall, possessed.*"

That last said by the leader. A familiar voice...

Isabella recognized her cousin and shouted his name, even as she ran past

Pietro to meet him. Pietro rushed after her. She could be mistaken, and then…

Mirandola lifted his torch, casting new shadows over the bone-dry dead that lined the walls all around them.

"Isabella. Could it really be you? I was worried when I couldn't find you in the cathedral." He embraced his cousin, who said, "I've much to tell you. You can't reach the bottega, it—" She caught her breath and said, "Pietro is here, too."

Mirandola looked at his apprentice and said, "So I see. What mischief have you been up to in here?" His words were stern, but his face looked haunted.

Pietro tried to explain what had happened, but the pain in his bandaged hand was excruciating. It exploded into his arms and chest.

He couldn't breathe and staggered backwards.

Mirandola tried to catch his apprentice as he fell, but it was like touching molten metal. He screamed in agony and jumped away from Pietro.

"Pietro…" shouted Isabella. "Your hand…is aflame…"

Pietro reached out to her and fell into bursting, blinding, exploding light. Isabella was thrown backwards by the blast and searing heat, as were Mirandola and his companions.

And as Pietro fell into curtained whiteness, he saw…Lucian.

EIGHT

Gathering in the Hand of Fate

Let an angel come into existence as my attendant.

—*The Gospel of Judas 47.1*

She is in the world, and another World will commence with that one.

—John Dee, *Quartus Liber Mysteriorum*

"*Stay back, boy. I cannot hold them. They finish me…and they will have you.*"

But the angel's warning came too late.

Belias' vines—his transparent, soul-depleting vines—suddenly released Gabriel and shot through the darkness toward Lucian. It was as if an arrow storm had been aimed at the boy from a thousand longbows, an arrow storm of twisting vines directed at the boy who had disobeyed Gabriel's command to keep his distance. The angel tried to follow after the vines, but Belias was still a presence enveloping him, holding him. However, now that the vines had removed themselves to attack Lucian, now that they weren't layered around the angel to form living winding sheets, Gabriel could once again see clearly…could *see* Belias' world in its entirety: the cold stars blinking above the ebon mountains that surrounded him; the silvery highlights of the cold cratered ground before him; the vines entering his ward, draining his life and soul, emptying him. Powerless, the angel floated in the lifeless darkness, his feet raised from the ground, his arms outstretched, as if Belias had secured him like a marionette to garrote wires. But all Gabriel could do was see…and hear.

Hear what Belias heard. See what Belias saw.

The angel heard Lucian call to him, just as he *saw* the contraption that held the daughter of light fall to the ground and quiver like a jellyfish stranded upon a black shore; and he saw, heard, and felt the agonizing and overwhelming presence of Belias, who now cloaked himself in angelic form as he pursued and spoke to the daughter of light. Then he saw the vines release Lucian and arc toward the girl, who was trying to crawl out of the contraption. He saw the aeon as he wished to be seen by the daughter of light: Belias, the dark twin of Gabriel, Belias whose thick straight hair cut across a face as chiseled and pale as Leonardo's statue of Judas, whose wings were the color and texture of silver, whose gown was as dark and deep as satin, and whose touch and voice were ecstasy itself. Belias—who was now a world, a middle-heaven, a spirit, an angel, and a thought—was infinitely stronger than Gabriel.

Gabriel was now but another soul trapped in his cold, cratered kingdom: too weak to help the boy and too weak to help the girl, who was now the prime focus of the aeon, which sought to bind and control her. Although it might take an eternity to drain Gabriel's soul, Belias had certainly won. Even when Gabriel sought to protect Lucian by capturing and trying to kill Belias' soul swallowing vines, the dark aeon was subtly capturing the angel's material soul, scattering it with every lunge and whipping caress of his snaking fingers. But like Lucian's soul-stealing serpent, which when distracted for but an instant loosened its deadly hold, so had the viney, crystalline fetters of Belias loosened slightly. Gabriel listened to Lucian's last, weak thoughts, thoughts of release, thoughts of reuniting with his material soul, thoughts of the crystal globe through which he had passed. And in that tick between ticking, that timeless instant, Gabriel gathered himself and wrested free of Belias.

The invisible garrote wires snapped, and Gabriel appeared before Lucian, who lay on the glassy ground. The boy hardly breathed. His face was as pale as the aeon. The vines no longer strangled him, for they had taken everything and hastened to the call of their master who was grasping at the soul of the daughter of light, the girl who was fighting Belias, even as he beckoned her to ecstasy.

"*Lucian...*"

The angel floated above the boy, his purple robe billowing as if in a storm, his wings slapping at the thin air and sounding like a great bellows. He could not hope to extract the daughter of light from Belias' grasp; but as the dark aeon's attention was now concentrated on the girl, Gabriel might have a chance of helping Lucian.

Lucian stirred.

"*You must return to your master Mirandola. You must return to the glass.*"

"*I am not...*"

"*You are not what?*" Gabriel asked.

"I am not."

"You are," Gabriel insisted.

"He has taken me."

"Not all of you. Your material soul is still whole. Seek it now."

"Too late," Lucian said, although his lips did not move, nor did he breathe.

Gabriel was having difficulty holding his position. His face was anguished; his wings were tearing in a great tempest, yet the air was still. Belias was again aware of Gabriel…and the boy. Even as he tore at the girl, he shifted some small bit of his focus back onto the angel. There was no time, no matter how compressed, to spare. Belias would soon master Gabriel again and, like sucking marrow from a bone, would diminish him, finish him.

"My physical soul is here," Gabriel said. *"Yours is not. Let yourself fall back into the stone."*

"Help me, Gabriel. I can't…"

"I can do little. I am weakened. Too much of my soul is here, in the grasp of Belias. It is time for you to help me."

"Me…?"

The angel smiled, and for an instant Lucian felt warmth, which was quickly lost to the deathly chill that overcame him.

"Call back your serpent," Gabriel said. *"It will take back what Belias has stolen."*

"I tried before. I can't. I don't even know where it is. And I cannot trust it. It tried to kill me."

"No, it was caught by the will of the aeon. You mastered it enough to release it. Now you must call it back," and with that Gabriel with great difficulty spread his arms as he had when he first sent the serpent to Lucian. His wings cast a shadowy light over Lucian, or perhaps a lighter shadow. *"Can you sense it now?"*

"Yes…I can." Lucian willed it to return; and like remembrance itself, it glinted across the darkness and snapped back to Lucian, strengthening him, returning what the aeon had stolen.

"Return to the stone now. *And tell—"*

But now Belias was concentrating all his power on the angel.

"It will not take me an eternity to destroy you, angel of weakness…"

The aeon's voice was a knife, eviscerating; and Gabriel made a sound like that of water trickling into a fountain, or perhaps a sigh, as he fell, wounded, deflated, to the ground. High above the angel, the stars were fixed points of light, as sharp as needles, as white as death.

"Go," he whispered to Lucian. *"I am lost."*

Lucian obeyed and willed himself back to the gazing-globe he imagined to be in his master's skrying room. He felt the serpent's power burning inside him; and in that last instant, as the demon Belias grasped at Gabriel, Lucian felt the snake's lust as it sought and swallowed the angel's soul.

As the snake tightened around his heart, Lucian fell back to the skrying crystal...back to earth...back to earthly time.

He felt overpowering bliss.

He could not contain the angel—he would surely die of it—and he also felt the dark, insinuating presence of a demon: Belias, poisoning him.

Angel and demon and serpent.

Killing him with flame and frost.

Pico Della Mirandola was the first to recover.

He moved his arms away from his face and retrieved his torch, which was still burning on the ground a few feet away from him. He had been thrown backward by an explosion. His head pounded in pain, his eyes stung, his face felt hot as if he had fever and sunburn. He leaned against the wall of the catacomb for support, held the torch high, and gasped in wonder as he watched his first apprentice Pietro.

The boy was kneeling, and he held Mirandola's gazing globe in his outstretched hands; yet the object kept losing its shape. It was smoke, mist roiling, snaking, curling, and expanding. Then the air snapped, as if the catacomb itself was cracking, and some of the smoke twisted away from Pietro's open hands and resolved itself into a human figure, a swarthy skinned, awkward, delicately built young man who just now looked much older than his twenty-one years. He had a flattened nose, piercing eyes, and a white scar that encircled his throat like a necklace.

"Lucian? Can that really be you...?"

Mirandola's servant Lucian might have been mist and smoke an instant before, but now he was flesh and bone...and lying beside Pietro. Convulsed in pain and still cloaked in snaking mist, Lucian reached out and snatched the gazing globe away from Pietro. Pietro groaned and then collapsed, as if the globe was his heart, breath, pneuma, and lifeblood. An image appeared in the roiling globe: a beautiful, chiseled, angelic face distorted in agony.

"Gabriel, I release you. Please...release me," Lucian begged, trying to stand up.

The globe shimmered and burst like a soap bubble, just as it had when Pietro had first picked it up in Mirandola's skrying room. Lucian collapsed on top of Pietro, and something skittered and clattered along the floor of the catacomb toward Mirandola. It looked like a small white stone. Mirandola called to Pietro and Lucian, then picked up the stone to examine it. But it burned and blistered his hand.

Dropping the stone, he swore and whispered "*Kyrie eleyson.*"

"It burned Pietro, too."

Mirandola turned, surprised and in pain. His cousin Isabella stood beside him. Her face was red as if sunburned. Her forehead was bruised from a concussion; and she seemed dazed, as if she was still fighting her way back to full consciousness.

"Are you all right?" he asked, holding his wounded hand, which began to feel numb.

She nodded.

"What just happened?"

"It's the stone," Isabella said. "It burned you as it did Pietro when he tried to save it from the black friars who broke into your bottega. But it burned Pietro differently I think. It burned into his soul. The stone and your gazing globe are one and the same now...somehow." She loosened a pomander from her neck and tied the resin saturated cloth around her cousin's hand. "This will have to do until we can apply some proper unguents to your wound. Now I must see to Pietro...I am afraid for him."

Mirandola followed her over to Pietro and Lucian; his two companions, soldier priests, had also recovered. They had retrieved their torches and stood beside him, as if he needed protection from his cousin and the two young men lying unconscious on the cold stone floor. One of the priests, the younger, gazed intently and somewhat quizzically at Lucian, who stirred, then looked up at his master with relief and joy.

"Thank goodness, Gabriel," Lucian said, speaking to himself, or to an angel only he could see. "I could not contain you one instant longer." As if suddenly recognizing Mirandola—and realizing he was not Gabriel—he looked this way and that for the angel. "Gabriel, Gabriel, where are you? Reveal yourself. Have you escaped Belias entire? I pray so." Then he turned to Pietro and shuddered. "You...you are the stone. No, you are not...you are—"

Dying.

Lucian recovered himself, although he had no idea what this dark place was. He could feel the icy presence of the demon as well as the tight, heart-squeezing presence of the serpent, and yet he knew this wasn't Belias' world. He was back home, but what had happened? His master was here, was talking to him. Isabella, beautiful dark-haired Isabella, was attending to Pietro. But Pietro was no longer the apprentice he knew. Just looking at him was a revelation. Phantasmic images passed before Lucian's eyes, as if he were looking into the gazing globe. Pietro was flesh and blood; but he had been changed, transformed by the skrying crystal, just as the skrying crystal—

the gazing globe—had been transformed into a stone. With a shock, Lucian realized that looking at Pietro was like…looking at Gabriel. Pietro seemed to appear and reappear, as if he was flickering back and forth at impossible speed from one place to another.

"Give him back the stone…quickly," Lucian whispered to Mirandola.

"I tried to pick it up, and I burned myself. If we wait a few minutes, perhaps it will—"

"No time to wait." Lucian said, trying to stand; but he was too weak, so he tried to crawl. "No time," he mumbled. "No time…"

"I'll get it." Isabella said; Mirandola tried to stop her, but she was too quick. She ran into the darkness, but she could see the stone as if it was the only star twinkling in the firmament. She grasped it. The pain was unbearable. She could smell burning flesh. Her hand and arm felt suddenly numb, then dead; but she managed to carry the stone back to Pietro and press it into his hand. He convulsed, as if shocked, then sat up. He stared at the stone, which had once again fused into his palm…become part of him like the bones in his fingers.

"What do you see?" Lucian asked him.

"I see where you have been…in the dark world that I showed you in the master's black mirror."

"And Gabriel? What of Gabriel? Tell me…"

But Pietro looked up at Isabella and grasped her wounded hand with his own. "Thank you, sweet Isabella," he said. "We must attend to your burn."

"I do not feel any pain," she said, blushing and crouching beside Pietro. "It just feels…numb."

"Yes," Pietro said, reluctantly releasing her hand and showing her his own, which had begun to cicatrize around the stone. "But you will not need unguents. Look, my wound is already healing."

The two priests attending Mirandola crossed themselves. The taller, who had the hard face of a soldier and the soft voice of a councilor, said to Mirandola, "We must leave this place lest we become caught in this prestidigitator's magic. Our orders are clear Maestro. We must leave now. And your hand, Maestro. Is *your* hand healing?"

"No, Antonio, not yet, at least; but I am not in pain. And the young man is not a conjurer. He's my apprentice, as is the boy Lucian." Mirandola nodded to Lucian, as if finally only now truly accepting him as an apprentice, as part of his family household.

"Our orders are to convey you to the appointed place," Antonio said. "No others are to accompany us. It will not be safe, and we do not have horses or supplies to—"

"Enough," Mirandola said. "*I* am ordering you. Would you resist?"

Isabella flinched, as she had never heard her cousin speak with such commanding force.

The priest inclined his head slightly in submission.

"Now, Pietro, answer Lucian's question," Mirandola said in a gentler voice. "What of Gabriel?"

Just then the angel revealed himself.

Lucian stood up, his eyes glittering in the torchlight.

"I think Lucian can answer that for himself now," Pietro said, standing, too. Although Pietro could sense Gabriel's sudden presence, only Lucian could *see* the angel flickering and shifting like a dream in the transparent darkness of the catacomb.

"Gabriel, I was afraid that—"

"*Fear not, young maskil,*" Gabriel said; but only Lucian could hear the angel's soft yet penetrating voice. "*We have both escaped Belias whole and entire. You may explain to your master that, as foretold in the Gospel, the Days of Grief are descending upon the earth; and the remembrancer, which your master has been so keen to acquire, is now in his possession.*"

The angel smiled, and Lucian smelled cinnamon and felt some slight warmth replace the chill that had captured his heart.

"*And perhaps you can help the remembrancer remember.*"

"Me...?" Lucian asked. "I don't understand."

"*When you learn to stop referencing yourself, perhaps you might understand,*" Gabriel said. "*In the meantime, your master can explain.*"

Lucian chuckled, even as he blushed in embarrassment at the angel's familiar rebuke, and said, "I will petition him to enlighten me."

"*Tell Maestro Mirandola that he and the others must go to the fortress in Urbino, but they must not tarry there or they will be lost,*" Gabriel said, flooding Lucian with a chill, desperate fear. "*You must find and free the girl... the daughter of light. She is the one. She is the fleshy incarnation of the aeon Sophia; and only she can defeat the demiurge that she conceived in ignorance and sin. Your master must gather enough force to free her no matter what the cost.*"

"No, you cannot ask me to do this," Lucian said. "*You* must ask my master. You must reveal yourself to him directly, for he will not believe me."

"What will I not believe?" Mirandola asked, looking quizzically at Lucian. "Whom do you speak to? Angel or demon? Gabriel or—?"

"*You must not speak of these things in front of strangers,*" continued the angel. "*And be warned that there is one amongst you who—*"

"Tell me...tell me who?" Lucian asked, but Gabriel was no longer present.

"The angel is gone, Lucian," Pietro said as he gazed into the space where Gabriel had been.

"Lucian!" Mirandola said, agitated. "I asked you a question. Tell me whom you spoke to."

"He spoke to the angel…Gabriel," Pietro said.

"Is that true?"

"Yes, Maestro," Lucian said.

"Are you sure it was not a demon?"

"It was not a demon, Maestro."

"And did *you* see and hear the angel, too?" Mirandola asked Pietro; there was anger in his voice, and anxiety: the anxiety of being the blind man among those who were receptive to the spirits.

"I sensed his presence, Maestro, but that is all."

"And what did the angel tell you?" Mirandola asked Lucian.

"I cannot tell you when there are…strangers present." Lucian took a furtive glance at the soft-spoken priest Gentile, who—torch in hand—had pushed past Isabella to be closer to Mirandola. The priest's proximity made Lucian very uncomfortable. The circlet scar around his neck burned and itched; and for an instant he felt soiled and suddenly dizzy with grief, which he attributed to the soul-searing shock of escaping with Gabriel from Belias' dark, cratered kingdom and falling back here…to this dark, earthy place: the grief was most likely some delayed psychic effect.

But Lucian would be wrong in thinking that.

"We are losing light," Gentile said as he turned his flickering torch this way and that to conserve the flame. The senior priest Antonio approached and said, "Maestro Mirandola, we must make our way out of here now while we still have light. Or we must find new torches." Mirandola nodded and turned to walk in the direction of his bottega. His torch flickered out, but he seemed unconcerned.

"You cannot go that way," Pietro said. "The bottega has been burned."

Mirandola sighed in resignation. "Lucian, Pietro…walk beside me."

"I will light the way for you, Maestro," Antonio said, stepping in front of Mirandola; Gentile stayed behind near Isabella: a soft shadow holding a guttering torch.

"I know my way through these dark corridors as well as blind Boethius knew his garden," Mirandola said, "and I will lead you to an exit…or find you another torch. Now please, Antonio, allow me a few words with my apprentices."

"What is this place?" Lucian whispered when they had left all the others a small distance behind.

"You are in the secret catacombs," Mirandola said, "but do not worry. I once spent two months living with the dead here. I can see with my hands in this place." His hand brushed against the wall as he walked; the soft slapping, sliding, and tapping of his fingers against stone and ancient bones seemed exaggerated by the darkness.

"What were you doing here?" Pietro asked.

"Hiding."

"When? From who?"

"I had to hide when the mad priest Savonarola accused me of sorcery and burned my bottega to the ground," Mirandola said, scowling in the darkness. "At the time it seemed a better solution than being burned on a cross."

"Which was what I heard happened to many before the—"

"*Permesso*...now tell me who has burned down my home this time."

"The black monks," Pietro said. "I saw them coming."

"Yes...?"

"Please forgive my disobedience, Maestro; but I sneaked into your skrying room and looked into the gazing globe. That's where I saw them."

"It appears that your disobedience saved the globe, your life, and that of my cousin's, isn't that true?"

"I think Isabella saved me."

"We saved some of your potions and jewels and your *Speculum Alchimus*," Isabella said. She had been walking quiet as a cat behind them.

"So you eavesdrop *and* steal my goods," Mirandola said, slowing his pace so he could grasp her by the arm.

"I—"

Mirandola laughed softly, grimly, then swore. "My skryer will pay dearly for what he's done. Dearly..."

"I do not believe Fra Baldassare was involved," Pietro said.

"No? And why would that be?" Mirandola asked.

"I think I sensed it from the stone burning in my hand. I, too, was furious with the priest; but as we escaped the bottega I felt...guilty, guilty for blaming him."

Mirandola said, "Wait," and when the priests caught up with their remaining torch, he pressed a lever behind one of a hundred skulls cemented into the wall. He pushed against the sainted remains, which creaked open like a heavy door. "Quickly now, for the heavy weight of the stone will pull the lych-gate closed."

They all slipped through the lych-gate into a chapel tomb. Mirandola pointed out the store of torches, and soon the tomb was bathed in harsh, flickering light and long, pooling shadows. The walls, ceiling, and even the monument columns were composed of human bones and mortar. The floor was a mosaic of marble and bone. The priests crossed themselves, and Antonio urged Mirandola to lead them out of here. Mirandola pointed out a lych-gate at the far end of the long, narrow tomb. "The passage branches into many corridors; but if you always orient yourself to the wall on your right, you will soon come to another chapel like this. Behind the north-facing lych-gate is a hidden stairwell. That will take you into the cellars of Santi Apostoli."

"That is Archbishop Salviati's parish," Antonio said.

"Indeed," Mirandola said, "and the parish connects with Salviati's palace… and the palace connects with his stables."

"Surely not," Antonio said in disbelief, "and even if that were true, he would have the ingress blocked."

"It was not when I last inspected it, perhaps because the holy swine is not aware of its existence."

"He must know that the catacombs—"

"Did *you* know they existed before this day?" Mirandola asked.

"No, Maestro," Antonio said, bowing his head. "Your knowledge saved us from the archbishop's traitorous attack."

"Just as your swords and courage saved me," Mirandola said, nodding to Antonio's quiet subordinate Gentile, whose efficient blade had released no less than twelve souls in the cathedral. The young priest bowed; and Lucian once again experienced an irrational yet potent malaise when their eyes met. Turning back to Antonio, Mirandola said, "We should allow the archbishop to provide carriage and horses for our safe passage. Can you take care of that?"

"I cannot leave you, Maestro." Antonio insisted.

"We will wait for you in the chapel I described. That seems to be the only safe course of action, do you not agree?"

"How can I be sure that—"

"You *can't*," Mirandola said. "As I trusted you, so must you trust me."

The priest nodded, and Mirandola continued: "Be watchful. We don't yet know what armies the cardinal and archbishop have employed. Trust no one, not even Fra Baldassare's troops. I fear the contagion goes deep."

"And what if we cannot get back to the chapel to find you?" Antonio asked.

"If you have not returned by the chimes of Compline, then wait for us by the Ponte Vecchio across the palazzo from the church, and we will find you."

"But if we cannot return, how can you—"

"There are many exits," Mirandola said. "But if you cannot get into the cellars, wait for us. We are not lost yet."

Antonio nodded again, and then he and his reluctant subordinate left. Mirandola listened for the distant creak of the lych-gate, and then said, "We will follow in a few moments. This is the only privacy we will have for some time."

"I should think we'd have an hour, at least, before the priests return," Isabella said.

"Yes, I'm sure," Mirandola said, "but I'm equally certain that the good priest Antonio won't have left us to our own devices."

Isabella looked at him quizzically.

"The priests would not leave us unprotected. I'm sure that Gentile will be close at hand."

"But you told them—" Pietro said.

Mirandola smiled and said, "Yes, I told them..."

"What does the stone tell you?" Lucian asked Pietro.

Pietro stretched out his hand before him as if it was an object that didn't belong to him and shook his head. "I just see..."

"Yes?"

"Darkness, ice and darkness, as if—"

Lucian grasped Pietro's hand, pressing the fingers into a fist to hide the stone, and said, "Yes, I know. Don't think of it right now. Not here."

"Don't think of what?" Mirandola asked. "Do you read his mind, Lucian?"

Lucian blushed, as if he had been caught naked, his welted scars exposed to all. "I see a little," he confessed; and then he told his master, Pietro, and Isabella everything that had happened to him after he heeded the angel's call and passed through the skrying globe into the cathedral that had been claimed by the demon Belias. "The Duomo is lost," he told Pietro, "and probably Florence as well. It all belongs to the dark aeon Belias now. It is part of him, of his world, which you saw in the Maestro's obsidian mirror."

"But I was *in* the Duomo," Mirandola said.

"Yes," Lucian said, "and the cathedral is now but an extension of the aeon. He is not just a god, a being. He is a world, the world that Pietro glimpses, the world that was mercifully hidden from you when the killing began in the cathedral."

Mirandola listened, as if Lucian was now the master and he the apprentice; and when Lucian finished telling him about the Days of Grief, which were now upon them, he simply looked into the darkness and whispered, "*Miserere nostri Deus.*"

"The angel also told me that the remembrancer you had petitioned for is in your possession," Lucian continued.

"And how am I in possession of such a thing?" Baldassare asked, hopefully.

"Well, I think that Pietro is in possession of the remembrancer."

"Me...?"

Lucian smiled sadly at Pietro. "Yes, I think you know that."

"What do I know?" Pietro asked, looking cornered.

"That *you* are the remembrancer."

Lost in thought, Pietro turned away from Lucian.

Isabella leaned closer to Pietro…embraced him.

"I think right now we have a remembrancer who cannot remember," Mirandola said.

"There is more," Lucian said, trying to conceal his jealousy over Isabella's attention to Pietro and also sensing that he must tell his master everything now while he could. "The angel said that you must make haste and go to the fortress in Urbino."

Mirandola looked startled. "You can see far, my young servant."

"Apprentice," Lucian said, even as he stole a quick, frustrating glance at Isabella, who was still fussing over Pietro.

"Go on then…my young apprentice," Mirandola said.

"The angel also warned that you should not tarry there."

"Why? What is to befall the castle?"

"I do not know, maestro. But Gabriel said the most important thing is to free the girl."

"The girl…?"

"In the tree," Pietro said. He stared at Mirandola and Lucian. He was involved now, focused. "It was the girl we saw in the obsidian mirror."

"Ah, the miracle…" Mirandola said, remembering seeing the outlandishly dressed girl clinging to the spectral upside-down ash tree in the cathedral.

Lucian nodded, then said to Mirandola, "No matter what the cost, you must gather a force to free her from the archbishop's authority. The angel calls her the daughter of light."

"And what does that mean?" Isabella asked, pulling away from Pietro.

"All I know is that she is the incarnation of an aeon: Sophia. She is the one…the one sent to us, the one who can defeat the demiurge. And if she is taken—"

"She has already been taken," Mirandola insisted.

"He means her soul," Pietro said.

"—if she is taken," Lucian continued, "all will be lost and the demiurge will win."

"*Who* will win?" asked Isabella, her eyes glittering in the torchlight.

"The aeon that created the world."

"*God* created the world," Isabella said. She hesitated and then said, "But you mean God, don't you?"

"It is not as you imagine," Mirandola said.

Isabella turned to Pietro. "And you? Do *you* believe this blasphemy, too?"

"Isabella, patience. You have been touched by the stone. You will understand, too."

She shook her head in amazement. "Are you *all* heretics who would blaspheme against the Lord—"

"No one here blasphemes," Mirandola said sharply. "But the holy church is not what you have been taught to believe...and right now while we are in danger, you must trust us. Later, when you have seen and learned more, you can decide for yourself."

"No," Isabella said, "I could not trust any of you now...or later, and I *have* decided." As she tried to leave, Pietro caught her by the hand. Isabella gasped in pain as her wounded hand once again felt the touch of the stone.

"What he says is true," Pietro insisted. "I have seen it. So will you...in time."

But Isabella wrenched her hand away from Pietro's, stood up, grabbed a torch, and rushed toward the gate at the other end of the tomb.

She was so very quick.

"I will bring her back," Mirandola said; but Pietro, quick as Isabella, held him back...burning him with the skrying stone as he had burned Isabella.

Although it pained him, Lucian made no move to chase her.

"Let me go!" Mirandola said as he tried to wrest himself away from Pietro.

"No, you must let *her* go," Pietro said before releasing Mirandola from the stone. Mirandola staggered backwards, and Lucian caught him. Pietro held out his hands, as if he were holding the weight of Mirandola's crystal globe, and gazed at the bone-white stone embedded in his palm.

Mirandola recovered himself and asked, "Well, what do you see?"

"I cannot see clearly now. I see only that the serpent in the stone is coiled.

"Why did you prevent me from rescuing my cousin?" he asked Pietro. Then turning to Lucian: "And why didn't you go after her?"

"If she remained, we would all be killed," Pietro said.

"How? Tell me how."

Pietro shook his head, looked to Lucian for support, then closed his hand into a fist, as if the stone was a terrible eye that could be squeezed shut.

"Tell him...tell him what you saw," Lucian said. "You owe the maestro the truth."

Pietro turned away from Lucian and Mirandola and said, "I saw that...we would be betrayed."

Mirandola laughed harshly. "If it was her intention to betray us, what is there to stop her now? She knows where we are."

"I am sorry, Maestro," Pietro said.

"For burning me or disobeying me or depriving me of my cousin?"

"For burning you and disobeying you and...and for seeing what I saw."

But Mirandola was suddenly distracted. He held up his hand for silence, then pressed his face against one of the skulls embedded in the wall. "Just as your stone speaks to you, these stones and bones speak to me," he said to Pietro.

"And what do your stones tell you?"

"That we must hurry, or find another way of escape."

Now Lucian and Pietro could also hear something.

A distant thunder…the sound of men.

NINE

Chains and Stratagems

They bound her with chains and lured her into their brightest of prisons.

—*The Secret Book of John, 25,16-30,11*

Know this, little children of light. Remember that Gabriel, the two-winged sapphire angel imbues his servants with fire, even those who do not know him.

Remember that they too burn with the fire of charity... [they too] can blister your flesh and sear your soul.

Know then their true heart, even if they appear in the raiment of the enemy.

—*The Gospel of the Damned, (Instructions from the Vision) 13.4*

"*Oh, Lord, am I to be judged by monsters?*"
Louisa Mary Morgan tried to wrest herself free of the grasping hands that squeezed her flesh and tore at her muslin cap and calico dress. She felt abject fear, adrenal terror: she had fallen from a silent dream of ice and darkness into this screaming, candle-bright, glittering nightmare. Where was she? It looked like a...cathedral, a great cathedral. Men in black hooded robes pushed the extravagantly dressed, sweat-stinking perfumed patricians away from her; but the hard-faced priests held her fast before the altar of this enormous cathedral as if she were a sacrificial offering. They spoke to each other in the quick, staccato language of her dreams. In the melee, Louisa focused on her hands, bruised and bloodied from trying to hold onto the upturned branches of

the upside-down ash tree that grew in the darkness…the tree that grew inside one of the aeon's invisible boles that connected his silver-dark heavenly realm with the cathedral. Belias had provided two miracles for the holy church: the tree and this outlandish girl dressed in lace and braid.

My hands are as red as Major Dunean's face, Louisa thought, remembering the popping grapeshot, which had torn it away as if it were chicken skin. Louisa stifled the gore rising in her throat and looked desperately toward the white-bearded archbishop, who wore a purple velvet tunic and a white silk gown. He appeared pale and kindly.

What is this place…?

Bowing his head, the archbishop smiled at her and continued to speak in Latin to the congregation. But the pox-faced cardinal standing beside him called out: *"Purifica Domine sanctum tuum, et dele iniquitatem inimicorum nostrorum."*

The signal for murder and mayhem.

The signal for the silent ones—those whose souls had been taken by Belias, those who were nothing more than automata ruled by Belias—to attack the richly clothed patricians who surrounded Louisa. A young man with a vacant, handsome face slit the throat of a blond woman with a shaved forehead and said, *"Che quant' era più irbatam era più brutta."* That was the language of Louisa's nightmares, and she could *almost* understand the words. Something about the one who is adored, no, adorned the most, she…she is the most hideous.

Blood spattered onto her face—it tasted bitter as wood—and as she screamed, the priests pulled her through the crowd, which parted before them. There were now soldier priests all around her, protecting her, their lancers and swords pointed outward to slice or pinion anyone in their way; the archbishop and Cardinal Caraffa followed calmly and purposely as if they were carrying relics from the tomb of Christ and thus preserved from the murder and mayhem surrounding them. The priests rushed her through one of the wide, pointed arches into the south aisle and where aisle met transept was a spiral staircase that led upward…and then down to a tunnel. Louisa was pushed into darkness. She could smell the dankness of stone and mold. She was afraid of the dark, afraid of closed spaces. She tripped on a step, but the priests held her upright. They descended into a huge crypt illuminated by a few shafts of grayish light. As the cardinal looked on, the archbishop kneeled before a nondescript marble tomb that was cracked and chipped. The archbishop placed both hands on the crypt, said a prayer, and pushed. The marble slab swung inward. Two priests stepped through and lit torches, which cast flickering red light upon the cavernous walls. Louisa tried to pull away from the priests. She had to get away from this place, away from the darkness that reminded her of…

She couldn't remember, but there was something she *had* to remember. She remembered the crack in the sky. She remembered the balloon and cold, icy ground. She remembered darkness and the howling, glass-breaking voices of her nightmares.

> —*Kũn mre*
> *lòc vo kis٢*
> *Sa ba vo kis٢* —

Something about vines…and who she was; and it came to her that she had looked upon the cold, chiseled face of God's dark seraph and was not worthy. Her father was right. She screamed, remembering that he was dead, too; and one of the priests covered her mouth and wrenched her arm, almost swinging her before him; and then they were hurrying through catacomb corridors. The cardinal ordered two of his priests to scout the dark arteries ahead for intruders. The black-cloaked men knew the way by memory and touch, for they carried no torches.

Louisa heard the stone slab swing shut behind her with a groan; reflexively, she recited the Lord's Prayer. Time and motion converged into echoes and coruscating torchlight; into whispers and grumbles; the slapping and soughing of stiff fabric on impatient soldiers; harsh yellow light flickering over walls of stone, cement, and human remains; half-glimpsed twists and curves; the successive smells of dampness, mold, and ordure; rats scurrying; claws clicking in the dark. She felt the walls and darkness closing in on her. She could hardly breathe. She looked to the archbishop, as if he might offer a safe haven of kindness amidst this nightmare, this dream that she had passed into through the crack in the sky.

"Be not affrayed, child of light," the archbishop said, turning to Louisa and then wiping both her hands with a costly needle lace *sudaroli* handkerchief that he had drawn from his sleeve. "Your bosky wounds are superficial and shall bleed no more."

She understood that! The voice sounded strange, the sentences seemed to be spoken as questions, and there was something reassuring about the *roundness* of the words…as if each were a perfect object to be rolled in the mouth. And, indeed, the scratches on her hands had stopped bleeding and itching and burning; it was as if the archbishop had applied some charmed healing balm.

"Be well comforted," the archbishop continued. "You are now safe…or shall be. Soon you shall be above all this in the heavens where you belong." Then he ordered the sour-smelling, brutish, heavy-set priest to let go of her arm and step away.

But the priest turned to the cardinal, who was just ahead of the archbishop.

The cardinal gave a slight nod, and the priest released her.

"You speak English," Louisa said to the archbishop.

"Of course I speak English…and Lorrayn, and the German tongues and at least five more. Do you not yet remember even a little Latin of the scripture?"

"I am a Catholic, and I know my prayers," she said.

He chuckled, as if he understood something that she could not yet comprehend. "Of course you do, beautiful child."

"Where am I?"

"Close to freedom. Close to the light. Yet still in prison, still bound in chains."

"What do you mean?"

"You will be bound until you wake yourself from your anamnesis."

"My what?"

"Your forgetfulness, my daughter."

"I am not your daughter," Louisa said sharply. She had had enough of this. "Now tell me right now what's going on." Several soldier-priests moved closer to the archbishop, as if to protect him from this red-haired, dangerous child; but he waved them away; and all but a torchbearer slipped back to accompany the cardinal who listened but would not speak a word.

"Take my hand, *Filia Lucis*, and I shall shew you," the archbishop said as he deftly slid around her and took her right hand with his left. She cried out in pain and almost fainted. She smelled flesh burning—her flesh—and tried to pull her hand away from him; but his grip was unexpectedly strong. He held her in fire and agony, and she gasped, "*Serpens sum.*"

"Ah, and do you understand what you say?"

"*I* am the serpent," she cried, and the archbishop allowed her to wrench her hand free from his. "What did you do to me?" Without even realizing it, she spoke in Florentine street dialect.

"I burned a path back to your soul to help you remember. Your soul remembers, even if you forget."

She felt the fire that had burned her hand coursing through her arm to her chest, her heart, and down into her loins; terrible memories followed the burning pain like silvery fish in the wake of a ship. She trembled with fear. As she remembered being marooned in that dead, cold place where she had been captured by Belias and his twisting, snapping vines, she could not catch her breath. She remembered the cratered ground and His dark presence all around her, inside her, speaking to her: *Ergo sum qui in re* I am the one who is *within you I serve the lord thy god and thou shalt not have any other gods before him Omnia pereunt a facie Dei Everyone perishes before me Et bonis et malis flagellum sum and I am the vine and the whip to both the good and the evil.*

"What did the Lord's servant tell you?" asked the archbishop. "And what else did you say to Him?"

"Deuoraui rampicantem," Louisa said in a whisper, her mind mazed and clouded with memory.

I devour the vine.

"I am satisfied you are the One...the one the church seeks," the archbishop said, making a pro forma gesture to the cardinal, who nodded. Then he grasped her hand again. The archbishop had the strength of a man half his age. Louisa gasped, expecting pain and fire, but now the old man's touch was once again like balm, a numbing, comforting unguent. "You would and you *should* devour your Lord your God, blessed is He, blessed is His name. Such is the miracle of the Eucharist, my dear one."

"The true God is not a grasping vine," Louisa said, feeling ill even as she said it.

"Did the Lord's dark seraph not tell you what he is?" the archbishop asked. "Did he not shew you what he is...and what *you* are?"

Louisa shook her head, once again denying her memory, but she could not deny that she had been touched by divine presence. But could God's servant bring night rather than light?

She could not deny that he had devoured her just as she was to devour him.

He had sanctified her, and she...she had fled from revelation and Holy Communion because he was darkness absolute, and she was terrified. Then she remembered what Belias had said to her, answering her even before she questioned him: *"Lux manet in tenebris."*

Light resides in darkness.

She choked and mumbled, "Forgive me, Father, for I have sinned.

The archbishop smiled sadly, put his arm around her, and said, "We have all sinned, daughter of light." He called to the torchbearer ahead to stop, and he opened Louisa's hand, the hand he had burned with his own heat, which he had channeled through faith, will, and his long experience with the holy arts. "Tell me what you see, daughter of light." She stared at the glassy-looking scar that had already formed in the palm of her right hand between the two creases her mother used to call her hourglass. It was a purplish striation that looked like a sapphire snake ready to strike. "Well?" asked the archbishop.

"It looks like a serpent." As she gazed at it, the serpent moved. It could be a trick of the torchlight, but, no, it had indeed moved: It curled itself into a flesh-red disk. She touched it and felt a stab of pain...and power as it uncoiled as if to strike.

"No," said the archbishop crossly. Then, catching himself, he said, "You must never mistake the holy vine for the treacherous serpent." Then, quoting scripture: *"Antiquus serpens extulit caput suum deuorans innocentes."*

Beware the ancient serpent that raises up its head to devour the innocent.

"But I *am* the serpent..." Louisa said.

"Do not be afraid," the archbishop continued. "The Lord will clear your eyes, just as he has cleared your soul. He will transform you, tear away all that is evil and willful within you. The serpent shall become the vine."

Louisa felt a chill snake down her spine.

"After all," continued the archbishop, the Lord of Hosts has placed his divine seal upon *you*. You are the chosen one. *You*, child, will come to know who you are."

"And who am I?"

"*Mater omnis creaturae.*"

Louisa understood that, but she was confused, disoriented, slightly nauseated... and certainly not the mother of creation. When the cardinal commanded the men to move forward, she stumbled.

"You will soon rest, child," the archbishop said.

"Tell me, please, what place...what time is this?" she asked again.

"You already know the answers."

"No, no, I don't. I seem to be able to remember a little, and then—"

"Just walk beside me. Soon everything will become clear, once we are away from these corridors of the dead."

"What did you do to me?" Louisa asked. "Are you some sort of piss-prophet or conjuror? You burned me without, without..."

"I am neither prophet nor physician, if that is what you mean," the archbishop said.

"I mean—"

"Neither am I a prestidigitator or spell-peddler," continued the archbishop. "You contain the same fire and force as I do, but, oh—so much more. And you will remember what it is and how to use it, just as you now remember how to speak in the proper language."

Louisa remembered the words Belias had spoken to her, the throat-tearing sounds from the language-before-languages. "Do you mean the ancient tongue? God's speech?"

The archbishop looked at her curiously, then said, "No, child, I meant the Latin of the holy book and the Tuscan tongue, which you are speaking right now."

That caught her, and she felt dizzy and frightened, frightened of the massing darkness all around her. "How do you know about me?" she asked. "What do you know about me? Do you know why I am here?"

He smiled and said, "You ask so many questions that there is no room for an answer." After a pause, he continued. "I knew only that you would be sent here by the Father in his perfect heaven...and that you are his revelation. You have come back a second time in the likeness of a female to tell of the coming end of this age and teach us about the beginning of the age to come. You will reveal his will and cast out the Adversary. Do you not remember these words from your scripture?"

"I never heard no scripture like that," she said, trying to come to grips with what was happening to her and who—or what—she had become.

"You will remember, child. In time, as you become more holy, you will remember everything."

"Who is the Adversary?" Louisa asked.

The archbishop looked at her with surprise and then said, "The one who serves a false god and calls himself archangel."

"Satan?"

"Call him what you like. He has many names. Satan or Gabriel or—"

Four figures suddenly appeared like ghosts out of the darkness.

The cardinal's burly advance scouts walked in lock-step behind a young woman and a tall priest whose hands were tied with silken choke-ropes that were also secured around their necks. When the scout dragged the young woman into the light, Louisa could see that she was frightened. Yet she maintained a haughty and determined composure. Her glory of raven-black hair framed her pale, beautiful face; and she was dressed in a simple yet expensive gown of white damask brocaded in gold. And she looked at Louisa as if she knew who she was.

The cardinal pushed past Louisa and the archbishop.

He stood in front of the captured priest and wrenched the cloth gag from his mouth. "So, Ser Antonio, my most dear and trusted paladin, I'm sure you have an excuse for being here without my permission. Then he turned to the girl. "And you...you are the bastard cousin of Ser Mirandola, are you not?" He squeezed her face and turned it side to side, as if he were examining a horse at one of the First Citizen's Palio races. She tried to speak through the gag. Cardinal Caraffa removed it and said, "Now tell me where your cousin is. If you have found your way into our secret places, I'm sure he has, too."

"I ran away," she said; then she glanced at Louisa, as if confused. Louisa watched her, concerned.

"From whom?"

"Be careful what you say," Antonio shouted to Isabella. "He—"

The cardinal smiled at the priest and said, "I did not think it would take you very long to betray yourself, Antonio." Then to the advance scouts: "Silence this apostate and take him out of my sight. He will speak quickly enough to the inquisitor's steel." Although Cardinal Caraffa had a narrow slash of a mouth and a weak chin, his power and authority—and a certain masculine potency—could not be denied. The flickering firelight accentuated his high, pockmarked forehead and deep-set eyes.

103

One of Caraffa's guards pulled the priest Antonio away from the light of the torches.

"Now tell me, who did you run away from?"

Isabella shook her head.

"You ran away from your cousin, didn't you, child?" said the cardinal. "But why? Could you no longer stand the stink of his heresy?"

She blushed, but did not look away from the cardinal, who—surprised that his little spear of irony had drawn blood—said, "Perhaps you won't need to accompany your companion when he speaks to my inquisitor. Perhaps—"

"Leave her alone," Louisa said. "Do not threaten her, she is a child."

"And you are not?" the cardinal asked, grimacing at her; then he caught himself. He glanced at the archbishop, then bowed to Louisa and said, "Forgive me, daughter of light. My voice is barbed and my patience short. Do you wish this girl as a companion?"

Louisa wasn't sure how to react. She had felt an immediate inclination to like this haughty, determined girl who would not give in to intimidation or her own fear. Yes, she was sure she would like her. She looked to the archbishop, who nodded. Emulating the attitude of her newfound companion, she said, "Yes, and untie the halter around her neck and her hands."

The cardinal gently removed her bonds himself, and the archbishop bowed his head toward Louisa and whispered, "The cardinal has humbled himself before you. Tread lightly."

Louisa nodded, thanked the cardinal for his benevolence, and then called on Isabella to accompany her. The cardinal ordered one of his captains to lead a contingent of his men to search the catacombs for Mirandola and another to hasten to the palace and ready reinforcements.

"And you can take my heretical priest with you…"

But an instant later, one of Caraffa's soldiers dragged the man who had been guarding Antonio into the flickering torchlight. The guard's throat had been cut.

The cardinal swore and ordered his men to search the catacombs.

Isabella grimaced and turned away.

Louisa stared hard at the gray-faced corpse. Her mother had been killed the same way, except—

Louisa forced her mind away from her memories; away from her big white house in Bartonsville, Virginia; away from the security of sleeping in her mother's big white bed; away from the slow drawl and enveloping hugs of Hamper, who had midnight skin and wiry curls and took care of her and her fire-and-brimstone father after her mother passed away.

"Come away, child," the archbishop said softly. "We shall soon be away from all this turmoyle and trubble, and you,"—he said to Isabella—"be not discomforted. You will be safe and protected in God's shadow. No wicked power will harm you."

Isabella nodded, and then the guards were jostling them forward, pushing and hurrying and guiding them through the twisting corridors of the secret catacomb. The cardinal led the party and whispered orders to his lieutenants; and as boots stomped over the cemented remains of martyrs and prophets, Louisa felt the serpentine scar pulse in her palm. She felt the serpent—it was *not* a vine—uncoil. She felt it burning and burrowing deep inside her. Chill and quick, it coursed through her arm and into her heart…and she *remembered*.

"Your friend with the crippled foot is wrong," she whispered to Isabella.

"How do you know about—?"

Louisa shook her head. "I don't know. I just do."

"His name is Pietro," Isabella whispered, "and what do you mean he is wrong?"

"You would never betray your cousin."

"I already have. I have probably murdered him, may God forgive me. He—"

The archbishop stepped closer and asked, "What are you two whispering about?"

"Nothing," Louisa said. "It just feels like we should be quiet in here. In deference to the dead." She caught Isabella's gaze and looked away.

The archbishop nodded and said, "Yes, it is a holy—and dangerous— place."

"Why dangerous?" asked Louisa.

The archbishop smiled, and Louisa *knew* that he had heard everything that had passed between her and Isabella. "Because it hides more than treachery."

"What does it hide?"

"The remembrancer." The archbishop looked at Isabella and said, "But you know of what I speak."

Isabella shook her head.

"Or of whom I speak," continued the archbishop. "But do not worry, for you shall both meet the Holy Father's own remembrancer." He addressed Louisa now. "He will know you, daughter of light. He is likely watching us right now. He will help you remember, for he is a physician…and he speaks your native tongue." Then he patted Isabella and said, "He is also our inquisitor."

Isabella did not respond.

"Ah, here we are," the archbishop said as they turned west into a passage that was so low and narrow that they had to crouch and queue single-file. He gently prodded Louisa and Isabella, but Louisa felt an overwhelming rush of claustrophobic fear. She backed against the wall of the main corridor and said, "I can't—"

The priests who had sworn an oath to protect the daughter of light prodded her forward. The archbishop ordered them to pass. They bowed respectfully, but would not enter the passage without her, nor would the soldier-priests who were their rear-guard.

"Your fears and phobias are *memoria*, nothing more," the archbishop said as he took Louisa by the hand. Louisa felt her scar grow warm and coil tightly in her palm. "Your soul remembers, but you...you are still blind to the past lives of your soul, so you feel only the shock instead of the recognition.

"We are almost there," continued the archbishop. "Your companion will go first, and I will follow. You will soon be safe in the heavens, I promise."

"What do you mean...?"

But the archbishop firmly prodded her into the passage. She felt moist air moving around her and gagged: the smell of decay was overpowering.

"It is the stench of the River Arno," the archbishop whispered. "The miasmas will evaporate in a moment. Keep going."

They followed the passage through a lych-gate and then up a narrow flight of stone steps to another opening so small that Louisa had to stoop and drop to her hands to get through it. She prayed and remembered her mother pushing her into a bedroom closet and locking the door when the Yankee deserters broke into their house. How she wished she had not broken out of that claustrophobic space...how she wished she had never witnessed what had happened to her mother.

She followed Isabella and the others into a dusty, dimly-lit room, a tomb guarded by gargoyles that lined the stone wall. One of the gargoyles was out of place, and one of the cardinal's Companions of the Night would have the task of sliding it back over the opening.

But it was too warm in the tomb. Dangerously warm.

The cardinal sent scouts ahead to determine if it was safe to continue. The heat seemed to be radiating from the walls, and the soldier-priests were sweating in their protective leather jerkins hidden beneath their heavy cloaks. The cardinal conferred with the archbishop as they waited.

"If the church is on fire, we will have to change plans," the cardinal said.

"Those with faith shall pass through safely."

"Not if this heat is any indication of what is happening above."

The archbishop looked at Louisa, smiled, and said, "Heaven's radiance can be very strong, indeed."

"It will not serve our purpose if the city burns," Caraffa said.

"It is only God's purpose that matters," the archbishop said.

"You dare lecture me about faith, just as your child would lecture me on the treatment of heretical prisoners?" The cardinal stepped back, as if preparing to strike the archbishop; but the archbishop bowed low and said, "I would never presume to lecture you, Eminence. Nor would I ever question your faith or intentions, for I serve God by my service to you."

The cardinal bowed in return and said slyly, "Holy father, your loyalty, devotion, and good works are never far from my thoughts."

The scouts returned from their reconnaissance, and the officer in charge said to the cardinal: "All is ready, Eminence, but we must hurry."

"The church and palace are unharmed?"

"Fire rages out of control all around the Piazza del Limbo. It is only a matter of time before it—"

"Yes, yes," the cardinal said. "And the ship? Is it moored?"

"Yes, Eminence, but it swings and shudders as if caught in a storm."

"It *is* caught in a storm," the cardinal said, and then hurried everyone through basements and storerooms and up a spiral staircase to a secret opening behind the wall of another staircase that led to the church's triforium. The mosaic floor of the Santa Apostoli was hot as a grill, but had to be crossed to reach the courtyard that separated the church from the archbishop's palace. The soldiers were protected from the burning pavement by their thick leather or wooden shoes, as were the cardinal, the archbishop, and Louisa; but Isabella was wearing fashionable laced *calze* with thin soles of felted wool. She gasped in pain and shock when her feet touched the stone floor, but the archbishop swept her up in his arms and carried her as if she weighed no more than an infant. Louisa stayed close beside him; and as they rushed down the aisle past the ancient green marble columns that had been stripped from an ancient Roman temple, the beautifully carved wooden ceiling caught fire.

"To the bronze door, there," shouted the cardinal; and the soldiers ran forward. They did not panic or break ranks. But instead of leading them out the door that opened into the courtyard...he ran past it. He slipped into a chapel and tried to remove something from the tabernacle. The archbishop called out to him, but it was too late.

A large stained glass window above the tabernacle exploded.

Clutching at the knife-shaped shards of glass that severed his windpipe, the cardinal fell to his knees. His officers rushed to help him, but the archbishop called them back. "Come away," the archbishop shouted as he stood in the doorway. "Come away brave servants of the church," he said as he released Isabella, who could stand comfortably in the soft verge of the courtyard. "You cannot help him now, so hurry, for this very minute the Lord is calling you to take action on His behalf."

But neither Louisa nor Isabella heard a word the archbishop said.

They were both looking up in awe at the huge golden-sailed airship that floated in the smoky, ash-laden air above the courtyard and the church.

A deep, thundering growl snapped Louisa out of her reverie. The growl was followed by bone-vibrating roaring that seemed to be coming from an ornately trellised enclosure attached to the church; and, as if in response, dogs barked and bayed and horses trapped in their smoky, overheated stables neighed in fear.

"What is *that*?" Louisa cried.

"I don't know," Isabella said, her neck craned as she stared at the airship that had descended to the level of the church's clerestory. It would be too dangerous for the ship to come any closer. Crewmen dropped tether ropes and a rope ladder to priests stationed in the courtyard below. The priests anchored the ropes and ladder to eye-posts in the ground; and the airship flickered in and out of sight above, as if it were constructed out of the stuff of angels.

"I mean the noise," Louisa said to Isabella, "the terrible howling."

The archbishop appeared behind them and said, "You hear the roar of my lions, daughter of light. They belong to the holy church."

"With all due respect, Eminence," Isabella said, "I believe they belong to the republic."

The archbishop nodded and said, "Yes, a common misconception;" and then he and his guards hustled Louisa and Isabella across the courtyard to the rope ladder shivering and singing in the smoke roiled air.

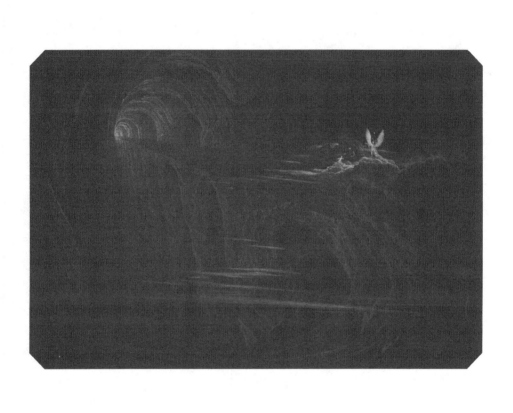

PARTITION THREE
Lions and Serpents of Light

'Trismegistus, please tell me then how a man can be here…and there at the same time?'

'I could not tell you that, Rheginus, for you confuse appearance with flesh.'

'Then enlighten me, Trismegistus.'

'Have I not told you that aeons are synchronous?'

'Yes, but—'

Listen to me, Rheginus. Have I not told you that aeons are not limited by time or space as we are?'

'Yes, I remember that, Trismegistus. But we are now talking of mortal men, not aetheric aeons.'

'Are you certain of that, Rheginus? Have I not told you that aeons can assume whatever form they desire and can multiply themselves like the sown men of Thebes?'

'If that is the case, Trismegistus, then the man of which you speak is but an appearance.'

'That is correct. And now might I explain the other earthly manifestations of the aeon under discussion…?'

—*Excerpt from the Third Discourse 90,29-92,10*

TEN

The Trappings of the Soul

And thus you shall know doubleness or more

In evil as well as good.

As aeons can be two... [themselves] or more

So can Belias be dark firmament, or Athoth ...flesh.

As two-winged Gabriel can be earth or crystal

So can you [repeated for emphasis] be stone and augury...
[or remembrancer and more].

—The Gospel of the Damned, (Exegesis of the Vision)
133.41-47 end

And he hearkened to the voice of Gabriel that called to
him in the night and went up and down among the lions
and became a lion; and he learned to catch the prey and
to devour men.

—Ezekiel 19:7

Pietro listened to the soft thunder of hurried, echoing footfalls.
It sounded as if an army was marching through the catacombs, yet he
could not be sure of its numbers or direction nor tell how far away it might be.
The tunneled walls confounded sound and distance, just as the curved sanctum
mirrors so lately favored by the nuns and courtesans in Venice distorted the
earnest faces of their suitors.

"Can you tell how many men there might be?" he asked his master. "Can
you tell where they are and—"

"*Silenzio!*" Mirandola said in no more than a whisper as he pressed his ear against a smooth, worn skull mortared into the catacomb wall. After a moment, he said, "The walls here magnify sound like a hearing horn, but distort direction. Yes, men are moving. How many I cannot tell, but I think they are moving south, as we are. If we hurry, we can still escape as planned. So clasp hands again, the archbishop's palace is not far."

Although the darkness was almost total, Mirandola would not allow them to use a torch. He led the way forward; his hands that brushed against the walls—and his memory of the catacombs' winding ways—functioned as sight. Mirandola, Lucian, and Pietro walked through seemingly endless corridors until they reached a tunnel the size of a boulevard, which in turn wound into smaller corridors. One was cut through by a pinprick of light from the ceiling. Dust motes blinked in and out, but the ray of light was so small and faint that it hardly illuminated the closest wall.

"We are nearing our destination," Mirandola whispered. They hurried on until they found themselves in another long, straight corridor without branchings. It seemed that they had been walking for an hour, but only about ten minutes had passed.

Mirandola stopped suddenly.

He listened, then whispered, "Pietro, do you sense something?"

After bumping into his master, Pietro pulled away and said, "No, master, except it does not seem so dark ahead." He could just about make out something hazy, in the distance, perhaps another small thread of dusty light escaping through the stone ceilings.

"I thought I heard something," Mirandola said.

"So did I," Lucian said. "Perhaps, as you surmised, the priest Gentile still follows us."

"No," Mirandola said, "it was not a proper footfall, but a—"

They all heard a low rumbling, a rumbling so deep it could almost be felt; then silence, except for the sounds of their own breathing. "Wait," whispered Mirandola, and soon enough they heard a scratching, the crush-crunch of friable rock or desiccated bone...and Mirandola saw a faint glint of something yellow.

"Quickly, fire the torch!"

Lucian almost lost the flint when he tried to strike it. He tried again. This time a spark, and the pitch ignited. After being in darkness for so long, the crackling torchlight almost blinded them; but, indeed, there was something ahead.

Now Pietro sensed it...something huge...something hungry.

Surprised by the blazing torch, a lion roared; and its yellow, almond-shaped eyes narrowed to no more than slits. The beast was tawny colored with a thick silvery mane and looked to weigh at least five hundred pounds. Pietro felt an ancient, overwhelming panic and without conscious thought drew his dagger, which flashed in the torchlight. The lion had to be eight feet in length. A female appeared beside him. She was smaller by a few feet and looked ghostly white. Behind her stood the rest of the pride, some seven animals in all, each one quiet and stock still, except for their tufted tails, which flicked back in forth. Their flame-yellow eyes—unblinking, calculating vectors and distance as vision rather than thought—stared at their frightened prey ahead.

"Stand perfectly still," Mirandola said, switching his own dagger into his left hand. "Lucian, give me the torch. I will see if I can turn them away."

"No, master, you can't," Pietro said. The stone buried in his right hand had suddenly became so hot that he dropped his dagger and felt the ghostly stuff that was his master's gazing globe appear as a sapphire cloud shifting shape, distending and contracting, and growing leaden in his hand. He compensated by trying to hold it with both hands—for he knew that if it fell away from him, he would die—and as he held the burning aetheric stuff, he saw what was about to happen.

He *saw* intention.

In his mind's eye, he saw the female cat leap forward, her retractable claws already extended, scuffing the ground. Then she leaped again, as if jumping and landing and jumping again were but one smooth motion, and she caught Mirandola by the neck in her jaws. She cracked his bones and brought him down as if he were a waterbuck; and in that instant—as the ghostly aether of the gazing globe transformed Pietro into Mirandola's promised remembrancer— he could feel the almost musical thrill of blood, bone, and muscle in the lion's jaw; could sense her thoughts, which were entirely physical and immediate: danger, flesh tearing gorging satisfaction, the deep fleshy odor exuding from her tawny mate, the butt-tingling sensations of sexual arousal, the warmth of sleep and satiation and close sleeping smelling of the pride and—

Pietro stopped her from attacking.

Arms outstretched and wrapped inside the envelope of what had once been Mirandola's gazing globe, he sent her to sleep...and the others, too.

Then he walked over to the sleeping beasts.

Mirandola tried to call him back, but Pietro ignored him.

He stood over them and willed them to awaken, willed their hunger to be sated; and as they rose up compliant if still weighted with sleep, Pietro felt a new and strange sensation: a sort of love for these killing beasts, but a love that was somehow entirely neutral and controlled. He wondered if the gazing globe would burst as it had before. Then he would be left at the mercy of these great beasts that huddled close together and watched him through half-closed eyes, just like the housecats he had adored as a child. He needn't have worried, however, for the aether dissipated like fog. His hand tingled as if it had fallen asleep, but was not burned; and still the cats were in his thrall. They gazed up at him, connected with him, and Pietro once again felt their warmth and emotion...and their memory. It was not sequential, but flickering shapes and chords of scent. What Pietro could only imagine as the past and present were in constant flux, each as present as the other. What the lions saw, he saw; what the lions could not understand, he could: a courtyard, cages, a dark tunic and a white gown, an extended claw impossibly large in the foreground, prey close enough to kill easily, and something great and bright undulating above and casting a huge shadow in the fire-haze.

"The archbishop is...escaping with your cousin Isabella," Pietro said to Mirandola. There was a quaver in his voice, and he was visibly upset. He turned to Lucian. "And he has the girl we saw in the mirror, the one Gabriel called the daughter of light."

"Where?" Mirandola asked, staring warily at the lions and wondering what spell his apprentice had cast over the animals.

Pietro shook his head. "In a courtyard, I think. He loosed the lions from their cages."

"It is his palace," Mirandola said. "He must know what we planned."

"Isabella," Lucian said.

"Even though the stone instructs me, I still...I just cannot believe she would betray us," Pietro said.

"Seeing you communing with beasts, I think I could believe most anything right now," Mirandola said.

"There is something else," Pietro said, "something such as we saw in your obsidian mirror, master, yet huge and shaped differently: a ship that plies the air."

"We must make haste," Lucian said. "Perhaps we can intercept them."

"It will be too late," Mirandola said.

"No," Pietro said, musing. "Perhaps not. Perhaps I am seeing what is about to happen."

"Even so, the archbishop will have his guards," Lucian said.

"But now we have his lions," said Mirandola, then turning back to Pietro, he asked, "*Do* we have his lions?"

Pietro nodded, but now he sensed—now he *knew*—that the lions never really belonged to the archbishop. Somehow they belonged to the living stone embedded in Pietro's palm...somehow they belonged to Gabriel, the sapphire angel.

"Yes," he said. "They will do what I—what we—ask."

"Then we must make haste."

As Louisa climbed the rope ladder that was vibrating in the soot-stinking wind, she looked up at the gondola of the airship. It was attached to the keel frame of the hull envelope and was some two hundred feet in length. The envelope above it was thin and long and didn't look like any balloon Louisa had ever seen. In fact from below, the gondola looked like the hull of a carrack with open gun ports. Shrouds were attached to dead eye blocks fixed to the gondola and the envelope, and what could only be described as a bowsprit projected from the front of the gondola. A half-deck was suspended below and behind the bowsprit, and what looked like retractable masts were fastened to the gondola; their webbed rigging snapped in the wind. Aft was a large triangular lateen sail that could be a rudder. Ropes and stays connected the gondola with the envelope...and the balloon—if, indeed, that's what it was—was covered with some gauzy material that seemed to shimmer and glow like heated metal.

Louisa glanced over her shoulder at the courtyard below to get her bearings: Red haze enveloped the stables and the trellised enclosure attached to the church. Burning embers caught in fire-born updrafts danced and swirled around the climbers.

Someone swore.

A priest's cloak caught fire, and he cried for help.

"Do not cast your eyes downward, daughter of light, lest you become dizzy," said the archbishop who was climbing the ladder behind her. He spoke loudly to be heard above the wind. "You shall be safe very soon now."

"Tell that to the priest on the ladder below you," Louisa said, leaning away from a spinning ember large as a leaf. "You keep promising I will be safe; but I am not afraid of heights, sir, and I've probably climbed more ratlines and shrouds than you or any of your guards."

"It would not be difficult to surpass me in such matters, child, for I am not crafty in the nautical arts, and I am most certainly fearful of climbing into the upper air." He stopped speaking to catch his breath and clear his throat, then continued, "You must become my teacher and enlighten me concerning your knowledge of such things, including the pneumatics of how you floated through the crack in the sky."

So he knows, Louisa thought; but before she could form a question, she swore loudly and slapped at an ember that was blackening her lace collar and burning her neck. One of the priest guards above turned around to make sure she was all right, and Isabella—who was below Louisa and the archbishop on the ladder—screamed at him.

"It's you...*you!*" she shouted, recognizing him as the soft-spoken priest Gentile who had accompanied her cousin Mirandola in the catacombs. "*Bastardo! Traditore! You* betrayed my cousin, *you—*"

"Do not turn around!" the archbishop shouted to Louisa. "Climb!"

Louisa ignored him and called to Isabella who had lost her grip on the ropes and was caught by the guard climbing behind her.

Then the wind changed, carrying ash and embers toward the church.

"You may be the daughter of light," the archbishop said to Louisa, "but even angels and aeons must bow before the authority of the church. Now *climb!*"

The gondola above her was a wooden shadow framed by the glowing nimbus of the airship's balloon envelope. The rope ladder Louisa was climbing disappeared into the main hatch of the gondola; and when she reached it, two rough-looking soldier priests pulled her and then the archbishop onto the deck. The priests wore narrow-brimmed black caps and leather doublets imprinted with the papal insignia: a crimson cross encircled by twisted vines.

"Get them away from the threshold," someone shouted with authority. "And be quick. Others are waiting to ascend."

The soldiers obeyed, although they were clearly awed by Louisa and continued to mumble paternosters and bow their heads before her.

Louisa was also awed as she stood in the center of the huge deck that could have been a quarter-deck if it were not covered. She looked through the dusty air turned golden by shafts of light from the many portholes, gun ports, hatches, and door-sized openings cut into the wooden walls and floor. There were four cannons the size of carronade guns on each side of the deck, and barrels, sacks, and boxes were secured along the bulkheads. Soldiers—which Louisa thought of as sailors—went about their tasks with practiced routine while officers in satin caps, doublets, and open-sided embroidered *guarnacca* tunics shouted orders at them. As Louisa also looked around for the plain-faced priest that Isabella had shouted at, the officer who had shouted at the soldiers to stand away from the main hatchway approached. He looked to be in his late twenties or early thirties; and although he was light complected with pale lucent-gray eyes, his affect was dark and brooding. He bowed to Louisa, then to the archbishop, and asked, "Reverence, is not His Eminence with you?"

"Cardinal Caraffa is dead," the archbishop said. "A terrible accident."

The officer's eyes narrowed; and after a beat, he said, "The captain is expecting you. May I—?"

"I imagine you have many other urgent duties to attend to, Count Ammirato," the archbishop said, taking Louisa by the hand. "I am familiar with the way to the wheel-deck. I presume that's where your captain awaits us?"

The uniformed count blushed, then stepped back and bowed. "As you wish, Reverence, and, yes, the Captain awaits you there."

At that moment the soldiers helped Isabella onto the deck. She looked this way and that for the priest she had seen on the ladder.

"He is not here," Louisa said to Isabella. She wiped her eyes, which stung from the smoke and soot in the air, and continued, "I looked when I first got here."

"Who is it you wish to find, daughter of light?" the count asked, in effect, dismissing the archbishop.

"A priest...he just came onboard," Isabella said. "He would be about your age, but fleshy-faced...and soft like a girl. He is called Gentile and—"

"It is no concern of yours," the archbishop said curtly to the count.

The count glared defiantly at the archbishop, but after a beat he bowed and obediently stepped away. He blushed again, and Louisa could almost feel the heat of his humiliation...and his distrust and hatred of the archbishop.

A shout repeated across the deck—

"Heaven up."

"Heave and pall."

"Unship your bars."

"Heaven up!"

—and Louisa heard the snapping of cables and felt a rush in her throat and stomach as the airship jumped and rose like thistledown in a draft. Isabella stumbled. The archbishop caught her and said, "You'll need to gain your sea legs. Look to your companion, the daughter of light. She is steady on her feet. Come. I shall now take you to the priest you maligned to all as a traitor and a bastard, but you'd best decide quickly where your allegiance lies—with the holy church or with filth, heresy, and eternal damnation."

"If I didn't believe in the truth of God's word, I would not be here now."

"Don't prevaricate, child. You haven't yet the subtlety...*recte sapere et intelligere.*"

Isabella looked blankly at the archbishop, who repeated, "You haven't yet the subtlety to perceive and understand properly; and you are only here now because of my dispensation and a nod from the daughter of light."

Isabella glanced at Louisa, then nodded and lowered her head.

"Good," said the archbishop.

Louisa touched Isabella's hand and then tried to distract the archbishop. "This ship is a miracle. How do you lift it...with coal gas?"

The archbishop smiled indulgently. "Fear not, little daughter, your friend will come to no harm. You have my word."

Believing him, Louisa nodded; and with Isabella in tow, they made their way toward the wheel deck.

Officers shouted orders.

Crewmen repeated them one to another.

"Heave hard, *ragazzi*."

"Heave round the capstan."

"Heave round the windlass."

"Release the masts."

"Release the yards."

Grunting and straining, crewmen turned the capstan wheels. Wood and metal groaned, and the ship rolled sickeningly as masts and yards swiveled into place. Louisa saw men jump through hatches and gun ports, as if they were winged angels leaping into the firmament; but they were mere mortal crew-men—top-men, nipper-men, tierers, and sail-loosers—climbing onto ratlines, scrambling to the braces and halyards, securing the rigging of shrouds, forestays, and backstays.

Louisa felt a sudden temperature change; it became cooler.

"Make sail!"

The order was echoed over and over, a jubilant shout from the officers of the deck to the men who climbed like monkeys over the wind-blasted rigging and choked in the air fouled with smoke and coin-sized flakes of dead ash.

The airship shook as the sails unfurled, and Louisa stopped before a gun port to watch. She imagined they were immaculately white and perfect clouds falling through the soiled sky, and as she thought of her father—

Oh, he would have loved to see such a thing as this.

—the sheets caught the wind and pulled the ship forward. She crossed herself and murmured, "Praise the Lord."

"Indeed," said the archbishop, "but the view is so much better here;" and he led them down a railed stepladder into the wheel deck. There they were met by two cardinals dressed in satin and furs and a priest who looked like he'd spent a lifetime in ill-lit libraries. The cardinals—one stooped and elderly, the other trim and middle-aged—were flanked by two very large Swiss guards wearing light armor and holding unsheathed swords. Behind them and in the center of the control cabin, which was constructed of steel and thick glass like a conservatory room, the captain bowed to the archbishop, Louisa, and Isabella. He said "*Uno momento*" in a voice so soft it could hardly be heard and then turned his gaze back to a compass set beneath the glass window of the binnacle box.

"That's *him*!" Isabella said. "That's the priest Gentile, who accompanied my cousin. But how...how can that be?"

Louisa wondered the same thing and turned to the archbishop who smiled and said, "Patience."

Wind howled and whistled through open windows and hatches.

Below, the River Arno was a fiery red wound winding through the burning city. Faint screams could be heard, carried like birds on the updrafts; and Louisa imagined she could see loose shrouds or stays swaying in the clouds of smoke. But they were not part of the airship. They were ghostly as the rising smoke. She shuddered, suddenly remembering fragments of a distant dream in which vines twisted and curled around her. She strained to remember the dream, but it dissolved like salt in cold water.

As the ship rolled and shuddered, the captain said, "Hard up as we go," and gave the steersman a course correction. The steersman adjusted the large wooden wheel and opened a valve beside the binnacle; an officer standing beside him noted the change in a large leather logbook. "Reef the sidetops if you need," the captain said to a young officer who leaned out of a bulkhead hatch and repeated the command to the crewmen. "Keep the watch," he said to the other officer and then he stepped in front of the Swiss guards and cardinals and bowed deeply to Louisa. Like his fellow soldier-priests, he wore a narrow-brimmed cap and a doublet imprinted with the cross and vine insignia; but his velvet cap, damask doublet, and gold-fringed tunic were rich crimson.

"So you are the prophecy revealed," he said to Louisa, glancing at the archbishop and nodding.

"I don't know about that," Louisa said, "but I saw your double climbing up the rope ladder ahead of me. Is he your twin brother?"

The captain smiled at the archbishop, then replied, "Yes, in a manner of speaking."

"Well, my friend needs to speak with him," Louisa said, suddenly feeling chilled. The captain had a kind face and the slightest swelling of a double-chin, yet Louisa could not help but think that the figure standing before her was in disguise.

She knew this man...if, indeed, he was a man.

If she could only see through the disguise...

If she could only remember...

The captain turned to Isabella and said, "You can speak freely to me, child."

"I want to speak to the priest Gentile."

"Ah, so you know my name," said the captain.

"I wish to speak to the priest."

"I am a priest, and whatever you wish to say...you can say to me."

"No," Isabella said.

"You think the priest is a traitor. Is that all you wish to tell him?"

"He killed many men to save my cousin. What kind of a man could do that and then betray him?"

"*You* betrayed him."

Isabella's eyes flashed with anger, and she said, "I am not a man...and I did not betray him."

"Then why are you here, child of the north, if you did not betray him?"

"I was captured."

"You ran away from him because you could not tolerate his heresy and blasphemy."

"How do you know that I—?"

"Certainly the priest you condemn as a traitor would reveal all he knows to me." The captain smiled at Isabella and reached out to touch her face, but she stepped away from him.

"You may come to regret that in time," the archbishop said.

"Make them both comfortable," said the captain. He looked at Louisa and said, "As my holy advisor told you, be not affrayed, child of light. You are safe." Then he whispered, "And I know the one who is within you." He smiled, as if that was their little secret, as if this soft-faced captain knew of her encounter with the dark aeon Belias. His eyes were soft, brooding, and sad, yet Louisa felt the deep penetrating chill of his presence. She returned his bow and then shuddered as she suddenly remembered being ravaged by Belias in his viney, ebon black world. Remembered how she had spat out the ancient words of power and retaliation, her words:

"*Serpens sum, et deuoraui arbustum.*"

I am a serpent, and I devour the vine.

As if in sympathy, the airship shuddered as it sailed away from the smoke and fire rising from the city...away from the frenzied fighting and killing in the streets, away from the ghostly vines that fell through the glowing, greasy air like cables from heaven that snapped and curled and swallowed the souls of the war-fevered unfortunates below.

It sailed eastward through a tempestuous blood-red sky toward the vulgar, filthy, beautiful, and most holy of cities: *Venezia*.

ELEVEN

Double Hearts and Tongues

In Nomine Jesu Christi, Quis tu es?

In the name of Jesus Christ, who are you?

—John Dee, *Mysteriorum Liber Primus*

Following his track, such was the will of Heav'n.

Paved after him a broad and beaten way

Over the dark abyss…

—John Milton, *Paradise Lost*

As he hurried through the tunnel-dark catacombs with Lucian and his master Mirandola, Pietro could hear the faint echo of other footfalls behind them. The cardinal's soldiers who had ransacked and burned Mirandola's bottega—if, indeed, that's who they were—would soon be upon them; and the air was becoming close, putrid, and incrementally warmer.

"We are approaching the archbishop's palace," Mirandola said in a hushed voice; he had extinguished their torch once Pietro seemingly tamed the lions, and the darkness was total. Nevertheless, Pietro could see. He could see the catacomb ahead as a vague, gray shape. He looked through the eyes of the lions that he followed, eyes that could see where men could not; and he looked through the shifting draperies of darkness into the cats' blind thoughts shot with raw images of blood and meat. The lions smelled flesh, and reflexively, Pietro's mouth watered. He felt repelled, for the flesh was human. The lions tried to resist his hold on them. They wanted to run ahead; the bloodlust was upon them, and Pietro could not help but feel it, too. It surged through him, driving him forward.

"The lions sense men ahead," Pietro said to his master.

"And there are men behind us," Mirandola whispered. "We are trapped." Although he couldn't see it in the dark, he visualized Pietro's wounded hand in which the transmogrified gazing globe was buried. "Does my crystal—your stone—show you anything?"

"No, Maestro."

"And you, Lucian. Can your angel help us?" After a beat, he called Lucian again, but there was no response.

"Pietro, where's Lucian?"

"I have no idea, Maestro. He was with us a moment ago."

"Ask your animals then."

"It doesn't work that way."

"Ask!"

Pietro willed the lions to stop and look back into the catacomb. As they did so, he felt their bloodlust increase. They smelled Mirandola...and himself. He felt a strange overwhelming urge to give in to them, to let them take him, feed upon him and his master; but he mastered the animals. He looked back through what appeared to be a fog-filled corridor, but Lucian was not behind them. Nor was he ahead."

"Well...?" Mirandola asked.

"He is no longer here," Pietro said.

"That cannot be."

"Of course it can," Pietro said impatiently. "His angel has taken him before. You should know that."

"You would speak to me that way?" Mirandola asked.

"Forgive me, Maestro. I spoke without thinking."

"No need, Pietro. You are right. It is I who—"

Suddenly, the lions roared at a dim flicker of light that appeared in the distance ahead...a light that only they could see. The huge tawny-colored male leaped forward toward the light, followed by three of the young lions; but the ghost-white female, also smelling the intoxicating odor of prey, turned the other way and led the rest of the roaring pride into the labyrinthine darkness of another catacomb artery. Pietro almost fainted as the stone embedded in his palm suddenly became red hot and leaden again. With dizzying double-vision, he could see clearly through the flame-yellow eyes of the cats. The male ran towards the torchlight, scrambling across loose stones and bones and charging at a contingent of household guards ahead, a few soldier-priests who were escaping the heat and destruction of the fire consuming the archbishop's church and castle above.

Pietro stepped backward as if he had been struck.

He was the male lion pouncing on a screaming soldier. As he clamped his jaws over the soldier's face, he could smell his leather jerkin sticky with dirt and salty sweat. He bit into flesh and bone even as he suffocated the man. The younger lions chased their prey back toward the archbishop's church, toward the increasing heat and the sweet cloying garbage stink of the river Arno; and as the tawny lion feasted, Pietro heard a voice calling him. The voice sounded as if it was coming from a great distance, but it was so close to him he could smell the garlic and tooth decay on the breath of his master Mirandola.

"Come, Pietro, we cannot remain here. We must hide ourselves."

As the lion tore at the soldier who was limp as a sack, Pietro smelled and tasted blood. *"No,"* he shouted, but it was a whisper; and the stone in his palm that had become so heavy, too heavy to bear, dissolved into a mist around him. It swallowed him, choking him just as the male cat had choked his unfortunate prey. *"No,"* he whispered again as he propped himself up against the blood-warm catacomb wall and stared into the darkness. Although he could still taste the flesh that the male lion feasted upon, his senses had shifted.

Now he saw through the eyes of the female cat. Her firefly bright soul and skittering senses became his own. Retinal explosions of red, multitudes of prey, sweat, fear, hunger. Instant coordinated desire and movement.

She leaped toward a tall soldier-priest cloaked in camphor, and incense.

Pietro recognized the priest.

"No..."

He summoned just enough psychic strength to distract the lioness and deflect her focus away from the priest; and an instant later the priest struck a mortal blow to her neck with his saber.

"No..."

Pietro felt the fiery rending of flesh and the stunned, slow freeze of the cat's thoughts into numbing darkness and hunger and yearning; and as she slipped out of his mind, he called the rest of her pride away from the panicked soldiers. Even in the throes of their bloodlust, he could master and command the young lions.

"To whom do you speak? Mirandola asked. His voice sounded insistent, but clear and no longer distant.

"To the lioness, who"—Pietro paused, then said—"who is now dead."

Once again, he felt the heavy stone burning in his hand; hard and familiar as a fingernail, it fused back into his palm.

"And now we must go back the way we came."

"Have you taken leave of your senses?"

"We have found safety, Maestro, for it is your own skryer who leads the soldiers toward us."

"My skryer...?"

"Fra Baldassare."

"But he—"

"I am certain he was not involved with the massacre at the church," Pietro said.

"And if you are wrong?"

"Do you believe me to be your...remembrancer, Maestro?"

"Yes, Pietro, I do believe that you are the one foretold by the angels in the crystal." After a beat, he said: "We can follow the lions to the archbishop's palace."

Reflexively, Pietro turned and gazed through the darkness toward what had been their original destination. He could sense the lions ahead; and he was careful not to expose his senses to the tawny male again, lest he become overwhelmed. But he was overwhelmed...not by the lions that feasted and kept the archbishop's few guards at bay, but by grief: an immediate, stabbing grief for the lioness and a hollow, aching grief for Isabella.

He had hoped to find Isabella, before it was too late.

But it *was* too late. Neither the archbishop's lions nor his men could return to the safety of the church and palace, for the buildings and grounds burned as hot as the stone in Pietro's hand. Even now the temperature was rising in the catacombs; Pietro and Mirandola were both sweating. The air was becoming steamy, and it stank of smoke and the river. They could hear footsteps echoing clearly above them.

"The walls are tricking us again," Mirandola said. "Let us hope your stone is not tricking us also." They walked back through the catacombs, away from the burning church; and even as the echoing footsteps of Baldassare's guards became faint, torchlight flickered in the distance.

As they walked toward the flickering light, Florence burned above them.

The heat was not only behind them now; it was everywhere.

"We may not get above ground," Mirandola said, wiping sweat from his eyes.

There was a deep-throated growling, and Mirandola and his apprentice could just make out two young lions advancing in the distance. Pitch and tow torches held high and swords extended at the ready, Baldassare's soldiers kept a safe distance behind them.

"So now it seems that your lions have become Baldassare's guides," Mirandola said. "Do you control the beasts still?"

"I think the stone controls them now, Maestro," Pietro said.

"Then let's pray it has not tricked us," and with that Mirandola shouted greetings to the skryer priest.

One moment Lucian was walking blindly in the pitch dark catacombs with Pietro and his master Mirandola…and then without hint or warning, he was falling through whorls of scattering white light. He had experienced the same attenuation, dislocation, and gorging pain when he had saved himself and Gabriel from Belias' dark, vine-ridden hell. Pain ignited memory; and as he fell, he felt the scar that encircled his neck begin to burn…and he remembered the blistering pain of the hangman's rope, the sun burning in his eyes like white fire; his father's strangled scream as the inquisitor's guard kicked the hanging platform out from under his wife's feet; the soft-faced, white robed Grand Master inquisitor gently patting Lucian's face and saying, "Now you must decide whether you will also murder your father."

"Yes, it was my fault," Lucian cried into the swallowing whiteness. "I broke the covenant. I revealed the location of the holiest of the holy tablets. I—"

"*Lucian…*"

The fragrant, crystalline scent of cinnamon tickled his nose.

"*Lucian…*"

"Gabriel…?"

Shapes roiled, but there seemed to be no perspective here. It was as if he was now floating inside the brightness of a heatless, benign sun: everything around him was intensities of white.

"Can that be you, Gabriel? Where…where am I?"

"*You would call it heaven,*" Gabriel said. "*Like my dark twin Belias who was almost our undoing, I can also embody both place and person. You've seen Belias' dark realm of crater and ice…now you see mine,*" and with that Lucian found himself standing on a high, narrow ridge in the desert near his childhood home in Palestine. He could smell the familiar lime and sulfur of *Yam HaMelah*, the Dead Sea, even as he gazed down at the caves that looked like shadows at the feet of the enormous precipices that rose in a crown around him.

"This was my home, the home of my parents," Lucian said. "It's certainly *not* heaven."

Gabriel appeared before him, coming into focus slowly; and his robes and wings seemed to take on the hues and textures of this dry land, as if this place was, indeed, but an incarnation of the angel. He smiled at Lucian who inhaled cinnamon and sulfur and shivered in the heat. Lucian turned from the angel and said in barely a whisper, "There, I can see The Ridge of Punishment where I was hanged…where my parents were executed for my sin."

Gabriel opened his hands and they were suddenly in that very place, deep in a glen at the bottom of the ridge. Above were the cracked towers of stone and broken mountains of yellow marl, sky, and the life-denuding sun. Lucian looked up at the plain where the wives and children of the priests and elders had been forced to watch his parents hang. Lucian touched the salt-sandy ground beneath the outcrop that had served as a gibbet and relived the last moments of his parents' lives.

"The sin was not yours."

"I told the inquisitor where the sacred tablets were hidden. Our purpose was to protect them, even if it meant giving up our lives."

"You chose your mother and father over a few scraps of parchment."

"I chose them over the Word, and they died for my apostasy."

"No matter what you told the inquisitor, they would have been killed."

"But *I* lived. I broke the covenant and yet I live…"

"The inquisitor was far more subtle than you, Lucian ben-Hananiah," Gabriel said as he settled into the stone precipice, as if into his robes. His angelic form—that of one of Botticelli's earth-born, feathery-winged gods— flickered, as if he couldn't decide whether to be soul-flesh or place. *"He punished you by taking your life, for you could not atone, nor could you take your own life, nor could your high priests and their council take your life."*

"In that, he succeeded," Lucian said.

The angel touched the scar that encircled Lucian's neck. *"Ah, but he left you his necklace."*

"It would have been better if the rope had broken my neck as intended. That would have been better than banishment by the elders and—"

"The inquisitor never intended to break your neck, Lucian. Nor was he an inquisitor."

"Then what was he?"

"He was an aeon like Belias. He simply doubled himself and took on a human incarnation. Do you remember when you *doubled yourself—?"*

"Me?"

"—When you transported yourself from your master's skrying room into the cathedral that the aeon Belias had fouled? Do you remember that while I was there whole and entire, you were attenuated?"

"Yes, as if I was stretched, and you—?"

"And you *saved me."* Gabriel's wings moved and fluttered inside the stone. *"You carried me with you. Carried me back into your master's gazing globe… into the crystal that now inheres in the palm of your friend Pietro."*

"He is not exactly my friend."

"Yes, of course," Gabriel said, acknowledging the nature of human rivalry, *"but you were in the cathedral…and in the gazing globe. Like the aeon/ inquisitor, you were in two places at once; or rather two places intersected within you."*

"And now, am I now in two places? I do not feel…stretched."

"Sadly, no, Lucian. You are here entire."

"I did not transport myself here."

"No," Gabriel said, *"I brought you here. I've stolen you from yourself."*

"Then where am *I*?"

The angel smiled, and Lucian could feel warmth radiating from the rock around him. *"If you wish, I will return you to your master in the catacombs; but if you decide to help me, then you will have to return the gift that both drains and sustains you."*

Lucian felt the snake as heat uncoiling inside him.

"Gabriel, I fear that I am too weak to—"

"Too weak to face the aeon that killed your family?"

And once again Lucian smelled the inquisitor's liver-breath and felt his soft dry hands clasping his face, the same soft hands that had humiliated his mother before he gave the order to execute her.

"Goccia di lei!"

Yes, he remembered...remembered how he, Lucian, had broken the sacred covenant of his people; once again he saw his father turn away from him and heard the priests tearing their tunics and chanting the prayer for the dead. For *him*. He was dead to all of them, dead because he was weak; and in that instant he was overwhelmed with hot, blind rage, which he directed at the angel who could see all that was the humiliating truth of his life.

Gabriel's wings fluttered as clouds passed across the sun, darkening the glen and the steep scarps around it. Lucian gasped, feeling a sudden, profound chill, as if he had just fallen into icy water. When he recovered, he whispered, "Forgive me... Forgive me, Gabriel."

"Do you wish me to return you to the catacombs?" the angel asked gently, calming Lucian with radiating warmth.

"I wish to confront the inquisitor—or aeon, whatever he is—that murdered me."

"You mean who murdered your family."

"It's one and the same."

"Well, you just met his most recent incarnation in the catacombs."

"I would have known if—"

"No, young maskil, you could not have known, for he hid himself from you."

"Who is he then?"

"The young priest Gentile who attended your master. Can you remember his face?"

"Of course I can," Lucian said; but hard as he tried, he could *not* remember. "Gabriel, I can't seem to fix it in mind. It's as if—"

"I know," Gabriel said. *"He is one of the demiurge's most powerful aeons."*

Gabriel removed himself from the stone scarp and floated in the air before Lucian. His delicate wings hardly moved, except when a gust of wind caught his feathers; and then, for an instant, they glistened like rainbows reflected in pure oil. "*He is called Athoth.*"

Lucian shivered with fear and hatred and said, "He is also called the whirlwind, or the reaper."

"*And how would you know that?*"

"When you and I were in the Duomo together, when I had taken Fra Baldassare's soul—I could see what he saw. I knew what he knew. I still can see into his thoughts a little."

"*Just as I can see into yours.*"

Lucian looked away from the angel.

"*Athoth is far stronger than I am, and he might surpass the one who created him. Some of your scriptures mistake him for Belias and call him Adversary. That is because he had once vanquished Belias and usurped his rule. But Belias has regained and reclaimed his power and is now in an alliance of sorts with Athoth.*" After a pause, the angel continued, "*Athoth is often privy to what Belias knows…and Belias still has some small part of you, does he not?*"

"No!" Lucian said desperately, reflexively. "The darkness is my own! My own sin. My—" He looked away from the angel. "Forgive me, Gabriel. It's easier to lie to myself than to you. Yes, I fear that Belias can look into me."

"*And that is why you must give up the seal I entrusted you with,*" Gabriel said as he reached into Lucian's chest and tore the seal—the sapphire snake— away from his heart.

Lucian gasped, experiencing a sudden, terrible emptiness. "Please, Gabriel…return it to me."

"You *must be the master of the seal.*"

"I am."

"*No, young theurgist, the serpent has been mastering you. You must be independent, even when you host the seal.*"

"But I am," Lucian insisted.

"*Ah, I see you have not forgotten the most important thing.*"

"And that is…?"

"*You.*"

Lucian felt the angel's laughter, and swore he would never refer to himself again; but the emptiness was so sharp that it seemed to cut through thought and marrow. It was *his* pain, and he could not pull himself away from it. Not even Gabriel's chiding and radiating warmth could fill his aching need.

"*If indeed you wish to play some small part to defeat the aeon that killed your parents, you cannot contain my seal,"* Gabriel said. *"Why do you think Athoth divided himself, took the form of a priest called Gentile, and then allied himself to your master Mirandola?"*

"Surely, I don't—"

The angel smiled at Lucian and said, *"I did not mean for you to answer that, even though I know you sense the reason. He was watching you, Lucian. Your master was but a means."*

"But why would he care what I might do?"

"Because you are special: yes, young maskil, like the daughter of light. And because of me: because of what I will give you."

"I am not special," Lucian said angrily. "If anything, I am—"

Gabriel just looked at him, and Lucian felt the almost physical impact of the angel's sadness...and guilt.

"What will you give me?" Lucian asked. "And how...how would Athoth know?"

"I will show you what he seeks, Lucian; and he knows because I let him know."

"You spoke to Athoth?"

"No, but I allowed Belias to look into my thoughts when I was imprisoned in his dark land, when he tried to destroy me with his vines.

"You *allowed* Belias to look into your thoughts?"

"Yes, Lucian. It seemed to be a reasonable strategy, as I was fairly certain that Belias would not be able to conceal the information from Athoth. My kind does not experience fear and agony—or time—in the same way as yours do. I could foresee many outcomes. One would be my destruction, oblivion from eternity. And one would be the outcome that appears to you to be in the past."

"You mean when Athoth came to my village in the guise of the inquisitor."

"Yes, for you...it happened in the past." The angel paused and then continued. *"Athoth believed that I gave you the sapphire tablet...he didn't realize that I would give you the tablet...now."*

"I remember the inquisitor asking for a sapphire tablet, but I knew of nothing called that."

"Not even your father knew all the treasures that your tribe was pledged to protect: ignorance is often the best safeguard. But the sapphire tablet is—and was—buried in the cave."

"Then why couldn't Athoth find it?"

"Because just as he hid his face from you, so was the tablet hidden from him."

"Did *you* hide it?"

"It is one of the keys under my control."

"Key?"

"*The tablet. Come, I will show you.*"

"Why did he—does he—seek out your tablet?" Lucian asked.

"*Power, young maskil…that which motivates all beings of the lower sphere, whether they be spiritual or material.*"

"But why would you let your enemy know about the tablet *now*?"

"*Because I have no choice. Because the balance is tipping against us. And because Athoth might be the one to shift the balance.*"

"*I don't understand.*"

The angel moved like flickering sunlight past Lucian. "*You will, if you can prevail. Now…follow me.*"

Lucian followed the angel up a steep ridge to the ledge that hid the entrance to the caves. He had climbed this many times as a boy, and the shadow-coolness and dust-dry smell of the hidden crevice wall brought the past back to him with the force of hallucination. For a grief-laden instant he imagined that his parents were climbing above him, reaching for the familiar handholds and footholds called the stairs, as they recited their climbing prayers.

> *Thank you, oh Lord, King of the universe,*
>
> *Who is the fortified wall upon which I cling,*
>
> *Who has placed these hands and feet upon your rock*
>
> *That I might guard your ways of eternity*
>
> *And the paths which you have chosen.*

Without thinking, Lucian murmured the familiar prayer as he climbed to the ledge that hid the cavern's mouth from those who would seek it below. The angel stood in the cave's twilight zone waiting for him, his wings drawn so tightly across his back that he could almost be mistaken for a man. He lowered his gaze as Lucian walked past him into the cave. The still air reeked of cinnamon and sadness. Lucian looked around the cave, searched all the secret places. Everything was gone. Not a scrap of parchment remained. "Athoth was very thorough," Lucian said.

"*Yes…*"

"How you must hate him."

"*Hate?*"

"Athoth. Stealing from you, tearing everything out of here…would it not be like—"

The angel smiled and said, "*Rape? Is that what you stumble to say?*"

"It would seem to be if this place is part of you…is you."

"*You should know better,*" Gabriel said. "*You contained me when you saved me from the aeon Belias.*"

"I could not see clearly. You overwhelmed me."

"*You saw clearly enough.*"

"You…dismiss him."

"*Yes, 'dismiss': perhaps that is our correlative to what you call hate.*" Gabriel nodded and said, "*Yes, I dismiss him.*" Then the angel pointed to a fissure in the stony wall. It was as long as the span of the angel's hand and narrow as a finger. "*There, Lucian. It is yours to remove.*"

"There is nothing there but—" and Lucian suddenly glimpsed a reflection in the wall crevice, a reflection as of the bluest water shimmering on a lake. He touched the crevice, slid his fingers against the smooth surface of the crystal contained within. "I feel something, like glass; but it—"

"*Yes, Lucian?*" the angel asked.

"It also feels somehow…familiar. Aetheric and alive. Warm."

"*Ah, does it?*"

"…just like the serpent you took away from me."

The hint of a smile.

"But I fear that if I try to pull the…sheet out of its place," Lucian continued, "I will break it."

"*It is stronger than the rock that contains it. Just pull your hand back. It will keep to you.*"

Lucian pulled his hand back slowly and the thin sapphire wafer came away from its niche. Only then did it seem to acquire weight. Awed, he held it carefully with both hands and examined it. Its surface was without blemish. It was smooth as a pool of mercury. "This is the tablet?"

The angel nodded and took it from Lucian, who reluctantly relinquished it.

"How can something so thin and fragile be so heavy?"

"*It is not thin, nor is it fragile,*" Gabriel said. "*It just seems so. It is more than you imagine.*"

"You call it a tablet, yet I can see no writing on its surface."

The angel angled the sapphire sheet. "*Look again, young theurgist. It will give you more than sight.*"

"I still cannot see anything," but then the surface of the tablet became clouded; and it was like looking into his master Mirandola's gazing globe. Perhaps the tablet and globe were *pari materia*…both made of the same aetheric stuff. Lucian saw Florence burning as if he was seeing it from a great height, and he heard wood creaking and sails snapping and men shouting. Then the tablet darkened; he saw bright shafts of light piercing the gloom, and Isabella…Isabella was walking with another woman and an officer in uniform. The officer's doublet was imprinted with the cross and vine insignia of the pope, and his crimson tunic was fringed with gold. Lucian took a sharp intake of breath. "I can recognize him now," he whispered. "It's the priest Gentile. He's dressed as an officer." And as if the scales had dropped from his eyes, he could see that the priest and the inquisitor were indeed one and the same: both incarnations—reflections—of the aeon Athoth. He remembered once again what had happened on the Ridge of Punishment eight long years ago; and his rage, grief, and loss turned to icy venom dripping into his chest.

The angel called his name; and as Gabriel's comforting warmth enveloped him, memory dissipated and his thoughts returned to the present. "If that is the aeon Athoth, what is Isabella doing with him?" he asked.

"*Do you not see the daughter of light?*

"Yes...I can see her, too."

"*But your gaze seems to be fixed on Isabella,*" Gabriel said, smiling.

Lucian blushed, but would not turn away from the tablet.

"Forgive my indulgence, angel."

"*Is that why you don't consider Pietro to be your friend?*"

"Because I am indulgent?"

"*No, because you are infatuated with Isabella, young fool...as he is.*"

"My only concern is to avenge my parents." Again, rage burned through him.

The angel sighed: wind whistling through stone cliffs. "*Isabella did not betray your master, but she is in grave danger, as is the daughter of light...as are we all.*"

"Why are we—?

"*Because in time they might both betray us.*"

"I cannot believe that."

"*Have you not felt the lures of darkness, heard the sweet voice of Belias? Perhaps you cannot feel toward the church as others do, but the light of the True God, the Invisible Spirit, is reflected in all of His aeons, just as the lesser light of their spirit is reflected in their creations.*"

"Such as the demiurge."

"*Yes. And the demiurge's spirit is reflected in his own aeons Belias and Athoth.*"

"And so have I, too, worshiped the demiurge," Lucian said in a hollow voice. "Have my people wasted their lives guarding false—"

"*Surely you felt the goodness of your parents and the priests of your assembly?*"

"Yes, but—"

"*And just so can the daughter of light and Isabella be captured.*"

Even within the familiar confines of the cave, Lucian felt suddenly dizzy. "So my parents served the aeon Athoth who murdered them..."

"*Just as Athoth serves his superior. The demiurge.*"

"And whom do *you* serve, angel?"

Gabriel moved deeper into the cave and beckoned Lucian to follow. "*You *have been chosen to have knowledge. You can choose light...or darkness."*

"But they seem the same."

Gabriel smiled and nodded.

"Does the demiurge—Jehovah—believe himself to be darkness?"

"How can I know the mind of a god?"

"Because he is an aeon. Like yourself."

"No, child, I am merely a seraph. But from my limited perspective and knowledge, I would imagine the demiurge considers himself painfully bright."

It was Lucian's turn to smile.

"I say that without humor."

Lucian nodded and asked, "Then there is little difference between the demiurge and..."

"And his master?" Gabriel asked. *"His master who is my master...the Invisible Spirit?"*

Lucian could smell ozone, as if a storm were breaking.

"The demiurge and his aeons will eat the world, young theurgist, if you allow it."

"If *I* allow it...?"

Gabriel smiled indulgently. *"Yes, you and others."*

"What, then, do you ask me to do, angel?"

"Take a journey. Find the daughter of light. And give her the sapphire tablet."

"Is that all?" Lucian asked sarcastically.

The angel nodded. *"I will show you the way, brave maskil."*

Lucian's face burned with guilty humiliation, but his mind raced: if he could find Athoth and the daughter of light, he would also find Isabella.

"And if I manage to do what you ask. What then...?"

"Stay with her and her companion. Protect them as best you can."

"But certainly Athoth will know me."

"Yes, and he will ingratiate himself to you. He will try to turn you, just as he has turned the daughter of light. And perhaps he will succeed..."

The very idea made Lucian ill, and he turned away from the angel. But perhaps...perhaps there might be a way to—"

"You do not have the strength to overcome Athoth. If you are to avenge your parents, you must treat with him; and to do that you must bury your hatred... and control your fear. If you can do that, you may find that he is not entirely as you believe. And if you succeed—if you can do as I ask—then perhaps Athoth himself might be turned." Gabriel smiled sadly and shrugged, sending shadowy blue ripples through his wings. *But it is entirely your decision to remain or go."*

"And what if I choose to remain here in heaven with you?" Lucian asked, gently yet carefully chiding the angel as he followed him farther into the cave and into a concealed room where the ancients had carved an altar out of the stone.

Lucian could barely see in the owl-light.

"*It appears that you are mature enough now to make a principled choice,*" the angel said as he placed the sapphire tablet upright on the altar. He stepped back from the tablet, which suddenly blazed, as if it were a mirror reflecting intense roiling white light. Lucian shielded his eyes. "*You will quickly become used to the light, and you will miss it when it is soon gone.*"

Lucian looked back into the tablet, which had enlarged into a doorway of light. The angel was right: the radiance no longer hurt his eyes.

"What do you mean...when it is gone?"

"*Patience, Lucian ben-Hananiah...*"

"Wait, I see something in there! I see an outline in the light...blue. I can barely make it out. It's light against light."

"*Exactly, and it will also be a light in the dark.*"

"It looks like a bridge, an impossible bridge without towers or trusses. I can see its span, but not where it ends."

"*It will lead you to the daughter of light...and Isabella.*"

"How?"

"*You need only step forward,*" the angel said. "*If possible, we will find you.*"

"We...?"

"*Go now, child, or stay.*"

Lucian shook his head as if to say "no", then mastering his fear; he stepped into the light.

Beneath his feet was the bridge, which appeared to be made of the same stuff as the sapphire tablet; it was hard and smooth and dangerously narrow—about the width of a *braccia*, less than a half stride—and seemed to extend as far as he could see. He looked behind, but he was surrounded by coruscating white light; reflexively, he began to pray—

> Who is the fortified wall upon which I cling,
>
> Who has placed these hands and feet upon your rock
>
> That I might guard your ways of eternity
>
> And the paths which you have chosen.

—and he felt a rush of panic.

He was losing his balance. He heard Gabriel's crystalline, impossibly faraway voice. "*Gaze forward, not downward, and make yourself ready. This is the easeful part of your journey...*"

Lucian took a tentative step forward and imagined he could glimpse something dark beyond the silent, swirling curtains of light.

TWELVE

The Paths of Light and Darkness

I have thrown fire upon the world, and look, I am watching it blaze.

On the day when you were one, you became two. But when you become two, then what will you do?

—*The Gospel of Thomas 11:1-4*

Then the time came when the child grew up. When he reached his maturity, the rulers sent him to the imitator so they might learn of our great Power.

—*The Concept of Our Great Power 44,31*

Two lions separated Baldassare and his troops from Maestro Mirandola and his first apprentice Pietro…and two of Baldassare's Companions of the Night stood beside the Dominican soldier-priest holding torches and extended swords. The lions were still, except for their tails which snapped back and forth with nervous energy.

"Call the lions away," Mirandola said to Pietro, "lest they panic."

"Panic…?"

But Pietro did as his master asked, and the lions, as if unleashed, bolted past Pietro and Mirandola; they rushed through the heated darkness of the catacomb, rushed out of sight to join the tawny male and the other young lions.

"They will return with the other lions, but will keep their distance."

"*Saluto*, Fra Baldassare," Mirandola said cautiously. "We are relieved to see you, but—"

"Yes…?" Baldassare asked, raising his head haughtily, his eyes narrowing in the flickering light. He looked haggard. His face was slick with perspiration, and his robes were torn, revealing slashes in his protective leather jerkin.

"Your presence would have been most appreciated in the church when your cardinal assassinated the First Citizen and your troops butchered the first families." Mirandola noticed that Baldassare's sweaty hands were speckled and smeared with blood.

"*My* troops? You would believe that *I* would allow such a thing?"

"There are many powers and influences that draw us away from our earnest intentions. I admit that I harbored ill feelings concerning your absence."

"Speak plainly to me," Baldassare said.

"Yes, for a time I thought you were in league with the cardinal, but…"

"But…?"

Mirandola glanced at his apprentice, then said, "Pietro saw that you were not involved."

Baldassare laughed. "Your apprentice *saw*? And you would believe him before me?"

"Yes, Agnolo, for the time being. He is the promised remembrancer."

He turned his gaze to Pietro who lowered his head in deference. "And you control the beasts?" Baldassare asked. "When the largest of the beasts was about to attack me, it suddenly hesitated."

"I called her back," Pietro said.

"And saved my life."

"Yes."

"And I returned the favor by killing your beast."

"She was not mine, Fra Baldassare."

"Well, she and her pride certainly no longer belong to the archbishop. Will they continue to do your bidding, young master?"

"As I told Maestro Mirandola, it is not I who influences them, but the stone," and Pietro held his right hand out to the priest to inspect. Baldassare touched the boy's palm, then grunted in pain and pulled his hand away.

"What is it? It looks like a key; yet it is hot as a grill, and it…moves."

"It is my master's skrying crystal, or was…"

"It seems that miracles as well as slaughter abound," Baldassare said to Mirandola. "And your servant Lucian, where is he?"

"Disappeared."

"Ah, another miracle."

"I thought perhaps *you* might know," Mirandola said, "as you seem to be able to see into each other."

Baldassare looked surprised and then said, "When we stopped for a short rest, I fell asleep for a moment or two and had a vision—a dream—about Lucian. I dreamed that he was enveloped in whiteness. He was afraid of falling from a dizzying height, and he said—"

"What did he say, Agnolo?" Mirandola asked.

"He said that Athoth would know him."

"The aeon Athoth?"

"I don't know. As I said, it was a dream." Then Baldassare abruptly changed the subject. "In the cathedral…it wasn't my troops, certainly none of the troops loyal to me."

Mirandola nodded.

"Let us leave this place and I will explain what I saw," Baldassare said.

"No," Mirandola said. "I must know what happened…and what you are doing down here."

After a few slow breaths Baldassare said, "Everything has happened so quickly. He drew the Gnostic's sign of the snake across his breast. "The holy church is no longer simply misguided: it has been murdered." He shook his head, as if he would not believe what he said. "Pope Innocent has been murdered, may he find bliss in his rest. His murderer is now Supreme Pontiff."

"Nunc sunt Dies tribulationis," Mirandola mumbled, shocked.

Now are the days of troubles.

"You know him, Maestro, and you know his son, the blond haired *condottiero* Cesare who calls himself Valentine: the one who slaughtered the children in Carthusia now wears a cardinal's crimson mitre."

"That whoring pig Rodrigo Borgia, pope?"

Baldassare nodded. "Although Innocent believed the demiurge to be the True Creator, he would not countenance Belias. In fact, his last encyclical declared the dark aeon a manifestation of Satan rather than the demiurge's archangel."

"He wrote his own death sentence," Mirandola said.

"Indeed, he did; and the new pope—who now calls himself Sixtus Alexander—has willingly enslaved himself to Belias. Thus he keeps his soul intact and gains what corrupt powers the aeon deigns to give him. But that is not the half of it. Those who murdered at Cardinal Caraffa's call in the church were all Belias' creatures…Florentine citizens whose souls he had taken. Belias is here in Florence, Maestro, stealing souls and creating an army to do his bidding out of our soulless flesh. And Valentine and all in his pay are here, too, laying waste to all that stands. A *condottiero* now leads the papal army."

"And you knew nothing of these…plans?"

Baldassare smiled grimly. "It seems that Cardinal Caraffa and the archbishop knew of my plans to, ah, reform the Holy Church. None of my spies could pierce their veil, and Valentine's troops took a circuitous route through the marshes. He traveled by moonlight and left none alive to sound an alarm…

"I fear our beloved Florence is lost. But I brought what men I could to find you. Most of my troops were poisoned in their barracks, and the Cardinal sent his *accoliti* cutthroats to dispatch me."

"How did you escape?" Mirandola asked, unaware that he was clenching and unclenching his fists.

Baldassare gestured at the men beside and behind him. "I have my own *accoliti*...and I don't dispatch so easily. But I assure you, Caraffa, the pope, and his bastard son will pay dearly for what they've done."

"Is this *all* your men?"

Baldassare shrugged. "Those who survived—those who kept their souls intact and are in my confidence—will make their way to Urbino. We shall know more then. Now let us leave these corridors before our flesh begins to roast."

"Tell me how you knew we were here," Mirandola insisted.

"Enough, Maestro!" Baldassare said, wiping away the sweat dripping into his eyes. "My patience is at an end."

"Pietro, how near are the lions?"

In response the lions—led by the tawny male—padded into the torchlight. Pietro strained to keep them under control, and they lay down each touching the other, as if to sleep. Baldassare nodded respectfully. "Your priest Antonio found me. He told me where you were and that you were in grave danger."

"*We* are in grave danger," Mirandola said. "The archbishop's troops are somewhere in the catacombs. We've heard them."

"Those that Caraffa and the archbishop sent down here will contribute their bones to the saints and the stones. We have dispatched most of them... and all their officers. Those who are left will stumble in the dark until they starve. Now may we leave?"

"Our intention was to go to the archbishop's palace beside Santa Apostoli," Pietro said, interrupting. "Maestro Mirandola's cousin and the one they call the daughter of light were taken there. But the palace and the church are on fire."

"And how does he know all that," Baldassare asked Mirandola.

"I know that because I looked into the memory of the lion you murdered," Pietro said. "Now please do me the kindness of addressing me directly."

"Much has changed, indeed," Baldassare said, as if talking to himself. "And what else did you see?"

"I think there was something in the air...a ship."

"Ah, so the cardinal was taking them to the *Ascensione*, the Pope's own heavenly gondola."

"The cardinal...?" asked Pietro.

Baldassare still directed himself to Mirandola. "The archbishop and the cardinal together abducted the daughter of light through the catacombs. That's where the cardinal's guards caught Antonio and Isabella. Antonio escaped by sheer luck…and by cutting the throat of one of his captors."

"And what about Gentile, his companion?" Mirandola asked.

Baldassare shrugged. "Nowhere to be found. Now if you are quite ready, and your apprentice is satisfied, Antonio and a contingent of my guards await us."

"Where?"

"By the Ponte Vecchio, as he promised."

"And then…?"

"To Urbino to gather our troops."

"That is what the angel said we must do," Mirandola said.

"Gabriel…?"

"Yes, he told Lucian that we must not tarry there lest disaster befall. We must gather enough forces to free the girl, and that will not be easy now that we have lost the First Citizen."

Baldassare smiled again, but his face expressed only pain. "Pico, we have not lost the First Citizen."

"I saw Caraffa thrust his dagger into his heart."

"Yes, but it was not Guiliano you saw murdered."

"I *saw* it, Agnolo, just as I saw his brother, his wife, and his daughters put to the sword."

"That they were," Baldassare said. "But not the First Citizen," and with that, he turned away from Mirandola and motioned his troops to follow him out of the heat-stinking catacombs.

Flanked by four very large and overly-solicitous guards, Louisa and Isabella left their cramped cabin on the covered upper deck to "take the air" with the captain of the airship *Ascensione*. It was almost dusk, yet the soft rippling unnatural light was as tangible and bright as the water in Capri's Blue Grotto.

"We are being treated as prisoners," Isabella complained.

"No, *signora*," said one of the guards called Rudolfo. "You are being treated as honored guests." Like his placid-looking companions, he wore a tufted crimson uniform with no indication of rank.

"Honored guests of the female persuasion should be accompanied by their own kind," Louisa said, "and certainly not by solders who might just forget themselves and—"

"Louisa, I don't think we're in any danger of that," Isabella said. She grinned, and the angry tightness in her face disappeared.

"I'm sure I have no idea what you mean."

"*Filia Lucis*," Rudolfo said to Louisa—and the other guards bowed their heads and intoned, "'*Ecce seruus Domini*'—you need have no fear of us. We are…different than other men."

"What does he mean?" Louisa asked Isabella. "And why are you smiling?"

"Don't you understand? They are eunuchs."

"I've never heard of such a word," Louisa said.

Isabella laughed and said, "How is it possible that you can know so much and yet be such an innocent?" Although Louisa's face burned with embarrassment, she continued to hold Isabella's hand as they walked. Isabella leaned toward her and whispered, "They have had their manhood removed."

But Rudolfo was close enough to discern what she said.

"Chosen one, allow me to correct your honored companion. We have all retained our manhood…we have just given back to our Lord the sacks that contained our seed and our lust. Our only lust and desire is to release the souls of the enemies of the holy church." He smiled sweetly and seemingly without guile said, "The edge of my sword has already released over a hundred souls… and with God's mercy and help, it will release many more of the Adversary's followers."

"You mean Satan," Louisa said, although it was really a question.

Rudolfo bowed his head and said, "Yes, the fallen one who has a hundred despicable names. You may know him as Abaddon, Adversary, Duma, Mastema, Sammael, Sathan, Shaitan—"

"Rudolfo!" The commanding voice seemed to come from above; and Louisa and Isabella looked up at the ceiling. The archbishop appeared in a flickering nimbus of the same blue-tinged light that shafted through ceiling grilles and the rectangular perimeters of closed hatches. He looked uncomfortable as he climbed down a narrow, almost vertical companionway. "Do you think it wise to utter the names of filth when we are in such proximity to the boundary of accursed souls?"

"If I had even a single doubt, Eminence, I would not have named the defiled one." Rudolfo did not look in the least intimidated by the archbishop who now stood before him.

"The captain is above," the archbishop said. "He awaits the daughter of light and her companion."

"Understood, Eminence," Rudolfo said. "But we have been directed to accompany her, and you have been invited to join the captain and his guests later in his quarters."

"I just left the captain. He said nothing of this to me."

The eunuch's soft face did not change expression; but he bowed low, as only a supplicant would, to soften the archbishop's humiliation.

The archbishop nodded stiffly and said, "Then I will be in my quarters. When the captain is ready to receive me, please send a servant to my chamber."

"I shall come for you myself, Eminence."

The archbishop nodded and turned to take his leave; but Louisa pulled away from the eunuchs and said, "Eminence, may I have the privilege of accompanying you to your quarters?" She glanced at Rudolfo and imagined that the slight tightness around his eyes indicated surprise. "And then we shall visit the captain, of course."

"I think you had best accompany the captain's *ennuci*," the archbishop said, but he stopped walking along the deck grating.

"I have questions I wish to ask you," Louisa said.

"And I too," Isabella said, taking her cue from Louisa.

The archbishop shook his head, although his expression softened. "The captain's wishes take precedence over all things on his ship...and *this* captain's wishes take precedence over—"

"Excellency, we shall all attend you," Rudolfo said with deference, "and once you are comfortably settled, we shall escort the child of light to attend the master."

The archbishop nodded and walked ahead of the eunuchs with Louisa and Isabella. "I thought your companion was eager to question the captain."

"I am," Isabella said, "but—" She turned to Louisa.

"Yes?" asked the archbishop.

"Perhaps you can enlighten her before we go before the captain," Louisa said.

Isabella looked relieved, as she was just trying to help Louisa preserve the archbishop's dignity.

"Ah, so you suspect his identity?" the archbishop asked Isabella.

"I suspect *him*."

"Of course you do," the archbishop said. "But who else could divide himself yet remain whole?"

"A magician...or a demon."

The archbishop smiled. "Or...?"

"Or an angel," Isabella said.

"More than that, child. Tread wisely and carefully when you ascend."

"Ascend?"

"When the captain's eunuchs take you above."

"You have not yet explained what lifts this ship," Louisa said.

"Do you still believe it might be coal gas?" the archbishop asked.

"No, I think not."

"Well, you will soon have the opportunity to ask the captain."

"But I'm asking you."

The archbishop appeared surprised and said, "Be careful, child. And be careful when you're on high."

"I shall endeavor to do so."

The archbishop smiled and said, "The envelope that buoys the ship is filled with…emptiness, utter emptiness which displaces the *materia* of the air itself and thus lifts us. Be mindful of the membrane that contains the emptiness, for it is an interweaving of souls; and even accursed souls have more density and strength than any form of corrupt matter."

"Is the ship's balloon membrane the boundary you spoke of earlier?"

"There are many boundaries; that is but one."

"And you use *souls* to lift your ship?" Louisa asked.

"Accursed souls."

"Their flesh might have been cursed, Eminence, but surely their souls are redeemable."

The archbishop laughed at that and asked, "Do you also believe your companion's heresy of the corrupted demiurge that created the world and all things in it?"

"I do not believe there are any gods but God," Isabella insisted, and "I am *not* a heretic."

The archbishop nodded, then asked, "And your cousin, the theurgist Mirandola, is he a heretic?"

Isabella blushed and said, "You can test my faith, but I will not be faithless to my cousin."

"Commendable…perhaps, perhaps not." Then he asked, "If you believe in the One God, do you also believe in the Adversary?"

Isabella said, "Of course," but she glanced at Louisa.

"And you, Child?"

"If you mean Satan, then, yes, I believe he exists," Louisa said, sensing a trap.

"The same Satan that the Sainted Gregory called the Bearer of Light, the beloved aeon who was so great in his glory, knowledge, and power that he wore all the other angels as his garment? The same one who declared war on God and Heaven and continues to ensnare the souls of humankind?"

"Yes," Louisa said warily, "the same."

"And of what stuff do you believe aeons are composed? Of spirit or corruptible flesh?"

"I would imagine either or both…if they wished."

The archbishop shook his head and chuckled. "Angels and their kin can be only spirit—"

"But Jesus—" Isabella interrupted.

"—and if an aeon or an angel appears in mortal guise, he is merely wearing the fleshy body as a garment to be discarded at will." The archbishop took Louisa's hand. She flinched and pulled away from his touch, which felt so hot as to be cold. "Can you not see that angels are entirely spirit, soul?" the archbishop continued. "If they weren't, then Satan would have...passed away long ago."

"Souls *can* die," Louisa said, even as she glimpsed, even as she remembered that she—her soul—had lived other lives in others' flesh. The touch of the archbishop had once again burned a path back to her soul...once again it awakened the serpent, the sapphire blue striation in her palm. The serpent was stigmata and memory, her soul's memory; and she remembered—she knew once again—that she, Louisa Mary Morgan of Bartonsville, Virginia, was merely the present incarnation of her soul.

And she also knew that souls *could* die.

"No, child," said the archbishop. "Souls may perish, but they cannot die; and once perished—accursed—they cannot be restored to what they were. There can be no salvation for perished souls, spirits, angels, or aeons such as the Adversary." He gestured upward. "The souls that make up the boundary above have perished. Although they are without salvation, they can at least be made to serve those who seek it. How well do you know your scripture, child?"

"Well, enough," Louisa said uncomfortably.

"Then you should be able to recite the first revelation from *The Acts of Thunder*. Well...?"

"I've never even heard of it," Louisa said.

Isabella squeezed Louisa's hand and said, "And then the Lord thy God chose his servant to gather up the darkness and make it shine."

"Excellent," the archbishop said, "and when you are above with the captain, when you look up at the boundary, remember the words you just spoke, for you will have to decide."

"Decide what?" asked Louisa, but the archbishop did not answer. Instead, he reached under his purple velvet tunic and pulled out a damson silk purse, which he gave to Isabella.

"Eminence, surely you don't need to—"

"Give this to the captain," the archbishop said to Isabella.

"What is it?"

"It is very valuable," the archbishop said softly. "I was going to give it to you, Daughter of Light," he said to Louisa, "but I think it might...protect your companion when she meets the captain."

"Why would I need protection?" Isabella asked.

"You accused and rebuffed the captain. If you recall, he guaranteed his protection to your benefactor and companion, but did not extend his protection to you."

"Surely he would not harm Isabella," Louisa said.

The archbishop slowed his pace as they were approaching his quarters, and pulled Isabella's hand away from the purse's tie string. "Do not dare to open it."

"What does it contain?" Isabella asked, kneading the purse gently. "It feels like stones, or, perhaps, jewels."

"Far more valuable than jewels, child. You are holding the flints from the Holy Sepulcher…from the tomb of our own Christ."

"Were they what the cardinal was looking for in the church when the window shattered?" Louisa asked.

The archbishop looked at her with admiration. "Yes, child, he sought to take them for his own purposes, but I anticipated his treachery. All he found was an empty drawer…and death."

"I cannot take part in this," Isabella said as she tried to return the purse to the archbishop. "These relics belong in Florence. They have always protected it from pestilence and—"

"And heresy?" the archbishop asked.

"I meant to say treachery."

"Relics belong only to the Church, not the state."

"Yet you would have me give them to the captain of this ship."

"I would have you give them back to their rightful owner."

Louisa felt the serpent coiling, twisting in her palm, and she restrained Isabella. "Eminence, when my companion realizes what you have done, she will enter a convent to show her gratitude."

The archbishop smiled, bowed his head slightly, and said, "I think a cloister might not quite suit your friend's high spirits"; then he nodded to the eunuch Rudolfo, unlocked the door to his chamber, and disappeared inside.

Rudolfo and the other eunuchs hurried Louisa and Isabella across the deck to another hatchway flooding with the rippling, watery light of the boundary.

"Captain Serafino awaits you, children of light."

"So now I too have a title?" Isabella asked.

"Only as a formality," the eunuch said. "Now please ascend."

Louisa looked into the hatchway; but could see only dim, slightly iridescent light, which seemed to swirl like mist. "Aren't you going to accompany us? We won't know where to go."

"You will have no need for directions, nor will you have any need of us now," Rudolfo said, bowing; and then he effectively dismissed the daughter of light by ordering the other eunuchs to turn away.

Isabella was about to say something to the eunuch, but Louisa shushed her.

"Come on, you wanted to talk to the captain."

"I'm afraid," Isabella whispered, shielding her eyes from the light streaming over her.

"Just follow me…I am not afraid," Louisa lied.

When they reached the landing above, it was indeed like standing in a bright mist. Louisa steadied Isabella and looked up toward the envelope. Although she couldn't quite make it out, she felt it as a living, thinking, grasping presence.

"I need to go back down," Isabella said; and Louisa could feel her trembling. "I've got to give the flints back to the archbishop. Something is—"

"Welcome, Daughter of Light…and you, too, Isabella Sabatini."

As the captain appeared—his kind, brooding face as soft as the eunuchs who served him—the mist seemed to dissipate.

"Can you feel the radiance of lost souls?" the captain asked. "It can be quite overwhelming. I have dampened the boundary's strength to make you more comfortable."

"Thank you, Captain," Louisa said, as she looked up into the shimmering blue-tinged light.

"The envelope is its radiance," the captain continued. "It has no substance, but if you gaze into it too long, *Filia Lucis*, it will weaken you."

"And you can control it?" Louisa asked. Everything around her—the decking, timbers, railings, and, beyond, the swiveling masts, yards, billowing sails, and the night itself—seemed wavery and washed out by the cyanic radiance. Even Isabella looked faded and somehow distant; only the captain seemed to embody substance and definition itself.

"Well, I must, mustn't I, if I am to control the ship and get you to your destination in safety," the captain said to Louisa.

Louisa nodded, but then looked up again at the balloon envelope: its radiance seemed to be a form of darkness itself. "So that's what the archbishop meant when he asked about scripture." She looked at the captain in his crimson tunic and damask doublet and also saw the priest Gentile. "Could it be *you* who gathers up the darkness and makes it shine?" With that, Louisa looked away from him. The serpent stigmata in her palm felt cold and dead; and she felt weak and dizzy, as if something precious was being leached away from her…as if something else was overwhelming her.

She felt emptied out, her arms heavy, her legs watery and—

The captain the priest the aeon caught her.

She expected his touch and aspect to be as cold as when she first met him, but it wasn't. He was warm, *human*, embracing; and he supported her weight as if she were no heavier than the gold-threaded epaulets on his shoulders. In that instant she felt absolutely and completely safe. Isabella reached for her hand, but stepped backward, as if she had just been gently yet powerfully pushed away. "The one who makes the darkness shine is within you," the captain said "Can you remember?"

Louisa shuddered as she remembered passing through the dark crack in the sky while trying to thwart the snapping, snaking, sapping vines of the cold, dark, and impossibly beautiful aeon Belias who was a world, a thought, an angel.

The one who made the darkness shine.

"You *aren't* Belias," Louisa said, relieved. She found her own footing and reluctantly stepped away from the captain. "The archbishop told me that I would have to decide who you are for myself."

"And so you have decided." Athoth smiled at her...warming her. "The archbishop is one of very few selected for revelation. He has power and sees many things clearly. But many of his enemies in the church confuse me with my dark cousin Belias, or with Satan himself." Then the aeon turned to Isabella and said, "I am also called Gentile, both priest and captain. Others have called me Reaper, Whirlwind, or simply Athoth. Which would you prefer, Isabella, companion to the daughter of light?"

Isabella stood before the captain; her hands were shaking and her teeth chattered as if she had suddenly been baptized in a bath of ice water, yet she kept her composure.

"Well...?"

"Gentile," Isabella whispered. "I would prefer Gentile."

"You wanted to ask me a question, and you also have something for me, isn't that true?"

"Yes," Isabella said, and she fumbled inside her finestrella sleeve for the silk purse the archbishop had given her.

The captain took the purse, opened it, raised it to his mouth, and inhaled. Then he retied the ribbon and handed the purse back to Isabella."

"But it's empty."

"No, little daughter, it is just no longer *materia*. You may open the purse and see for yourself."

She did so, and the radiance emanating from the flints bathed her face. She looked away and squeezed the purse shut.

"Well, what did you see?" asked the captain.

"I saw...you."

"Look again."

"I can't. It hurts my eyes."

"Look again."

She obeyed and peered into the purse. "I see the flints, but—"

"Yes..."

"They look like they're on fire, and—"

The purse disappeared, as if swallowed by its own fire.

Isabella screamed in pain and then caught herself. Suddenly calm, she looked at the captain who said, "I've blessed the stones."

"But they've gone."

"No, child." He touched her face as he had when they had met in the control cabin, but this time she didn't flinch. "Now," he continued, "do you still wish to ask my why I killed men to save your cousin, only to betray him?"

Isabella maintained eye contact with the captain, but would not speak.

"I did not betray him, Isabella Sabatini, for I owed no fealty to your cousin who would wage war with Heaven itself."

"He would not—"

The captain waited for her to continue, but she did not. "It is a war, and all the destruction we leave behind is only the beginning...a skirmish."

"Do you mean Florence?"

"Which now burns like Sodom."

Isabella crossed herself, and the captain smiled at her again. "But then why save my cousin?" she asked with difficulty.

"Because he set certain things in motion. It was not Ser Mirandola I sought, but another." With that he turned away from Isabella and gazed happily into the radiant night. "And he seeks you even now."

"Who...?"

The captain touched her lips to silence her, then turned to Louisa and said, "The radiance enervates you, *Filia Lucis*. You must go below. Now."

"No, Captain, I'll be fine."

But it was too late.

The captain stepped away from her and disappeared in the radiant mist, which seemed to swallow everything—words, intention, and vigor.

"Isabella," Louisa called.

She felt so very weak.

"Isabella..."

She felt a gentle but overwhelming force guiding her down the hatchway to the deck below and found herself in the arms of the captain's eunuch guard Rudolfo, who smelled of musk and sweat and supported her effortlessly. The other guards bowed their heads in her presence.

"We will return you now to your quarters to rest, holy daughter."

"I don't need to rest," Louisa said, trying to push the eunuch away, "and I cannot leave my companion with—"

151

She stumbled, and Rudolfo caught her. "I'm sure the captain will return her safely to you," he said as he took her in tow.

Louisa felt bereft and cheated; and against all reason and common sense, she yearned to be back in the captain's presence.

"Unless, of course," the eunuch continued in his soft, comforting voice, "it is his will to make her his own…"

PARTITION FOUR

The Sapphire Tablet

'Trismegistus, why does this scripture call Belias a traitor? Is he not the favorite aeon of the demiurge?'

'Yes, Rheginus, he is the demiurge's archangel.'

'Has he then fallen like the aeon of light, Satan?'

'No, Rheginus. Belias is secure in the arms of the demiurge.'

'Then how can Belias be charged a traitor? Do you mean to say that the *Lamentation of the Aeon Athoth* is… incorrect?'

'Not at all, Rheginus. I would not presume to dispute holy scripture. I simply mean to say that Belias will betray Athoth.'

'But, Trismegistus, isn't Athoth a lower aeon like Belias? And isn't Athoth—like Belias—a favorite of the demiurge?'

'Yes, Rheginus, but it matters not. Belias must punish those whose loyalty to the demiurge is inconstant.'

—*Excerpt from the Fourth Discourse 11,19-31*

THIRTEEN
Burning Bridges

And how will you be able to perceive his way of entry,
that is how will he enter your soul? And how will you be
able to perceive in what garment he will enter you?

—*The Teachings of Silvanus 94,29*

And the souls mounting up to God
Went by him like thin flames.

—Dante Tommaso Rossetti

Pietro warned Baldassare and Mirandola that it would be too dangerous to cross the Lungarno Accialo, a cobbled boulevard that led along the river to the Ponte Vecchio where Baldassare's agents were supposed to be waiting with news and horses. The boulevard was strewn with clothes, weapons, broken furniture, smashed ceramic pots and bowls, and torn sacks of flour, beans, and other foodstuffs; suckling pigs lay in puddles of congealed blood…as did the bloodied corpses of men, women, children, and Baldassare's soldier-priests.

"Holy Mother of God," Baldassare whispered, but without pause he collected himself and said, "It appears that the danger—at least the immediate danger—has passed." He stood beside Pietro, Mirandola, and his second-in-command, the battle-hardened aristocrat Jacopo di Pecori, under the arched overhang of a tower stronghold. The empty fortress behind them had once belonged to the powerful Mannelli family, and its cellars had a hidden access to the catacombs. It was from there that they had gained access to the streets; and these were their first moments in the open air, if it could be called that. The air was hot and thick with smoke and fire and putrefaction. The river shimmered and sparkled, reflecting the light from burning buildings and the slivered moon.

It also ran red with blood and black with shadows; and its coursing waters magnified the not so distant screams, explosions, and clanging of metal. With the help of the soulless ones—hapless Florentines lost to Belias' soul-stealing vines—the condottiero army of the new pope's son Valentine was taking the city. Baldassare pressed a scented cloth to his nose, then wiped his face, which was slick with perspiration. "But we must not tarry," Baldassare continued and, ignoring Pietro's warning, motioned his men to cross the avenue and make for the bridge.

"Can you not see them?" Pietro cried.

"See *what*?" Baldassare asked impatiently.

"The columns and the viney things that snap and twist, they fill the air everywhere."

"Pietro, there is nothing here, but corpses and desolation," Mirandola said. But Pietro could see the translucent columns that floated in the smoky ochreous miasmas above; he could see the glistening, transparent vines that slowly twisted around and between the ghostly boles like slithering eels in their thousands. Mirandola nodded to Baldassare, who told him to be quick with his apprentice and then headed toward the bridge.

Pietro watched the priest disappear with the last of his men into the bridge that had become a village over the Arno with overhanging rooms, apartments, *bottegas*, and shops built one atop the other and supported by brightly painted wooden beams constructed over the stone arches.

"You see?" Mirandola said. "They have come to no harm. I do not deny that you may see what we cannot, but—"

"Fra Baldassare was right," Pietro said...*I am not the promised remembrancer.* The stone that had become part of the glassy flesh of Pietro's palm felt cold-dead and heavy. Pietro looked back at the rusticated fortress and tower behind them, but he could not see the lions...nor could he sense their presence. "Let us make our way to the bridge, Maestro, before it, too, catches fire," he continued, stepping over a filth sluice onto the cobbled Lungarno Accialo. His movement was awkward, as he compensated for his club-foot.

As they crossed the boulevard, Mirandola asked, "Have you lost them, Pietro?" He meant the lions.

"I don't know, Maestro, but I fear so...and"—raising his eyes—"I fear what lies before us."

It was stifling on the bridge, or, rather inside the bridge, much warmer than in the shadows of the towers; and they had to step over the bloodied corpses of guards and aproned men and pigs, for this was the butcher's quarters. Even the few old prostitutes who worked the bridge had had their wrinkled throats cut. The smell was overwhelming. Gagging, Pietro and Mirandola rushed down the walkway to find Baldassare and Jacopo di Pecori talking with a young soldier priest, who looked deeply frightened. His right eye was bleeding and crudely bandaged with a torn piece of cloth; and blood was caked on his hands, one of which was curled into a distorted ball. Baldassare's men stood well away from him.

"It is just as I told you," the young priest said. "Our orders were to stay with the horses and wait for you." Even though the heat was unbearable, he gathered his black *lucca* gown tightly around him and pulled his hood over his face.

"I see no horses," said Jacopo, whose voice sounded as if gravel were rattling in his throat.

The priest looked away from Jacopo, lifted his head to take a quick glance around the bridge, and directed himself to Baldassare: "There were only five, Excellency, for you and your party. But we lost them."

"*Lost* them? How?"

"They was tethered tight, right and safe as could be," the priest said. "They shouldn't have been able to, but they broke away." He gestured at a broken tether bar, and, indeed, the iron buckles had been ripped right out of the flooring. "They must have sensed what was going to happen because they broke away just before we were attacked by foreign soldiers, the Pope's soldiers and—"

"Well, continue, and be quick about it," Jacopo said.

"—by our own troops."

"What do you mean?"

"The ones whose souls had been taken by the vines. One of them had been my friend since childhood. I remember him smiling at me...before he tried to kill me. He was with the foreign soldiers, killing with them and doing what he was told."

"And what did *you* do?" Jacopo's war-scarred face was grim.

The priest glanced upward and made the sign of protection over his heart.

"You ran, didn't you?"

"Enough," Baldassare said to his second-in-command, then directed himself to the young priest. "The horses. Did *anyone* try to recover them?"

The priest glanced at the corpses around him and said, "There was no time...not a minute before—"

"Quickly, search for the horses," Jacopo said to his guards.

"My lieutenant Fra Antonio, where is he?" Baldassare asked the priest, who blinked, shrugged, then bowed his head. "Surely *some* of the men in your unit survived. Where are they?"

"They took a pigsman's carrack down river," the priest said in a low, barely audible voice.

"Do you mean to say *one* boat?" Baldassare asked, his voice flat and cold, hiding his anxiety.

"Yes, only the one. I heard someone say the other boats were holed."

"How many men in the command?"

"Including myself, forty-eight, Excellency."

Baldassare kicked at a corpse wearing the red and yellow uniform of the pope and winced when he saw the words CESAR VALENTINUS embroidered in gold thread on the front and back of its bloodied jerkin. "How many of our own men lie here on this bridge?" he asked Jacopo. "Fifteen at the most? It's just not possible. Caraffa and Salviati could not have turned my own guards. I won't believe it...I *can't* believe it."

The priest started to speak. "It was—"

"What?"

"It wasn't only those you see here...those who were killed. The vines... they took most of my company." The priest looked around, gazed slowly upward and then said distractedly, "Maybe the blood leaking from the corpses holds the vines in thrall. Maybe we're safe for the moment, but soon...soon—"

Acknowledging the arrival of Mirandola and Pietro, Baldassare just scowled in frustration and shook his head.

"*Padre*," Pietro said, addressing the young priest, "the vines in the air are visible to you, are they not?"

"Can *you* see them, too?" the priest asked.

"Yes, but I don't understand what I see."

Pietro bowed and stepped past Baldassare and Jacopo.

"I thought I was mad," the priest said, "but perhaps being mad was my salvation." He laughed, a mirthless croak.

"Tell me."

The priest stepped back from Pietro and said, "First tell me what *you* see."

Pietro looked up into the shadow-shifting rafters above. Ghostly vines twisted around each other, closing and releasing, forming capricious, ever-changing patterns in the air. "The vines twist slowly," he said to the priest. "They grasp each other and then separate. They form tapestries in the air, do they not?"

Satisfied, the priest nodded and pulled his hood away from his face. He looked barely eighteen. He was pale skinned, pimply, and already had a high forehead. "I can tell you that they are not so slow when they feed." He started to look upward, then caught himself and lowered his head again. "I think they are waiting."

"Waiting for what, *Padre*?" Pietro asked softly, trying to calm the boy.

The priest shrugged. "I think they're waiting for the ones who have lost their souls to return and attack us…and then *they* will attack us." He gestured toward the vines roiling above.

"Do you mean those who have conspired to betray Florence?" asked Baldassare.

The priest laughed and then humbled himself before the superior cleric. "No, Excellency, I mean those who have lost their souls: soldiers, townspeople, peasants, priests, and grandees alike. Ordinary people. *They* did all…this"— he waved his hand, indicating the carnage all about them—"and I'm sure they will return. The city is lost. We are lost." The boy turned to Pietro, as if for confirmation.

"We have not seen the ones you speak of," Pietro said. "We have been below the city in the catacombs." The priest nodded and seemed to draw himself into his cloak, as if he could disappear in its recesses.

"Do you know who they are…the ones you claim have lost their souls?" Baldassare asked, insistent.

"They are the ones who were touched by the things circling above," the priest said. "Your own men, Excellency. Your own soldiers who will come back to murder us."

"What about those you say escaped in a carrack?"

"I don't know, Excellency. They ran, or hid, or—"

"Like you?" Jacopo asked in his harsh, ragged voice.

The boy was shaking, but he stood his ground. "I don't know…exactly." Again, he turned to Pietro for support. "I fought alongside my brothers, and then something struck me in the back of the head. I don't know, but I must not have been benumbed for long because I heard the clangor all around me, and someone stepped on my hand, and God's blessed witness, I didn't feel anything." He extended his hand so Pietro could see the broken fingers. "I tried pulling the bones right, but now it hurts like buggar-man; and it was when I was lying there looking up that I saw the snaking things twisting and sliding into our priests even as they was fighting. I think the things were taking—"

"What…?" asked Pietro. "I believe you. Tell us."

"I am not one to say, but—"

"Yes…?"

"I saw the viney things feeding on my brothers who were fighting the Pope's soldiers and the rabble whose souls had already been lost…I saw the viney things drawing something out of them, something smoky and wispy and shiny like the snake things themselves. I could only think they was snatching away their immortal souls; but may our God Almighty forgive me, *verum est, et incredibile*. In fact—" The young padre paused again, considering, then said, "What they took looked like glowworms."

"I wouldn't compare imperishable souls to...worms," Baldassare said.

"Lucian told me that when he stole *your* soul, it appeared just as the young padre described," Pietro said.

Furious and humiliated, Baldassare turned to Mirandola. "You allow your apprentice to speak without leave to his superiors?"

"I think perhaps he is no longer my apprentice, Agnolo." Mirandola gave Pietro a significant look. "Although he has become his own man, I'm sure he means no disrespect."

Pietro quickly kneeled before Baldassare and said, "Forgive me, Lord Spiritual, Maestro Mirandola is correct. I shall try harder to contain my thoughts in future." Baldassare gestured Pietro to rise and said, "Do not try, young master...*do!*" Then he turned back to the guard. "Continue, my son." His voice had a gentler tone. "You may speak freely to us."

The boy looked around the bridge nervously and said, "Once the viney things took their...souls away, our men turned on their own kind. They killed their friends, their brothers; and those that were left...they left with the rabble like they'd been with them all along. That's all I know, Excellency, except—"

"Yes?" asked Baldassare.

"When the viney things were attacking my brothers, I had the thought that..." The priest looked upward into the shivering darkness, his eyes vacant.

"*Padre, Padre*, please continue," Pietro said.

"I could not help but believe that the vines were actuated by anger, by hate. Perhaps...perhaps they could even feed on love." He turned his attention from the shadowy rafters and trusses to Pietro and asked, "Can you see the change?"

Pietro looked up and saw that the vines were moving faster, coiling and twisting as if agitated. "Yes, *Padre*, the vines quicken."

And what does that tell you?" asked Baldassare.

"That we must leave now. I have obeyed my orders, I have waited for you and the First Citizen's sorcerer," he said to Baldassare, referring to Mirandola, "and now I—we—must all leave. Quickly!"

The streets echoed with approaching footfalls. Troops on the run. Yet there were no shouts or cries, just an eerie, thundering...silence.

One of Baldassare's lieutenants rushed over to him and Jacopo. "Excellency, we have recovered four of the horses and"—he was interrupted by a shock that could be felt on the bridge: a tower had exploded nearby—"we have also found Fra Antonio."

"Is he alive?"

"I think you must see for yourself. He murdered one of our men—a priest he had known and seemingly cared for—before he could be subdued, but when I left him he was quiet as a lamb, as if..."

"Well, speak!"

"As if he's not inside himself," the lieutenant said, shaking his head. He was a burly middle-aged man with a thin, gray beard that accentuated rather than hid his weak declivity of a chin. "Also, Excellency…"

"Yes?"

"Can you not feel something unwholesome and strange in the air? The men are nervous and eyeing the horses. I fear for discipline."

Baldassare nodded. "We will attend to this immediately." Then he turned to Jacopo and said in a voice so low no one else could hear, "Once we are away, retreat to the hermitage as quickly as you can…and any way you can."

The Dominican looked surprised.

"I will not risk a battle with an enemy I do not yet understand. You may leave a lancer or two to reconnoiter and report, but they must be told the nature of the danger."

"Understood, Excellency.

"*Hijs nostris benefacite.*"

"*Fiat voluntas Dei.*"

With that, Jacopo di Pecori backed away into the darkness and disappeared.

"We leave immediately," Baldassare said to Mirandola. "You…and your apprentice."

"We must take your priest," Pietro said. Turning to the young priest who could also see the vines sliding and snapping with increasing agitation, he asked, "What is your name, *Padre*?"

"Vincenzo, Vincenzo Antellesi from—"

"Fra Vincento *must* accompany us," Pietro said.

"*I* will determine who will accompany us," Baldassare said.

"When your other priests ran away, *he* was the only one brave enough to stand his ground; and I would wager ten gold florins that he was the only one who could see the invisible agents of the aeon Belias. He should be rewarded, not excluded." Pietro could feel the scar in his palm warming, coming assuredly to life; and reflexively he grasped Baldassare's hand.

Baldassare's eyes narrowed in pain, but he didn't try to pull away. "Would you swear to having ever possessed even *one* gold florin, Ser Neroni?" he asked Pietro in a controlled voice. "Now unhand me." He smiled grimly at Pietro, who released his grasp. Baldassare looked at the key-shaped burn blistering on his palm and said, "My compliments, Pico Della Mirandola, it seems you have transformed lead into gold twice."

"Twice?" asked Mirandola.

"Yes, first with your Jew servant Lucian ben-whatever-you-call-him and now with your one-time first apprentice here." Revealing rotting teeth, he looked at Pietro with something that might almost be interpreted as affection.

"I have no intention of leaving Fra Vincenzo behind and—"

With a loud crack and a long, noxious sigh, the bridge caught fire.

Hoping he could reach the horses before they bolted, Baldassare propelled Mirandola and the young priest forward. Reflexively, Mirandola grasped Pietro by the sleeve and pulled him along while Baldassare's captain and lieutenants forced their men across the bridge, lest they be stranded and have to face the armed and silent mob of soldiers and citizens that would soon be upon them…the soldiers and citizens that had lost their souls to creatures just like the ones that snapped and flickered and twisted in the burning rafters of the bridge.

When Baldassare reached the other side of the bridge, he found the horses, each one hooded and reined in by a guard; in fact, the horses were fitted out better than the soldiers, with chamfrons, mail trappings, and neck, withers, crupper, and flank defenses. Two nervous guards stood steady beside the lieutenant-in-charge and held the bound and beaten priest Antonio upright between them. "But Baldassare had no time to examine Antonio. He climbed upon a huge armored roan; and after Mirandola, Pietro, and the Priest Vincenzo were in saddle, he took the reins of the remaining horse and called his lieutenant to "Heave your man over." The lieutenant and his guards bound the compliant Fra Antonio to horse and saddle as best they could; Antonio, his face devoid of expression and his eyes empty as heaven, sat upon the shivering horse and gazed calmly at Baldassare. Baldassare said something to him, but Antonio could not or would not respond; yet he seemed to be just on the cusp of recognition and a smile.

Baldassare nodded to his lieutenant, who ordered his men to unhood the horses; and then with an uncharacteristic shout from Mirandola, who had a wild look in his eye, they were away. Baldassare's troops, who were marching in the same direction, cheered him. Behind them, part of the bridge's superstructure, fueled by rotting frames and timberwork, stores of satin and damask, furniture, paints, and explosive chemicals, crashed into the red and orange waters of the Arno.

"At least Belias' soulless rabble will not easily catch up with my troops," Baldassare said to himself as they rode away from the heat and fire. It appeared that only the city on the other side of the river was under Belias' shadow. On this side, at least, the air was cool and breathable; but there were no lights flickering in the streets or their overarching buildings, only moonlight and shadows and the fiery reflections of the great fire in the sky and on the rippling surface of the river. The only sounds were the crunch, rumble, and distant thunder-sighs of the fire; the soughing of the wind; and the steady, rhythmic clomping of their horses' hooves upon the cobbles of the Via Spirito. "If the soulless ones are to cross the river, they will have to find another bridge…as I will," he thought as they passed the broken arch of an ancient Roman bridge. "But, oh, how I would have loved to engage them and determine for myself who, or what, they are…"

They passed the Ponte Santa Fondazione, a ruined Roman bridge, and both Pietro and the priest Vincenzo warned Baldassare and Mirandola that something was amiss.

"What is it?" Mirandola asked Pietro.

"Above us…the air is thick with vines."

"They sense blood and emotion," Vincenzo said, looking upward. "They are revived…refreshed, they—" and the young priest gagged, his body convulsing so hard that he tumbled from his horse.

Pietro shouted and turned back to retrieve the priest.

Baldassare could not see what Pietro and the boy saw, but now he could sense something sudden and unnatural in the air; and now he could also see men, women, and children appearing from the shadows as quietly as smoke from a chimney. Those who had once been soldiers and his own guards were armed with swords, lancers, spiked maces, and crossbows, while the others carried whatever tools could be converted into weapons: axes, hammers, scythes, slings, and knives. But just as Baldassare was about to shout, "Quickly, away from here," the priest Antonio came to life. With dreadful strength and speed, he snatched the reins of his horse away from Baldassare and twisted their link-chain lengtheners crosswise around Baldassare's neck, effectively garroting him.

Baldassare was wrenched from his saddle…and as he fell into the spinning, tumbling moonlight, he glimpsed Antonio's innocent beatific smile.

Lucian could see something shadowy and malignant beyond the angel Gabriel's swirling curtains of light; but it was so very far away, and the sapphire bridge was so long and narrow that he feared he might collapse of exhaustion before reaching its end. He stepped carefully upon the span, which was as smooth as the surface of the tablet from which it was created. He had long since stopped crying out for Gabriel. He was completely and profoundly alone; and if he slipped or took a misstep, he was sure that he would fall through the eternities of Gabriel's bright heaven until he stopped breathing. Nevertheless, he continued to move forward. Heeding the angel's warning not to look down, he stared straight ahead. The span of the bridge shimmered like a shaft of coherent blue light; and although there was only the shifting, sapphire-tinged light that surrounded him and the dry scents of salt, lime, and sulfur—the smells of the country of his childhood—he could *feel* the fearsome distance and bright vertiginous depth below him. Although he was still in the heart of Gabriel's realm, he also had the odd sensation that everything around him was flat: that the shifting clouds of light were merely motions and disturbances on the surface of the tablet he had removed from the wall of the cavern. His very thoughts seemed to be playing in the light, or rather on the light, like the cloudy phantasms and images he used to discern in his master Mirandola's skrying crystal. Indeed, he had the unsettling thought that crystal, bridge, and tablet were one and the same, and he was caught in the vast insubstantial reaches of the skrying crystal, caught in the thin, yet infinite sapphire tablet: Gabriel's sapphire key.

And who, he wondered, might be watching *him*?

· Like a sleepwalker balancing high on a familiar balcony, he gained a new-found sureness and grace. He had started to become used to the narrow span of the sapphire bridge, the warm, breezeless air, and the monotony of the shifting yet never defining light; but he almost lost his balance and fell when the curtains of light suddenly parted to reveal a clear image of Isabella in the embrace of a soldier priest.

It was like looking into a tower window or, as he would describe it later, like gazing at a painting that was suddenly imbued with life and motion. As Lucian squinted to close out some of the peripheral light, the priest turned his head away from Isabella's cheek and looked directly at him...and as Lucian looked into the soft, dark eyes of the aeon who had had his parents murdered, he felt the heart-stopping impact of the contact—

> *Athoth...*
> *Gentile...*
> *Whirlwind...*
> *Reaper...*

—and as he stepped toward the image, he felt a slight, sudden resistance and found himself in utter darkness, freezing crystalline darkness. He tried to back away from the dark, tried to push his way back into Gabriel's light-swirling heaven; but he had crossed a dangerous threshold and could not return. The darkness and the cold were with him now, whether he retreated or went forward. His eyes stung, his teeth chattered, and his bladder was full to bursting. He relieved himself, then wrapped his robe around him; but nothing could keep out this chill: his doublet, which was meant to give warmth and protection, was constructed of thin cheap fabric and still damp from perspiration that became a coverlet of ice. He felt a murderous rage toward Athoth; and even though he tried not to think about Isabella, the gorge rose in his throat. *Faithless, fickle whoresome—*

He took a step forward and then another, for if he lingered, the cold would put him to sleep, and he would surely fall. His eyes became accustomed to the darkness, his temper settled (although he constantly had to force his thoughts from drifting back to Isabella and to the death of his parents), and he remembered Gabriel telling him that the bridge would become a light in the dark. The bridge did indeed glow, but it was with a dull flat phosphorescence, as if it were weakening, coming undone, succumbing to the icy miasmas that enveloped it. As he hurried forward, pumping warmth into his legs and slapping his chest and thighs with his aching hands, he glanced downward and was amazed: there were constellations twinkling below, thousands upon thousands of pinprick tears in Athoth's dark firmament, for surely this was Athoth's realm, and—like Belias' icy heaven—his pit and domain and the very embodiment of himself.

But the stars were *moving*; they were alive with a shivering energy, more like fireflies than the eternally fixed stars, which were beyond passion and human conception. Lucian imagined that the points of light were far away, but he sensed they were close, sensed that they were caught in this waste just as he was: displaced souls searching for warmth and light, attracted like insects to the dying glow of this bridge that spanned the frozen miasma of Hell.

The fireflies, the entrapped wormlike souls, slowly moved toward the bridge in their thousands, perhaps in their millions, and as they did so—as the slow hours passed, if, indeed, there was such thing as time in this frozen waste—they covered the span with their own flickering, dying light. The same weakened light that burned in the bridge, burned in them. But it was to no avail, for as they absorbed the bridge's wan light and almost imperceptible heat, so were they absorbed into numbingly cold darkness until there was nothing, no embers of souls, no sapphire gleam to define the span of the bridge...nothing but roiling darkness. Lucian heard a distant cracking, yet he continued walking: that would be his only chance. He trembled in terror and realized that he was crying for his mother and Gabriel. He prayed that the bridge would remain whole, that the poor souls that might be underfoot would not take hold of him and carry him back into the void with them, and that he might not step off course and fall forever into darkness.

He intoned the Hymn of the Rock—

> *Thank you, oh Lord,*
>
> *Who has redeemed my soul from the Pit,*
>
> *That I might be raised to everlasting heights,*
>
> *To walk upon the level and limitless firmament.*

—and felt something warm and moist envelop him.

He had passed through a thin membrane akin to the crack in the sky that the Daughter of Light had traversed. In an instant, he passed from pitch dark into familiar night: immoveable stars flickered in their panoply, cool erratic breezes spun past him as did moist swirls of cloud, and beneath his feet and extending through the elevated atmosphere was the narrow span of the sapphire bridge; its light was now strong and steady…and Lucian could see the bridge's terminus: the huge, golden-sailed airship that carried the Daughter of Light, Isabella, and the aeon Athoth. Above the gondola hull with its projecting masts, sails, and webbed rigging—with its own constellations of gun ports and hatches that leaked the soft buttery light of habitation—was an envelope that radiated its own soft iridescence. The envelope glowed with the same light as the bridge, the same light as the souls that had been swallowed in the universe he left behind. But the bridge seemed to end somewhere short of the hull, just above what might be identified as a mizzen topsail, except its mast extended horizontally from the hull rather than vertically from the deck. Lucian noticed that the airship was moving, occluding the stars behind it, and the bridge span moved in perfect harmony with the ship. As he stepped carefully to the end of the bridge's span, he felt that he was being watched. He crouched low, balancing, calculating whether he could catch one of the shrouds or ratlines creaking and singing through the air below him; and as he surveyed the ship, he spied a partially open hatchway and wondered when an unseen lookout would notice him and sound the alarm; but there was nothing for it: he couldn't go back, only forward. But what about the tablet, Gabriel's key…the bridge?

He kneeled and touched the edges of the span to balance himself; as he did so, the bridge simply ceased to be, or, rather, was transmogrified, and Lucian found himself clutching what was now a small sapphire tablet, and falling.

Holding the tablet to his chest with one hand, he grasped at a ratline with the other: he slammed hard into the rigging, catching the shroud and ratline with his feet, securing himself. The rough fabric of ghostly white sail billowed behind him, taut and tight to the wind. After securing the tablet inside his doublet, he crawled toward the gondola. His face and hands were bleeding from the harsh contact with the webbing; and he kept slipping, as this was not his element; but before he could manage to reach the hatchway and pull himself to safety, someone shouted, "Ho, crippled spider, *riconoscimento!*"

A mariner reached out of the hatchway above Lucian, shouted, "Belay there" in a low but carrying voice, and then grasped Lucian's shoulder and pulled him through the hatchway as if he weighed no more than a sack of flour. Still holding Lucian in a viselike grip, the mariner leaned out of the hatchway and called to the master of the watch, "Forget your eyes, this is the Captain's business."

Lucian tried to pull away from the mariner, who instantly let go of him and said, "Forgive me, child, I meant only to preserve you, not constrain you."

The room was dark—a storeroom lined with banded grog barrels on floor-to-ceiling shelves—but the lamplight flickering from the doorway was enough; and Lucian could make out the huge man's features: a wide, soft face, fleshy, friendly-looking, and hairless. His tufted, crimson uniform appeared purplish-black, and a strong scent of musk and sweat permeated the close air; and Lucian noticed something else, something that looked like a body—or perhaps it was just a sack—lying crumpled in a corner.

"I am *not* a child," Lucian said, regaining his composure.

"Of course not, ser, it is merely a form of address."

"And you are...?"

The fleshy-faced mariner bowed and said, "I am Rudolfo, master of the captain's *ennuci*, and I give you the captain's greetings. He has been expecting you."

"And just how would he know to expect me? Lucian asked.

"Why, he saw you, of course," Rudolfo said, "but I'm sure you know that and only wish to test the waters, hey?" As Lucian took a sharp intake of breath, the room suddenly blazed with light: two of Rudolfo's eunuch guards carrying lanterns appeared in the doorway. One of them said, "*Difensore*, we were patrolling up on the orlop deck when we heard you shout the watch, and we came as soon as—" Rudolfo silenced his guard with a subtle hand gesture and said, "It's blessed and not to be spoiled with apology. We've caught the swab that broke into this locker and saved the child from a terrible fall." He nodded to Lucian, smiled kindly, and turned back to his guards: "There is a barrel of kill-grief missing and also a barrel of laudanum ardent, so they must have been handed out to someone on the watch. Whoever you find drunk or sleep-dizzy will follow our purloiner," and with that he stepped diagonally across the room and dragged an unconscious sailor crumpled in the corner to the hatchway. The sailor was an old scruff: mostly bald, but with enough hair to make a gray, waist-long pigtail. His eye was bruised an angry purple and his nose was broken and bleeding. He began to waken as Rudolfo picked him up, swung him through the hatchway, and—careful not to tangle him in any netting—dropped him over the side. After he did so, he said, "*O quanta est hois infirmitas et corruptio*," which was followed by a distant scream as the sailor realized that the prickling sensation of falling through rarefied air was not a dream.

"Now, child, it is my privilege to take you to the captain," Rudolfo said to Lucian, who had not yet recovered from what he had seen: it had happened so fast; and as the other eunuchs did not utter a word or blink an eye, it seemed that such actions were commonplace.

Lucian swallowed hard, stood as stiffly as he could to appear taller, and said, "Not quite yet, eunuch, for there is someone I must see first."

And to his great surprise, he was granted an audience with the one they called the daughter of light.

FOURTEEN
Desires and Destinations

'All human souls are immortal, Ascelpius, but they are not all immortal in the same way. They differ depending upon matter and time.'

'Do you mean then, Trismegistus, that all souls have not the same quality?'

—*Corpus Hermeticum, Asclepius 2*

This thing is the fortitude of all fortitude because it overcomes all subtle things and penetrates every solid thing.

—*Tabula Sapphirus of Hermes Trismegistus 9*

What power was contained in these diviners that they could bring down the very stars? This they could not do, but for the power of the fallen one called לזאזא, Azâzêl, who deceived them, seduced them, and taught them sorceries whereby they made use of them.

—*Hebrew Book of Enoch by Rabbi Ishmael ben Elisha 5,9*

The daughter of light was a prisoner, locked in her stateroom.
The room was spacious, as measured by what she was used to aboard her father's steamer; the cabin was, in fact, part of the captain's three adjoining apartments. He had relinquished the great cabin to his guests and maintained one of the apartments for meetings and entertainments with his guests and officers; the other cabin was securely locked and presumably used for private

storage: however, it was common knowledge that the captain rarely retired to the great cabin and never slept there.

Louisa called petulantly to the eunuch on the other side of the door.

The bolt rattled as it dropped, and one of Rudolfo's men leaned into the room and asked, "Yes, *Filia Lucis*?" His bulk filled the doorway.

"We need a physician for my companion."

The ennuci guard looked across the room at Isabella who was asleep on a feather-stuffed pallaise atop a neatly tied and squared pallet of folded jib-size sails. She wore a white *camisa* chemise that revealed her curves yet covered her flesh, and her long black hair fanned over her silk pillow. She snored quietly and evenly.

"Please do not worry, *Filia Lucis*," the guard said, smiling, "she is in no danger and will awaken soon, I assure you."

"And you are a doctor then?"

The eunuch lowered his gaze and said, "Actually, yes, child, I am a theurgist."

"And you can tell her condition from across the room?"

"Do you not remember your condition when you returned from the boundary?"

"I was not insensible for twelve hours."

"You were not exposed to the boundary for as long as your companion," and with that the eunuch bowed his head, murmured "*Ille est lux noster*," then closed and locked the door behind him.

Louisa sat down on a cushioned bench opposite her friend. She folded her hands as if she were sitting beside her father in church, but her hands were trembling. She felt utterly lost and alone, and a sudden emotional realization of how far away she was from everything she knew and loved overwhelmed her. The stigmata that the archbishop had burned into her palm felt cold and numb; and the revelatory memories that the aeon Belias had poured into her after her balloon had passed through the crack in the world and landed in his cold, dark heaven were clouded by the unwavering influence of the boundary above: the melancholy radiation emanating from the poor captured souls that lifted the ship. Louisa sobbed quietly and cried for her father rather than her mother—when she thought of her mother, her blessed mother, she could only remember the terrible violence of the Yankee deserters that murdered her. Even now, she could see their faces and hear them laughing as they hurt and befouled her.

Isabella awakened.

"Louisa, Louisa, what is the matter?"

"I am forgetting who I am," Louisa said, speaking to herself, lost in her own emptiness; and then, coming to her senses, she rushed over to Isabella, sat down beside her, and stroked her face. "I was so worried about you. You have been asleep for hours and hours."

"Have I? I seem to remember Gentile—"

"You would call the aeon Gentile?" Louisa asked.

"Do you not remember that he asked me how I wished to address him? I felt Gentile was more appropriate than Captain."

"Were you intimate with him?"

"No more than you, but why would you accuse me? You are clearly the chosen one?"

"I'm sorry, Isabella, I—"

Isabella shook her head, propped herself up on her pillows, and grasped Louisa's hand. "No, please don't apologize. I felt jealous when Gentile caught you as you stumbled under the boundary...I reached out for you, or for him, I don't know, and felt something pushing against me, keeping me from you. Perhaps it was only natural that you might feel something like that."

"Jealousy...?" Louisa asked, wondering; but before Isabella could reply, she said, "Yes, it was something like that. But why? We don't even know him."

"He is an aeon, an angel, or—"

"Yes, Isabella?"

"Or a demon. Either way we are in his thrall, are we not?"

"We do not have to be in anyone's thrall," Louisa said, her eyes narrowing. "We must be sure of him."

"Yes," Isabella said, lowering her eyes. "But how?"

"I don't know yet, but we must. Everything depends on it." After a pause. She said, "I'm so relieved you're all right. I feared that you would not awaken."

"Like the little girl in the fairy tale?" Isabella asked, smiling playfully; but then her expression suddenly darkened, and she let go of Louisa's hand.

"What is it, Isabella?"

"Nothing. Just a dark thought."

"Tell me," she asked as she gently clasped Isabella's hand. "We can share each other's dark thoughts."

"It is just that I cannot rest thinking that Pietro and my cousin Pico could be heretics and damned. It could not be true. I won't believe it's true!"

"Who is Pietro?" Louisa asked.

Isabella explained that he was her cousin's apprentice, a theurgist who would one day wield great mastery over his art.

"You smile when you speak of him. Is he your lover?"

Isabella blushed, as if it were true, but said, "Are you going to ask if everyone we meet is my lover? No, Pietro is just a friend."

Louisa smiled back at her. "But I think you wish him to be more than that."

"Well, you have certainly regained yourself," Isabella said. Louisa gave her a questioning look; Isabella apologized and squeezed her hand. "You said you were forgetting who you are, and I can see that you've been crying, and that—"

"No, Isabella, I have not regained myself. I am…lost."

"But you behave as—"

"As what?"

"As the chosen one. *Filia Lucis*."

"And you know how she would behave?"

Isabella smiled, and so did Louisa. "Perhaps we are both lost, led only by circumstance."

"No," Louisa said. "We must not allow that."

"There, you see? *Omnis hora, est hora nobis*."

Louisa looked at her, questioning. She felt a familiar tingling in her palm as her glassy serpentine scar came alive with heat and strength and then suddenly understood— *"Every hour is our hour"*—suddenly remembered, just as the archbishop told her she would. "You taunt me."

"Perhaps a little, perhaps because I believe that *you* are circumstance."

"How could you believe such a thing?"

"Because you are the daughter of light, because the tree of knowledge reached into the cathedral and transported you from Heaven."

"I *fell* from the tree," Louisa said, shivering, remembering again.

Isabella ignored Louisa's interruption and continued her argument, but Louisa interrupted her again. "Isabella, tell me…why were you so long with the captain?"

Isabella seemed taken aback, confused. Reluctantly she said, "I can't remember. I can't remember how long I was with him, nor what he said, except…"

"Yes…? Please try."

"Something about the blessed stones. The flints." She shivered. "Perhaps he did touch me, but it was about the flints that the archbishop gave to me." She looked past Louisa and out the inclined ceiling windows: the stars were sharp, unblinking.

"What about the flints?"

"He said they will show you the way."

"Me?"

"Yes, my dear one, he also said I would show you the way. He said—"

"Isabella?"

"It's difficult to remember; it's as if the memory slides away." She paused and said, "He said I would carry all but one of the flints to the holy church in Venice." She shook her head, not understanding what the aeon had meant by "all but one," and then glanced up at the windows again, as if she could find knowledge and solace in the steady stars and eternal heavens, and shivered. "He said the flints were *inside* me, part of me." She looked at Louisa and said, "Just as Pietro has become my cousin Pico's gazing crystal, his remembrancer." As Louisa embraced and comforted her friend—and was about to ask her what she meant about Pietro becoming a skrying crystal—there was a soft tap on the door.

"Yes?" asked Louisa, not moving from beside Isabella, who was still shivering, as if with fever. The door opened, and Louisa almost gagged on the pungent odor of musk: the eunuch Rudolfo must have recently applied it, more likely drenched himself. Better a bath than perfume, she thought as Rudolfo bowed to her, then stepped aside and gently propelled a gangly, swarthy-skinned boy into the room. The boy was tall and awkward, and the eunuch ordered him to bow, lest he crack his head on the ornamented lintel; but both Rudolfo and Louisa were caught by surprise when Isabella shouted "Lucian" and stood up to embrace him.

"How is my cousin?" she asked, sizing him up and seeing that he looked older and somehow stronger. "And Pietro, is he safe?"

"When I left them, both were fine."

Isabella looked relieved; Lucian turned to Louisa and bowed.

"Forgive me, Louisa, this is Lucian, servant to my cousin Pico Della Mirandola."

"Apprentice," Lucian said.

Isabella smiled and said, "Yes, of course, I remember. I misspoke." Lucian blushed and looked away from Louisa who found his shy awkwardness attractive, although he was hardly handsome. She turned away from the dusky skinned boy and asked Rudolfo to remove himself, which he did reluctantly, although she was sure he would send his guards off in a clatter and remain quiet as a soul behind the door. She shrugged, remembering that there could be no real privacy on a ship, anyway.

"How did you come to be here?" she asked Lucian.

"Was it the angel Gabriel?" Isabella asked, interrupting. "Did he take you, as he had done before?"

"Yes, but not quite as before, Isabella Sabatini," Lucian said. "This time I am here entire and cannot return to Pietro or my master like a soul passing through the aethers." With that, he stumbled, although the ship had not heaved; Isabella and Louisa caught him and helped him to the pallet where Isabella had slept. Without thinking, Louisa touched the dead-white scar that circled his neck. Isabella looked at her, surprised, and then settled beside Lucian. Louisa, however, stood away from the pallet, even though she felt drawn to this boy who seemed simultaneously anxious and in control. "I was surprised that I have been allowed to see you," Lucian said to Louisa, and then, as if speaking only to himself, "although perhaps I should not be…" He pressed his hand against his chest and continued: "So pray allow me to tell you why I am here while I may. I come on behalf of the angel Gabriel." He turned to Isabella, who took his hand; again he blushed. "The angel has sent me with a gift for the aeon, the one known as Athoth." Lucian's expression hardened when he said the name.

"If it is meant for the aeon, why would you give it to me?"

"The angel told me to put it in your hands."

"Why?"

"He did not tell me."

"What did he tell you, Lucian?" Isabella asked.

"That you are both in trouble, and…I am to do what I can to protect you."

Isabella laughed, then caught herself.

Lucian blushed with humiliation and tried to stand, but Isabella would not release him. "Please—"

He squeezed her hand, withdrew his own reluctantly, and admitted, "Yes, I thought the same when he told me." Then he removed the sapphire tablet he had secured in his doublet. Although he was still weak and unsteady on his feet, he rose from the pallet, bowed to Louisa, and handed the tablet to her.

"It's…beautiful," she said, turning it this way and that, mesmerized by the depths and reflections in the perfect gem. "Yet how can it be so heavy?"

"Forgive me, daughter of light," Lucian said, and he stepped unsteadily back to the pallet. Isabella fussed over him, but he would not put his head on the pillows. He looked exhausted now. "If you keep it close to your person, it will weaken you. While it was my passage, my bridge to you, I did not feel its effects; but as soon as it resumed its natural form and I had to carry it, I—"

Louisa touched the surface of the tablet: her hand disappeared, and then she leaned—or fell—into the sapphire sheet, even though it was only as large as one of the small window-panes that curved around the cabin behind her. Isabella called out to her: it seemed that rather than falling into the tablet, the daughter of light had somehow stretched it around her like a cloak. For an instant the tablet hung in the air, slowly twisting, and then it was back in Louisa's hand, as if she had never left the room.

"What did you do?" Isabella asked. "Where did you go? What did you see?"

Louisa smiled at her friend, then stumbled, as Lucian had; Lucian caught her and brought her back to the pallet where Isabella fussed over her. "You are right," she said to Lucian, whom she thought smelled faintly—and delightfully—of cinnamon, "it weakens the flesh like the boundary above."

"Boundary?" Lucian asked.

"The fabric that lifts the ship has the same effect as the tablet," Isabella said.

She touched the tablet on Louisa's lap, but its surface was hard as diamond: "Let me move the tablet away from you. Even I can feel its effects."

"No," Louisa said sharply, looking into it as if it was a mirror. "I saw the angel."

"Was he robed in purple?" Lucian asked, leaning toward her.

Louisa nodded.

"And was there a white circlet around his head...and the smell of cinnamon?"

Louisa smiled at Lucian and said, "Yes, but the smell of cinnamon—"

"It was Gabriel," Lucian said. "Did he speak to you? What did he say?" Lucian was about to reach for the tablet when the lock turned and the door opened suddenly, as if on cue; but it wasn't Rudolfo who entered: it was the captain. He wore a simple yet sumptuous monk's gown with hanging sleeves: *azzuri* silk, the same color as the tablet. He bowed to Louisa and Isabella, whom he acknowledged as *filiolae lucis*—little daughters of light—and then to Lucian. "Welcome, ser, to the church of true light."

Lucian felt the scar around his neck burn and wanted to lunge for the aeon...wanted to strangle him for what he had done to his parents, for—

Lucian fought for control, then nodded to the aeon...slightly, stiffly. But he looked away as he did so.

"I quite understand your hesitation, Lucian ben-Hananiah." The aeon seemed to radiate empathy and understanding. Then he turned to Louisa and asked: "Do you believe you saw a dark angel in the tablet, *Filia Lucis*?"

"She saw the angel Gabriel," Lucian said, "and he is *not* a dark angel."

"Ah, bravery and timidity combined: an endearing trait..."

The aeon smiled at Lucian, all benevolence and good will, as if he were lecturing a favorite yet slightly wayward child.

"But may I suggest that if you fail to respect those who are disposed to you, you might find yourself to be...disposable."

Lucian nodded, disgusted with himself for acknowledging this deceiver and the poisonous vapours that were his words; but he remembered Gabriel's advice and took the wise course: to listen, learn, and keep his own counsel.

"Indeed, I would wager that you saw an angel when you wrapped the tablet around you," the aeon said to Louisa.

"And you could see that without being in the room?" she asked.

"That...and other things," said the aeon, appearing impatient. "Tell me now, *Filia Lucis*: did you see an angel inside the tablet?"

Louisa gazed down at the sapphire tablet on her lap and nodded. She looked drawn and tired, as if her strength and humours were bleeding away into the roiling surface of the tablet.

"Can you see him now?" asked the aeon.

Louisa nodded again. She could see a figure forming and reforming deep in the tablet; the angel, if that's what it was, did indeed wear a circlet around his head and was wrapped in purple robes. His wings suddenly appeared crystal clear, feathers shivering and occasionally falling into the mercurial light in which he floated; and then she could see his face, his beautiful, constantly shifting face. Every shifting plane was beautifully etched and perfect as mathematics itself...and she remembered Belias. The angel in the tablet was his bright twin, yet there were subtle differences: this angel, though shining and warm featured, seemed to be somehow weak, almost puerile, while silver-dark Belias and his millions of viney appendages had contained the potency of all the heavens and hell combined.

"And do you believe him to be Gabriel?"

"How would I know?" Louisa asked, careful not to give too much away. "I've never seen him."

"You've seen God's aeons and angels," the aeon said as the air in the cabin pulsed with anger; and then he reached into the tablet on her lap and, as if from a pool of quicksilver, pulled out something quick and bright.

Lucian gasped, for it was as if the aeon had plucked a soul from the tablet; Lucian felt a sudden, aching emptiness, a yearning for the soul-stealing snake that had lived in his blood and pneuma: the sacred seal that Gabriel had bequeathed to him only to reclaim it by tearing it out of him like a still-beating heart.

There was a sharp, cloying smell of cinnamon.

An angel took form, appearing beside the aeon in a nimbus of the same intensity as the light from the flickering lamps on the walls...golden light resolving, materializing.

"Gabriel, it *is* you," Lucian cried, as he reflexively stood up and reached toward the angel; but the angel drew back.

"And what would you do if you could grasp me?" the angel said. "Inhale me? Swallow me as if I were a soul?"

"No...you cannot be Gabriel," Lucian said, crestfallen, suddenly doubting his own memories and experience of the angel. He backed away until his legs touched the edge of the pallet where Isabella and Louisa were sitting: Louisa reflexively took his hand to steady him and then quickly released it; Isabella, entranced at its presence, blinked at the angel and held her hands to her chin in prayer.

"You still bear your scar," the angel said to Lucian, "but not the seal I gave you: the seal that gave you the power to inhale the knowledge of souls."

"You are a poor imitation of Gabriel, and your knowledge is imperfect."

The angel smiled, and as he did so Lucian could feel its warmth and smell cinnamon. The angel's folded wings, too large to be unfurled in the cabin, fluttered, and as they did so, they shimmered like rainbows reflected in oil. Lucian felt the stabbings of his old connection with Gabriel.

"I can still see into you, young Lucian ben-Hananiah," the angel said, his voice gentle, familiar, and comforting, "just as I saw into you when we stood on the ridge above *Yam HaMelah* where I instructed you how to find and use the key."

It was Gabriel, Lucian thought, but...

"Gabriel—the true Gabriel—would not betray me."

"I have not betrayed you, Lucian ben-Hananiah. I have only led you here bearing the gift ordained for Athoth...as was your proper destiny." The angel bowed to the aeon who nodded in acknowledgement, even as he kept his gaze firmly upon Lucian.

Lucian did not—would not—flinch from the aeon, but said to him directly, "This apparition is not Gabriel."

Both the aeon and the angel smiled. "But you cannot be sure, can you, young theurgist?" the aeon asked. "Everything that has passed is now uncertain, is it not?"

"No," Lucian insisted; then turning to the angel: "You are not Gabriel."

"*Sum quod sum*," said the angel. "*Unus in uno*."

I am who I am. One within one.

"You are *not* Gabriel," Lucian insisted.

"Tell him," said the aeon.

"*Nomen meum est...*"

My name is...

"Tell him!"

"לזאזא" said the angel, his voice the buzzing of bees.

Azâzêl.

A look of shame and disgust flickered across his face as Lucian raised his hands to the winged apparition of Gabriel and dispatched him with a learned placement of mind and the cantrip: "*Decedite in nominee eius, qui vos huc misit.*"

Depart in the name of that which has sent you here.

There was a cracking sound like wood splitting, followed by the hot smell of iron; and then the demon Azâzêl was gone. No longer was there a lingering hint of cinnamon in the air.

The aeon bowed to Lucian and said, "Well done, young theurgist. My compliments."

"I suppose I should not be surprised that you would barter with demons such as Azâzêl," Lucian said, challenging the aeon.

Again, the air vibrated with anger; and the aeon said, "I would choose my words—and thoughts—most carefully, Lucian ben-Hananiah. And make no mistake: your master Mirandola and his skryer priest have unknowingly bartered—as you put it—with the fire demon Azâzêl. Can you be so sure that they have not been led astray? That *you* have not been led astray?" And with that the aeon-the captain-Athoth-Gentile turned away from Lucian and bowed to the daughter of light.

As he extended his hand to her, she felt his warmth and sincerity: it seemed only natural to hand the tablet to him.

Lucian said, "No! Wait!"

The aeon left the room; and Louisa looked up at Lucian. "What...what did you say?"

"I was trying to stop you from giving him the tablet."

"But why? You told us that you brought it for him."

"I am not so sure now...perhaps he—and Azâzêl who serves him—deceived me...deceived us."

Isabella drew breath sharply, a sob catching in her throat.

"What is the matter, Isabella?" asked Louisa.

Isabella shook her head, as if angry, and brushed her tears away with the back of her hand.

"What troubles you?"

"You don't believe what Lucian says, do you?" Isabella asked Louisa. "You don't believe that Gentile...you don't believe the aeon is a deceiver like the demon he pulled out of the tablet, do you?"

"No," Louisa said softly, "I don't believe the aeon is a deceiver."

"Well, if you're right—and I believe you are—then my cousin Pico is damned." She turned to Lucian and said, "As you are. All this time you and your master and...Pietro"—she choked when she said his name—"have been led astray by demons."

"That's not true," Lucian, said, agitated. "I would know if that apparition was Gabriel. I carried Gabriel when we escaped from Belias. I would know."

"Carried?" Louisa asked.

"Gabriel—or Azâzêl—gave him the power to steal souls," Isabella said to Louisa.

"It *was* Gabriel."

"Is that how you helped him escape?" Isabella asked Lucian. "By using the power he gave to you?"

"Something like that."

Lucian paced back and forth across the room. He needed to work out his feelings. He needed to think, consider. He would not make eye contact with Isabella and addressed Louisa. "Your captain—Athoth—is the first authority of the one you believe to be your god. Athoth rules his own Hell, as does Belias, his ally and your god's twelfth aeon."

"*Our* god?" Isabella said

"They are both servants of Yaldabaoth, the demiurge who created the world."

"*God* created the world," Isabella said, feeling disgust...and sudden, blazing hatred for Lucian.

"My parents worshipped the same god," Lucian said quietly. "They too thought he was the True One, the Invisible Spirit"—now he was speaking to Isabella—"and Athoth murdered them to get the tablet your friend just handed him. His gift to me was a hanging rope," and he touched the scar that circled his neck. His hand trembled: anger and memory.

"Then why would your angel send you *here* with the tablet?" Louisa asked.

Lucian turned away from Isabella and Louisa—*Yes, Daughter of Light, why would Gabriel, the true Gabriel, hand a key as precious as the sapphire tablet to an aeon such as Athoth?*—and there was a sharp knock on the door.

The eunuch Rudolfo entered the room, bowed to Lucian, and said, "Ser, the captain wishes to receive you."

"Receive *me*?"

The guard bowed to Louisa and Isabella, then clasped Lucian firmly by the arm and led, or rather pulled him out of the cabin: the eunuch's appearance belied his prodigious strength. Louisa rushed to the door, but was not quick enough; and as the bolt dropped, she could faintly hear Rudolfo say, "Please do not struggle, young ser, and be not afraid. The captain only wishes to present you with a gift."

FIFTEEN

The Broken Tablet

3.27 Prophesy and choice [theft?]…

The tablet of sapphire will be sundered

The Sacred Seal of Gabriel reclaimed.

—The Suppressed Gospel of the Exarch Teth 3.7

It is written in the *Hexapla* that Origen, father of our Christian Church, once cried out in hopeless desperation: "The vines, the vines, what can stop them?"

An answer to Origen's plea might be found in the *Third Book of the Damned*: "If the sapphire tablet of the two-winged Gabriel be cast down from the heavens, the air and the very earth would be divided as if by a wall higher than the stones of Babel."

And in our own time the great theurgist Pico Della Mirandola of Florence witnesseth that those who can find the eye-blinding crack in the sapphire wall might escape the shadow of Belias and pass into the light.

—Agrippa of Nettesheim, Of Occult Philosophy, Or Of Magic, Book 4, Chapter LXXII

Baldassare's great sorrel roan dragged him across a colonnaded piazza, away from the Via Spirito, which ran beside the river that reflected moonlit clouds, smoke, and fire.

The soldier-priest felt no pain, just numbness and a sense of time moving so very slowly as his legs banged against the cobbles and his arms, head, and chest struck the horse's sharp-mesh flank mail. He held onto the link-chain rein lengtheners that the priest Antonio—soulless and seemingly animated by the aetheric vines quickening in the vibrating night air above—had twisted around his neck. He tried to pull the chains apart, but they were knotted together like a kinked necklace. He tried with all his strength to take a breath, to expand the chains just enough to ease the gagging emptiness convulsing him; but even that was too much. He realized it was too late and wondered what passages death would open for him. Resigned, as if suddenly immersed in a great calm, his thoughts became prayers, prayers without breath, prayers of light and the promise of revelation—*Finis tenebrarum Halleluyah Omnia gaudent fine Mysterium nobis reuelandum.*

But what he thought of as death was not the end of darkness: it was an *explosion* of darkness.

As if darkness was thick and tangible.

As if it could blaze and burn like light itself.

Much later—or perhaps it was but a moment later—he heard a voice cry in the darkness. He shivered and without thought brushed at his face—his thin black beard was crusted with ice—and suddenly the world came back to him, resolved. No longer was he in motion, no longer gasping for breath. He was lying on ice-slippery cobbles; the air was impossibly wintry; his hands and neck were raw and bloody; and he was looking up into the face of the priest Antonio. He cringed, shaking his head as if he could throw off this nightmare and whispered, "*Benedictus Dominus, am I dead and in hell...?*"

"No, no, Lord Spiritual," Antonio said to Baldassare, his voice hoarse and his breath steaming in the air, but his expression was intent and intelligent. "You are not dead, and I am no longer...soulless. Forgive me, Excellency, but it was not *me* who twisted the chains around your neck, although...although I remember it as clearly...as clearly as if—"

"It *was* you," Baldassare said, still mazed.

"Yes, Excellency, as you will," Antonio said, "but I was not under the control of my soul, but that of another. Whom—or what—I do not know. But, somehow, that part of me is returned, and I am now whole and entire."

Baldassare blinked his eyes, comprehending, and murmured, "Yes, my friend, I too was once lost—" He grimaced, reliving his connection with Lucian, as if the recollection was as painful as the bruises now swelling and blooming purple and black on his face, arms, torso, and legs; and then he forced himself upright, looked around the piazza, and saw the glistening veins and arteries of ice melting and runnelling between the cobbles. "What in God's name has happened?" he whispered.

"I don't know," Antonio said. "I can remember...being as I was, and then there was an explosion—yet it was without light; how could that be?—and then here. With you." Then, as if admonishing himself, he continued, "But I *must* remember. I *must* know." His voice sounded harsh, angry. He picked up a shard of ice, thin as Venetian crystal, which melted in his hand. Shaking his head in wonder he said, "This cannot be...and there, Excellency, across the river..."

Baldassare gazed southward, following Antonio's hand.

There were only scrims of shifting darkness, veils, and deep, tomblike silence, as if everything on the other side of the Arno had simply disappeared... and where were the others—Mirandola, his apprentice Pietro, and the pimple-faced priest Vincenzo?

Baldassare turned away from the Arno and looked across the piazza: although he could see alleys, arcades, fortified towers, and Roman ruins beyond the shadowed piazza, the distances, elevations, curvatures, and angles—the entire measure of perspective—were somehow displaced and flattened. This part of the city was drowning in Belias' dark, cursed glamour; it was segregated, walled off from familiar reality. But Baldassare could see *something* ahead: a wavering shadow that resolved into a razor-straight line, a crack in the night that grew brighter and brighter as he watched, until he had to avert his eyes.

"What is it? Antonio asked, pressing his hands to his face. "I swear I could see something coming out of it, something..."

Baldassare looked again. The crack darkened and widened; and, indeed, before it dimmed into chiaroscuro, he perceived that something dark and poisonous was pouring through the crack in the darkness, a miasma that twisted and boiled as if caught in a storm. It reached upward like some bloated creature from the depths of the sea and expanded into the cold air. In that instant he understood that the miasma was not a unitary materialization: it was a violent expulsion, an explosion of thousands of the viney things that Pietro and the young priest Vincenzo had seen so clearly earlier. And Baldassare saw something else in the darkening, widening crack, something on the other side: figures moving.

"We have to leave this place...now," he said to Antonio.

"And go where?"

"There, toward the crack. Perhaps we can pass through it...perhaps it is like a door. Or a bridge."

"I can't see it anymore, Lord Spiritual...can you?"

But Baldassare could still see it...like an afterimage that would remain even if he closed his eyes. He could also now see the snapping tendrils gathering, accumulating above; and it seemed like the unnatural, wintry air itself was pressing down on him.

"That crack...could it have been lightning?" Antonio asked.

Baldassare looked around for his horse, but it was long gone, as was Antonio's. He shrugged, replied distractedly to Antonio—"*Figlio mio*, you are seeing only with your eyes. Have I not trained you to see with more than your eyes?"—and started to walk toward where the crack had been. He stumbled on an icy cobble, and Antonio supported him—strong, earthy, trusted and trusting Antonio, single-mindedly simple, yet subtle as a courtier.

"Thank you, I can support myself," Baldassare said, but he did not pull away from Antonio's firm grip; he felt an old, familiar yet distant affection return for this soldier who had traveled and fought beside him for the last twenty years—long and bloody years.

"You are shivering, Lord Spiritual."

"Of course I am!" Baldassare said. "It is cold."

"But how can that be?" Antonio asked; and then he said, "Excellency, there it is again." He gestured toward a fluorescence ahead, a perfectly straight slash in the shadow-shifting darkness. "I can see it now."

"Shield your eyes," Baldassare said as the crack in the darkness brightened, then exploded.

A bursting of sapphire blue behind eyelids.

"Can you not see them?" Antonio shouted in utter panic.

Baldassare nodded: he too could see the unnaturalness ahead, the twisting vines shooting like a cloud of arrows through the crack in the aether.

"The vines!" Antonio cried. "I remember now...how they pierced me... violated me. They belong to the aeon. Belias. And this place...this place belongs to him, too. I can sense his presence, his—"

"We must hurry," Baldassare said, staring straight ahead, thinking, concentrating as he recalled a dream of Lucian wreathed in whiteness: the image of a sapphire tablet and a narrow bridge spanning the dark heavens formed in his mind. "I don't know how long we have before the...bridge closes."

He grasped Antonio's arm, urging him forward.

"The bridge?"

"The crack in the aether before us," which darkened until it was a darkness against darkness, a darkness that widened to reveal shadowy figures moving on the other side.

But Antonio pulled away from Baldassare.

"No, Excellency, I cannot accompany you there. You would walk into the very place where the vines spawn?"

"*Here* is where the danger lies," Baldassare said, gesturing upward toward the swirling vines. "Can you not see that?"

"We can take shelter."

The crack began to flare once again and Baldassare said, "I'm leaving now. *Andiamo!*" He hurried forward, his left leg thrumming with pain, and stumbled once again on the slippery cobbles. After a few seconds Antonio caught up with him. Shouldering some of Baldassare's weight, he said, "I fear that what we will find, Lord Spiritual, will be worse than death."

"But not worse than disobedience, good soldier?" Baldassare asked wryly, still staring determinedly ahead as if he were going into battle. The crack appeared to be just on the other side of the piazza. As they approached it, alleys, towers, arcades, and the canopied roofs of shops and houses became more and more distorted. "There, its light increases. Our chance will be when it is at its brightest…when it explodes. Then and only then, I think, will we be able to pass through."

"How can you know?" Antonio asked.

"It is but a guess."

Antonio laughed derisively, then caught himself. "Apologies, Excellency. I mean no disrespect, but why would you think—"

"Light expels darkness. Just as it expelled Belias' viney creatures, so perhaps it might—"

"*Perhaps…?*"

"Now!" Baldassare shouted as the crack flashed into exploding cyan-white light.

They rushed across the glistening, ice crusted piazza, and Antonio whispered a prayer and followed Baldassare into the blindingly bright curtain of light. He had entrusted his life to his captain before: this was no different. The crack, the bridge was a point, or a series of points that confounded distance…or any sense of distance. Antonio felt a rending, as if his very flesh was being peeled and torn; and as he screamed in pain, he remembered being harrowed by Belias' vines…remembered how they had wrapped themselves around him in the cold snaking darkness and ripped out his soul as if it was a fleshy organ.

Baldassare experienced a viscous pressure that was deathly cold, and then he blinked and found himself looking at his own sapphire tinged reflection in what had once been Mirandola's gazing globe. The globe was a huge, infinitely curved mirror that shattered as he and his priest Antonio passed through its ice-rimed surface…

Passed back into the warm, burning Florentine night.

As the eunuch guard Rudolfo propelled him down the covered quarter deck of the airship *Ascensione*, Lucian recalled a dream of the priest Baldassare being dragged along the cobbles of a piazza by a large armored horse. But there was more: he recalled Baldassare and another priest running along ice-rimed cobbles toward a crack of blinding light in Gabriel's sapphire tablet.

Gabriel's sapphire tablet...

"I beg your pardon? Rudolfo asked.

"I didn't say anything."

"Ah, but I think you did, companion to the light. Shall I repeat it to you?" Lucian did not respond, and the eunuch smiled at him. "You must learn not to think so loudly."

Blushing—and feeling suddenly violated and vulnerable—Lucian said, "I'm sure I don't know what you mean."

"You must imagine yourself inside a castle or, better, a cathedral larger than any that exists in your city; and only there, deep within its thick walls and silent darkness, will you be protected. You must build it in your mind, stone by stone, until you find its inner sanctum."

Rudolfo led Lucian toward a bright coruscation of light at the end of a long, wide corridor. They walked past a series of staterooms and high cladded doors marked with the Pope's insignia of twisted vines encircling a cross and the single word *PROIBITO* stamped in red. Blue-tinged light pierced through ceiling grates, hatches, and mirrored portholes cut at angles high in the walls. Dust sparkled then disappeared into ever fading blue shadows...blue, the blue of souls, the blue of Gabriel's tablet.

"Why would you tell me this?" asked Lucian.

"Because I have been charged to protect you."

"Me...?"

"And also the daughters of light whom you are also charged to protect."

The eunuch stopped before a steep companionway bathed in iridescent light. The hatch was open at the top of the narrow staircase.

"The captain awaits you."

Lucian looked up into the bleaching, eye-aching light above.

"Has the daughter of light told you about the boundary?" Rudolfo asked, his eyes averted from the watery light.

"Yes, she told me of the boundary...of the accursed souls that lift this accursed ship."

"You might begin building your cathedral now, young companion," the eunuch said, then lifted Lucian onto the steep, narrow staircase.

"I am not a child, leave me."

"That I will, but before I do so, child, one last suggestion: do not think you can shade your words to dissemble. The captain sees your thoughts as clearly as you saw him when you walked upon the sapphire bridge. Do you remember? As he embraced the girl called Isabella, he turned to meet your gaze…just as he does now."

Lucian heard soft laughter from above; he tried to look up as he climbed, but the light was too bright. As soon as he reached the landing, he felt the crushing pressure of the lost souls trapped above him. He was suddenly weak, dizzy, and disoriented; and if the aeon had not grasped his arm at just that moment, Lucian would have fallen backwards down the staircase. Nevertheless, he resisted the aeon.

"Welcome, young theurgist," the aeon said, holding him even tighter. As he spoke the dazzling light became bearable; and Lucian could make out his kindly features: soft yet piercing eyes, a prominent aquiline nose, and a full, generous mouth, all of which gave him a regal, almost handsome appearance despite his slight double chin and fleshy girth. He wore a velvet cap, damask doublet, and a gold-fringed tunic.

"You do not appear as I remember," Lucian said, still trying to pull away from the aeon. He tasted angry bile, the black bile of hatred. The aeon released him; but this place—the lost souls above, the noxious, enervating aethers that swirled around him like motes of dust caught in unblinking light—seemed to be sucking away all his strength, his very life-force. He stumbled backward again. The aeon smiled and caught him: this time Lucian did not—could not—resist.

"Shall I raise the temperature?" asked the aeon.

"I'm sure I do not understand," Lucian said weakly. He wanted to put out the aeon's eyes, pull the flesh from his soft face (if flesh it was), but the enervating aethers radiating from the lost souls trapped in the airship's envelope swallowed Lucian's anger, grief, and hatred.

"The poor, denuded souls above are as cold as darkness itself," the aeon said, "and you—sweet, angry child of light—you are too warm. You radiate the very heat of life itself, and they can do naught but try to take nourishment for themselves."

"Is that why you summoned me?" Lucian asked. "To murder me here because you neglected to do so when you executed my parents?" As the aeon caressed his face, Lucian felt a permeating warmth…and strength.

Revolted by his own feelings, he pulled away from the aeon's touch.

"Would you prefer to lean against the balustrade rail for support?"

Lucian nodded.

The temperature was indeed rising, and as it did so, the light dimmed… clarified. Now he could see the vast expanses of decking, which looked as dry and brittle as autumn leaves. Iron rails seemed to define the long, narrowing perspective lines, and they, like the scattered stores of armor and cannon, were all pitted and coated with rust.

"If I had meant to murder you, child of light, I would simply have—" The aeon made a sweeping gesture toward Lucian, who felt a pleasurable tingling around his neck.

"The scar...it's gone," Lucian said as he pressed his fingers along the smooth flesh that had an instant before been a necklace of scar tissue. "What did you do?"

"It's not what I did; it's what I've...what has been undone."

"You can't undo what you did to my parents! You can't—"

"Ah, but *that* is my gift to you, child," the aeon said. "Your parents live."

"You are a liar," Lucian said; immediately after he spoke, the temperature dropped, and once again he felt weak and nauseated. He clung to the balustrade rail for support.

Weaker, weaker...and cold, so very cold.

"You should have taken my eunuch's advice," said the aeon, reaching out to Lucian. "Your choler is palpable." He touched the boy's shoulder, and Lucian felt better, stronger.

"What do you mean?" Lucian asked, trembling; he had no choice but to allow the aeon to caress him.

"It is not only the words you speak that wound me, little messenger, but the raw seepage of your thoughts. Take my eunuch's advice and build a cathedral to hide your thoughts. Then you will not only protect yourself, but you will protect others from the poison that leaks from here"—the aeon touched Lucian's head and then pressed his fingers against Lucian's pounding heart—"and here."

Lucian gasped, for the aeon had stopped his heart, then released it.

"What do you want from me?"

"Firstly, just the respect you would give your parents," said the aeon, "and then loyalty, your complete devotion."

"Never!" Lucian said. "You could never be trusted, aeon."

"You are either very brave...or simply foolhardy." The aeon paused as he reached under his tunic to draw out Gabriel's sapphire tablet. "You may call me Athoth...or father."

"I have a father...or rather had a father."

"You do have a father, child. A living father."

Lucian shook his head. "To me you are as you were. Inquisitor."

"What did Gabriel promise you?" the aeon asked, tapping Lucian's chest lightly over his heart. "Tell me."

Lucian inhaled sharply, as if he had been struck.

"Revenge?" asked the aeon. "A capable and wide revenge?"

Lucian tried to meet his gaze, but couldn't. "I don't know what—"

"He promised that you could play a part in my demise...my defeat, didn't he?" Athoth smiled at Lucian. "But now you have no reason to avenge your parents, for they live."

"And you would expect me to believe that? You would expect me to believe *you*?"

"Yes, my son, I would...I do," and with that the aeon held the tablet before Lucian as if it were a mirror. "Are you so afraid to see the truth and your heart's desire?" asked the aeon. "There," he said smiling, "can you not see *Yam HaMelah*, the Dead Sea? And there, child, past the purple scarps...is that not your home?"

Lucian could not help himself: he looked into the tablet, which like his master Mirandola's gazing globe, seemed to contain its own depths of roiling, misty light. The tablet's light looked to be as deep and iridescent as the souls' boundary above; and Lucian felt as if he were being gently, yet powerfully pulled into the tablet as shapes resolved in the shining, mercurial mist. He could see a street cut into the living stone of a cliff, and, there, as clear as if he were looking through perfectly blown glass, was the home of his parents—his home—which looked like a rough-cut, two-story block of marble squeezed between two three story dwellings. He smelled lime and sulfur and his breath quickened when he saw a basket of star-shaped *dibbaihh*, his mother's favorite flowers, next to the doorway. The doorway was so low that an adult would have to bend over double to enter. A dark, curly haired woman gracefully pulled herself through the entrance, using her hand as a fulcrum. She looked around, waved at a neighbor, and then, grinning and waving and seemingly looking out of the tablet and directly at Lucian, shouted, "*Dahuf, Loo'cian!* Hurry. We have been waiting prayers for you, and your father is hungry." Lucian felt a blast of dry heat, the seasonal sirocco wind, and tasted gritty sand. It was as if he had passed through Gabriel's sapphire tablet and was home. Reflexively he raised his hand to wave at his mother, to call to her, and—

Found himself facing the aeon.

"You see, you believed," said the aeon, shifting the tablet away from Lucian.

Dizzy and disoriented, Lucian grasped the balustrade rail. "But I would have discovered the truth, just as I did with your demon Azâzêl."

"I laid the truth before you, companion of light, and now it will be up to you to choose."

"To choose...?"

The aeon smiled sadly at Lucian and said, "But every gift has its price, as you well know." He bowed his head slightly. "Allow me to return what Gabriel has taken. After all, there is no need for disguise. I can see your angel's intentions as easily as I can see yours...perhaps our intentions are not so different, after all." With that he drew his index finger across the tablet, gouging its perfectly smooth surface to create an aetheric coil, which he snapped, raking it away from the tablet. It stretched and twisted like one of Belias' aetheric vines, and then shivered into the shape of a glittering, jeweled serpent.

Lucian stepped away in fear.

"Have you lost your need for Gabriel's gift?"

"That is not—"

The snake raised itself, curved backwards, and struck.

Lucian fell backward as the serpent lunged toward his eyes, his windows of the soul; it thrust itself into his right eye, blinding him, then flashed through artery and pneuma, binding him, and finally coiling like a wreath of fire around his heart to make him whole and entire once again. Lucian could sense the many rooms of memory and experience that had been closed to him, could sense the shadowy presences of Baldassare and the angel Gabriel: it was as if he was, indeed, a cathedral; and when the angel Gabriel had taken back his serpent seal, Lucian was left completely and profoundly alone, trapped in one small, narrow, windowless room.

"Well, Lucian ben-Hananiah, do you believe me now?" the aeon said, supporting him.

Lucian wrested free and nodded. "Yes, Inquisitor, I believe you...but I do not trust you."

"Are not belief and trust cut from the same cloth?"

"Are you finished with me?"

The aeon remained close to Lucian. "No, my son, I am not. As I told you, you must choose."

"You pulled me back from my mother—if she was truly my mother and not a demon or a phantasm—and you have either recreated Gabriel's seal or poisoned me with an imitation so finely wrought that I cannot tell the difference. Just as you *tried* to do with the demon Azâzêl." But after a pause, Lucian asked, "What then would you have me choose?"

"This," the aeon said sadly. He pushed the tablet toward Lucian, but did not let go of it. The tablet's mercurial surface darkened and then blazed so brightly that Lucian could only see the geometries of purple-edged afterimages. Seconds later Lucian could see—could feel as he held it—the tablet's true size and depth, could see it as a wedge, a crystalline wall, a bridge that could pass through all the spaces of the world and its contiguous heavens and hells...and he could see Florence in the tablet, could see that the tablet had become a discontinuity that divided the city from north to south; and there, reflected and magnified in its shadowed surface was a dark colonnaded plaza divided by a deep, almost iridescently black line of aetheric energy that was about to explode. On one side of the thickening divide the priest Baldassare helplessly pulled at the rein-lengtheners that were twisted around his neck as his great roan dragged him along the cobblestones. On the other side, the snapping, agitated vines attacked Lucian's master Pico Della Mirandola and a boy dressed in priest's raiment. As the boy fell from his horse and Pietro reached out to retrieve him, armed men, women, and children converged upon the party: a silent army of fleshy, soulless ghosts seemingly conjured out of the unhealthy air.

"What is this?" Lucian asked Athoth.

"The tablet is both sword and shield. It can divide powers and possessions. Just as the aeon Belias has claimed your cathedral with its pretty Duomo and now casts his throne across Florence, so too can the tablet lay claim to what you see. Like a lodestone, it will pull Belias' tendrils—what you call his vines—away from your friends and those around them, thus releasing and returning their souls."

"But it divides Fra Baldassare and his companion from the others."

"Yes, and watch..."

Lucian saw the snapping vines being sucked into what could only be a crack, an opening in the tablet's dark surface...saw the air above Baldassare turn thick and dangerous. "The tablet looks to be cracked, broken."

Athoth smiled. "No, it is aetheric like a soul and can divide itself, open itself, or change its shape for a purpose. Thus are the vines expelled to the other side, and there they will be contained. Your friends will be safe."

"But they will attack Baldassare."

The aeon shrugged. "He tried to kill you, did he not?" The aeon paused, gazed kindly at Lucian, and then continued. "But if you choose to return to safety—if you choose to return to your parents and your previous life—then the tablet will cease to divide Florence and contain the vines."

"And my master?"

"Maestro Mirandola will no doubt...ah, use his considerable talents as a theurgist to try to defend and retain his immortal soul."

"They will all lose their souls," Lucian said grimly, watching the tableau unfold; and as he did so, Athoth scratched out another aetheric coil from the tablet, which he palmed for himself like a street magician disappearing a coin.

And then he snapped the tablet in two.

One half was bright with the long light of early evening; the other was dark. One radiated warmth and the dry, salty odors of home and childhood; the other emanated darkness and a chill so deep that for an instant Lucian could not catch his breath. The bright tablet that the aeon held in his left hand seemed to be expanding. There was Lucian's home. There his mother calling him. By the time he took another breath, the golden light would envelope him, transport him home—

"*Dahuf, Loo'cian!*"

—and as Lucian fell into the soft, sandy light of home and childhood, he reached out to wrest—*to steal*—*both* parts of the tablet away from the aeon, who just laughed softly. "Ah, so you have made your choice, young thief and theurgist. But I predict it will not be as you expect."

Pietro pulled hard on the braided reins and turned his horse so that he might reach the young priest Vincenzo who was wrestling with the aetheric vines that were entering his eyes and nose and mouth, twisting and coiling around his neck and face, and extracting the silvery ribbon that was his soul. As Pietro reached for him, the boy convulsed one last time and lay still; and Pietro felt the stone that was fused into his hand begin to burn. He also felt something pulling at the stone, some near yet invisible force as large as the Mountains of Moses and as high as the heavenly spheres. And he screamed in pain as the glassy striation that looked like a coiled snake uncoiled in his palm and exploded into a swirling wall of mist. Both the swirling mist and the stone embedded in Pietro's palm were manifestations of Gabriel's sapphire seal and sigil: the same ghostly yet material stuff that had once been Mirandola's gazing globe; and both mist and stone combined with the tablet that Athoth had snapped in two to form the towering discontinuity that divided the city... combined to become the enormous crystalline wall that would isolate Belias' realm of icy, shining darkness from the rest of Florence.

Pietro found himself lying beside the young priest.

Although his hand still burned, he shivered and discovered that his clothes—like the cobbles of the colonnaded piazza—were wet and rimed with ice: vestiges of Belias' presence. Yet it was warm. Except for the fires raging across the Arno, it was a clear Florentine night. The moon cast a bright, almost coruscating light; and the air was wholesome...emptied of the clouds of snaking, soul-stealing vines.

"Ser Pietro, Maestro, are you all right?" asked Vincenzo, kneeling over Pietro.

Pietro nodded. He felt weak and dizzy; yet he also felt relieved, as if a great burden had been lifted from him. He stared at the priest—or rather into him—then forced himself to his feet.

"Can you not see the miraculous wall that reaches into Heaven?" Vincenzo asked as he gazed in awe at the dark, glittering discontinuity that divided the city.

"Yes," Pietro said, "I can see it." He watched the discontinuity, mesmerized by the way its shifting surface reflected and magnified the cyan-tinged moonlight.

The priest crossed himself, his thumb extended toward the heavens, and intoned "*Lux in æternum*." Then he asked, "Do *you* know what this miracle might be?"

"Perhaps...it is our salvation. A gift from an angel."

Although he did not quite understand what the young maestro meant, Vincenzo nodded.

"Where are you?" Pietro asked, but he was not addressing Vincenzo. He surveyed the towering discontinuity, which could not be more than a few stadia from where he was standing, then scrutinized the deserted, isolated piazza, which was now filling with men, women, and children. They might be mazed and frightened; but no longer were they soulless automata willed by Belias: they had regained themselves when the vines were expelled. Baldassare's lost guards and other Florentine soldiers also massed in the piazza: they, too, looked confused and disconcerted, as if they had all just awakened from a lucid dream.

"Who, Maestro?" Vincenzo asked.

"I am not a magister," Pietro said absently, "and you need not address me as such."

"Who are you looking for, Maestro Pietro?" Vincenzo insisted. "Ah, there, I see, look...look, there is Maestro Mirandola. He looks fine." He gesticulated to Mirandola who remained mounted on his horse and although shaken was also trying to gain his bearings.

Pietro nodded to Mirandola, but his thoughts were elsewhere. Silently, wordlessly, he called to the lions: an uncertain sorcerer summoning his familiars.

"*Where* are *you*...?"

"*I* know *that you are here*...

"*I can feel you, I can*—"

Suddenly, there was shouting and great commotion; and the frightened townspeople, guards, and soldiers who had just regained their souls ran towards them. And still they clutched their scythes, knives, hammers, crossbows, and swords.

"*Deus, Deus, noster*," mumbled Vincenzo. "We are done for."

"No, *Padre*," Pietro said, feeling sudden satisfaction, vindication, and a wild thrumming joy—

They're here!

—and he pulled the young priest behind an upturned vendor's stall that stank of mold and rotting fruit.

Vincenzo yelped in pain at Pietro's touch.

"Your hand, it burns—"

Pietro released him and said, "I'm sorry, but do not be fearful. The rabble isn't after us." And, indeed, he was correct, for the stampeding crowd ran right past him and the young priest. "They're running away from...*them*," Pietro continued, pointing to the west; and Vincenzo gasped when he saw two huge lions following the crowd as if they were dogs mustering sheep.

Pietro grasped Vincenzo again and said, "No, no, they will not harm us. They are...mine."

But where...where are the rest of the cats?

The priest didn't pull away in pain this time. "Yours...?"

"Yes, in a way," Pietro said, musing, "just as I seem to belong to this." He released Vincenzo, extended his right hand, which felt numb, and gazed at the bone-white stone embedded in his palm. The glassy blue striation—the snake—was coiled once again.

Vincenzo crossed himself when he saw the stone, but his attention was fixed on the young lions that were approaching them. "I will not run...I *will* not run," he whispered to himself.

The lions sat down before them.

Behind Pietro and the priest the soldiers and townspeople began to drift back. They kept a respectful distance, but were abuzz with astonished conversation.

"We live in a time of miracles," Vincenzo said in awe, "and I—"

"Yes?" asked Pietro reflexively, almost mechanically.

"I...have regained myself."

"I could see that you were whole and entire when you awakened me. Your soul has regained its proper place."

"Yes, Maestro, if not yet my courage."

When Pietro's master Mirandola appeared, the priest bowed and made an effort to smile. But Mirandola kept his distance. Although his black and gray courser bucked and pulled its head against his tight hold on the reins, the lions did not even turn to notice.

"You seem well recovered," Mirandola said to Vincenzo, although it was obvious that he, Mirandola, was still unnerved: he was short of breath and his hands trembled. But Vincenzo understood that he was being asked about his soul, not the state of his mind and humours. Mirandola glanced at the crowd of soldiers, guards, and citizens and said, "As do all the others."

"Thanks to the...miracle, we are all restored," Vincenzo said. "Were you attacked by the vines, too?"

Mirandola seemed distant. "Yes, *Padre*. And you...Pietro?" he asked anxiously. "Tell me about the propitious appearance of these two lions and, please God, tell me what you know of all...*this*?" He waved his hand in a circle, as if he could circumscribe everything that had just happened. Droplets sprayed from his water-soaked sleeve. He gazed at the discontinuity and asked, "Perhaps my old apprentice—who is now my promised remembrancer—can explain what *that* is. Perhaps he can also explain how ice can form in heat, only to dissolve again.

"Well...?"

Pietro answered his master, but his attention was elsewhere...

"The wall," he said, meaning the discontinuity, "has something to do with the aeon Belias, with Lucian, and...this." Pietro held out his hand, showing him the stone buried in his palm, the stone that had once been Mirandola's gazing globe. "And the ice didn't form in heat. It formed out of the cold presence of the aeon Belias; and it dissolves because the aeon has been thwarted, his power diminished. For the moment."

Mirandola continued to question him, but Pietro no longer heard what his master was saying. He was gazing into the golden, black-flecked eyes of one of the lions...looking into its memories as if watching images resolving in Mirandola's crystal skrying globe. Although the cat could not comprehend what it saw and remembered, Pietro could. He could see the rest of the pride padding back and forth along the edge of the discontinuity, the crystal-sparkling spectral wall that dwarfed any imagined Tower of Babel. And Pietro saw someone passing through it, as if slipping through parting curtains or veils. It was Baldassare, followed by the priest who had tried to kill him. He also saw something else: a body lying just behind where the lions patrolled.

Lucian...

"Pietro, are you befogged? Answer me."

But Pietro was already running across the piazza. He hurried past ice-encrusted ramshackle vendors' stalls and hutches that still smelled of offal and spices, past a gang of frightened, confused-looking *armeggiatori* wearing the black and red colors of their fighting confraternity, past unfinished stone gargoyles scattered around an abandoned stonemason's cart. Mirandola tried to follow, but his courser was too frightened; it shook its head, bucked, whinnied, and turned in circles.

Pietro ran toward the discontinuity, which was now but a few yards away. As he approached it, he could feel the stone burning in his palm. From this vantage the discontinuity looked spectral, almost transparent; and it was so high that it seemed to curl back upon itself, disappearing into a confusion of perspective lines. Pietro could feel its awesome power throbbing within him like an excited heartbeat, draining him; but he did not stop until he reached the prone figure that was being guarded by the largest of the lions: the tawny colored male.

"Thanks be to God! It *is* you, Lucian."

The other three lions stood menacingly around Baldassare and his companion Antonio, who did not dare move. Pietro could feel the lions' staccato thoughts, the comfort of being near each other, the sweat stinking smells of the two men exciting hunger and arousal. He could sense that they considered Lucian one of their pride and would not harm him. But Baldassare and Antonio...they were simply intoxicatingly fresh, oily-smelling meat.

Pietro willed them away from Baldassare and Antonio.

Reluctantly, the cats backed away.

"Thank you, son," Baldassare said.

Pietro nodded. He looked toward the boundary and felt his skin tingle, but all he could see were shifting shadows and the natural glinting of moonlight on wet cobbles and the ice-crusted facades of Florentine towers, arches, and palazzos. Above, the sky was astir with streaming smoke and scudding rouge colored clouds.

He kneeled before Lucian and said, "Thank God you're alive."

Lucian looked up at Pietro and a tear runneled down his cheek. He sat up, wet and shivering, and whispered, "I failed them, Pietro. *I'm* the traitor, I'm—"

"What do you mean...traitor? Baldassare asked. "And whom did you fail?"

"Not now," Pietro said sharply.

Baldassare's hand reflexively closed on his sword; he would not be dismissed by a housecarl.

The lions turned their great heads toward him, menacing.

"I saw you," Lucian said to placate Baldassare. "I saw you and your man pass through the crack in the sapphire tablet that divides our city."

Baldassare looked into the discontinuity...looked at the distorted streets and buildings on its other side. Then he made the sign of protection over his heart and turned away.

"That took great courage, Lord Spiritual. Great courage." Lucian looked at Baldassare's man Antonio: "And you, too, Ser."

The leather-faced guard actually blushed and said, "I just followed my captain, child. The choice was either the Adversary's snapping things or... the exploding dark." The immediate tension alleviated, Lucian turned back to Pietro. "I was supposed to protect Isabella and the daughter of light."

"Did you see Isabella?" Pietro asked, his heart quickening. "Is she all right?"

"Yes, I saw her. She is well, but—"

"But...?"

"I fear that both Isabella and the daughter of light have fallen under the influence of Athoth, the aeon that killed my parents." He mumbled something about a gift and his parents being undone.

"Lucian?"

Lucian shook his head and apologized. He clasped his knees and said, "I fear Isabella and the daughter of light will soon be lost to us."

"But we divined that they were taken aboard the ship that sails the heavens," Pietro said. "How could *you* reach them?"

"The angel...Gabriel."

"Was that when you disappeared from the catacombs?"

Lucian nodded; and as the lions allowed Baldassare to come closer, the other two lions returned with Mirandola and Vincenzo a safe distance behind them. Mirandola walked beside his horse; although he had managed to settle the spooked black-and-gray, he was still keeping a very tight hold on the reins. Acting upon Pietro's subliminal needs and desires, the cats held back the silent, now reverent crowd that followed. Some of the soldiers crossed themselves and kneeled, an old crone clicked her rosaries, children wriggled in their mother's arms, and anyone who even whispered was shushed by the uniformed *armeggiatori*; but most citizens just stood, watched, and tried to listen.

"I had a dream that you were surrounded by light," Baldassare said to Lucian. "Then you were crossing a sapphire bridge through an eternity of darkness."

Lucian smiled wanly at Baldassare. "Wish it or not, Lord Spiritual, we are still connected." Then to Pietro: "As we are, too."

Pietro nodded.

"What have you done, Lucian?" Mirandola asked.

"I made the wrong choice, which was no choice at all. The angel Gabriel provided a path to Isabella and Louisa."

"Louisa?"

"The promised one...the daughter of light." Lucian paused, then said to Baldassare, "The bridge you saw in your dream, Lord Spiritual, and the boundary you just passed through with your lieutenant are one and the same: Gabriel's sapphire tablet." Then he grimaced, for he could not truly be sure whether the tablet was Gabriel's key or an imitation conjured by the aeon Athoth. Neither could he be sure that the serpent curled around his heart was Gabriel's seal or Athoth's.

Pietro could discern Lucian's pain, and then he suddenly felt cut off from him, as if Lucian had erected an invisible but tangible wall around himself. He moved closer to Lucian, as if proximity would make any difference, and asked, "How did you fail, Lucian? Tell me: what did the angel ask you to do?"

"Gabriel asked me to protect Isabella and the daughter of light. He asked

me to keep them from turning to the aeon, and yet I am here instead of there...
where I should be. Gabriel asked me to give Louisa the sapphire tablet, the
sacred key, which was to be a gift to Athoth."

"What?" cried Baldassare, who could not come any closer to Lucian for
fear of being attacked by the lions. "Gabriel would never traffic with angels
of darkness."

"Please speak softly, Lord Spiritual," Pietro said, bowing his head to
Baldassare, "lest those who kneel and pray behind us hear you."

Baldassare did not acknowledge Pietro, but lowered his voice: "Why
would the angel send you? And why would he give a sacred tablet to the
Reaper?"

"I don't know, Excellency," Lucian said.

"Perhaps to buy the aeon's allegiance," Mirandola suggested.

Lucian just shook his head, as if he didn't know; then continued: "Athoth
broke the tablet. He snapped it like it was nothing but a thin piece of ice. He
offered me—"

"What, child? What did he offer you? Tell us...please."

"Each half of the tablet was a bridge," Lucian said to Pietro, as if only he
could understand; yet Lucian protected himself as the eunuch had suggested:
he could not let Pietro know how he felt about certain things...about Isabella.
"One led back to my home and my parents."

"But your parents are dead," Mirandola said.

"The other led here," and then he said to Pietro: "One would protect you
from Belias and his vines...and save you and our master."

"And me...?" Baldassare asked.

"You saved yourself, Lord Spiritual." Lucian looked to his master
Mirandola and feeling ashamed, turned away from him and gazed upward
into the sapphire limned discontinuity. "The aeon offered me a choice: you...
or my home, my life, and my family."

"But you chose *us*," Mirandola said gently. "You made a difficult decision
and chose what you knew to be real rather than the aeon's phantasms."

"No, Maestro, I tried to steal *both* halves of the tablet from Athoth."

"But you are *here*."

Lucian smiled at his master. "Yes, I am here." Then, as if musing to
himself: "He told me it would not be as I expected."

"Who, Lucian?"

"Athoth."

"You seem overly familiar with the Reaper," Baldassare said. "As if..."

"Yes, Lord Spiritual?"

"As if you were under his thrall."

"Yes, perhaps that's true," Lucian said, "and if I am, then you would be better off without me."

"We will not leave you," Mirandola said. "That is my decision."

"And mine," Pietro said.

"Ah, the boy who would also be king," Baldassare said, smiling at Pietro, then addressing Lucian: "My choice, child, would be to kill you. That would at least dissolve our…connection and ensure that you would not betray us. But as you seem to be protected by your friend's beasts, I think necessity demands that we keep you very close." With that he looked around and said to Vincenzo, "*Padre*, you've been given another chance. Find our horses, and no excuses," and then he motioned to Antonio: "I'll comb through this rabble and find guards enough to form a command. Don't let Gabriel's Jew out of your sight."

After Baldassare and Vincenzo had disappeared into the crowd of armed, and still haunted-looking worshippers, Mirandola noticed something in the fire-crazed moonlight. He looked quizzically at Lucian and reached toward the boy's doublet collar. "*Figlio, mio*, your neck, it's—"

"Yes, Maestro, I expected you would be the one to notice. The aeon Athoth said he undid my scar…just as the death of my parents was undone."

"I cannot believe that even aeons can bring back the dead," Mirandola said.

"He told me that he healed the scar, but he didn't say that *he* brought back my parents. I think he spoke the truth, and the snare was in his words."

Mirandola shook his head, pulled a stray lock of hair away from his eyes, and said, "How can one know the mind of an aeon?"

"Or an angel," Lucian said; and with that he stood up, as if revived. He gazed fixedly into the shimmering discontinuity that towered above them and then said, "Maestro, you must leave this place right now."

"Why?" Mirandola asked.

Lucian took a step backward. "Because I sense…danger."

"I sense something, too," Pietro said.

"What danger?" asked Mirandola.

"I fear that Belias and his vines are stronger than Gabriel's sapphire tablet…stronger than the aetheric wall that protects us." He turned to the priest Antonio. "And *you* must leave with him. Take the maestro away from here *now!*"

It was then that the priest Antonio saw a familiar flash of lightning in the distance. But this was not a flashing in the blood-lit sky. No, this was a new crack in the aether, a new crack in the discontinuity that he and his superior Baldassare had so recently traversed: the protective boundary had been breeched.

As the towering crystalline wall—the discontinuity, the tablet—shattered, everyone ran, bolting away from what could only be described as a rushing avalanche of lightning and shining darkness. The priest Antonio grabbed Mirandola by the arm, and ran, too. And later, in the vine-shot, icy darkness, he remembered the Jew's last words to the apprentice theurgist Pietro:

"If we leave with the others...we die."

SIXTEEN

The Isle of the Dead

Behold the viney sigils of the church

Behold [the traitor] Belias that bringeth them forth

To devour the children of the light

To devour the aeon of many appearances

—*Lamentation of the Aeon Athoth the First Power, Hymn 8, [fragment]*

Methinks that time moves very fleet

  For aeons and angels.

Methinks that time moves very slow

  For aeons and angels.

Couldst be that flippant time is beguiled

  By aeons and angels?

Couldst be that time is twisted and shifted

  By aeons and angels?

—Robert Burton, *The Twelve Antimonies*

Francesco Salviati, the archbishop of Florence, slept fitfully this night aboard the Pope's airship. He dreamed once again of the carnage in the Duomo cathedral after the beautiful, precious, and promised daughter of light fell from the tree of judgment: the black rivers and streams of blood spurting and flowing from men, women, and children alike; the stinking smells of sweat, fear, and bloodlust; the screams echoed and magnified by the expanses of dressed stone, by the high-ceilinged chapels, apses, and the great domed roof; the First Citizen clutching the hilt of Cardinal Caraffa's dagger buried in his chest and falling to his knees as if in silent prayer; and Salviati dreamed of the terrified little altar boys hiding behind him, pulling at the hems of his purple, archbishopric robes and pleading *"Aiuto, aiuto, mio padre"* in singsong over and over and over.

Help, help, help…

The archbishop woke up sweating and choking on his tongue. Strands of his coarse gray hair were plastered to his face, and his shot silk sheets were soaked and twisted around him like Shrove-tide shrouds. He pushed away the tangled sheets, reflexively grasped the dagger he had secreted in the crack between bulkhead and pallet, and stared up into the darkness. It must be close to dawn, he thought, for he had awakened to relieve himself at four bells, which would have been around two-o'clock in the morning. He could smell the reek of the chamber pot on the other side of his cabin. Nevertheless, his stomach growled with hunger, for he had not eaten with the other priests: he had learned long ago never to trust wine and victuals carried by servants. Although fully awake now, he did not move; and as darkness gave way to the dim hazing of dawn twilight, he listened to the wood creaking with the movement of the ship and the occasional shouts and swearing of the officers of the watch. He listened for soft, nearby footfalls, but none came…yet.

The archbishop sensed danger, although he could not discern why. Yet *something* was wrong. Something in the aether…?

He could hear his heart beating loudly yet steadily, and his thoughts returned to the cathedral. His troops had escorted the daughter of light to safety; that much had gone according to plan; and it would forever be on his conscience that when he spoke the *Laudate Dominum*, he had given the signal to destroy the enemies of the church. But the murder of all the patricians and the First Citizen's family…that was unnecessary. That was not the plan. Had circumstances been different, he would have challenged the cardinal. But the cardinal had intrigued to include his own guards and some of the condottiero Valentine's invading hirelings, and could not be challenged: the safety of the daughter of light was at stake. She, and only she, was the archbishop's charge and purpose. And had not the Lord of Hosts taken his own revenge upon Cardinal Caraffa? Had not—

The archbishop heard something, a creaking that seemed a half-tone higher than the constant sighing and groaning of the timbers above. Someone stepping onto the deck grating? He quickly bundled his pillow, gown, robe and tunic under the bedcovers. Then he pulled off his sleeping cap, slid it half under the covers to complete the illusion of a figure sleeping with his face toward the wall, and crouched behind a carved high cassone positioned at the head of the pallet. The cassone also hid a hatch and a tightly furled tussore ladder. As he waited, he smiled grimly and shook his head: an old man— himself once a papal *assassino*—still spending his last days playing hide-a- way and squeezing the hilt of a dagger instead of the soft hand of a nurse.

Softly, a key turned in the door. A slight creaking as a man robed in night- watch black, dirk in hand, made his way quickly and quietly to the pallet. As he leaned over to thrust his knife into the bedclothes, the archbishop reached out and grabbed the man by the hair. He pulled hard, his grip strong as a manacle, and knocked the would-be assassin's head against the wall with a sickening thump. Leaning over him, knife held so tightly against his throat that it drew blood, the archbishop whispered, "Who sent you to do this thing?"

The assassin, a servant in the officer's mess, was still dazed by the blow.

"Speak now or I'll split your apple in a most painful manner," the Archbishop said softly as he pressed the blade incrementally harder against the man's throat.

"No, *Santità*, please...I cannot."

"Your last chance, my child," and the archbishop remembered his dream of rivers and streams of blood.

The servant gasped, his neck and chest wet with blood and said, "*Santità*, please, it was...""

"Yes? Quickly, child, before any more of your lifeblood leaks away."

"It was...Conte Ammirato. Now, please, Santità, mercy. I—"

Ammirato. Of course, I should have known.

The archbishop whispered "*Valeas in Cælis*"—*may you be well in Heaven*—as he slit the assassin's throat deeply and neatly and held him tight through his death throes. Then he pulled the cassone away from the hatch, which he opened. Below, at 44°13'N, 11°17'E, illuminated by first light, were the shallows, mudflats, swamps, and islets of the crescent-shaped salt-water lagoon that surrounded the greatest, brightest and most dangerous city in the world: Venice. Fishermen looked up at the miracle floating high above them. They stood knee-deep in gunge-marsh and water inside their basketwork fishing enclosures. The archbishop saw them and could not help but remember the sea-salty and earthy taste of crayfish, crabs, and morels fried in fat— as he pushed the mess servant through the hatch. There should have been sufficient clearance through the airship's web of ratlines and shrouds, but the airship suddenly lurched as if it had come aground, which was impossible. If the archbishop had not grabbed the leg of the cassone, he would have certainly followed the corpse into the netting. The archbishop felt sudden claustrophobia and a deep chill descend upon him, and in the pallid light of his cabin he could see his breath curl in the suddenly frigid air. Then there was another shock, as if the airship had been slapped on the broadside. The dead assassin was shaken from the shrouds and fell headlong toward the watery plain below; the archbishop, still holding onto the cassone, slid across the cabin. Officers shouted the alarm and swabbies cried out as they were thrown against bulkheads, hogsheads, hatches, gratings, and gangways. The air remained abnormally frigid; and the archbishop sensed something else, something even more sinister: an encroaching emptiness, a coiling nothingness as deadly and enervating as the boundary of accursed souls above. He felt separated, isolated even from the familiar things around him, as if he was circumscribed by some living, invisible membrane.

The ship shuddered again.

Then all was quiet, deadly-still quiet, and *cold*.

An unnatural lethargy descended upon the archbishop; and he fought it, using a cantrip the Pope's theurgist had taught him. He felt his fatigue lift; but his bones ached as if he had been doing hard physical labor, his head throbbed with dull pain, and the frigid air seemed to be pushing against him, resisting him, needling him. Certain that the daughter of light and her companion were in mortal danger, if not already dead, he shivered into his robes. His warmest robes. He wiped the blood from his dagger on a coverlet and was about to step out of his cabin when he remembered the furled ladder.

Take it!

Well, perhaps…just perhaps.

He slung it over his shoulder—it was thin and weighed less than his cloak—and carefully opened his door. The light was dim and debilitating: the same dolorous light that emanated from the boundary above—from the captured, perished souls that lifted the airship—overwhelmed the pearl and crimson glow of dawn. But Athoth, the aeon that captained and guided this ship, should be controlling the souls' icy emanations…and protecting those below.

Should be, but why wasn't he?

The archbishop looked up and down the corridor and saw two of Rudolfo's eunuch guards. One was sprawled against a bulkhead, his neck broken and head resting on his shoulder as if it belonged to another. The other, whom the archbishop knew as Augustino, had fallen onto a grating; and the light from below wrapped odd shadows around him. His arms and legs were askew, obviously broken, and he had lost an eye; but he was alive.

The archbishop knelt beside him and said, "*Figliolo*, tell me…tell me what has happened."

The eunuch's fleshy, yet once handsome face was crusted with blood. He blinked and looked up at the archbishop. "*Difensore* Rudolfo sent us to protect you." He smiled wanly at the irony, more a grimace. "We received word that an *assassino* had been sent to you by—"

"Yes, I know. Go on."

"And then...then something happened. We were *struck*—" The eunuch's head suddenly jerked back and forth, and blood sprayed from his ear and eye socket as he frantically looked this way and that.

"What is it?" the archbishop asked, clutching the eunuch's hand.

The eunuch gazed upward, shuddered, and mumbled "*I vitigni...i viticci*". *The vines...the tendrils.*

His remaining eye, which looked green in the unnatural, shifting light, began to glaze. "Can you not see, *Santità*?" he said in a whisper. "Can you not see...?"

The archbishop looked upward and saw *something* in the blue-tinged light, but it was like looking at a quick, passing reflection in a mirror. He allowed his eyes to become unfocussed, so he that might better discern anything malignant dwelling in the aether; and, indeed, he could now clearly see a vine—the deadly sigil and substance of the dark aeon Belias. It twisted and writhed, snapping and glittering in the blue-tinged light. Shivering from fear and the unnatural chill in the air, the archbishop prayed, "*O Lux Deus noster, novi januam mortis.*"

O Light, our God, I have seen the gate of death.

He watched the vine curl backward, about to strike. It would be useless to try to hide or run from the aetheric, soul-devouring creature. The archbishop was as vulnerable as the prostrate eunuch beside him. *Belias is here, on this ship; and Athoth, our Captain, God's first scepter of light, is surely under attack.*

We are all under attack.

God's own archangel Belias has betrayed us, has betrayed his own Church; and by taking—or destroying—the daughter of light, has betrayed the Lord God in Heaven, Holy be His Name.

The archbishop had no doubt that Belias had slapped and shaken the airship as if it was no more than a bird in his hand.

But then the vine suddenly withdrew, as if it were a coil of steel that could not resist the demanding pull of a lodestone. "It is so cold..." whispered the eunuch; and the airship groaned and shuddered again, as if caught in an unnatural rip, and made a gut-wrenching, gore-raising descent before righting itself.

The archbishop gasped for breath and looked frantically about him, much as the eunuch had done a moment ago. The aetheric, soul-stealing vine had disappeared. The wintry air felt like needles in his lungs, and shadows now defined the corridors. Morning had somehow passed into dusk, and the eunuch looked like he had been dead for many hours: his blood crusted face had hardened into a rictus smile, and he smelled of rot and feces. A silence permeated the ship so heavily that the archbishop imagined that all natural time, motion, and consequence had ceased. He exhaled, and his breath curled in the air.

Had Athoth, the aeon of light repelled Belias' attack?

Or had the invading Belias won and taken the daughter of light?

The archbishop grimaced and forced himself forward. As before, the very air itself seemed to be pushing against him, slowing him, making each step an effort. He held his dagger in one hand, as if he could cut his way through the resisting *matèria* of the blue-tinged air; his other hand seemed to have a will of its own: it pressed against his chest, securing the rope ladder that hung like a bandolier over his shoulder. He encountered crewmen in all the corridors, all dead or unconscious, all broken, as if they had been thrown against bulkheads and racks of caulked storage boxes and tonel barrels; but he did not tarry to investigate who might be dead, soul bereft, or suspended in abnormal sleep. He made his way directly aft to the restricted area, which was always heavily guarded; and indeed the captain's *eunuci* guards were all there: scattered or thrown together, as if they were sacks that had been tossed into the narrow corridor that led to the expansive T-shaped deck. It had become noticeably colder. The oak planks of the corridor were blood-rimed and sticky, and the archbishop had to step carefully over and around the tangled bodies to reach the captain's private deck. There he found the captain—Athoth—standing in front of the red-cladded door of the great cabin where the daughter of light and her companion had been held captive for their protection. But the captain looked more like an exhausted, war-wearied paladin rather than one of the Eternal's first aeons, a king of arms to the silence and living light. He was not dressed in his captain's uniform of velvet, damask, gold, and crimson, but wore instead a simple tippet over a white linen cassock. His brow was knit with strain, and he stood still as a statue. Indeed, he might have been made of fixed stone.

It was difficult to gaze upon the aeon. The air that surrounded him seemed to have acquired vital substance and whirled around him like mercury spinning in an alchemist's beaker.

"Shift your gaze!"

"What?" asked the archbishop, startled: the aeon had not moved his lips; the whispery voice—the aeon's voice—was inside his head. As he obeyed the aeon and allowed his eyes to shift focus so that his gaze might pierce the aether, he shivered and said, *"Dio meo!"* Thousands of vines, translucent as glass, were writhing around the aeon like a storm, snapping, whipping, squirming, attacking, and absorbing his vital energy. Or perhaps it was the vines themselves that were under attack...perhaps the aeon was absorbing *their* vital energies and preventing them from escaping and attacking the archbishop. But the archbishop could see something else in the storm of vines: the swirling vines resolving into the towering figure of the dark aeon. For one terrible, heart-hammering instant, the archbishop beheld Belias' achingly beautiful face; and Belias' Gorgonian gaze met the archbishop's.

The dark aeon smiled at him; and the archbishop felt his throat close, as if he was being throttled. He was suffocating. The aether pressed against him, painfully sharp yet porous, thickening and thinning, squeezing and slackening, as if the very air itself was breathing.

"Shift your gaze!" Athoth repeated; and once again the archbishop could see Athoth through the translucent cloud of attacking vines. *"That's time you feel, son of the church. I created a path for you, but—as you can see—my will is being somewhat deflected. I cannot restrict natural time and resist and contain the coils of Belias. You must—"*

For an instant the living skein of vines completely obscured the aeon, and a few of the glittering vines escaped the twisting mass and flew toward the archbishop, who stepped backward in fright and tripped over the body of Rudolfo, the aeon's personal eunuch guard. But then the aeon pulled the vines back, and once again the mass of vines was hazed and aetheric and the aeon whole, substantial, and visible.

"The key to the cabin...around the eunuch's neck. Open the door and get them away."

"The daughter of light...she is safe?"

But the aeon disappeared once again into the swirling storm of vines; and suddenly everything quickened, seemed sharper. Although the air was numbingly cold, it was no longer suffocatingly oppressive...it no longer muffled the sounds of groaning men, the creaking of the airship as it descended fitfully, and the whistling and soughing of wind through planks and masts and torn shrouds.

"Holy Name," the archbishop implored, but the only word he heard, word without sound, was *"Hurry..."*

But even as he said, "I cannot pass through the vines," he knew that he must act now or lose his soul where he stood. He bent over the dead eunuch and pulled the looped gold necklace over the eunuch's head. Then holding the attached key before him as if it were a crucifix, he whispered *"Sit nomen Domini benedictum"* and rushed toward the cabin door. Vines snapped and coiled as he passed through them. They felt like icy spiderwebs breaking across his exposed hands and face. He did not have time to glance at Athoth, who was now behind him, but intoned his prayer as he tried to fit the key into the lock with his shaking hands.

Surely the vines would attack...surely they would pierce him and take his soul, wrest it from him as if it were nothing more than a sweetmeat.

The bolt clicked, then dropped, and the archbishop rushed into the room, slamming and locking the door behind him.

He found the daughter of light and her companion Isabella wrapped in blankets and sitting on the pallet set against the bulkhead wall farthest from the door. Louisa was shivering and cradling Isabella in her arms to keep her warm. Isabella was either asleep or unconscious; her breathing was irregular, her skin pale and pasty.

"How did you get through the vines?" Louisa asked, blinking, as if unsure that someone had actually unlocked the door and stepped into the cabin.

"You must ready yourself to leave," the archbishop said as he glanced around the room. The last rays of twilight filtered through the high windows and outlined the closed hatches.

"I will not leave Isabella."

"She is already lost, and we have no time to—"

The room suddenly grew darker and colder. The archbishop glimpsed thin shadows arcing toward him and the daughters of light, snaking around him... snaking around all of them. The vines had finally escaped Athoth's restraints and penetrated into the room.

We have failed, Holy Name...now we are all lost to the furies of darkness.

But a voice spoke inside the archbishop's head. Athoth's voice.

"Wake her up. Now."

"The companion?"

"No, child, awaken the daughter of light! You must once again burn open her soul's memories. I can no longer protect..."

Even as he felt the vines threading through him as if they were substance and he was aether, he reached out to the daughter of light. He grasped her hand and pressed his thumb hard against the glassy pebbly seal that he had burned into her palm in the catacombs. And in that instant, just as he glimpsed the dizzying intensities of light and darkness that pulsed through her, he was thrown across the planked floor. He landed feet first against the opposite bulkhead and experienced piercing, nauseating, overwhelming pain. But it was not bruised flesh or broken toes that caused him to cry out: it was the vines tearing and twisting hungrily inside him. Cold, they were so cold... cold needles piercing him, winding sliding knifing through his innards as if he were butcher meat. He mumbled his last prayers. Like his benefactor Athoth, he was beaten; and with each thrumming of his heartstrings, he could feel the vines tearing away the layers of his soul.

He thought he could hear the daughter of light shouting, as if from a great distance—

"Serpens sum," she cried.

I am the serpent.

"Deuoraui arbustum."

And I devour the vine.

—and then the archbishop felt the shock of another explosion in the aether.

When he regained himself, he saw that Isabella was awake and gasping for breath; and the daughter of light was standing stock-still in front of the pallet. Her arms were outstretched, and the vines that had invaded the cabin were silently shattering all around her in the blue-tinged air. It was as if they were twisting creatures of living crystal being thrown and broken against invisible diamond-hard walls: thrown and broken by the dangerously uncontrolled will and strength of a sixteen-year old girl…the promised incarnation of the anointed one.

A sixteen year old girl more powerful than an aeon…

Then Louisa stepped backward, her calves striking the pallet, causing her to fall back onto the pallet. "Are you all right?" she asked Isabella, then turned to the archbishop. She looked confused, as if she had just been wrenched from a terrible nightmare. Would she remember what had just happened…what she had just done?

The archbishop prised open the dead-man hatch and gasped: the airship was skiffing dangerously low over one of the Venetian islands. He could see sparse lights glowing below, and through the high windows above he could see the carnival blaze of the Castello and San Marco in the distance. He shivered with distaste, for they could only be floating over the island of San Michele, the isle of the dead.

"Hurry, we must leave the ship."

"But surely the captain will protect us," Louisa said, still shivering. She sounded like a child pleading.

"Look into your memory."

"No, I cannot," Louisa said. "I *cannot*," but she could, and she did. "Oh, God, the captain is so weak. But an aeon, an aeon cannot die…he cannot." She looked around, terrified. "And the vines, they return—"

Indeed, the vines were slipping through the cabin door and bulkheads like fingers of mist; but there they stayed, as if caught. Louisa was too weak now to destroy them…too weak to restrain them. It could only be Athoth still trying to protect them, even as Belias was putting him to the sword.

The archbishop unfurled his tussore ladder, secured the tie-downs, and threw it out of the hatchway. "Hurry to me now, or lose your souls forever."

Isabella helped her dazed companion across the room to the hatchway; but when the daughter of light looked at the grotesquely asymmetrical spires, towers, and cenotaphs below, she stiffened: the spires were rising toward them like pikes.

The airship creaked as it lost altitude.

"Our best chance is to drop onto one of those rooftops," the archbishop said as they passed over dimly lit sepulcher palaces.

"I…can't do that," Isabella said. "Why can't we just wait until we're closer and—" She glimpsed something moving in the air and shuddered.

Louisa saw a curling, twisting vine trying to reach Isabella and the archbishop. "You *can* do it," she said and lowered herself over the hatch, securing her heels in the rungs of the rope ladder. She looked up at the archbishop, as if to say farewell, and said to Isabella, "I'll be right below you. You won't fall, I promise. Now hurry."

The archbishop helped Isabella onto the ladder, holding her wrists until she could secure her feet. Louisa climbed down carefully, looking at the roofs sliding past below, looking ahead to the next roof. Below, lights guttered in piazzas and avenues formed by the convergent towers, palazzos, cathedrals of the dead. The ladder swung and twisted as the airship descended erratically, as if buffeted by high winds. Louisa looked up. Isabella was but a few rungs above her, and the archbishop was just climbing onto the ladder. The airship suddenly stopped moving forward, and the ladder jerked backward in response. Isabella screamed but hung on.

"Climb down," Louisa called to Isabella and the archbishop. They were hanging over great dome, a minaret encircled by a parapet balcony.

The archbishop shouted, "Jump."

Louisa took a deep breath and released her hold on the ladder. She fell about six feet and landed onto a smooth sheet of marble and slid down to the parapet. "Jump, Isabella."

Isabella hesitated, and the airship began to rise.

"Jump…*now*!"

Isabella let go and fell near the parapet. She was still screaming when Louisa caught her. They both looked up for the archbishop, but the airship rose precipitously, its sails billowing and nacreous white in the moonlit sky, and then shot forward as if jerked by some unseen hand. The airship's carrack gondola disappeared behind a huge pyramid covered with thousands of green porphyry gargoyles; but they could still see the balloon with its skin of accursed souls glowing like algae in the sea.

And then they were blinded by an explosion.

For an instant the island of graves turned to sapphire as the gondola and its envelope of souls were torn out of the sky…

As the archbishop was thrown from the airship by the blast—and as he fell toward scattered graves and a copse of cypress trees, his arms and legs still entwined in his twisting, burning rope ladder—the aeon Athoth blessed him with a revelation.

> *Jehovah proditum eclesia.*
> *Pertinetis ad damiurgus.*
> *Non ad Verum Deum.*

> *Our god Jehovah betrayed his own church.*
> *He is the demiurge.*
> *Not the* True *God.*

And as Athoth fought to escape the dark aeon's viney death grip, the First Citizen of Florence awoke with a start in the mountain fortress of Urbino.

He dreamed that an angel, an aeon, had just penetrated his very soul.

SEVENTEEN
Ministering Angels

And do thou, Gabriel,

Lay low our foes…

—Alcuin, *A Sequence for St. Michael*

Do not torment yourself
With melancholy thoughts.
Come with me in the gondola.
Let us step upon the sea.

—Boatman's barcarole

Pietro tried to pull Lucian away from the boundary, away from the lightning and shining darkness that seemed to be crashing down on top of them like an ocean displaced by a falling star. It was as if the aether itself and the shapes and shadows it contained had become as solid and smoothly sharp as hailstones. The boundary that was the sapphire tablet—the boundary that reached to the darkest heavens and separated them from Belias' snapping vines—was shattering: it shimmered like a speculum and distorted all perspective as it fell. Lightning frizzled in the air and scorched the ground, followed by ear-splitting claps of thunder. Pietro could smell roasted flesh, could hear screams of terror; and the hair on his arms and scalp tickled and stood on end as if he were being swept up into a maelstrom.

But Lucian held tightly onto Pietro and with God's strength wouldn't allow him to flee in panic with the others: with the mob of soldiers and townspeople…with Mirandola and Baldassare and the young pimply priest Vincenzo.

"If we leave with the others, we die," he said.

"We'll surely die standing here," Pietro said as icy shards spun around him as if caught in a vortex.

"No, we must grasp what is ours."

"Ours...?"

Lucian took Pietro's hand, which burned him; for Pietro's stigmata was on fire. Pietro cried in pain as their flesh seemed to boil together...and then everything was suddenly still: a storm of crystal caught in amber.

"Absorb it," Lucian said. "Make it your own. Can you not see what is before you? It is your glass, it's Mirandola's gazing globe"; and indeed Pietro saw—through Lucian's mind's eye—what the soldier-priest Baldassare had seen and felt when he had passed through the boundary. Baldassare had seen the gazing globe arching before and above him; and it was pure sapphire: the color of Gabriel's tablet...the color of concentrated souls.

Pietro said—or perhaps he only thought—"How do you know?" And then he remembered Lucian's connection with Baldassare: Lucian, who had once stolen the priest's soul. But that thought was interrupted by another voice. In that terror-shot second, Pietro could not be sure if he was hearing the echoes of his own thoughts, Lucian's voice, or the voice of a spirit—

"What you see before you is your master's gazing globe, Pietro; and it is also the sapphire tablet I gave Lucian to pass on to the aeon Athoth. And now, I have instructions for you both."

—or perhaps, just perhaps he had heard the growling of the lions that stood beside them, facing the boundary. The lions seemed unconcerned, as if they could not see, hear, or sense what was crashing over them.

And then Pietro found himself blinded by light, by intensities of bright white light. He found himself in a place without perspective, without form. It was as if he had suddenly been swallowed by a cloud that contained the pure white power of the sun itself, and the only tangible was Lucian's strong and bony hand, which clutched his own.

"Do not be afraid," Lucian said. "The light-blindness will pass."

Pietro knew it was indeed Lucian's voice. "Where are we?"

Lucian released his grip on Pietro's hand and said, "I would call it home. You would call it heaven."

Pietro inhaled the sudden smell of cinnamon and heard the voice of the angel Gabriel...

Heard laughter that tolled like a thousand tiny bells.

Mirandola, with his skryer Baldassare, the priests Antonio and Vincenzo, and a ragtag command of guards, ran for their lives when the boundary shattered in an explosion of lightning and thunder, falling sheets and stacks and pillars of ice...and darkness. They ran through the twisted boulevards, streets, and alleys, and only stopped when the chill in the air dissipated and all was still except for a strangely distant rhythmical ratcheting and cracking. Several hundred townspeople and soldiers were also in the street, huddling together like pups trying to get at their mother's teat, and repeatedly making the sign of the cross. The smell of fear was as strong and acrid as the stink of perspiration.

"We must find Pietro and Lucian," Mirandola said to Baldassare. Mirandola had not yet caught his breath and his heart was still pounding in his throat. He looked around the crowded street and said, "I cannot see them. Can you?" But Baldassare seemed oddly distracted: he had closed his eyes and tilted his head, as if he were seeing distant events that others could not."

"Agnolo!" Mirandola said, pulling at the priest's sleeve.

Baldassare shook his head, as if irritated by the question; but the priest Antonio, who stood beside his master Baldassare, said, "I don't think they ran with the rest of us. I was near them and heard the Jew say to the other apprentice that—"

An enormously loud and hollow cracking came from the direction of the piazza; and the rabble, like a herd of spooked deer, ran away from the noise, ran down the street and away from the boundary, away from the center of the city that the aeon Belias had claimed with his vines and ice-sharpened darkness. If the mob continued fleeing eastward, they would soon come upon the elevated church of San Miniato where lay the ancient remains of the martyr Léonello who was said to have carried his own severed head through the streets of Florence.

"Tell me what Lucian told Pietro," Mirandola said to Antonio, who was nervously gazing this way and that. But Antonio ignored him, turning instead to the meditative Baldassare: "Lord Spiritual, *please*, we must leave this place. The cloth-cap rabble runs, and so should we. Our own men will not stay here. Can you not sense the danger? Can you not feel the—"

"Antonio!" Mirandola said, demanding attention.

The priest made a growling noise, turned back to Mirandola and said, "The Jew told the other one that they would both die unless"—his exasperation and impatience were palpable—"unless they stayed where they were. And that's *all* I know, Maestro."

"I'm going back to find them," Mirandola said: perhaps he was speaking to Baldassare, perhaps to himself.

"No!" Baldassare said, himself once again. "Your apprentices are no longer there."

"Then we must find them."

"We cannot go where they are, Maestro."

"You mean they are dead?" Mirandola asked quietly.

"My unfortunate connection with your soul-robbing apprentice still remains, so I think your Jew, at least, is alive, but—"

"Lord Spiritual, look!"

Antonio pointed to something dark and poisonous in the distance, a roiling, spidery cloud that distorted the shapes and lines of street and building. It looked like elongated fingers pushing and then closing into a fist, coming nearer with every stretching and clenching movement.

Baldassare nodded and said, "We leave *now!*" He motioned to his guards to follow. "When we reach safety—*if* we reach safety—you'll form the men-at-arms into ensigns and, if we have enough, into banners," he said to his gravel-voiced second-in-command Jacopo di Pecori. Jacopo nodded, shouted for his lieutenants, and quickly began rounding up his troops. Baldassare calculated the speed and distance of the spidery dark shapes moving toward them and shuddered. With a voice as gravelly as Jacopo's—gravelly from fear—he said to Antonio, "I told you to find me a horse. I cannot run from the vines with this damnable leg."

"And I told you that there are none to be found," Antonio said, returning his belligerent stare as if they were soldiers of equal rank. "Horses sense the vines like birds sense a storm, Lord Spiritual." With that Baldassare leaned on Antonio to relieve the pressure on his sprained ankle and ordered Mirandola to help him so that they might move faster.

But Mirandola could not, would not leave his charges.

He made a cursory bow to Baldassare, asked for the prelate's forgiveness, and then ran back toward the piazza. He ignored Baldassare's shouts, for he could not see the twisting cloud of aetheric vines speeding towards him, just as he had never been able to see the angels in his own gazing globe. But he knew the danger that was ahead. *I'm blind as a beggar*, he thought sourly as he looked into the dizzying, perspective shifting darkness ahead. Even the cloud-shrouded moon above appeared distorted, and Mirandola imagined that it was folding in upon itself. His legs ached, his breath grew short, and he suddenly felt bone-chilling fear as something icy cold and needle sharp passed through him. He had experienced that terrible sensation earlier, when something quick and aetheric and invisible had pierced him, violated him, left him empty and bereft. His soul had been taken...and was then somehow restored.

He stopped dead and reflexively turned around to see what had swept past him; and then, as if the proverbial scales had suddenly fallen from his eyes, he could see a dark mass receding: a cloud, a swiftly moving miasma of twisting, writhing vines. He whispered *"Purifica Domine, et dele inquitatem inimicorum nostrorum."*

Lord, cleanse me and destroy the evil of our enemies.

He pressed his trembling hand against his chest.

He was whole and entire.

The vines had not emptied him, and as he watched them disappear he had the sense that they were growing weak, losing potency. He turned and retraced his steps back to the boundary. He walked along the narrow, claustrophobic Via di Salva, which was bordered by heavy stone walls and balconies that threatened to crush him. He should turn back, he could turn back, but he could not leave Pietro and Lucian.

He felt nothing but purpose, cold, implacable purpose.

Perhaps the vines *had* taken something vital from him.

No, he insisted to himself, *I am whole and entire. I must see this out, even if, even if*—and he realized there and then that something was drawing him, something was pulling him back to the boundary. The air became increasingly colder. He shivered in his white linen theurgist robes and prayed that he was not being held in thrall by Belias or some other demon or aeon of darkness. The street widened and opened into the piazza. He tried to turn back, to test himself, only to discover that he was indeed in thrall.

And before him was a mountain of ice. Yet as he gazed at it, the huge tumble of glittering shards, boulders, blocks, and shimmering stalactites and stalagmites seemed to be somehow inverted. It was as if he was looking into an immense cavern of shifting perspectives, shadows, and reflected light.

He pulled against the force drawing him. He squeezed his eyes shut: it hurt to gaze upon the mountain that was folding into itself like the moon he had glimpsed earlier…folding itself into an ebon emptiness that pierced the earth and sky like the inverted tree in the doomed cathedral. But even in that instant when his eyes were closed, he could *see* something watching him. He opened his eyes and found himself staring into the golden, almond shaped eyes of one of Pietro's lions: the huge tawny male with the silvery mane. It stood before the shifting, glittering immensity of ice waiting for Mirandola to approach; and Mirandola realized that he had been drawn back to the boundary, drawn to this place by the lion. He could see himself reflected in the lion's eyes…could see himself as the lion saw him. He was a lean danger bleeding sour smells; yet he was also an aspect of the lion, an integral part that moved and breathed and hunted outside the lion's sight and skin. Just as the lion experienced time and memory as a constant present, so did Mirandola glimpse an infinity of whiteness that would be his immediate future.

The lion turned toward the boundary and leaped into the crack of ebon darkness that was the heart of the collapsing mountain of ice and aether. It might be said that Mirandola followed the lion, but that would be like trying to follow one's own shadow. He simply found himself in darkness, in utter absence and emptiness, which was in an instant—or an eternity—completely overwhelmed by the pure, blinding, white light of Heaven.

"There's no way to get into this...*mausoleo* from here," Isabella said as she slapped her hands in frustration against the marble dome of the huge, cathedral-shaped mausoleum. Then she turned around, leaned against the ornately carved balustrades of the balcony, and looked at the moonlit palazzo below. "And there's no way down. We're trapped." She shivered and backed away from the edge: just standing so close to it made her feel dizzy and nauseated, as if the ground below were pulling at her. Even now, she could still feel the heat from the explosion of the airship; and the image of the fiery starburst appeared for an instant as a dark pattern every time she blinked.

"Hush!" Louisa said. "Your voice will carry." Louisa had walked along the circumference of the balcony, checking the walls below the crenellations of the decorative porphyry battlements, and, indeed, could find no way down.

"I doubt the dead can hear us," Isabella said, but the peevishness in her voice was only bravado to mask her fear. She thought of the aeon Athoth, the captain of the airship, the one she had elected to call Gentile; and her hand trembled as she touched her forehead, which was bruised and weeping through a makeshift linen bandage. *Oh, Dio mio, Dio mio, how could the Adversary destroy* you, *an angel of God?* As she made the sign of the cross, her fingertips left faint bloodstains on her white *camisa* chemise.

"Do you think the dead lit the lamps on the avenues and in those windows?" Louisa asked sarcastically as she nodded toward a dimly-lit building that could have been another cenotaph or perhaps a church or monastery. Then she turned, looking across the black water toward San Marco and the Castello. "And *there*!" she pointed. "Do you also think the dead can row boats...?"

Louisa and Isabella watched yellow lantern light skittering and reflecting on the water of the opposite shore as swift green and black *vipera* picket boats rowed away from the Sacca della Misericórdia. A slower cortege of black plumed funeral barges, small *sandolos*, *topo* skiffs, and gondolas followed.

"They're coming this way," Isabella said, alarmed.

"No, look, they're going where the airship exploded."

"No, Louisa, they're coming for us. They're coming for *you*, daughter of light." Isabella sounded suddenly out of breath. "But perhaps...perhaps landing atop this *mausoleo* was a godsend.' She started to say, "At least we'll be safe here until—"

And was interrupted by a voice calling them from below.

"*Filiolae lucis!*"

The voice—a woman's voice—was not that far below.

"Just behind you, *Filiolae lucis*, come around here."

Louisa and Isabella moved along the parapet until they could see the woman who called them. She was clinging onto the slippery smooth black marble wall like an insect on glass.

"Who are you?" Louisa asked.

"A friend, but there is no time." With that the figure dressed like a young man in a doublet, tight black calze and a camicia blouse grasped the edges of the merlons and pulled herself onto the balcony. Her hands and bare feet were stained and blackened. Her long hair was as blond as Pico Della Mirandola's and wound in a plait around the crown of her head. Her face was elfin, marred only by her nose, which had been broken and had healed unevenly. Her jaw jutted slightly, giving her an appearance of hauteur, but it was her eyes that fascinated: even in the hazing moonlight they looked witched—haunted—as if she had witnessed too many sins and lost all the innocent, mischievous joy of youth. "You have been seen by the priests in the monastery," she said and pointed out the dimly lit building Louisa and Isabella had looked at before: a white façade of Istrian stone as grotesque as the gargoyle-guarded towers that surrounded it. "And they intend to do you harm."

"Harm?" Louisa asked.

"By what magic did you climb up here?" Isabella asked, accusing.

"None, companion to light. The masons always leave climbing indentations. Is it not the same in your country?"

Louisa kneeled between the merlons and could see the indentations, which appeared to be no more than shadows in the moonlight.

"It is a trick of perspective," the intruder said to Louisa. "The towers look straight, but are not...like the Coliseum in Rome." She spat when she said Rome. "The angle is slight, but enough to ease climbing and repair."

"Why would the friars wish to harm us?" Louisa asked. "We were being taken to the Pope at his behest."

The woman looked impatient, then her expression changed, and she spoke softly, sadly: "You could not know this, Mistress of Light, but white smoke has risen from the Basilica. There is a new Supreme Pontiff, the father of the bastard Valentine who even now marches against your country. The pontiff is in league with the Adversary and his dark angel who reaves men of their souls...the one who transforms God's light into shining darkness. Surely you have seen his handiwork." Remembering the aeon Belias and his twisting vines, Louisa shivered and looked away.

"Innocent is dead?" Isabella said, disbelieving.

"Poisoned. The new Vicar of Christ is Cardinal Rodrigo Borgia. He has taken the name Alexander, the Sixth Alexander."

"Rodrigo Borgia? How could that be?" asked Isabella. "How—?"

"How else? With a few drams of hellebore and many sacks of gold. Now"—the woman turned away from Isabella and addressed Louisa—"do you wish to be taken by the Adversary's new pontiff or remain free?"

"And where would such freedom lie?" Louisa asked.

"Only with those Christians who retain their faith." The woman pulled out a small pouch secreted in her bodice. She shook out a portion of black powder, spat into it, and then rubbed it into her already blackened hands and feet. Bowing her head slightly, she handed the pouch to Louisa. "This will help you to grip the marble, *Filia Lucis*."

"I cannot do it...I cannot climb down a sheer wall," Isabella said.

"Then you will have to stay here."

"Who *are* you?"

The woman smiled. "You may call me Sister Maria Theresa."

"You are a nun?"

Sister Maria Theresa gave Isabella an ironic smile and said, "Why else would I watch the holy friars of San Michele?" Then, lowering herself over the balcony, she said to Louisa, "You must come with me, *Filia Lucis*. We don't have much time. And you *must* not be captured."

The nun looked into Louisa's eyes. Supplicant to infanta.

Louisa nodded, turned to Isabella and said, "Open your hands."

"No, I cannot do it," Isabella cried. "Oh, *Dio mio*, I cannot climb down a wall. My head hurts. I am not an insect, I am not a—"

"We have no choice, and I will not leave you here."

Isabella composed herself, then held her hands out, palms up.

"And your feet, too," Louisa said, as she leaned against the balustrade and rubbed the sticky alum onto her toes and the balls of her own now bare feet. "You won't fall, my dear companion. I promise you. I shall be right below you. All right?"

Isabella nodded, her hands shaking, teeth chattering as if Belias' vines and cold aethers were swirling around her. "But what about my shoes?"

"Leave them," Maria Theresa said with a slight smile. "God will provide."

Louisa signaled to Maria Theresa, who lowered herself four or five handholds to give Louisa room; and then Louisa was over the balcony. She could feel the nun's hands on her ankles, gently helping her to find the masons' indentations. "Come now," Louisa said to Isabella. "Slowly, pull yourself over. You won't fall, I promise. Steady. I'm positioning your foot. And now the other. There, feel how your toes stick to the openings?"

"Yes," Isabella said, her voice thin. "Like an insect."

Handhold by handhold, foothold by foothold, they slowly climbed down the sheer marble precipice: fear-sweat running oily and slippery, hands and toes sticky, breath rattling like paper in wind, and muscles tight and threatening to cramp.

Maria Theresa directed and guided Louisa in a soft flat voice; Louisa, looking upward, did the same for Isabella; and with each searching tentative movement, Isabella mumbled to herself: a chant, a prophecy from the yellow-haired North, a childhood song that was older than church or empire:

> *Descend, descend, through force of magic*
> *Bring down the golden moonbeams*
>
> *Bring down the moon shining high*
> *And the gnarly tree called night*
>
> *The tree that pierces all nine realms*
> *The tree 'round which all revolves*
>
> *Bring down the bright heavens*
> *Welcomed by the black abyss*
>
> *As you fall, a-howling*
> *Screaming in despair*

And finally—after what seemed like a slippery, sweaty, aching eternity—they all felt the delicious sensation of soft, dew-cool earth and grass between their toes.

Solidity. Ground. *Erth*. Expanses of moonlit piazzas. The frightful glances of leering gargoyles perched on cenotaphs. The acres, towns, cities of shadowed gravestones, gardens of cypress trees shuddering in the breeze like ghosts that had seen a ghost, sculptures surrounded by wrought iron, gates inviting the dead to enter and rest while their flesh putrefies into nutrient mulch. Maria Theresa led them through a sickly-sweet smelling garden filled with circles of small, pink gravestones.

"What is this place?" Isabella asked.

"Speak softly," Maria Theresa said. "Your voice will carry over water."

"Water?"

"There," she said, pointing. "We are very close...and the pink stones are the graves of children." She guided Louisa forward toward a small quay where a funeral gondola was moored. The sculpted image of a saint was mounted on the prow, and a gondolier in a gilded uniform, black scarf and sash stood behind it. "Domenico..." she called softly.

"*Si, Suor Maria Theresa. Sbrigati!*" said a gondolier with a scarred, pockmarked face and a freakish smile. Then he made an odd, chuckling noise.

"And who rows with you?"

"*Non preoccuparti!*"

She nodded and led Louisa and Isabella to the boat. Another gondolier dressed exactly like Domenico bowed low to Louisa, uttered a prayer, and helped them all aboard. There were three other gondoliers, five in all; and as they rowed the long black mourning gondola through the oily, refuse feculent water, Louisa and Isabella were seated in the dark, crepe-draped cabin and watched over by two of the gondoliers. Louisa felt uncomfortable with the two heavy-set, sweat-stinking men so close, but at least she could hear Sister Maria Theresa talking outside to the chief gondolier. He kept chuckling; it sounded almost like a cough. Then she heard what she imagined was a hard slap—or, perhaps, oar against bone—and then a splash: dead weight striking dark water. She and Isabella both tried to get up, but the gondoliers, who were as silent as the eunuchs in the airship, held them in their cushioned seats.

"What's happened?" Louisa shouted. "I demand—"

Domenico's pockmarked face appeared between the curtains. "Please do not be distressed, little daughters of light. The one who found you was a traitorous whore."

"What have you done to her?" Louisa asked, still trying to wrest herself free of the gondoliers who seemed implacably, impossibly strong and... uninvolved.

"We do not suffer traitors and heretics," Domenico said.

"Who do you mean by 'we'?"

"Why myself...and the Holy Father, of course." Then he smiled, as if he had just been touched by a saint, and said, "We are taking you to him now, *Filia Lucis.*"

The angel Gabriel parted the infinities of intense white light as if they were curtains, and Pietro and Lucian found themselves standing on the ledge of a cliff that overlooked the yellow-tinged waters of the Dead Sea. A familiar smell of cinnamon wafted around them. To their right and to their left was a vast sweep of calcareous mountains that contained the many hidden caverns of Lucian's Essene community; and far below were thorny shrubs, stunted cypresses, and expanses of pebbles and stones that led to the sulfurous salt lake. Still clutching Lucian's hand, Pietro stepped backward in shock. His club-foot slipped on the gravelly stone, and before he could recover, he struck his head against a marly cliff wall.

"*You'd best train yourself not to be so easily startled now that you are stone*," Gabriel said to Pietro. A wry smile flickered across the angel's perfect face as he floated in the clarified air beyond the ridge, the opalescent ridges of his feathered wings refracting the harsh desert light into soft rainbow shades.

"Stone...?" asked Pietro, rubbing the back of his head.

Gabriel moved closer to Pietro and Lucian, his bare feet just touching the solid rock; and Pietro imagined that the angel's movements were like the smooth shuffling of playing cards. "*Yes, remembrancer, you have become the stone that once burned in your palm.*"

Pietro lifted his hand and looked at it as if it belonged to another. His palm was smooth, creased only by the natural lines of life and fate: the stone had disappeared. Surprised, he looked back at the angel and asked, "What...? What do you mean?"

"*And you, Lucian,*" the angel said, ignoring Pietro's question, "*you have regained the seal that I took away from you. I see that Athoth has gouged a new serpent for you out of the sapphire tablet.*"

Lucian shuddered. "I had hoped it would be your seal, angel. Is it his?"

"*Let's just say it is ours. But now you contain more than the serpent, impetuous thief. Just as your master's skrying stone was transformed—transformed into young Pietro's living flesh and bone and spirit—so has my sapphire tablet been transformed.*"

"*Your* tablet?" Lucian asked.

"*Yes, Lucian, mine...and yours.*" The angel turned to Pietro and smiled sadly. "*The tablet also belongs to you, young ser, just as you belong to Lucian.*"

"*I* don't belong to anyone," Pietro said. "I—"

The angel's soft, tender gaze stopped Pietro's words, just as it could stop his heart. "*Yes, young ser, you* do *belong to him now, just as he belongs to you. But it doesn't stop there: You both belong to me, but that is just a matter of perspective.*"

"I don't understand," Pietro said.

"Nor I," said Lucian.

"*Of course you don't, but you will. Venite filij lucis.*"

Come, sons of light.

And with that Gabriel stepped forward, passing through Pietro and Lucian as if they were made of the same aetheric stuff as angels and sweeping them into the cliff face with him. Overwhelmed with bliss—and a sudden, aching emptiness—Pietro and Lucian reappeared inside a concealed cavern on another cliff face. Lucian recognized this place at once: it was where the sapphire tablet had been hidden. The Cave of Light. He felt a poignant combination of grief and yearning as he wondered if his parents were indeed alive and living in the village hidden beyond the scarps below, as Athoth had promised.

The angel stood in the twilight zone of the cavern before them, himself as ghostly and evanescent as the motes of dust dancing in the dim, misty light. "*And just as you both belong to me and to each other, so do I belong to you,*" he continued as if passing through a mountain of stone should not have distracted them.

"How can that be?" asked Pietro as he gazed around the cavern. He sensed something imminent; but what it was, he did not know.

"*When Lucian stole both parts of the sapphire tablet from Athoth—and when both of you came together to try to stabilize and preserve the boundary that was crashing down upon you in Florence—you sealed your fates as one. You shared what you had taken.*"

"I took the tablet," Lucian said, "but—"

"*And when you did so,*" Gabriel continued, "*you released it, and it chose you, young theurgist.*"

"How can a 'thing' make a choice? Lucian asked. "It may be holy, but it is not a being. It is object not soul."

"*There you are wrong,*" the angel said. "*It is exactly that. It is soul pure and protected. It is…my soul.*"

"No," Lucian said, "souls must reside within—"

"*Within what? Within your breast? Where is the seat of your soul? Within your heart? Your liver?*" The angel rested against the wall of the cavern and, indeed, took on the coloration and substantiality of the stone itself: became a restless, shifting, magnificently beautiful gargoyle. "*Where then would my soul reside, young theurgist? I have no heart. No liver. No soily substance. What you see is but an extension of what we might as well call my soul.*" The angel leaned toward Lucian, frightening him with his proximity. "*If you believe your souls can reside in such temporary casements as earthy flesh, why is it so difficult for you to believe that mine can repose in pristine crystal?*"

"What I can't believe is that you would give your soul to Athoth," Pietro said.

"*Ah, so the remembrancer has recovered himself,*" Gabriel said. "*What do you think would convince Athoth of my intentions?*"

Pietro would not meet the angel's steady gaze.

"*I have nothing else of equal value.*"

"But to give your soul away as if it were nothing more than a jewel for decoration."

"*Ah, but only a fool would wish to steal it.*"

"Do you then call Athoth a fool?" Pietro asked.

"*No, but perhaps my aetheric cousin was not as…bright as he is now.*" Satisfied with his twist of wit, the angel turned to Lucian and smiled sadly: "*And so now, young son of light, you contain my soul—and many others, too.*"

But my spirit also rests within you, Pietro, for the skrying stone—the gazing globe you stole from your master—is of the same stuff as the sapphire tablet."

"I did *not* steal Maestro Mirandola's skrying stone," Pietro insisted, missing the angel's point—or perhaps unable to accept it—and reacting as if he were a child who had just been caught opening his father's purse. "I was only curious to see..."

The angel radiated disappointment: heat wafting from a hearth.

"If it makes you feel better to believe you were but borrowing the stone, then that will have to suffice for now. But the 'thing'—the gazing globe— also...borrowed you, Pietro. It chose you."

"Your soul was also in the gazing globe?" Pietro asked, comprehending. "And you can just divide your soul like...like a loaf of bread?"

The angel laughed heartily at that, and both Pietro and Lucian felt tingling, tickling warmth. *"If the demiurge and his aeons would destroy me, I thought it best to give them some little difficulties."*

"But I cannot sense you within me as I did when we escaped Belias," Lucian said. "I—we—could never contain you."

"You can, and you do. As long as I can retain my senses, I can relieve you from feeling the weight of my soul."

"And if you cannot?"

"Then you must find your own way."

Pietro sensed something again and stared into the cave, into the darkness beyond the twilight zone. An instant later he heard a groaning and the low rumble of a lion. "That cannot be!"

"Come forth, Maestro Mirandola," the angel said. *"Do not fear, you are perfectly safe here."*

Dazed, Pico Della Mirandola stepped forward; and the great tawny lion paced around him, as if guarding him...or protecting him. Pietro could not help but imagine that the lion had somehow become an extension of his master. But he, Pietro, could not sense the lion's thoughts; he felt as blind as Mirandola.

"What are *you* doing here?" Mirandola asked when he saw Pietro and Lucian. "What is this place and—" But the maestro was no longer blind to aetheric creatures and forms, and took a step backward when he saw Gabriel. Then he fell to his knees and tented his hands in prayer.

"No, Maestro, raise yourself," the angel said as he passed into Mirandola and lifted him to his feet. *"Would you pray to the air you breathe, or the voice of the wind that whispers in your ears?"*

For an instant Mirandola's face was a mask of fright; but then, as the angel passed out of and away from him, he regained himself.

"Did you understand what I've been discussing with your former apprentices?" Gabriel asked Mirandola.

"I—yes, I heard what you said, but I didn't understand until you..."

"*Until I lifted you.*"

"Until you passed *into* me, *angelus mirabilis*," Mirandola said. "But this place is not the whiteness I experienced as your heaven. Where are we?"

"*What you call whiteness is my..heaven, if you like. But unformed. This*"—the angel gestured to include the cave and the world around and below—"*is the same, but formed. Like the boundary from which you fled, the boundary that held back Belias' darkness and his soul-seeking creatures.*" Then the angel turned to Lucian and Pietro and bathing them in warmth said, "*The boundary you risked your lives to strengthen and preserve...that you prevented Belias from destroying.*"

"But it *is* destroyed," Pietro insisted. "It has fallen and is now ice and—"

"*And what?*" asked the angel.

"Ice and emptiness," Pietro answered, standing uncomfortably before the angel, afraid to look into his eyes.

Cinnamon wafting like warm sweetness.

"*When you brought those portions of my soul contained within you to the boundary, you strengthened it just enough to weaken Belias.*"

"But how could we—?"

The angel's attention encompassed both Pietro and Lucian.

"*Even with the added strength you brought to the boundary, I could not long hold back the onslaught of Belias and his poisonous familiars. But I could grasp my pound of flesh...or soul. Thus, when Belias and his poisonous familiars attacked the boundary, the boundary also attacked them. The ice and emptiness you describe is Belias himself. Part of his soul, if you like, has been captured by my soul. But make no mistake. Weakened he may be, but he has enough strength to recover.*" The angel's eyes narrowed as he turned his gaze inward. He shivered and for an instant seemed to lose substance. "*In fact, he has already done so.*

"*And, Lucian, what you told Pietro was correct. If you or Pietro had run away from the collapsing boundary, Belias would have destroyed you.*"

"Because of you?" Pietro asked.

The angel nodded, radiating sadness like heat. "*Because you carry the burden of my soul.*"

Lucian took a step toward the opening of the cave. As he looked at the sun-bleached land beyond, he felt the ache of memory and loss. "Is this the same place...the same land where I grew up?" he asked Gabriel.

"*Yes, son of light, the same.*"

"If it is the same stuff as the boundary...is it also your soul? All of this?"

"*It is...me,*" the angel said. "*You now contain the very place where you grew to manhood. It is inside you like a chick in an egg."*

"But that cannot be," Mirandola said.

"Yes, it can," Lucian said, remembering, understanding. He spoke to the angel: "Like Belias, you are both a place—a world—and a being: a god."

"Not a god, Lucian, merely an angel."

"Whether you be god or angel, how can your heaven be part of the world that the demiurge created?" Mirandola asked. "Unless...*you* are a creation of the demiurge."

"No, Maestro, I am not a creation of the aeon you call Demiurge, but his creation is a part of me."

"How can that be?"

"Because he stole it. That is how he created the world that you know, and all the others like it."

"Others...?"

Gabriel shook his head, and Mirandola felt as if he had suddenly lost his tongue. But Lucian hadn't. Unable to help himself, he asked, "Did Athoth lie to me? Are my parents alive? Are they here?"

"No, Athoth did not lie to you," Gabriel said, the sadness in his voice a keening in the air. *"He just tricked you a little."*

"Then my mother and father aren't here," Lucian said, gazing in the direction of his village carved into the scarps.

"No."

"But they are alive...?"

"Inside you," the angel said gently.

"Now *you're* tricking me a little."

"Only a little, son of light, for the truth is too large for you just now."

"Then what truth would be the right size for us?" Mirandola asked.

The angel looked at Mirandola and nodded. *"Your beloved Florence is lost, Maestro. Belias, the new pope, and his bastard son Valentine now rule Florence, Venice, the papal states, and the Anjou Protectorates."*

"Then all is truly lost," Mirandola said.

"Before the lion led you here, you were on your way to Urbino, were you not?"

"My skryer Baldassare was leading his soldiers there, yes, but whether he can—"

"He can and he will."

"You know that?"

The angel smiled and said, *"Yes, Maestro, I know a little."*

"What else do you know?"

"*That Valentine and his troops have already taken Urbino, and Guiliano de Medici, your First Citizen—Florence's real First Citizen—is ill and imprisoned in the palace.*"

"Then Baldassare will be too late."

"*Not if you intercept him.*"

"Me?"

"*Now you are beginning to sound like your youngest apprentice*"—Lucian blushed and looked away from Mirandola—"*who might well be attending you.*"

"But what could *we* do?" Lucian asked.

"*Perhaps tip the balance.*"

Mirandola just stared at the angel who seemed to dissolve into the dim, dust agitated light of the cave.

"*Every soul that Belias takes tips the balance. Valentine is merely the vanguard here. Belias' snaking creatures will follow and devour every soul... eventually even Valentine's.*" For an instant the angel looked as if he were in pain. "*Belias already has his enemy within his grasp.*"

"Athoth?" asked Pietro.

"*You see, remembrancer, you see more than you know. However, you're seeing into the past. Look into the present. What do you see?*"

Pietro closed his eyes. After a beat, he said, "I'm not sure, angel. I see moonlight on water. I see marble towers. Pink gravestones.." He moved his hand across his face, as if to brush away spider webs, then looked at Gabriel, questioning. "I see—"

"*Yes?*"

"An explosion, a terrible explosion. But I can't...I can't see anything more, angel."

"*No matter, remembrancer,*" Gabriel said, his voice soft and comforting. "*I was, in fact, referring to the daughter of light.*"

"But she is only a child," Mirandola said. "How could she be enemy to an aeon?"

"*Why is air the enemy of a fish? Can't you discern who she is?*"

The angel looked at Pietro to answer, but Pietro shook his head.

"*Like you, Maestro, she is still blind to the transfigurations of her soul. But if Belias can take her before she awakens to who she is, all will be lost.*"

"Who is she?" Mirandola asked, insistent.

"*The distressed soul of an aeon who created all you know and see.*"

"Jehovah...the demiurge?"

"*No, maestro, the daughter of light is the aeon who created the demiurge. His aetheric power derives from hers.*"

Mirandola marveled at the idea. "But if he destroys her, he would destroy himself.

"*Or she might destroy him first, which would ruin his...plan.*"

"What is his plan?" Mirandola asked.

The angel turned toward Lucian. "*Have you regained your memory of what I told you in this very place?*" And with a sickening almost physical jolt Lucian remembered and relived everything that happened on that terrible day: the day he had reached his majority. "*So now, finally, you regain yourself, young maskil. Tell the maestro what he wishes to know.*"

Repeating the remembered words of the angel, Lucian said, "The demiurge's plan is to destroy all creation, all that has been, is, and will be."

Gabriel nodded, acknowledging but not lifting the boy's grief.

"Surely, the demiurge would not destroy himself," Mirandola said, addressing himself to Gabriel, as if the angel and not Lucian had just spoken. "He could never hope to destroy the source, the Invisible Spirit, the true creator."

"*Ah, but that would be the pinnacle of power, Maestro: to be able to destroy God and creation itself...to end eternity and destroy oneself, one's own soul.*"

"Perhaps he believes he would survive," Pietro said.

"*Remembrancer, if you are to fulfill your promise, you must learn to face what frightens you and what you do not immediately understand. The demiurge Jehovah needs to possess and then destroy every soul. But the object of his destruction is himself. Only by ending all of creation can he deny the Invisible Spirit. In one final implosion of hubris he can achieve his heart's desire.*"

"Which is...?" asked Mirandola.

"To become the One," Lucian said.

Pietro scowled at Lucian, unable to conceal a momentary flush of jealousy.

"I cannot believe that Belias and the other dark aeons would follow him to that end," Mirandola said. "Not if they knew."

"*Disbelieve if you will, but the demiurge and his aeons...they are all one and the same.*"

"How can that be?" Pietro asked.

"*Because he made it so!*"

"And Athoth, what about him?"

"*He is like me.*"

"But he is, or was, in league with the demiurge—"

For an instant, Pietro could not catch his breath.

"*He is like me,*" the angel repeated, signaling he was unwilling to continue the conversation. Then he turned to Mirandola.

"*Now, Maestro, you must decide what you wish to do.*

"I can but do as you wish, *angelus.*"

"*No*, you *must choose your path, theurgist*."

"Well, what choice do I have but to intercept my skryer, as you suggested?"

"*You could choose to intercept the daughter of light*."

"But how—?"

Gabriel glanced at Lucian and said, "*Your apprentice knows*"; and, indeed, Lucian did know. He felt drawn like a lodestone to the fissure in the stony cave wall that had once held the sapphire tablet, and he remembered a small divination psalm from *The Words of the Heavenly Lights*:

> *I see the gateway for the blessed.*
>
> *I see the walls which hide the stone.*
>
> *For Thee the stone shall open.*
>
> *For Thee to cross its endless space.*

Gingerly, he touched the crevasse where Gabriel had hidden the sapphire tablet and remembered the oily-smooth feel of the sapphire sheet against his fingers...remembered how easily he had slipped it out of its niche...and how it had blazed into a doorway of light when the angel placed it upon an altar deep inside the cave...and he remembered what the angel had said when Lucian stumbled backward, stepping away from its searing radiance. "*You will quickly become used to the light, and you will miss it when it is soon gone*."

Yes, Lucian thought, I miss it even now; and in that instant he—or the angel—transformed memory into light and heat.

The sapphire tablet appeared in a blaze before him, then dimmed and expanded into a doorway of roiling white light perfectly contained. But this time Lucian did not stumble backward. He gazed into the light; and there it was, barely visible, an outline limned in blue: the sapphire bridge that had led him to the daughter of light.

Mirandola gasped and asked, "What is it?"

"*Your bridge to the daughter of light*," Gabriel said, "*or to your skryer*."

"I see only...light."

"*It's there, Maestro. Your apprentice can demonstrate*." The angel smiled. "*Or you can take it on faith*."

"How can I decide what to do, *angelus*? I—"

"*You are a magus. Decide!*"

Mirandola nodded and began to speak, but Pietro interrupted. "Angel, I think I should go with Lucian."

"*So you should*," Gabriel said. "*Do you know why?*"

"I sense that we—the tablet—"

"*Go on, Remembrancer*."

"We would be stronger together."

"*Because of Athoth.*"

"Yes, angel," Pietro said averting his eyes.

"What do you mean, Pietro? Lucian asked. "What about Athoth?"

"*Tell him.*"

"It is as if I'm looking into a gazing globe, but nothing is clear. I just know that the...fortunes of the aeon and the First Citizen are somehow intertwined."

"How?"

Pietro shrugged. "And our fortunes are tied to theirs."

"*Are you afraid to say* fate, *Remembrancer?*"

"Yes, angel, I am afraid..."

"*As well you should be. That still leaves you to decide,*" Gabriel said to Mirandola. "*Or perhaps...perhaps you have already done so.*" The angel watched the great lion sniff like a housecat at the light roiling in the doorway that Lucian had opened and then disappear into it.

Mirandola nodded to the angel and asked, "Is it safe to follow?"

"*I see what your remembrancer sees: destiny, not safety.*"

With that—and a great deal of awkwardness—Mirandola stepped into the light.

The angel turned to Lucian and asked softly, "And you, *maskil*, can you overcome your hatred of Athoth...?"

"I will do what I must," Lucian said, looking away from the angel as he remembered what Athoth had done to his parents; and after a few last words with the angel, Pietro and Lucian reluctantly stepped into the roiling light of the sapphire doorway.

PARTITION FIVE

The Scales of Fate

'Trismegistus, why does the *Canticle of Reversals* speak of the defeat of the Invisible One?'

'Because, Rheginus, my young friend, it describes the aeon Sophia's vision of the entire span of measure and the weight of fate.'

'How could that be, Trismegistus? The Invisible One alone controls fate and measure. Is He not in fact their embodiment?'

'What you say is true, but have you forgotten that the *Canticle* also describes Him as "The Many in the One."'

'And the demiurge, Trismegistus, what then is he?'

'He is the vine that strangles the serpent, the part that poisons the whole.'

'But if what you say is true, Trismegistus, that would imply that the demiurge is part of the Invisible One?'

'Certainly, Reginus, as are you and I and that pretty sapphire ring on your thumb.'

—*Excerpt from the Fifth Discourse 9,1-3*

EIGHTEEN
Smoke and Crystals

I approached a bodily dwelling…and I went in.

—*The Second Discourse of Great Seth 51,20*

Thou best of thieves; who, with an easy key,

Dost open life, and, unperceived by us,

Even steal us from ourselves.

—John Dryden, *All for Love*

The young priest Vincenzo Antellesi thought he saw a lion in the thickening gloom: a mirage, there, high above him on the ancient, powder-gray Roman road that led to the towering stronghold of Urbino. He blinked again, for then something appeared in the overcast sky: a crack that opened and closed as quickly as his eyelid. Vincenzo grimaced and turned away from the sudden sharp incandescence that was so bright that he could see its perpendicular afterimages through the bandage that covered his right eye. Yet no one else turned…no one seemed to notice.

Vincenzo had been marching, or rather climbing, beside his commander Baldassare who kept his troops—which numbered less than three hundred—well away from the narrow road that wound up and around the precarious slopes and recesses of this edge of the eastern Apennines. After Baldassare had lost Lucian, Pietro, and then Mirandola to the boundary that for a time had separated Florence, he made Vincenzo his body servant and kept him close. Vincenzo could not help but feel that Baldassare somehow blamed him for the loss of his men and horses at the *Ponte Vecchio* Bridge. In fact, he felt more like a prisoner of war than a sworn and sanctified Dominican guard.

"What is it?" Baldassare asked him.

"Nothing, Lord Spiritual," Vincenzo said.

"You saw *something*." Baldassare noticed the clean dressing that covered the boy's right eye: no doubt the barber had attended him again because his broken fingers were splinted and covered with new linen. "Something made you flinch, and your pimply face is white as a winding sheet."

Vincenzo blushed, then said, "I thought I saw something on the high road. But it must have been a trick of the light."

"What did you see?"

"It looked like a lion, Excellency."

Baldassare tried to see what the priest saw. Indeed, it must have been a trick of the shifting light. He craned his neck, looking up toward the heavens, searching, and asked: "Did you see anything else? *Anything...?*"

The priest bowed his head and stared at the gravel scattered around his feet as if the igneous rays that enabled sight could burn right through stone. "I thought I saw something flash across the sky. But it could only be illusion, Lord Spiritual. Like the lion I thought I saw."

Baldassare turned back to Vincenzo and said, "Illusion? From someone who claims to see what others cannot...who can see aetheric creatures and protect himself from their deadly influences?"

Vincenzo shuddered and said, "No, Lord Spiritual, I was *not* able to protect myself. And *you* can see the creatures that dwell in the aether as well as I."

Baldassare looked at him with dawning respect—*perhaps the hobbledehoy has a spine, after all.*

"Did you see anything, Lord Spiritual?"

"No, *Padre*, but I sensed something—"

"Yes, Excellency?"

"I don't think I am quite ready to make you my confidant," Baldassare said, feeling a familiar, uncomfortable presence. He called to his second-in-command Jacopo di Pecori to discuss whether they might be able to reach the Hermitage of the Zoccolanti before nightfall, but Jacopo could not be found.

"Where *is* he?" Baldassare demanded.

"He was just called away, Lord Spiritual," said one of his officers; his voice lisped through broken front teeth. "Something important about—there, Excellency," the guard said, pointing, "There he is now"; and indeed Jacopo di Pecori was hurrying toward him pulling two boys in tow.

Pietro and Lucian.

"Maestro Mirandola's young apprentices have something to tell you, Excellency," Jacopo said. He held onto both boys as if they might suddenly decide to escape.

"Kindly ask your underling to unhand us," Pietro said. "He's hurting us."

"*Underling?*" Jacopo said, grasping the boys' arms even tighter.

"Restrain your insolence and respect your betters, young ser."

When Pietro bowed his head and begged forgiveness, Baldassare gestured to Jacopo to let them go. After ordering his other officers to leave, he said, "There may soon come a time when your superiors will not be so gentle with you."

"Yes, Excellency, pray forgive me," Pietro said.

Baldassare responded with the customary benediction: "*Vos es venia.*"

Pietro nodded to the young priest Vincenzo—*Why is Baldassare keeping him by his side?*—who nodded back and nervously shifted his weight from one foot to the other.

Baldassare looked to Lucian and asked, "Tell me what news you carry."

"The pope's bastard has—"

Pietro felt Jacopo's gloved hand on his neck.

"We've come to warn you that the *condottiere* Valentine has taken Urbino and its castle," Lucian said quickly.

Jacopo laughed hoarsely. "Impossible! We have no intelligence that the castle and the First Citizen have been captured."

"Belias and the new pope have won," Pietro said.

"If that is indeed true, then all is lost," Vincenzo said.

"Maestro Mirandola said the same thing," Lucian said, "but Gabriel believes there is a chance."

"You saw the angel?" Baldassare asked. "And Mirandola, too? Where?"

"In heaven," Pietro said.

Lucian scowled at Pietro, and then explained to Baldassare what had happened to them since they parted company. When Lucian was done, Baldassare merely nodded. After a long moment he asked Vincenzo, "What do *you* think, Padre?"

"Me...?"

Baldassare waited.

"I don't know what to think, except..."

"Yes?"

"That now it is not even safe to go to the hermitage."

"Why?"

"You told me that the duke of Urbino often retreats to the hermitage to study and pray. Surely the *condottiere* Valentine would know that and secure the hermitage before climbing the road to the fortress."

"Whatever troops we may have are waiting for us there upon your order," Jacopo said to Baldassare. "Our only chance is to rendezvous as planned."

"Can we reach the hermitage tonight?"

"Yes, I think so. The moon should provide enough light, but these heights are treacherous."

Baldassare nodded and then turned to Vincenzo. "Tell the maestro's apprentices what you saw."

"What *we* saw."

"I saw very little," Baldassare said, "and you, like the clubfoot, begin to take liberties above your rank."

Pietro felt a hot flush of anger crawl across his face and neck, but said nothing: Baldassare would keep baiting him until he was satisfied that Pietro was truly contrite.

"I saw the sky open," Vincenzo said to Pietro and Lucian.

"You saw Gabriel's sapphire tablet," Lucian said.

"The tablet carried you here?" Vincenzo asked. "That is the bridge you spoke of?"

"You also saw it as the boundary," Lucian continued. Then, to Baldassare: "It is the same stuff as the gazing globe you used to peer into. Now it belongs to Pietro."

"Reveal it," Baldassare said to Pietro.

Pietro extended his hand and said, "I cannot, Lord Spiritual, for it has disappeared into my flesh." Baldassare hesitated and then gingerly touched the smooth surface of his palm: the bone-hard, key-shaped stone had indeed disappeared, as had the raised red weal that resembled a curled snake.

"If you are truly a remembrancer, then reveal what must pass," Baldassare said; yet he spoke in a low, more respectful tone.

"I glimpsed something when we were attending the angel." Pietro looked to Lucian, as if for affirmation; but Lucian only said, "Continue, *Memoria*. I did not penetrate your vision." Pietro nodded. "Just as I told the angel, I saw that the fortunes of the aeon Athoth and the First Citizen are somehow bound together."

"Once again both of you invoke the demiurge's angel," Baldassare said, crossing himself; Vincenzo and Jacopo did the same. "I will not stand here and believe that Gabriel would commerce with—"

"The aeon is not as he was," Lucian said, feeling revulsion and hatred even as he said it. "That's what Gabriel and the sapphire tablet have been all about: to turn Athoth toward us. You must trust us on this, *Mignolo*. The aeon truly is our ally—"

"*What* did you just call me?" Baldassare asked: His blessed and long dead father had nicknamed him *Mignolo*.

Little Finger.

"The words just…came out of my mouth, Excellency."

Baldassare felt a slight vibration around his neck, felt the old uncomfortable connection with the boy: *The twisted Jew had stolen my soul, and still I am in his embrace.*

"If I've caused offence, Excellency, please, I apologize with all my heart."

It was rare for the blush to come to Baldassare's cheeks. He looked away from Lucian and directed himself to Pietro: "What of Athoth, then? Will he help us?"

"I think first we must help him."

"Speak straight, child, not in riddles."

"You have looked into my master's gazing globe, Excellency. What do *you* do when it is clouded?"

"Tell me what little you do see, then."

"Athoth and the First Citizen have both been captured. They are both in mortal danger."

"An aeon in mortal danger? I think you might still be more clubfoot than remembrancer."

Pietro started to speak, but thought better of it and bowed his head.

"Although aeons are immortal, their substance can be transformed and diminished, Lucian said. "And just as Belias can swallow our souls, so can he swallow Athoth."

"What else does your vision tell you?" Baldassare asked Pietro.

"If we can free the First Citizen, we free the aeon."

"And how are we to do that?"

"By climbing to the castle. We cannot overcome the castle with numbers, only with guile. But a few men just might be able to rescue the First Citizen." After a beat he said, "That's what I saw in my vision, Excellency: I saw shadows climbing to the castle."

"Fra Baldassare, we must leave now for the hermitage," Jacopo insisted. "While we waste our time with the cripple, we lose the light."

Pietro knew better than to respond; he simply clenched and unclenched his fists.

"What else did you see, *Memoria*?" Baldassare asked, ignoring his lieutenant.

"You were one of those shadows, Excellency. And I can also point out the others who appeared in my vision. I...know who they are."

Baldassare nodded.

"Lord Spiritual," Jacopo said. "*Please!*"

Baldassare felt the connection with Lucian break—as if the pressure of elevation had been relieved in his sinuses—and he dismissed Jacopo. "You will get your way, crucifer. Once I have taken the men I need, you'll lead the rest to the hermitage and determine whether it is safe or not. I leave all that to you—"

"But—"

"—and you will wait my signal. Tell no one what is afoot and sleep in the dirt without fire if you have any anxiety that there is unusual activity. If I cannot get word to you by the first cast of dawn, you may engage the enemy as you see fit."

"*If* there is an enemy," Jacopo said, nodding curtly to Pietro. "Still, Lord Spiritual, I would go with you."

"No, crucifer, I need you strong if we fail," and with that Baldassare looked to Pietro and Lucian. Pietro averted his eyes, but Lucian said to Jacopo: "Forgive my insolence, but if you must fight, you…"

"Yes, go on, tell him what you have to say," Baldassare said.

"You must somehow numb yourselves," Lucian continued. "If you do not—if there are aetheric vines present—then they will gladly capture your souls and leave you to fight on the side of the enemy."

Jacopo laughed and shook his head. "And how would you suggest that I benumb myself and my men?"

"I know of a potion that might work," Lucian said. "It numbs and shadows the heart."

"And what is this potion called?"

Lucian paused and said, "It is known as *Datura stramonium*."

"You mean Devil's Weed," Baldassare said sourly. "I would not feed such poison to my men. Would you have them all seeing visions of the Naked Virgin instead of the enemies that might await them?"

"Yes, crucifer, I would have them benumbed," Lucian said, "benumbed enough to resist the Adversary. If your men succumb to the bloodlust of combat, the aetheric creatures that appear to us as vines will take their souls. You will have no chance, that is certain. No, crucifer, to conquer, you and your men must kill without feeling or sensation."

"Like wreaths…like the vines themselves."

Lucian nodded.

"And you have enough of this potion to…protect all the men?"

"I can compound enough to shadow their souls, but once taken, the salutary effects will not last long."

"How long?"

"No more than a quarter of an hour."

"That is not enough," Baldassare said.

"If I increase the dose, it might release the madness of dreams."

Baldassare looked at Jacopo and then told Lucian to make the preparation. "You will go to the hermitage with my crucifer, young theurgist, and attend to their welfare. And you'd best prepare enough of this potion for my men…in case the need arises." Then he turned to Pietro: "And *you* will point out to me the 'shadows' you saw in your vision."

Pietro started to say "But I saw Lucian climbing with us to—" and then realized he had only *assumed* that Lucian was one of the shadows in his vision.

"Well?" asked Baldassare.

"Nothing, Excellency," Pietro said. "I saw you, the priest Antonio...and you, too, Padre Vincenzo."

"Surely not me," Vincenzo said, looking pale.

"I also saw him," Pietro said, pointing out the officer with the broken teeth.

Baldassare nodded. "Take the Padre and find the others you saw in your vision. Tell them to report to me immediately."

Within the hour Lucian was heading west toward the Hermitage of the Zoccolanti with Jacopo di Pecori and his troops, while Pietro was climbing with Baldassare and fifteen 'shadows' toward the stronghold of Urbino.

And above, lying still as the broken stones in a misting mountain crag, a lion caught Pietro's familiar, musky scent.

Sister Maria Theresa da Rieti had been standing behind the black *felze* cabin of the gondola with the pox-faced gondolier Domenico who was, in fact, a mendicant priest and trusted agent of her superior, the prioress of the convent of Santa Sophia dei Miracoli. She had always felt uncomfortable with this man whose scarred cheeks pulled the corners of his mouth into a grotesque smile.

"Does Prioress Christina have further instructions for me?" she asked.

"No, sister," Domenico said—he also had an unnerving habit of chuckling after he spoke: a nervous disorder—"your task is complete."

"Not until I have delivered the daughter of light and her companion to the prioress."

"Ah, but your task was to deliver the little daughters of light to *me*." His eyes narrowed as he chuckled.

Maria Theresa noticed his gaze shift. It was a subtle thing, and then she glimpsed a quick movement behind her. She sidestepped reflexively and felt a thud across her back and neck that had been aimed at her head. She felt throbbing, vibrating pain, which turned to numbness, and saw the oarsman who bludgeoned her with his oar twisting in the canal-stinking night air. But it was she who was twisting and falling into the cold black water; and as she fell—even as she smelled the offal that perfumed and floated on the water—she imagined that she could hear Domenico blessing her from above: "*Your reward*" chuckle "*awaits you*" chuckle "*below*." She held her breath and sank into the feculent water…she held her breath until she thought her lungs would burst, lest Domenico and his men think her alive. Even though her eyes were closed to relieve the acid sting of the polluted water, she saw pinpoints of light; and her chest hurt so much that whatever the consequences, she had to surface. Taking a deep, gasping breath, she looked around and was almost struck by another gondola. The gondoliers, dressed in festival colors of red and blue stripe, shouted "*A-oel!*", which meant "Look out!" while a young man wearing a gold mask and smelling of wine, sweat, and pungent perfume, reached out to her and—with the help of his companion—pulled her aboard.

"Well," the young man said, slurring his words slightly, "we've caught a fish, hey, Alfonso. Why, it's a *girl* fish."

The other man, Alfonso, who was unmasked and did not seem as drunk as his friend, steadied Maria Theresa and helped her into the sumptuously furnished, curtained cabin. A single small lamp cast a guttering roseate light, and a beautiful, half-dressed courtesan retreated behind satin curtains but did not pull them closed. Maria Theresa sat down, or rather collapsed, onto a pallet of gold and silver brocaded velvet cushions.

"You're hurt," said Alfonso as he applied a cloth to Maria Theresa's neck, which was bloody and bruised. Maria Theresa remembered brushing against the forked stump of an oarlock when she fell. Her head, shoulders, and back were already aching, swelling, and bruising black and purple. "What happened to you?"

She thought quickly; and rather than pretend to faint, she said, "The gondola I was riding in collided with another. The gondoliers were screaming at each other and then began to fight, and I was struck with an oar. That's all I can remember."

"Shocking," said the man in the mask who squatted opposite Maria Theresa. He had a full mouth, a rather weak chin, and a patrician accent. "But you're… dressed in men's clothing. Not a very clever disguise, I think…not with your hair, pretty sprite." Maria Theresa's plait had come loose in the water, and her long, blond ringlets were plastered against her face and shoulders. "Now are you *sure* you're telling us the complete truth?" he continued, smiling. "Might the real truth have something to do with an act that might be…*au rebours*, as they say? A jealous lover, perhaps? After all, all forms of love are countenanced during *Carnivale*."

"Leave her be," Alfonso said.

"*I* know who she is," said the young woman, parting the curtains and leaning forward. "She is a nun from the Miracoli Convent and the Count Ammirato's paramour. Isn't that right, sister?"

"Who are *you*?" asked Maria Theresa.

"Katerina Vescolli." She laughed and said, "And I'm a whore, but at least I admit it." The man in the gold mask crawled toward the woman, pulled her *gamurra* undergarment open, and before closing the curtain invited Maria Theresa to join them.

"Forgive my friend," Alfonso said. "We've been to a wedding celebration and—"

"I would be in your debt if you could take me to Rio di Cannaregio," Maria Theresa said. "It's not far."

"You see, I told you," said Katerina from behind the curtains. "She wants to go to the convent."

"Then so she shall," Alfonso said; but as he called to the gondoliers, he slid his hand between Maria Theresa's legs and deftly pulled away the laces that attached her woolen stockings to her doublet. "By the time we reach the shore, sweet sister, you may consider the debt paid in full."

Although it was late, the prioress received Maria Theresa immediately in her private rooms. The old woman looked like she hadn't slept in days: her white, coarse hair hung in a disheveled braid over her shoulder; her skin, wrinkled and textured like parchment, had a pallor Maria Theresa had not seen before; and there were deep shadows under her startling, piercing green eyes. Those eyes and the strong, yet delicate architecture of her face were all that remained of her legendary beauty. She sat at a table piled with papers, books, and scrolls and motioned Maria Theresa to sit down on the bench beside her. An armillary sphere hung over the table, as if it could give off its own light, and the plashing sounds of water whispered through an open arched window. "You failed, daughter," the old woman said matter-of-factly as she riffled through the quartos on her desk. Maria Theresa could not help but notice that the pages were covered with musical notations. The prioress composed as well as played. "Well...?"

"Yes, mother, I failed."

"The theurgist will attend you forthwith. In the meantime, remove your wet clothes." She nodded toward a large cassone beside her bed. "Take one of my woolen robes and a scapula." As Maria Theresa changed clothes, the prioress said, "I pray you have broken no bones."

"I don't think so, mother."

"Are you in pain?"

"Yes, mother."

"Good. You look terrible."

"As do you, mother."

The prioress looked up at Maria Theresa and smiled. "At my age it is of no difference whether I appear to be in or out of health. One is as ghastly as the other." She paused, then said, "It wasn't your fault, Maria Theresa…it's mine."

"How could you know that—"

"I received word as soon as that traitorous bastard Domenico delivered the daughters of light to the new pope." She patted an hourglass on her desk as if it were a pet. "He will soon be floating in a canal, but that is of little consequence…except to me. He succeeded and I failed."

"He was your agent for many years."

"He was more than that," the prioress said. "He was my flesh and blood."

Maria Theresa looked surprised.

"He was my youngest brother, child, and I won't be able to bring him back…at least not to this world." She sighed and said, "But we must bring back the daughter of light, and quickly, or all will be lost. There might be a way."

"Yes?"

"If you are whole and entire…and able." The prioress pulled a bell-string on the wall beside her desk, and, immediately, there was a knock on the door. "*Avanti*," said the prioress, and an old man whom Maria Theresa knew to be the prioress's private theurgist and skryer entered and bowed. "Examine our wounded dove," said the prioress, "and then be so kind as to unlock the gazing crystal."

"Are you sure?"

The prioress glowered at the theurgist. "I am sure, now attend to the girl."

The theurgist directed Maria Theresa to a bench chest with scrolled arms that sat in the far corner of the room and, after much probing, pushing, squeezing, and applications of salves and bandages to the wounds on her back and shoulders, he said, "Mother Allesandra, the appearance is worse than the injuries. But she was very lucky; if she had been struck a finger's width on either side"—he drew his brown fingernail across the bandage he had affixed to her neck and spine—"she would be paralyzed." He patted her paternally. "Now you must remember to dress your wounds daily with the white of an unblemished egg and ointment of *Apostolican*. If you fail to do this, they will turn pustulant and—"

"Marin…the gazing crystal," interrupted the prioress.

"The grace of God be upon you," the theurgist said to Maria Theresa as he crossed the room to the heavy *prie-dieu* that stood beside the bed. He knelt upon the kneeling step and, after a brief hesitation, mumbled something in a guttural language that sounded more like a cough than a prayer. The solid walnut base suddenly seemed to shimmer like water in a lake. With a quick darting motion, his hands penetrated the surface and he pulled out a small tablet that Maria Theresa imagined was a blue-tinged mirror. But it was not a mirror. It was a perfectly smooth, thin wafer of sapphire. She had heard of substances that took on the appearance of pure crystal. They were said to be celestial keys: the captured souls of aerial beings more powerful than angels.

"Do you wish me to read the crystal, Holy Mother?" the theurgist asked.

"No, Marin, that won't be necessary. I am giving it to Maria Theresa."

"You are going to do *what*?" asked the theurgist, forgetting himself. He held the crystal so tightly in his trembling hands that if it were any ordinary substance it would have cracked or splintered into pieces.

"What am *I* to do with it, Mother?" asked Maria Theresa.

"You are to give it to someone who can deliver it to the daughter of light."

"And who might that be?" asked the theurgist.

"Marin, remember your place!" the prioress said harshly, but she looked gently at him, as one old lover upon another. Turning to Maria Theresa, she said, "You will deliver it to the archbishop of Florence. You should remember his face. You were introduced to him at the *Basilica Papale*, and he—"

"*Miserere nostril Deus!*" Maria Theresa said. "You would gift the man who murdered the entire congregation in the Duomo...who murdered the First Citizen and abducted the daughter of light. The filth who worships the Adversary and is catamite to his angel Athoth."

"I know very well what he did. I also know that men, gods, and angels are not always what they seem; and sometimes they are not always what they were."

"He's a murderer," Maria Theresa insisted.

"So am I...and so are you."

"Not like—"

"When you see the archbishop, you can ask him to explain himself," the prioress said. "In the meantime you must trust me as I have trusted you. Or would you fail the daughter of light again?"

"You must not allow the crystal to be removed from its seat," the theurgist insisted.

"I can, and I will...and you, Marin, will accompany Sister Maria Theresa. And protect her as best you can."

"From whom...the archbishop?" Maria Theresa asked. "Pray, Mother, let me take the crystal to the daughter of light directly. I can find her, if anyone can. She knows who I am, and I know the secret tunnels into the papal palace."

"Even with the aid of Marin's hermetic arts, which are considerable," the prioress said, "you would not stand a chance of reaching the daughter of light. The new pope's protective magicks are too powerful. His Angevin theurgist has contaminated the palace with all manner of *bruta animalia*...noxious demons that would blind you and bind you. And after the Angevin had captured your intelligence, he would feed your souls to the vines that, in turn, feed Belias and the Demiurge."

Marin made the sign of the serpent upon the sapphire wafer he was holding, but as he squinted into the crystal, his expression changed to fear.

"What is it?" the prioress asked.

"We have been found out," Marin said, staring at the crystal as if he were looking into a window. The papal guards are already in the building."

They could hear shouting and screaming and the thunder of footsteps.

The prioress stood up. "Then we will deal with them."

"No, Allesandra," Marin said, "there will be no dealing with them."

She met his gaze and nodded. "Give Maria Theresa the crystal."

After a slight hesitation, Marin handed it over; and as he did so, there was a pounding on the door.

"You must try to climb down, if you can," the prioress said to Maria Theresa. She gestured toward the window.

"But what about you and—?"

Someone shouted, "*Apri la porta!*"

"Give us the heretic whore, holy sister, and you'll be spared."

"Hurry," said the prioress as soldiers pounded on the door.

"*Apri la porta!*"

"But if I manage to escape, how do I find the archbishop…if he is, indeed, alive?"

"If you have the crystal, he will find you. Now *go!*"

Before slipping the tablet into her jerkin, Maria Theresa glimpsed flames rushing across its surface: a doleful augury. And suddenly she felt the true weight of the crystal tablet. Its size and dimension belied its enervating influence on its bearer. She looked at the prioress for one last time, then clambered out the arched window just seconds before the soldiers smashed through the door.

As she climbed down the wall, pulling herself out of line of sight and bloodying her hands on the rough siliceous bricks, she heard the theurgist cry "*Benedictus Deus*"…and later, she heard the screams and saw the thick smoke rising from the flames that enveloped the convent.

NINETEEN

Lodestones

O, strong of heart, go where the road
Of ancient honor climbs.

—Boethius

For Thee the stone shall open.
For Thee to cross its endless space.

—*The Words of the Heavenly Lights, 7.14*

As Pietro climbed toward the fortress town of Urbino, which was silhouetted against a purple streaked twilight sky, Lucian struggled to keep pace with the forced yet stealthy march of Jacopo's soldier priests. Baldassare's second-in-command had divided his men into 'banners' of twenty-five, and the twelve autonomous units slipped quietly on foot through the long-shadowed, darkening countryside. Should they be seen by anyone who had quit the well-trodden trails or highroads, be it man, woman, or child, they were under orders to execute the unfortunate. Luckily, there were no such reports.

The troops reached the thick wood below the vineyards and cemetery of the hermitage of the Capuchin Friars. Jacopo sent scouts to reconnoiter and then, finally, acknowledged Lucian. "Take some water, child, but not too much."

But Lucian didn't need water. He simply needed more time to regain his strength after he and Pietro had tried—and failed—to preserve the boundary that had divided Florence.

"Can you smell it?" Jacopo asked Lucian.

The wind had changed, and Lucian smelled roasted meat. He salivated, even as his stomach rolled.

"They're burning bodies," Jacopo said, his gravelly voice little more than a whisper. He cracked a branch in two with one hand, the only evidence of his anger and frustration and called one of his officers to make sure the men were settled. "They must be assured by their officers and decurions that everything is under control…and that all will be clarified in due course." The officer nodded and left, quiet as a ghost.

"And you, young alchemist," he said to Lucian, "keep close to me. I may have need of you."

"For what, ser?"

But Jacopo did not answer. He stood motionless in the oak wood as the shadows lengthened into darkness, and the glow cast by unseen pyres seemed to be reflected in the storm-clouded sky that turned the rising moon into a purplish smear. Lucian rested his back against a tree and inhaled the faint odor of roasting flesh combined with the dry scents of forest and earth. He nervously squeezed and reshaped a small leather purse of powders, balsams, unguents, and alexipharmacum stones as if he was manipulating a rosary. Fireflies blinked like stars, small animals scurried through undergrowth, and occasional muted human sounds filtered through the air. Drunken laughter and swearing.

"*Via a cagare.*"

"*Va' a fare in culo.*"

"*Fottiti!*"

Hours later a soft voice whispered, "*Cancelliere.*"

"I can see you, Fra Sassetta, and I eagerly await your survey report; but tell me, why have you hidden a child there"—Jacopo shifted his gaze, indicating direction—"by the creek bed?"

The black-robed soldier made a 'phutting' sound and gestured toward his follower. "He's not a child, *Cancelliere*, he's a—"

"I can see now what he is," Jacopo said impatiently.

A dwarf stepped gingerly out of the shadows. Although he appeared to be bruised and dirty, he was dressed in house-carl's livery: a shot-taffeta shirt, a knee-length velvet *mantello* tunic with side openings for his arms, and green and white hose. The white stripes of his hose and the front of his shirt had been darkened with charcoal; in the partial moonlight, he looked for all the world like the fabled green man of the wood.

"Who do you belong to, little man?" Jacopo asked.

"To myself, none other," the dwarf said fiercely. "I am neither slave nor wyvern. But my fealty is to the noble mistress of Montefeltro, just as it was to my Lord Guidabaldo, the legitimate ruler of Urbino. I was his servant and advisor."

"Was?"

The dwarf looked as if he were made of stone, implacable stone, "He was murdered by Borgia's executioner. Murdered right in front of his queen, Signoria Elizabetta."

"And how would you know this?"

"Because I was there! Oh, that pretty son of a whore Valentino pretended it was a terrible misinterpretation of his orders. He swore on the church that the perpetrators would be drawn and quartered. He purred and cooed and begged for the Madonna's forgiveness. He swore on the Pope's soul that no harm would ever come to her or to any citizen of Urbino... And he also promised she would not lack for fucking."

The dwarf spat. "*Pote de Cristo, guzzo, mariulo!*"

Christ's cunt, brigand, thief!

"But you abandoned her and ran," Jacopo said.

"Valentino would not allow the Queen to leave, but I am of no consequence...and I am, as you remarked, small. I escaped when I overheard that Florentine soldier priests were sighted. That was two days ago. I thought to warn them, but I was too late."

"And I am to believe that?" Jacopo said.

The dwarf shrugged and said, "Believe what you will."

Jacopo's officer said, "*Cancelliere*, I believe he speaks the truth. He slit the throat of a guard who spied me and my lancers in the wood, and...he also saved me from stepping into a pike-hole."

"I see no sword on your belt, dwarf," Jacopo said.

"A knife suffices me, ser; and I prefer to be called by my name. Achille Bentivogli." He made a quick, snapping motion with his arm, and as if by magic a double-spiked dagger appeared in his left hand.

Jacopo didn't smile, but nodded with respect.

"We've seen the pyres, *Cancellier*," said Fra Sassetta. "And the papal encampments."

"How many of our soldiers are dead?" Jacopo asked Bentivogli, ignoring his officer. "They couldn't all be—"

"They fought with courage, holy captain, but the *stronzo* Valentino was well prepared. He murdered them at the passes and threatened to kill the peasants and their families if they didn't keep him abreast of any strangers traversing the land."

"But surely he could not have killed or captured *all* our soldiers," Jacopo said, his voice so gravelly with anger that he seemed to be speaking in another dialect.

"They are dead, holy captain. Those he captured were tortured for information. His lancers were offered a gold florin for every head they took. They combed the woods. Valentino must feel secure, for he has sent most of his troops back to the fortress atop *Pian del Monte*. Only a small garrison of his trusted guards remains here." The dwarf spat again. "It's a humiliation for us all. For your holy soldiers dead and burning"—he nodded toward the pyres burning inside the grounds of the hermitage—"and for our duchy and the ancient House of Montefeltro.

"We welcomed him as an ally, and he took us as easily as Joshua took Jericho. All he had to do was fire a few cannon shots at the castle and march his Spanish cunt mercenaries around the city."

The laughter and shouting and swearing of Valentino's troops had become louder and more constant. A great flash of lightning lit the forest, ravines, vineyards, and the fortified walls of the hermitage, followed by rolling thunder. Lucian felt a spatter of rain on his face. An instant later, pelting rain.

"How small?" Jacopo asked, seemingly oblivious to the downpour.

The dwarf shrugged, pulling up the collar hood of his tunic . "Perhaps five hundred men here and the same number at the Palazzo Ducale."

"And he didn't think that more of us would come?"

"The son of a whore has conquered Florence, Pisa, Lucca, and Modena; and his main force at Pian del Monte numbers some ten thousand paid *condotti*. He's killed your priests to a man, and he has the dark cloud that steals souls at his command. No, *Cancelliere*, I don't think he fears your Dominican Companions of the Night."

"You have seen the vines?"

"No, but I hear the stories of the country folk. One of their healers who claims to have the sight swears he saw them. The peasants are superstitious. And terrified."

Jacopo turned to his lieutenant and said, "Matteo, we might well have been seen and reported."

"No one reported seeing anyone, *Cancelliere*," Sassetta said.

"That's of no import. They could well have seen us."

"It's possible," said the dwarf, "but you came through the northeast passes and kept away from paths and roads. The peasants go into those woods only when necessary; because it's dark even in the day, they believe it's haunted by shades and ghouls."

Jacopo nodded, then, after an uncharacteristic hesitation, asked, "And what of Lord Guidabaldo's...guest?"

"If you mean your Lord Guiliano Medici, then, yes, *Cancelliere*, he was alive when I left the castle. But my queen told me that after he heard how his wife and children had died in the cathedral, he begged the Borgia pig to kill him."

"And where is the First Citizen being kept, Ser Achille?"

"I accompanied my queen to pray with him in the king's *studiolo*. It contains a small chapel. He is imprisoned there with all the courtesies due his rank, but very well guarded."

Jacopo nodded in relief. "So he is in the palace, not the fortress."

"He could well have been moved by now," Achille said. "But what difference could that make to you, *Cancelliere*?"

"Do you wish revenge for your king?"

"I wish to free my queen and rid my country of the pestilence that now rules it."

Jacopo nodded. "How well do you know the troop emplacements in and around the hermitage here and...the palace?"

The dwarf smiled. "The moon will soon escape from the clouds, *Cancelliere*, and I will make you a map."

"Are you also an aereomancer, that you can foretell the weather?"

"One does not have to be a theurgist to know local conditions. Just observant."

Jacopo laughed at that, a dry laugh, more a cough; and, indeed, the downpour had stopped and the storm clouds were scudding northward. "Then leave us and do your work, aereomancer. Fra Sassetta will watch over you." But before he dismissed them, he embraced his officer and whispered something into his ear. Then to the dwarf: "We will consider you a friend, Ser Achille. But should you prove yourself to be otherwise, I will not need a blade to tear out your heart."

The dwarf bowed and followed Sassetta into the moon shadows.

"And the time has come for you to prove your worth, too, child," he said to Lucian. "I will need enough of your Devil's Weed to benumb and protect all my men for at least half of an hour."

"*Cancelliere*, with all respect, I already explained to you and Fra Baldassare that such a dose risks madness. It could be as dangerous as the vines it is meant to—"

"And after you distribute your, ah, protective balm to all of us, I presume there will be enough of the substance left for another dosage, should it be necessary."

"Yes, but..."

"But what, theurgist?"

"Didn't Fra Baldassare order you to await his signal before taking any action?" Lucian asked.

"And I await his signal even now."

But Lucian didn't hear what Jacopo said; he dropped his leather purse, groaned, and pressed his palms against his temples.

"What is it, child?"

"It's Fra Baldassare. He's..."

"He's what? Tell me what you see?"

Lucian concentrated on the images fluorescing behind his closed eyelids, then staggered backwards. His legs gave way, and with a gasp he fell into crimson pain and vertiginous darkness.

Hidden in the darkness beside Baldassare and the priest Vincenzo, Pietro gazed upward with trepidation at the looming bulk of the ducal palace. It was a man-made outcrop of the hillside salient, a fortress of dusty brick and stone pocked with arrow loops and square putlog holes and crowned with spiked merlons. Although the city of Urbino with its piazzas, arcades, towers, domes, and tiered loggie descended from the palace in steep angles and narrow, labyrinthine steps and declines, Pietro could not see it. But he could see the gaping hole and protruding window spikes just below the wall walk where Valentine's cannon had struck one of the garderobe toilets. The stink from the toilet and the cesspit mingled with the smells of damp earth, hay, and stale gunpowder.

"Ready yourselves," Baldassare whispered.

Pietro nodded as he watched Lucca Parenti—the officer with the lisp and broken front teeth—direct five of his lancers to the wall. Parenti was wearing the green and yellow uniform of a papal guard whose throat he had slit moments ago. His lancers looked like menials in their loose shirts, doublets, and unattached hose. Each man carried a sectional ladder, which they expertly joined together with leather bands to form an escalade: the top rung just reached the twisted window spikes of the garderobe. One at a time, they climbed, each squeezing past the dangerous iron spikes, and into the window. After a few minutes Parenti signaled an all-clear to Baldassare, who directed the rest of the men to cross over a bridge of rubble to the wall. The men climbed quickly and efficiently; they had all learned their siege craft the hard way. Pietro followed the priest Vincenzo, but had difficulty climbing the escalade because of his game leg; Baldassare prodded him impatiently.

As Pietro neared the spikes that jutted from the window, he felt his throat close. He gagged on the overpoweringly concentrated stink of feces and urine.

"Hurry, we're exposed," Baldassare whispered as Pietro hesitated before slipping over and between the spikes, which were encrusted with dried shit.

Pietro climbed through the twisted and broken window grill, then dropped down to the safety of the debris-littered stone floor. As he backed away from the opening to give Baldassare room to lower himself, he reached for the pomander around his neck and pressed it tightly against his mouth and nose.

"*Sei un finocchio…?*" one of the lancers whispered to Pietro.

"*Are you a cock-quean fairy…?*"

Humiliated, Pietro slipped his pomander into his doublet as he reached for his dagger; but Baldassare stayed his hand and told the whippet-faced lancer to respect his betters and regard his own business. The lancer bowed in submission, begged forgiveness, and backed away into the shadows. Although Pietro appreciated the ironic twist in Baldassare's words, he made no acknowledgement. While the last two lancers, who were perched precariously on a ledge, pulled up the escalade and quickly and efficiently maneuvered the ladder sections through the window, the gap toothed lieutenant asked Baldassare's permission to reconnoiter and discover where the First Citizen was being held. Lucca Parenti was a good choice: he had once accompanied a Florentine delegation to the ducal castle when he was a young corporal; and as a consequence of chasing ladies' maids and servant girls for favors, he became familiar with the palace's labyrinth of torch-lit corridors and pitch-dark shortcuts.

"Take as many men as you need," Baldassare said.

"It's safer if I reconnoiter alone, Lord Spiritual. "I can slip through the passageways unnoticed. But if I am not back by the first call of Matins, then—"

Baldassare dismissed his lieutenant with a nod, ordered half his guards to take defensive positions where three corridors joined outside the garderobe, and positioned two guards by the doorway: they stood in the flickering shadows, their 'ox-tongue' short swords drawn. The laddermen broke the ladder down into sections that could quickly be rejoined and placed them against a wall where they would be effectively out of sight. The remaining guards just kept as far away from the stinking toilet holes as possible. Vincenzo positioned himself near Pietro and Baldassare like a trusted dog keeping track of his pack masters, but didn't engage with either; he seemed lost in his own thoughts.

Pietro felt nervous. Although he sensed something ominous, he could not 'see' into the darkness; he was blind to the future. A sightless remembrancer. He was about to ask Vincenzo if he, too, sensed something untoward when he heard footsteps, heard the swish of cloth and a stifled cry. Ready to engage, he drew his dagger and quickly stepped into the shadows behind the doorway. Vincenzo did the same.

But when Pietro saw the guards drag the limp body of a boy through the doorway, he returned his dagger to his doublet in disgust. The lancer who had called Pietro a *finocchio* obviously had no compunctions about killing children. "You see, Lord Spiritual?" he said to Baldassare. "Not a drop of blood on the uniform."

Baldassare looked at the boy, who was gangly and quite tall for his age, which could not have been more than twelve or thirteen. "Hide him," he told the guard, "and not down a shit hole. Vincenzo, help him"; then to Pietro, "Remembrancer, take the unfortunate child's clothes. They should fit you."

When Parenti returned, he told Baldassare that the First Citizen had been accorded Duke Guidobaldo's private contemplation room. "However—"

"You saw him?" Baldassare asked.

"No," Parenti said. He seemed impatient. "Something must have changed, Lord Spiritual, because the First Citizen has been taken from the Duke's *studiolo* to the Chapel of Absolution."

"And why would that matter?"

"When Duke Guidobaldo's father was a *condottiere*, he used one of the two *tempietti* chapels as a torture chamber."

Baldassare swore softly.

"Duke Guidobaldo has been murdered," Parenti continued. "His corpse has just been hung upside-down from one of the chapel's finials. And his men are gossiping that he has given the Duke's queen to his red guards."

"I cannot believe Valentino would kill hostages he could barter," Baldassare said.

"Unless..." Pietro said.

"Unless what?" Baldassare asked.

"Unless it is not who we think."

Baldassare gave him a curious look, then pulled him aside, out of earshot of the others. "If you are truly the remembrancer you claim to be, tell me what you mean...what you see."

"I—"

Pietro suddenly sensed Belias as a faint yet palpable presence, a dark, twisting emptiness. *But what of the aeon Athoth and the First Citizen?* he asked himself. *Gabriel had said they were...No, it was not what Gabriel said: it was what I said, what I saw*; and now he could clearly see what had been clouded earlier: Isabella and the daughter of light trying to escape from a ship that would explode in the sky, the dark aeon strangling Athoth with his vines, and Athoth escaping, escaping into—

Pietro could feel the substance of Gabriel's sapphire tablet, his soul, vibrating inside him like light, vibrating softly in the marrow of his bones, in his blood and viscera and humours. Groaning, he mumbled, "*Et finis est.*"

"What? What is finished?" Baldassare asked, insistent. "Quickly. We cannot linger, for—"

"Valentine no longer attends the First Citizen," Pietro said, seeing now as a remembrancer, seeing through eyes of sapphire. "It is now Belias who imprisons him. Belias has swallowed Valentine's soul and now wears him like a garment. "

"Belias? Why would he be *here*?"

"The aeon Athoth had been protecting the daughter of light from him. In the Pope's airship. But Belias was the stronger; and if Athoth hadn't retained a shard of Gabriel's tablet, Belias would have certainly destroyed him. Athoth used the tablet as a bridge to escape Belias, and since the tablet is drawn to itself, like a lodestone, he was drawn here. And Belias pursued him. To swallow and extinguish him forever." After a pause, Pietro squinted as if trying to pierce the darkness and said, "I'm to blame, Lord Spiritual. I'm the lodestone that drew them here because…I'm part of Gabriel's tablet."

"But why would Belias be keeping watch over the First Citizen?"

"Because the First Citizen now contains Athoth's soul."

Baldassare looked vexed. "But if you are the lodestone, remembrancer, why would the aeon not be residing within *you*?"

Pietro just shook his head, his aetheric senses once again clouded.

"And the daughter of light whom Athoth was protecting? What has become of her?"

"I don't know, Lord Spiritual. But I'm certain she is alive."

Baldassare nodded. "We've come to get the First Citizen, and that's what we will do."

"We can't fight an aeon," Pietro said.

"We have to try," and with that Baldassare directed Parenti to lead them to the Chapel of Absolution by the most surreptitious route.

"Wait," Pietro said, uncomfortable in the dead boy's green and red uniform, which was too tight around the waist. He could smell the boy's sour odor; the clothes smelled of death and fear.

"What now, remembrancer?" asked Baldassare.

"Lucian's potion…each one of us must take it. Just one dose to protect our souls. Who knows what disturbance killing the child might have caused?" Pietro looked at the guard who had called him *finocchio* and said, "Who knows what the dark aeon can sense?"

Baldassare ordered his lancers to swallow one of the wrapped potions of Devil weed they had been given. They swore, grimaced, and gagged as they gulped down the poisonous powders wrapped in intestine. Pietro's portion caught in his throat, but he swallowed and swallowed until he could feel it pass like a lump down his esophagus. "And *you* will remain here," Baldassare said to the priest Vincenzo. "I could see that you palmed the potion I ordered you to take."

"I am not a coward," Vincenzo said; and although he whispered, there was heat in his words. "And I do not want to be left behind." Then he bowed his head. "Forgive me, Lord Spiritual. I will take the bolus."

"No," Pietro said, staying the priest's hand as he addressed Baldassare. "Perhaps one of us should remain clear."

"That's what I thought," Vincenzo said. "That's why—"

"You will remain here," Baldassare said. "If we haven't returned by late Vespers, or you perceive trouble or disorder, you must make your way to the hermitage and alert my crucifer Jacopo. Can you handle the ladders?"

Vincenzo just nodded and glanced at Pietro, as if there was something more to be said.

Parenti led the party single file through secret and little used corridors. He held a small candle before him, which he shielded from air currents. As they passed into a small vestibule, its high walls covered with illusionistic intarsia panels and religious paintings, Pietro felt the first effects of the drug. Heartburn, reflux, lightheaded nausea; and then he felt as if everything around him had become suddenly magnified, that he could see through time and darkness. He had a terrible apprehension that everything was locked into place, unchangeable. He found himself staring at a painting of a stoic Christ being feasted upon by lions.

Lions, my lions, they have deserted me. They have—

"Here," Parenti whispered as he slid back an inlaid intarsia panel that revealed a servant's door, which he opened. Pietro followed the others onto the stone landing of a stairtower; and for a vertiginous instant, as he looked down the well of a spiral staircase, he thought he was going to fall. Light flickered from the vicinity of the stables or perhaps from the duke's thermal baths below. "The Chapel of Absolution is on the *piano nobile*," and with that Parenti led the way down the staircase and through a secret corridor used by spies, envoys, and favored concubines and servants. He stopped before a doorway. No light leaked onto the rough stone floor of the corridor. Parenti put his ear to the door and listened for what seemed an eternity before he nodded to Baldassare who unsheathed his short sword. The others followed suit, except for Pietro who still felt as dizzy as he had when he looked down the spiral staircase. The drug had numbed him to Belias' strong presence; only now could he feel it coruscating through him.

He reached for Baldassare.

Too late.

The door latch creaked. The hallway was flooded with light.

Pietro fumbled for his steel, but again too late, for Valentine/Belias had set the trap, had sensed the murder of the child, and had alerted his guards, who were as soulless as the swords they wielded. One of Valentine's guards stabbed

Parenti in the heart—the guard was perhaps a year older than the boy whose uniform Pietro wore. Without a sound or a hint of emotion, Baldassare pushed past his fallen lieutenant and slashed at Valentine's throat. But Valentine/Belias was too quick for the aging captain. He seemed to shimmer backward in the yellow torchlight, and as he did so, he snapped his jewel-pommeled dagger in an arc that split Baldassare like a sausage. Holding his entrails, the soldier priest collapsed.

There was movement behind Pietro, as troops closed off any escape back through the corridor. Pietro fought, wielding both dagger and short sword, killing expertly until he was overwhelmed, beaten into unconsciousness; and as he descended into darkness, he heard, felt Valentine/Belias' orders to his soulless avatars—he could feel the aeon's leaden joy: *"Do not swallow their souls yet, wait for the potion that shadows them to weaken."*

And Pietro also sensed something else, something subtle as aether, subtle as dust or thought passing through him, into him, expanding like light inside him; and he mumbled "Gabriel?"

But it was not Gabriel.

It was Athoth.

Now hiding inside him.

Waiting...

After the priest Vincenzo finished rubbing dried feces and filth onto each of the sectional ladders to camouflage them, he maneuvered a ladder between the twisted window spikes of the garderobe window, pulled the last rung over a spike, and connected another ladder, balancing the upper section against the exterior stone wall as he fastened the leather straps. He lowered the ladders four times and then dropped the fully-connected escalade the few feet to the ground below. Satisfied that it was indeed indistinguishable from the stone wall it rested against and would facilitate a quick escape, should it be necessary, he kept the watch and nervously waited for word from Baldassare. He balanced himself on the broken ledge below the twisted window grill; and as he looked out into the darkness, he felt something slide into the back of his neck. He had no chance to turn or cry out as one of Belias' aetheric vines wrapped itself around his spine and drew out his soul like marrow from a bone, but in that instant before his soul was wrenched from his living body and transported heavenward into the demiurge's cold, dead prison of eternity, the little priest drew upon his last vestiges of courage and strength: *"Consummatum est.* No, Belias you will not enslave me I will break my body first."

He threw himself over the ledge; and as he fell, he heard a roaring in his ears.

But just before his skull struck stone and cracked into blood and splinters, he whispered "*Leo vicium omnim colorum*" and marveled at the huge golden-eyed lion standing over him.

TWENTY
Paths of the Lions

There is a lion in the way: a lion in the streets.

—*Proverbs 26.13*

The chains, the noose, the lead, the snares, the lure,

Our dismal heroes, our souls sunk in night.

—Tommaso Campannela, *La Città della sole*

A huge tawny lion appeared on the Ponte della Paglia.
It padded past the torch-lit marble and porphyry statues of lions that silently guarded the Pope's Venetian palace. It moved through the awed and terrified *carnivale* crowds of masked harlequins, beggars, black robed nobles, harlots, mountebanks, notaries, tourists, Punchinellos, inquisitors, courtesans, counselors, scaramouches, bull-baiters, rope dancers, chestnut vendors, acrobats, chambermaids, children, women dressed as men, men dressed as women, tinkers, merchants, and priests. And as it cast its shifting shadow over paving stones littered with confetti, ribbons, trash, oranges, and pumpkin seeds, the crowds parted like the Red Sea. Children stopped flinging eggs filled with sweet water. Peasants and grandees alike made the sign of sanctification and intoned the "Ascent of the Soul". A woman dressed as a nymph in white lace fell to her knees and cried, "*È un miracolo.*" A cardinal, or a reveler dressed as a cardinal, crossed himself and said, "*Misericordia Dei,*" while the nymph tore at her bodice as if offering herself to the lion: "*Locus est hic sanctus…sacer est a te Domine.*"

This place is holy…consecrated to you, Oh, Lord.

The lion became frantic with the smells of roasting meat, sweating flesh, and human ordure; its open mouth dripped with saliva as its kaleidoscopic memory reproduced the voluptuous sensations of breaking bones with its jaw—the tannic bursting of blood, the bite of steaming flesh—and reflexively its senses vectored onto the white meaty tangy fleshy salt-sweet-sour nymph who was so near, so close to the ground; but the lion felt a greater need, a greater compulsion; and even as the lion strained against its need and hunger, it ran.

It ran across the piazza, gnashing and tearing at anyone unfortunate enough to be in its way. Its sensorium overwhelmed, it ran through screams and smells, slipping once on wet stones, swiping its claws at a porphyry statue of a crouching lion as it crossed a bridge. It paused behind the church of San Zaccaria, sniffing at its moon-white façade, then circled the convent. There was something inside the squat brick building, a sapphire lodestone that the lion perceived as comfort and satiation; but against its will, the lion moved on, moved away from the discordant clamor of nuns and the daughters of patricians who were entertaining eligible guests. Although it yearned for raw flesh and warm blood, the lion skirted around the crowded piazzettas and campos and made its way north through *ramo* side streets and dead-silent alleys.

It followed the increasingly dark and bitter scents of smoke and ash until it found what was left of the convent of Santa Sophia dei Miracoli.

And there it waited…

Pico Della Mirandola had made his choice.

He had accepted the angel Gabriel's challenge to find the daughter of light. He had followed the lion through the doorway of roiling white light that was the angel's sapphire tablet. And he had fallen into darkness.

Into the gagging, smoking Venetian night.

He found himself standing in a square overlooking a white marble church wreathed in smoke. A group of men—their faces wrapped in cloth—ran past with buckets and long fire hooks. Bells pealed from the church tower. The streets and piazzas were crowded with curious revelers and the faithful alike. Soldiers and liveried *armeggiatori* confraternies kept the peace; neighbors watched from recently dampened rooftops.

Mirandola tried to get his bearings. He was still dizzy and disoriented.

I have spoken with an angel, followed a lion into Heaven…and followed it here. But where is it? Where is the lion?

Shivering in the heat and humidity, he intoned the *Mysterium nobis reuelandum* and was startled when an old woman slapped his hand and said, "Don't waste your prayers on them. They deserve what they got."

"I don't—"

"They're whores and heretics. That's why the Holy Father burned them alive in their fouled convent." She spat. "Do you know they used their scriptorium as a gaming room?"

Not wanting to reveal his ignorance, Mirandola simply nodded.

"I see you looking; but trust me, ser, you don't have to worry about the church." The old woman wore a loose black woolen dress tied with a leather belt; there was no veil attached to her wimple, and her intense blue eyes seemed trapped by the wrinkled skin around them. "The church itself it's unharmed," she continued. "The bones of the Virgin will protect it forever. Not for nothing did the Holy Fathers name it Miracoli. And I'll tell you sumtion else, ser, about…"

Mirandola caught sight of something yellow in the hazed distance.

"…them's worse than the Benedictine whores of San Zaccaria." The old woman spat again, then made the sign of protection over her breast. "They'll be next mark my word. But…"

It could have been one of the costumed spectators, Mirandola told himself; but no, he glimpsed it again: it *was* the lion. He excused himself, but the old woman grasped his sleeve and nodded pointedly toward her other hand, which was palm up. Mirandola gave her a few soldi and then headed through the crowds toward the far corner of the piazza.

The lion stood behind a bronze monument to one of the ancient doges.

When Mirandola approached, it padded across the perimeter of the campo; and Mirandola felt an odd tingling at the base of his spine as he followed the huge creature, followed it through labyrinths of alleyways and deserted squares and parks. Although he couldn't *see* clearly into the lion's thoughts, he could sense its intention and feel its impulsive desire as direction. The lion was looking for something…for someone: a woman who did not smell like meat.

It skirted the carnival crowds of San Marco and led Mirandola into a small graveyard beside the double storied convent of San Zachariah.

And there they waited.

The Pope's black robed soldiers were looking for her.

The nun Maria Theresa might have escaped the environs of the burning convent, but she had spent the last three hours vomiting under an archway in a deserted street near the Ponte del Cristo. After she had emptied her stomach of the poisonously feculent canal water, she mercifully fell asleep. She held both arms tightly over the small tablet that she had concealed in a pocket under the rough-weaved scapula the prioress had given her; and in a fever-dream she relived her rescue of the daughter of light and her companion from the *mausoleo* on the Isle of the Dead.

Once again she was bludgeoned by an oarsman…once again she fell into coal black water as the prioress' traitor of a brother blessed her from above: "*Your reward*" chuckle "*awaits you*" chuckle "*below.*" And then something shifted, and even at the bottom of sleep she sensed that her ordinary memory-charged dream was over and something else had captured her: a lucid dream. As her sleeping self gazed into the prioress' tablet, she saw what awaited her.

She awakened with a start. The prioress had told her to find the archbishop, but it was other people, other beings, that she saw or glimpsed or imagined in her dream: one she recognized as the Florentine mage Pico Della Mirandola; another was hidden in someone else like a luminescent pearl nestled in an oyster; and lastly all she could see were two golden eyes gazing hungrily out of the darkness. She shrugged, as if she could throw off the last thin vestiges of both fever and dream, and then took her bearings. Three small canals came together here. On her right the massive façade of the Pallazzo Marcello-Pindemonte-Papadopoli rose above the waters like a mythic wood turned to stone. Maria Theresa realized that she had not travelled far from the convent before becoming violently ill, but she had chosen well: this wedge below the bridge had always served as a good hideaway when she was a child…a very naughty and willful orphan who had been given refuge by the nuns.

Again she vomited, another dry heave; and as she did, she heard the crunch of a heel on gravel. She pressed her back against damp stone, but too late. She was seen by a papal guard. Gagging, she started toward the canal. That would be her only chance of escape, but the priest was young and quick and upon her…which gave her an idea, a real chance, perhaps.

"Are you the one we've been looking for, sweet *puttana?*" the priest asked, grabbing her arms and pinning them behind her back. He was young, lanky, and strong, but his comely features were overwhelmed by welt-like eruptions. His breath smelled of decay, and like all men, she thought, his member purposely pressed against her was hard as a pike. "And what's this?" he asked, feeling the sharp edge of the tablet against his abdomen.

She kicked at his shin.

"*Porco dio,*" he swore, slamming her hard against the wall. "We were warned that—" She felt hollow thunder as the back of her head hit the wall. She purposely went limp in his arms; and then—bracing herself against the wall—she hard-butted his nose with her forehead, pushing bone into soft brain tissue. He dropped like a sack, convulsing only once as he died. Lest he evacuate and soil his *veste togata*, she pulled his clerical robes away from him. She prayed for his eternal soul as she smoothed her hair back into a knot and took off her vomit damp habit, which she replaced with his *camicia* and hooded black *togata*. And then, with the precious tablet safely secured and flat against her breasts, she kept to the deserted *calle* laneways and alleys before stepping into a crowded and noisy square. She pushed past the patricians waiting their turn outside the moon-white convent of San Zaccaria: waiting to be called inside to visit the nuns or the eligible daughters of other patricians posing vivaciously behind silver-netted grilles; and when she was denied entry at the portico by two stolid-faced nuns, she whispered, "*Benedictus qui venit in, nomine Domini.*" The nuns nodded, accepting the shibboleth; and one of them accompanied the disguised Maria Theresa through the crowded reception room and lavishly ornamented galleries of the *mezzanino*, then upstairs to the prioress' private apartments.

"What is your business?" the prioress asked Maria Theresa. She did not rise from her seat beside a study table: *this callow-looking priest certainly could not be long out of ordination.* "I have already met with—" Then her expression changed. "Ah, yes, Padre, I do remember now." After she dismissed the guardian nun, who bowed and closed the cambered door, the prioress crossed the room to Maria Theresa. and pulled back Maria Theresa's hood. "*Magna est Gloria eius!*" she said, making the sign of the snake over her breast. "It was rumored that you were drowned, then resurrected…that you were seen going into your convent, but not found within. Again, someone saw you, saw you hanging from the convent wall like a fly. The Pope's guards searched, but—"

"I hid right under their noses," Maria Theresa said. "But one luckless guard found me." She shuddered, thinking of his smashed face; overcome by a surge of nausea, she tried to loosen her tunic; and the next thing she knew, she was lying naked in the prioress' canopied bed. The apartment was suffused with first light, and Maria Theresa, still raveled in dreams, thought that the prioress attending her was a nurse. "You're handsome enough to have been a courtesan in your day," Maria Theresa mumbled. Still mazed, she wondered whether she—herself—was a courtesan or a nun. "Better to be old. You don't have to keep your legs open and get poked by ugly, sweaty—" Coming to her senses, she opened her eyes wide and said, "Forgive me, Mother Dolabella, I don't know what I was saying."

"Actually, little sister, I am a nurse, and I was a courtesan. Like our great father Augustine, I found my way to truth by way of error." The sweetness of her smile belied the irony of her words.

"Where, where is—?"

"Don't fret, the crystal tablet that Mother Lorenzetti gave you—may she rest in peace—is safe," and with that the prioress retrieved it from a hidden cache and handed it to Maria Theresa who clasped it tightly. "It always feels warm, like blood."

The prioress nodded and she sat down on the edge of the bolstered bed. "Its very proximity weakens me, but you are young, so perhaps…"

"No, Mother Dolabella, it does the same to me. I struggle against it even as I embrace it."

The prioress nodded again and with a long look said, "Maria Theresa, neither you nor the crystal can remain here. We are too near the pope's palace. His Angevin theurgist will sense its presence…if he has not already. He is a great mage, even greater than our own Pico Della Mirandola, and was once a true seeker." After a pause, the prioress said, "But you had no intention of leaving it here, did you?"

"No, Reverend Mother. I just—"

"What, child?"

"I was weak and ill, and I had a dream that seemed to push me toward your haven, Mother Dolabella."

"We are no haven in these times. However"—she tapped the fresh, tightly wrapped and unguent-sticky bandages that covered and protected Maria Theresa's chest and midsection—"our nurses are the best in Venice. The poisons in your stomach have been purged, and your wounds and bruises will heal without scar or sulcus. I worry only about the effects of the tablet so close to your breast."

"Please don't worry, holy mother," Maria Theresa said, "I—"

The prioress lifted her hand: a sign for silence.

"You've told me enough, child. Any more, and I will become a danger to you, our cause, and everyone in our convent, whether she be nun, courtesan, or noble's daughter being groomed to wed. Now…do you feel strong enough to get dressed." She smiled. "I have some very rich clothes for you, and some jewels, too. You will look the very picture of a noble's daughter, or a successful courtesan; and the sisters have arranged your bandages to give you some proper cleavage."

Maria Theresa blushed, but allowed the prioress to help her dress: a linen chemise, a white damask *cotta* with flowers brocaded in gold and sleeves decorated with pearls, and a *gornea* gown open at the front and sides to reveal the rich fabric of the cotta beneath. "I can hardly move," she said, "and the slippers are squeezing my toes one over the other."

"You're even beginning to sound like a *fille de joie*," the prioress said.

There was a hard knock on the door, and the burly sister who had accompanied Maria Theresa to the prioress' apartments looked very pale and unnerved. "Reverend Mother, there is a man with a very large lion standing in the north portico."

"Maria Theresa felt dizzy and sat down on the bed. "Mother Dolabella, they're from my dream."

"Well, don't just stand there," the prioress told the nun. "Let them in. And bring them through the escape corridors."

It had been no use shouting at the pockmarked gondolier called Domenico. The man simply bowed and snapped the curtains closed, leaving Louisa and Isabella, the little daughters of light, with the two heavy-set, silent guards who looked ghoulishly yellow in the flickering lamplight. The gondola cut through the dark waters, rocking slightly, splashing through the wakes of other boats; and Louisa thought better than to speak to her companion in front of the guards, who tapped their chests in obeisance every time Louisa looked at them. The gondola's black *felze* cabin was private, and all Louisa and Isabella could see was the fuzzed lamplights of other passing gondolas and the smeary lights of the palaces that overlooked the canal. As the gondola approached the Pope's palace, bright light bled through the tasseled curtains. Then there was a soft bump as the prow skipped against the landing stage and came to rest. Domenico pulled back the curtains, bowed, and said to Louisa, "His Holiness himself has honored you with his presence. He stands in the open with the other supplicants." He bowed again, gave her a twisted smile, and made his characteristic chuckling noise.

"Now come out of the darkness, *filiæ lucis*. Come into the light."

The burly gondoliers firmly escorted Louisa and Isabella onto the deck and then helped them over to the landing stage; and, indeed, it was like coming into the light: as if the gondola had passed through the shadows of darkness into coruscating glory. Isabella gave Louisa a frightened look, then mumbled "*miracolo*" as she stared in awe at the impossibly lit façades of the Papal Palace. It was just as the archbishop had promised: the pope's palace *was* the City of Light. Darkness had been banished; and lights seemed to be burning everywhere, burning on columns, niches, and pinnacles, burning in *calli* and *campos* and courtyards, in archways, and arcades…seemingly burning in the very air itself: golden, shifting lights reflected and magnified by the Papal Palace's palisaded tiers of cupped windows and glittering facades of alabaster, marble, jasper, granite, marmot greco, and cipollino. And flanked by two phalanxes of heavily armed and sumptuously costumed papal guards, the pope stood waiting on the ground-level portico under the pointed entrance arch of the waterfront-facing loggia. He was a bear of a man with a large, fleshy nose that overpowered his thick-cheeked face. Although the few chosen cardinals standing behind him were magnificent in their voluminous crimson cloaks and hoods made of the finest camlet, he wore a simple brimless cap, a satin-lined *mozetta* mantle, and a bright white rochet. But it was the tall, smiling man beside him that caught Louisa's attention. Although he looked clownish in his conical hat with its overly large, flouncy crown, he was wearing white theurgist's robes…and he radiated the kind of power Louisa had felt when she had touched the sapphire tablet.

"Who is that?" she asked the gondolier Domenico. "The theurgist who…"

But Domenico and his gondola had disappeared into the crowded, shimmering canal; and after making an obligatory obeisance to the pope, the theurgist was making his way toward the daughters of light.

He stopped before them and bowed to Louisa, who felt that something was amiss. Rather than sensing a magnification of his power, she felt its diminution: as if someone—or something—else had focused on her. But somehow… somehow it had been reflected through this excited-looking exaggeration of a theurgist. She couldn't help but look past him…at the Pope, his cardinals. No, not them; but she saw someone who looked like the theurgist moving in the shadows behind them, a tall figure—a shadow amongst shadows—which disappeared as did the pressure of its powerful glamour.

"*Venite filiæ lucis,*" said the theurgist. "*Lux in aeternum.*"

He shifted his balance from one foot to another; that he was used to power and command was belied by his nervous affectation and genial, ingratiating smile

Isabella tapped Louisa's arm, waking her from her reverie.

"I'm sorry, ser," Louisa said; "I was"—she shook her head—"distracted. Please forgive me."

He grasped her hand and squeezed it gently. "It is only natural to feel overwhelmed in the presence of the Holy Father, even for someone as blessed with grace as the daughter of light." He spoke with an odd staccato-like accent. "But, come, we must not keep him waiting."

She nodded, noticing the cross and vine insignia embroidered in gold on his sleeve, and allowed him to lead her toward the waiting convocation. Isabella had taken her other hand and, shaking with fear, squeezed it tightly. She leaned her head against Louisa's and whispered, "Are you all right? You seemed…*inhabited*, somehow." But then they were standing before the Pope, who greeted them equally and graciously, his gaze warm, hypnotic and comforting, yet somehow lascivious.

"Welcome home, *filiæ lucis*. We have awaited you for a thousand years."

TWENTY-ONE
The Walls of Flesh

So share thy victory,
  Or else thy grave,
Either to rescue thee
  Or with thee die.

— Peter Abelard, *Lamentations*

There is another way, full of meanders & labyrinths, whereof
aeons and spirits have no exact ephemerides: so look thou to the
wals of flesh, wherein these soules doth seeme immured.

— Sir Thomas Browne, *On Revelation*

"Lucian...child. Awaken!"
Jacopo di Pecori stood over the prostrate boy, who felt a stomach-gnawing surge of hunger and then, once again, revulsion when he realized that the distant, wafting odors of roasting meat were not kine.

The painful hunger pangs were but a physical manifestation of his sudden, harrowing emptiness, the emptiness of loss, the loss of his connection with Baldassare: Baldassare, the priest whose soul he had once stolen, the priest who once would have killed him without passion or regret, had his master Mirandola not intervened. But although Lucian had returned Baldassare's soul, a faint, rogue connection remained; and only now, now when the connection had snapped, broken, when Lucian had seen, felt, heard, and experienced Baldassare's last moments of astonishment — the dawning of pain and grief, the hard-fought swallowing of darkness, the gloating blue-eyed gaze of

Cesare Valentinus Borgia—did he realize how much of himself belonged to Baldassare.

He looked up at the hazed stars, their brightness diminished by moon glow, and heard rasping, tearing sounds: Jacopo's voice.

"Are you all right?"

Jacopo settled on one knee beside Lucian, who, coming back to himself, was trying to sit up. "Slowly, slowly does it, child."

"Water and, pray, something to eat. How long have I—?"

"You have been out of consciousness for over an hour," Jacopo said, helping Lucian rest his back against a tree. Then he gave him a water skin and ordered a guard to bring some salted meat. "Messer Bentivogli has been administering to you. He was the only one able to awaken you."

Lucian nodded to the dwarf standing beside Jacopo.

"Yes, indeed," Jacopo said. "It seems our friend is not only an aereomancer and a maker of maps"—the soldier priest tapped a parchment roll he was holding—"but a theurgist as well. He asked my permission to cast a cantrip... and here you are."

"Are you a theurgist, ser?"

"Merely an advisor, a humble servant," said the dwarf. "Nothing more."

Lucian nodded, distracted, for he was remembering what he had seen, remembering that in those last minutes of connection with Baldassare, there was something interfering with the connection: blocking clarity. He shook his head.

"Lucian!"

He turned to Jacopo, who was staring at him intently. The soldier dismissed the others, including the dwarf; and his sword-scarred face was humorless, cleansed of sympathy and concern, the relationship of master to servitor reestablished.

"What caused you to faint, child? What did you see?"

"Why would you think—"

Jacopo slapped him: not hard, but now he would have absolute obedience. "The dwarf said that your syncope was a presentiment, that it was no ordinary loss of sensibility. Now speak while there is still time, for we will soon advance upon the enemy: I have authorized Fra Sassetta to distribute your potions of Devil Weed."

That was it! Lucian thought. *Baldassare had taken a potion of* Datura stramonium. *That was what I sensed as interference...* His mind and vision were becoming more clear; his strength was returning (even though his hands shook and his breath was uneven), but the empty hollowness remained.

"*Cancelliere,* you asked what I saw." Lucian paused, then said, "Our master, Fra Baldassare is killed by Valentine's sword."

Jacopo's face betrayed no change of expression: it was still as hard and cold as chiseled stone. "And the others?" he asked quietly. "The First Citizen?"

"In pain, that's all I saw…being tortured, perhaps, yes, I think that is correct."

"But alive," Jacopo said, as if speaking to himself. "And what else did you see?"

"Pietro…Pietro is there, and he contains—"

"Go on!"

Lucian shook his head, as if that could clear it. "Belias…"

"Do you mean to say that Pietro contains the dark aeon?"

"No, *Cancelliere*. I—I don't know. The aeon Athoth is there…and so is Belias. I can't be sure what I saw, or what I see." Lucian closed his eyes, trying to see truly. He felt a stab of pure dread and terror, imagined Belias' aetheric vines slithering like tentacles around him, through him, as they sucked his soul away, leaving him as hollow and empty as he had once left Baldassare. Poor dead, bleeding Baldassare. He jerked backward, suddenly sensing realizing understanding that Belias had, of course, taken Baldassare's soul after he murdered his body. And Pietro would be next.

Pietro…

Lucian imagined that he could sense a tenuous connection with Pietro, as if they were both shadows in the stone, both broken pieces of Gabriel's sapphire tablet. Was the remembrancer trying to see *him*? Calling him? No, but Lucian heard a *voice* that chilled him to the bone: *"Do not swallow their souls yet, wait for the potion that shadows them to weaken."*

"All is lost," he said, thinking out loud; but then his expression changed. "Unless…"

"Unless what, child?" Jacopo asked.

"I must go." Lucian tried to stand up; but feeling immediately lightheaded and dizzy, he stumbled on a stone concealed in a tangle of brush.

Jacopo caught him.

"You're in no condition to go anywhere yet."

Lucian nodded, but remained on his feet.

"Now tell me what you saw and where you wish to go!"

"I may be able to help Pietro…and the First Citizen."

"You? How?"

"Both Pietro and I host Gabriel's sapphire seal. We each contain a small part of him within us. A small part of his soul. And perhaps a small part of his power." Taking strength from his visceral faith in Gabriel and accepting that Athoth could no longer be his enemy, he continued: "Together—and with the help of the aeon Athoth—we might save the First Citizen."

Jacopo spat at the mere mention of Athoth.

"If Belias has already defeated Athoth, then we are all lost," Lucian continued. He closed his eyes for a few seconds. "But I think I can sense Pietro's presence." His face tightened in fear, anger, and disgust. "Among others."

"You...*think*?"

"It is only a small chance, *Cancelliere*," Lucian said, meeting Jacopo's gaze directly. "But perhaps our only chance."

"If there is a chance, it will be by destroying his troops here"—Jacopo nodded in the direction of the hermitage—"and then taking the Ducal Palace."

"By then it will be too late."

"If you would allow me to finish, young ser, I will send three banners commanded by Fra Sassetta with you to free the First Citizen. And when we are finished here, which I pray will be quick, we will gain the town and the palace." He smiled grimly at Lucian. "If we are all fated to lose our souls, we will at least diminish our enemy."

"**O**h, how I yearned to join your excellent crucifer Jacopo, or one of his captains, to slit the throats of Valentino's sleeping host," the dwarf Achille said to Lucian as their banner of twenty-five men led by Fra Sassetta began a forced march through brush and forest toward the hilly eastern outskirts of Urbino. Jacopo—who was even now slaughtering Valentine's drunken, sleeping soldiers in and around the hermitage—had sent other banners, consisting of almost a hundred men in total, to infiltrate and slit the snoring throats of those in the camps outside the town and then, if possible, to make their way over the walls. These other banners were under Jacopo's command but led by other captains. They all took different routes, which had been expertly laid out by the dwarf; and, like Sassetta's banner, would keep to the forests as best they could: away from the more exposed grain fields.

"Of course, you must first dispatch the sentries (efficiently and with the least disturbance) and then replace them with your own men," continued the dwarf Achille. He spoke in barely a whisper; but to Lucian, who had been forced by Jacopo to take a double bolus of *Datura stramonium* with the rest of Fra Sassetta's seventy-five soldier-priests, it was as if the shifting shadows of leaf and branch were speaking: whispering to him in a susurration of vegetal voices, which interfered with his perception and the normal flow of his thoughts, frustrating any possibility of his being able to hear or sense the thoughts of Pietro or Athoth...or Belias. Lucian reflexively tapped his chest. *May the Invisible One protect me. Magna est gloria eius.* And he wondered how he might counteract the numbing effects of the phantasmagoric drug he himself had prescribed as a protective anodyne.

"But my responsibility is to preserve my queen Elizabetta and the house of Montefeltro; nevertheless, I hope to carve up my own goodly portion of the pig." Achille looked up at Lucian and grinned, but Lucian did not notice as the light of the moon was obscured by tree and cloud.

I told the fool Jacopo that I must not take the potion...That it would—

"Did you say something?" Achille asked.

Surprised, Lucian hesitated; the soldier behind him swore and pushed him forward. The dwarf grabbed Lucian's hand and pulled him along.

"Well...?"

"No," whispered Lucian. "I didn't say a word."

The dwarf nodded, still smiling; and not another word was spoken as the soldiers worked their way through dense wood, ravines, and dangerous inclines toward the moonlit towers, walls, and cupolas of the town and palace until the bells in the town towers and the castle began to peal their alarm, followed by a more muted clangor emanating from the hermitage's church tower.

"Now it will be more difficult," the dwarf said, motioning to Sassetta.

"But I know a way," he said to the lieutenant. "We will need rope, and we will have to contrive a scaling hook."

Sassetta nodded, as he listened to the shrieks of battle emanating from Valentine's camps outside the city walls and contemplated the uncertain situation at the hermitage: Baldassare's crucifer Jacopo would be in the thick of battle now, as would his captains, all plans of stealth and surprise extinguished.

Lucian closed his eyes, trying to concentrate, trying to penetrate the interfering miasma of the Devil Weed, trying to establish a connection with Pietro. But he might as well have been deaf and blind. He shivered as an unseasonably chill wind swept past him: it carried the acrid taint of blood and feces.

It was like gazing into a diorama.

Even as the hallucinatory, numbing affects of the Devil's Weed dissipated, Pietro felt that he was looking into the chapel that had been converted into a torture chamber from a great distance...as if he were looking into the room—the room in which he was standing—through a long and narrow tunnel. The room was brightly lit with torches and candles in sconces, and the exquisitely wrought intarsia paneling that covered walls and ceiling seemed to glow from the depths of its mirror polished wood. And there, at a great distance—which was in reality little more than a few *braccio* away from Pietro, double the length of his arms—Guiliano de Medici, the First Citizen, hung naked in the vine-laden air: his arms had been pulled around his back and his wrists were tied to a thick rope that passed through a *strappado* pulley affixed to the ceiling. His stretched and rotated shoulder sockets were supporting his entire weight, and to heighten his suffering, a heretic's fork had been secured between his breast bone and throat, lest he lower his head or fall unconscious. Controlled by Belias who inhabited him, Cesare Valentinus Borgia stood before the First Citizen and spoke to the aeon he assumed was hiding within the young Florentine ruler.

"Come, come, my brother, you must be feeling the pain of your host. Leave him be and confront me"—Belias laughed softly—"*mano a mano.*" With that, Valentine/Belias pressed an index finger to Guiliano's forehead and pushed gently; the First Citizen swung backward and forward, the whites of his eyes as glazed as the white bands of marble that edged the room.

Pietro suddenly felt the secret presence of Athoth buried deep inside him, a shadow around his heart; and his neck, chest, and limbs felt stiff, as if the presence of the aeon had turned him to stone. Straight ahead were Valentine/Belias and the First Citizen, the latter swinging in and out of Pietro's field of vision; and the air was thick with shadows, with vines twisting and passing through Valentine's guards, passing through Baldassare's men: extracting their souls and leaving only obedient meat behind.

Thinking it was an effect of the potion he had swallowed, Pietro strained to gain control over his body; he tried to turn his head. Valentine's guards, perhaps thinking that he was a soulless shell like the others, did not restrain him.

"*No, no, do not try to move,*" a voice whispered inside Pietro's head, a voice so soft, so quiet that it concealed itself in the autonomic musings of his heart and the diastolic murmur of blood and viscera.

Athoth.

"*You must appear as empty as the others. I cannot conceal you, protect you, otherwise. Nor can I protect the maskil.*"

"The maskil...do you mean Lucian?" Pietro asked; and through the thinning miasma of the Devil's Weed, Pietro imagined he could sense Lucian, could sense the color, the texture of his friend's thoughts and emotions; but the connection was so tenuous and fragile that it might only be a phantasm brought on by the drug: as perhaps was the voice of the aeon Athoth.

"*He is trying to reach us,*" Athoth said, "*and if I can continue to deceive my dark brother, perhaps, just perhaps...*"

"What?" asked Pietro.

"*Small and several as we undoubtedly are—you and I and your maskil compatriot—just might become the many in the one."* Pietro felt Athoth's ironic laughter as a juddering in his chest, a deep feathery tickling. *"Young remembrancer, are you prepared to die? Are you prepared to lose both your celestial soul and your terrestrial body, with no hope of redemption or deliverance?"*

"Isn't that what Belias has in mind?"

Athoth smiled or silently laughed; Pietro felt a tickle, as if a spider had just scurried down his spine, and then, suddenly, he, Pietro, could feel Lucian's presence, could feel Lucian trying to break through the drugged miasma that separated them. Pietro called to him, re-establishing their sapphire connection, but Athoth usurped it: he was calling Lucian, directing him, explaining that if he, Lucian, were to save them, save his friends, the aeon, and the First Citizen from Belias, he would have to forfeit his life and his soul for theirs.

"Would you be willing to do so, young maskil…?" Athoth asked the distant, transpontine Lucian.

A s the influence of the Devil's Weed diminished, Lucian heard Athoth's call: at the same time the atmosphere thickened and viney shapes wavered in the air. Sassetta tried to form up his scattered banners, but it was too late: the bolt of a crossbow split his skull. Enemy troops were suddenly everywhere, attacking without care for their own personal safety, hacking with sword and skean and axe, clubbing with knobsticks and shortstaffs. They uttered no oaths or curses: they were silent and soulless automatons intent only on killing; and moments later, as blood-rage and blood-lust overwhelmed the weakening affects of the drug, Sassetta's men were overcome with war-fever. As they hacked and grappled with the enemy, Belias' vines swept through them: the vines, as transparent and insubstantial as a sharp wind, cored the men of their souls, leaving them to obey the ever-strengthening will of the dark aeon and turn on their compatriots.

"This way," said the dwarf, pulling at Lucian's sleeved tunic. "Our only chance," and Lucian followed him, lacerating himself as he ran through brush and burdock. Lucian was no coward: he felt pangs of guilt and remorse for leaving the troops behind to die or be emptied by the vines. But the aeon had called him, had saved him for his own purposes; and as Lucian followed the dwarf, crossing the edges of open fields, Lucian listened to the aeon's tickling, itching thoughts: he could also see them as ghostly images that seemed to scatter before his eyes; and when the dwarf tried to lead him to a secret opening in the town's walls below the castle, Lucian said, "No, Ser Achille, we must follow our course to the hillside behind the palace. It is only from there that we can gain access: Valentine opened the way for us when he besieged the castle with his cannon."

The dwarf gave Lucian a curious look. "I know about the breach in the walls, theurgist, but how do *you*?"

"No matter, I just do," Lucian said.

"And how then do you propose to climb up to the breech without rope and hook?" asked the dwarf. "I know just where to acquire all we need…which is where I was going. But perhaps you're right: there's no need for us both to risk being seen. Follow the footpath north until you reach an old charge-gate. The climb is easiest from there. I'll meet you under the breach. There are enough stones and rubble to enable us to cross over to the wall. Wait for me there on the hill side." He chuckled to himself. "You'll find it easily enough. Just follow your nose."

Lucian shook his head with impatience. "All that we need is already there."

"I need to know how—"

"I'm being called and directed, Ser Achille. That will have to suffice for now."

The dwarf said, "No, theurgist, that will not—" but he checked himself and followed Lucian, who moved quickly and sure-footedly, even though he seemed distracted, as if he were listening to directions or seeing paths that Achille could not. Indeed, Lucian was preparing himself, stiffening himself for the worst; and he felt that fate and the aeon Athoth controlled him now. He gained a strength in his resignation; and he obeyed Athoth's stern directive to bury as deeply as he could all fear, pain, need, and regret, all emotion and all memory…lest his presence be detected by the dark aeon. Indeed, that's what the aeon himself was doing.

When they reached the rock salient that became the north-eastern wall of the castle and made their way over the bridge of rubble and stone, Lucian found the broken body of the young priest Vincenzo. He stopped and damping his regret, he slid his hand under the priest's tunic and touched the cold, hairless chest. He pulled his hand back as if he had been burned, but it was not heat he felt: it was emptiness, searingly cold and utterly dark. *Cold and dark as fate*, Lucian thought, feeling simultaneously moved and distanced.

Push such thoughts down. Conceal…

"He was one of ours," Lucian said to the dwarf; but Achille had moved off. "Here," Achille said in not more than a whisper, "there is an escalade. You were right." He pulled the escalade back to gain a better balance and began to climb. "The stink here is more than a maggot could bear."

"Wait," Lucian said. "You know of the dark aeon."

"Yes, of course…the vines," the dwarf said, stepping down from the first rung of the ladder and standing back against the castle wall for cover.

"He is in the castle, and most of our men are probably dead, or soulless. The vines are real, Achille. They are no mere peasant superstition."

The dwarf nodded, as if they were of little import.

"And my queen, Elizabetta?"

"I don't know, small warrior; but would you risk your soul for her?"

"What would you think?" Achille whispered.

It was Lucian's turn to nod. "Then search for her. I will find the First Citizen. We go separate ways. If all goes well, we meet near the cottage west of the charge gate."

"Do you believe your chances better than the others?" asked Achille.

"No."

"And how will you find him. You don't—"

"I will find him," Lucian said, listening for the now familiar purling voice of the aeon and suddenly realizing its absence: and the absence of ghostly images.

Something must be wrong…

But he remembered the aeon's directive: no emotion, no panic. He must continue to think himself invisible, lest Belias grasp his presence.

"If the First Citizen is being tortured," Lucian continued, "he must be below the *piano nobile*."

"No," said the dwarf, "if he is being tortured, he will be in the chapel. I will show you the way." He would brook no argument, and they climbed, maneuvered their way past the garderobe's twisted window grille and worked their way through the secret unlit corridors that Achille knew so well. He led Lucian down a spiral staircase that was eerily lit from below and said, "The chapel is two levels down. I will show you."

"No, I must go alone," Lucian whispered. "Just tell me how to find it."

"It will be the second door to your right when you step onto the landing. If a torch burns in the corridor, you will see the inscription *Sacra deo est* in its frieze: you do not want the first door, which is inscribed to the muses." He nodded to Lucian and said, "My queen's apartments are on this level. Good luck, young…maskil."

It was Lucian's turn to be surprised; but there was no time to interrogate the little man because if the aeon had gone silent, there was not a moment to spare. Lucian climbed quickly, but carefully down the staircase. He concentrated on the aeon, listened for his voice inside his head, but heard nothing except ambient scratchings, groanings, and susurrations: the ever-present melody of a great castle.

The hallway was dark, and Lucian felt his way through it, his fingers sliding against the intarsia-fitted wall on his right until he felt the outcrop of a door pillar. He moved on until he found the lock style of the next door; and as he touched it, he felt a sudden, overwhelmingly painful connection with Belias and Athoth and Pietro, a blindingly bright connection that exploded in the dark hallway, and he heard sensed felt Belias, who was concentrating all his energy and focus on Athoth: for an instant, Lucian felt and experienced reality as an aeon did: saw the past, present, and future superimposed one upon the other; heard the rattle of the latch before he touched the door; saw the twisted, agonized First Citizen hanging by his wrists from ropes straining from a pulley attached to the icon-lavished ceiling; felt the dark aeon's calm, almost amused discovery that Athoth had fooled him, as a ventriloquist his audience; and then the dark aeon's sudden shift into cold-focused anger as he directed his vines in concert toward Pietro as well as turning his Spanish forged sword to the remembrancer with the intention of rousting Athoth and taking Pietro's life and soul in one fell swoop—the soul, which would be collected and especially tortured. He also glimpsed the terrible darkness which awaited him if—

No time to wait, to pause, to fear.

There was nothing to it, he told himself, but to barge right in, which he did: all was as he had seen through the eyes of an aeon.

As the dark aeon rushed toward Pietro, simultaneously sweeping his sword in an arc that would decapitate the young remembrancer, Lucian heard Belias say to Athoth, "*And now, my foolish and traitorous cousin, I will relieve you of the house in which you hide.*" Belias' vines were also twisting around Pietro, as if to strangle him, rather than pass through bone and viscera to suck out his soul like an egg from its shell. It was then that Lucian stepped between Valentine/Belias and Pietro/Athoth, dagger in hand, intending to deflect the sword sweeping toward Pietro's throat; but that could not meet with success, even if Valentine were not strengthened and possessed by Belias. Valentine was known for his strength and physical prowess; by comparison, Lucian was no more than a child. But that did not matter, for with intention all its own and speed that confounded any human notion of time, Gabriel's sapphire snake uncoiled from around Lucian's wildly beating heart and coursed like wildfire through his blood. It pierced Valentine's right eye, seeking the dark aeon nestled in the viscera, pneuma, and pumping blood of the handsome blond *condottiere*. The prince of the church lurched backward, and all of Belias' familiars, his twisting vines, rushed to protect the dark aeon: but Lucian's sapphire snake had shifted the delicate balance of power, and as the snake tried to swallow Belias' soul—tried to swallow the raging force that was Belias entire—Athoth removed himself from Pietro, passing out of the remembrancer's flesh and bone and soul to attack the scourging vines, destroying them *en masse* and further weakening the dark aeon who, no longer able to maintain himself within Valentine, tried to make his escape.

An explosion of cold air iced walls and ceiling and instantly extinguished torches and candles as Belias transported himself, shifted himself into his dark heaven; but even in that instant, that twisting of time and place, Gabriel's snake overcame and imprisoned his soul in its glittering aetheric coils.

And Lucian, connected to the sapphire serpent as an arm is to the shoulder, was transported, swallowed whole into darkness and isolation. This was the fate, the destiny that Athoth had intimated to him: if Belias was to be trapped and isolated—if everyone and everything he loved were to be protected from the dark aeon and his familiars—Lucian would have to consign himself and his soul to this endless darkness and empty isolation.

Cold and dark as fate...

PARTITION SIX
Trust and Consequence

'Trismegistus, tell me, what is a body without a soul?'

'Rheginus, do you refer to a body that still lives after its soul has been taken?'

'Yes, Trismegistus, that is what I refer to.'

'Such a thing is a mere...*automatos*, Rheginus. A slave without will.'

'Trismegistus, tell me then, can a soul that is taken ever find its way back to its self?'

'Only if it is released, Rheginus. And only if its body, its envelope *materia*, remains alive.'

'And if its fleshy self perishes, Trismegistus? What then?'

'Then the soul is severed, Rheginus.'

—Excerpt from the Sixth Discourse 13,74-87

TWENTY-TWO

Fealties

Scrutinizing, with greater penetration, that harmony of the universe which the Greeks called *sympatheia* and grasping the reciprocal affinity of things, the theurgist draws forth the miracles which lie hidden in the storehouses and secret vaults of nature, as though he himself were their artificer.

—Pico Della Mirandola, *Oration on Sympatheia and Natural Magic*

Let lions dire this naked corse devour.

—Robert Burton, *The Anatomy of Melancholy*

In the more confined, almost Spartan labyrinth that was the second floor of the Convent of San Zaccaria, Pico Della Mirandola could smell the lion that paced obediently beside him like a dog trained to heel for its master.

The rank, sour odors of fur; the almost fishy fragrance of decaying particles of flesh trapped in gums and caries; and a palpable emanation, a prowling hunger, were suddenly transformed into a kind of feral, shared knowledge. Mirandola discovered that he could shift in and out of the beast's sensorium at will: the frightened yet stolid, wide-hipped nun leading them to the prioress's rooms was fresh meat, raw living meat perfumed with an intoxicating perspiration, a tangible essence which he could taste at the back of his throat. Her anxious fear was a pressure in his groin; and the lion's fear— more an adrenal thrill akin to sexual need—mingled with his own rising panic over what he was presently (and unexpectedly) experiencing. Panic.

Blind panic…

But the great theurgist of Florence was no longer blind, no longer removed from the enormous cache of knowledge he possessed as a cabalist, geomancer, mathematician, astrologer, alchemist, theurgist, theologian, and natural and occult philosopher. It was said that he knew more about *goetia* and *theurgia* — black and white magic — than anyone alive; he had deciphered the anagrammatic *Tabula Smaragdina* of Hermes Trismegistus and had demonstrated its great Hermetic principles by turning a brace bit into a quintessence of gold of exact weight; but until now he had not *become* his knowledge. He had not breathed it in like a Sybil her vapors, and he had needed the services of his skyrer Baldassare to penetrate the roiling mists of his own crystal gazing globe. He had, however, seen Belias' aetheric vines; but now...now as he looked through the eyes of the lion and experienced reality as a kaleidoscopic eternal present, he knew that he could no longer hold the reactive power of his knowledge at bay, could not protect himself from it; and that is what frightened him: how could he control this wellspring overflowing within him, threatening to carry him into the shadows and dark depths of his unexamined soul?

Mirandola made a guttural sound, as if he could physically expel such thoughts and fears; and as if in reply, the broad-waisted nun knocked sharply on a heavy door at the end of a narrow corridor. There was a muffled reply from within: the nun nodded and turned the latch, then edged away, pressing her girth as close to the wall as she could to distance herself from the two ungodly creatures that had been granted an audience with her prioress. Was it not enough that a priest who looked like a girl had proceeded them?

"Please to go in, ser," she said: to her credit, she did not move or say a word when the lion sniffed at her before pushing its way through the unlatched door. It entered the room and sniffed again, turning its great head this way and that; and ignoring the elderly prioress standing near the doorway, it headed directly toward a sumptuously dressed young woman sitting on a narrow, curtained bed in the far corner of the room.

"*Vi ordino di fermarvi!*" Mirandola shouted.

Indeed, the lion did stop.

As it looked back at him, Mirandola felt a hot spurting of adrenaline in his chest and tasted iron in the back of his throat as he slipped again into the lion's very being even before he realized he had willed it so. But this time there was not the snap-snap succession of disconnected images, no synesthetic smell-sight sensations of hunger or surfeit. Mirandola just saw a reflected image of himself and then, as the lion turned back to the young woman, he comprehended that the object of the lion's desire was not meat and blood, but a luminous presence that could not be completely hidden by any human contrivance, no matter how deftly and expertly concealed, no matter how deep or thick or opaque the materia: the small sapphire tablet secreted under the young woman's brocaded and jeweled *cotta* gown was a gifted fragment of Gabriel's precious soul.

As the lion sat before the young woman and put its head on her lap, the prioress made the sign of the serpent over her breasts and intoned, "*Viuo sicut leo in medio illorum, et misericordia tua Domine magna est.*"

I live as a lion in their midst, and your mercy, Lord, is great.

"Amen," said Mirandola, bowing to the prioress and feeling the lion's thrumming joy of the young woman's caress. As she scratched and massaged the loose flesh behind the lion's ears, she looked up at the theurgist and said, "I am Sister Maria Theresa, and I dreamed of both you and the golden one." The peaceful expression on her elfin, yet slightly odd-angled face indicated that she might still be within her dream.

"I but followed the lion here," Mirandola said, standing awkwardly before her and feeling a strong sexual attraction, which surprised him, for he rarely felt physical passion; he was surprised again when he realized that he was also petting the lion. He felt heat come into his face and stepped back.

Perhaps it is the presence of the tablet…

"What else did you see in your dream…and why are you not dressed in a habit?"

Sister Maria Theresa smiled and exchanged a quick glance with the prioress. "I am in disguise: the Pope's men are searching for me." She looked at the prioress again and said, "And I fear that neither one of us can remain here"— she turned her attention to the lion, which was immobile yet purring like a housecat—"now that *you've* come to visit." She raised her head and said, "Forgive my lack of manners, Magister. Please to meet Reverend Mother Arcangela Dolabella of San Zaccaria. She has risked everything so that I—so that we—may be here."

Mirandola bowed formally to the prioress and thanked her; she returned his courtesy and said, "Those of my community who have seen you can be trusted not to tell their sisters, and I have intelligence that your…companion was not seen by the rabble or petitioners in and around our piazza. However, as I told Sister Maria Theresa earlier, it is too dangerous to remain here, especially now with—"

"I know about Sister Maria Theresa's tablet," Mirandola said.

"Please, Maria Theresa will do," said the nun.

"The magister asked you about your dream, Maria Theresa," Mother Arcangela said; then she nodded to Mirandola and walked toward the door. "One of the nuns will come for you shortly. God's blessings upon you…both."

"Reverend Mother, please…" Maria Theresa said. "I understand your reservation, but please stay. Ignorance might be even more dangerous than knowledge."

"Is that in your dream, too?" asked the prioress.

Maria Theresa blushed and said, "Yes, Mother Dolabella. You were in my dream, just as you are here."

The prioress nodded and sat down at her desk: a safe distance away from the lion.

Gazing once again at the lion, Maria Theresa said, "The dream ended with—"

"With what, Sister?" Mirandola asked.

Maria Theresa shifted position. The lion sat back on its haunches, purring and watching her expectantly as she reached under her gown and loosened the bandeau that secured the sapphire tablet. "With this, Magister," she said, holding the tablet upright on her lap like a mirror. The lion rose, backing away from her, even as it watched its reflection floating upon the surface that was so blue it appeared black; and then it leaped, leaped toward Maria Theresa as if to devour her...and disappeared into the roiling surface of the small tablet. Mother Arcangela gasped and crossed herself.

Maria Theresa held the tablet out to Mirandola and said, "That is how my dream ended, Magister."

Mirandola felt a weakness come over him as soon as the tablet was in his hands. He gazed into it and saw the lion's golden eyes staring back at him: he felt the lion's presence and had the odd and immediate notion that if he, Mirandola, were to cast a shadow, it would be the lion's.

"Doesn't the tablet weaken you?" he asked, relieved after giving back the tablet, which she secreted behind the heavy, brocaded bed curtain.

"Yes, it weakens me, yet—somehow—it also strengthens me."

"Then perhaps you are meant to bear it."

"Does it weaken you?" she asked, leaning toward him; and as she did so, Mirandola felt as if he were once again holding the tablet. He nodded and said, "As it seems do you."

She smiled at that and said, "But the lion is yours, is it not?"

Mirandola felt a dizzying jolt as his sensorium shifted, and he passed through the infinities of sapphire that lay beyond the crystal surface of the hidden tablet: he was the lion wrapped in liquid light; and all thought and sensation was a combination of disconnected memory and prescience, flickering shades and smells of blue: and for an instant the scene shifted, and the trembling theurgist saw a priest—no, not a mere priest, but a cleric of high rank—being dragged along a jetty in chains.

Could it be—?

But there was more: he glimpsed Lucian and cried out.

"Are you all right, magister?"

Mirandola found himself once again standing before Maria Theresa. He composed himself and said, "Please, call me by my forename: Pico."

"Very well…Pico. Tell me, what did you just see?"

"I thought I saw Francesco Salviati, but my vision was—" He paused and said, "Blurred."

"You saw the archbishop?"

"I can't be sure, but I believe so. Why?"

"Because we must find him," Maria Theresa said.

Mirandola's expression hardened. "I think you'd best tell more about *your* dream, sister."

"I glimpsed you and the golden one, but there is more, which you may or may not already know."

"Yes?"

Maria Theresa looked again at the prioress, who seemed to be praying, and said, "The prioress of my own convent—Santa Sophia dei Miracoli—gave me the tablet."

"And who gave it to her?" Mirandola asked.

"She said it had been passed from each prioress to the next. I do not know who gave it to the order originally, just that it would remain under the order's protection until—"

"Until the final struggle," Mother Arcangela said, reciting, "when it will be given to one who has been chosen by the angel who is both brother and sister to the serpent and the lion. *Ecce seruus Domini.*" She paused, her once beautiful face even more lined in concentration; she also seemed…angry. Unable to contain herself any longer she asked, "But why in God's arms would you seek out such a man as the archbishop of Florence?"

"I have been made to understand that he is not as he appears, Reverend Mother," Maria Theresa said softly, almost tentatively.

"And did this vision of yours show you where you would find the archbishop?"

Maria Theresa shook her head.

"When I looked into your tablet, I saw a cleric," Mirandola said to Maria Theresa. "In chains. Being dragged away. Water…"

The prioress watched Mirandola, as if he were the lion himself, only perhaps more dangerous and closer to the motions of angels. "It is whispered that Archbishop Salviati was found barely alive by the good monks of San Michele. It was a sign from God that the Pope's flying gondola was destroyed on the Isle of the Dead. But that Salviati should have survived…" She spat, then stepped on her spittle, grinding it into the floor as if it was an insect. "Like the new Borgia pope, he's catamite to Belias and the—" She stopped herself, made a quick sign of protection. "But it is dangerous to speak or even think of such presences, lest we alert the Angevin," she said, referring to the

Pope's theurgist. *Still*, she asked herself, *why would the archbishop be brought to the pope in chains?*

There was a knock at the door.

"*Avanti*," said Mother Arcangela, and a nun who could not have been more than twelve or thirteen (although she wore a full habit with a red thread signifying that she had taken simple vows) entered the room and handed the prioress a sealed note. The prioress broke the seal, read the note, and then dismissed the nun who was gazing steadfastly at the floor. Unable to help herself, the young nun glanced furtively at Mirandola and Maria Theresa as she left the room. "The prioress looked up at Mirandola and said, "It seems that your presentiment was correct, Maestro. The archbishop had indeed been taken to the Pope's palace. In chains."

"*Perfetto*," Maria Theresa said.

Turning to her in surprise, the prioress said, "I would think that the archbishop will find his situation far from perfect."

"But it *is* perfect for us, Reverend Mother, now that the archbishop and the daughter of light are both in the palace."

"And do you intend to walk right in like a beautifully dressed and finished *zoccola* whore? I'm sure the Angevin and the Pope would greet you with open arms."

"Perhaps they would, Reverend Mother," Maria Theresa said, grasping hold of the tablet and holding it once again against her chest; Mirandola could see himself as if floating in its roiling depths. He shook his head and said, "Are you so sure I could slip inside the mirror like the lion? And even if I could, what good would it do? *You* certainly can't carry the tablet into the palace."

"She can't," said the prioress. "But I can…"

"No, dearest Mother, the pope's theurgist would sense its presence on your bosom as easily as a lamp in the dark."

"And your carefully worked out plan, daughter. How would that work?"

Maria Theresa looked away from the prioress, who held the note the young nun had brought her over the flame of a candle on her desk and then made a fist around the char before rubbing the lampblack from her palms. "As I thought. And even if I were exposed, even if the tablet was discovered, you and Maestro Mirandola might find a way inside the crystal to serve destiny. But my chances are more than even, Maria Theresa, for I will seek an audience directly with the Angevin theurgist; and I'm certain he will receive me."

"Can you be so sure the theurgist will receive you?" Mirandola asked.

She nodded, smiling sadly, and a blush came to her face. "I must look like Methuselah's wife to you, Maestro, but there was a time when he was happy enough to be received into my bed: I might add that was before I was initiated into true gnosis."

"You know him?" Mirandola asked, taken aback.

"As a theurgist, I would have expected you to know," she said.

"And you never thought to—" Maria Theresa.

"The Angevin wasn't aware either," said the prioress. "It was an eternity ago, and my secret...the card in my palm, you might say. Gian was not who he is now, and as his sometimes mistress, I was his great guilt. But that was before he, shall we say, misplaced his family."

"Gian?" Mirandola asked.

"His surname was Dei." She smiled grimly and said, "But he also liked to be called Jack Day." She pronounced the name as a guttural: *J'ach*. "He was, however, never an *agnus dei*." Mirandola had heard rumors of a great mage referred to as Agnus Dei, but had dismissed them as superstition. "Nevertheless," continued the prioress, "I learned many secrets from him, the Anevin tongue being only the least. He taught me how to hide whilst in full view, how to—"

"Forgive me, Reverend Mother, but do you mean the theurgist murdered his family?" asked Maria Theresa. Her hands trembled as she held the tablet, which no longer felt warm; suddenly enervated, she put it down on the bed, then pushed it away from her.

Noncommittal, the prioress shrugged and said, "You should indeed be fearful, daughter. A much more rational reaction; and now you must take your leave. As I said, it is dangerous for you to remain here. Once you are both inside the crystal, I will hide it."

"As you have been doing all along," Maria Theresa said.

The prioress made no acknowledgement; she seemed lost in thought. "I wonder, does one sense the duration of time inside the crystal?" She looked to Mirandola and said, "You might take some bread and wine to sustain you. One cannot tell how long you might be...imprisoned."

"I think not, Reverend Mother," Mirandola said. "There is no sense of duration inside the tablet. Only—"

"Yes, theurgist?"

"It's instantaneous. You step into it, and then you find yourself somewhere else."

And yet, Mirandola told himself, Lucian claimed to experience duration. For him it was a visible bridge, a place. Once again Mirandola felt his inadequacy: his one-time servant had probed more deeply, had perceived more.

I am, indeed, still blind!

He nodded to Maria Theresa, who retrieved the small tablet and gave it to Mother Dolabella. The prioress stood up and faced her guests, holding the tablet before her: in a blink, in an instant of blinding blue, a retinal flash, both Mirandola and Maria Theresa disappeared. From their perspective, however, the tablet had expanded; and they simply walked, hand in hand, through what seemed to human senses to be a perfectly squared doorway.

The lion was waiting for them in the roiling, timeless light.

"**C**ut me down," said the First Citizen, who was hanging naked from a rope attached to the *strappado* pulley affixed to the ceiling of the Chapel of Absolution.

After Belias had shifted himself and Lucian into his dark heaven, the few candles and torches that remained alight cast a cold coruscating radiance; and that light was magnified and reflected by the skim of ice that covered the intarsia walls and ceiling. It revealed the extent of the carnage: Baldassare, his lieutenant Lucca Parenti, and eight of his lancers were dead, as were Valentine and all his soulless guards who had been slaughtered in retribution by Pietro's compatriots...slaughtered in savage fury by soldiers no longer under the soporific influence of Devil's Weed.

With the help of a ladderman with a mottled gray and red beard and two of the other lancers, Pietro lowered Guiliano de Medici gently onto the blood-stained tiled floor. "No, I can stand," he said, planting himself solidly and stretching himself to full height; he checked for broken bones, surveyed the destruction, and then addressed the lancers, who were traumatized, confused, and shivering in the unnatural chill that filled the room: it was as if they had just awakened from a dream, only to discover that it was real: "Wait for me outside the chapel." But when Pietro stepped away to leave with the others, the First Citizen said, "*No, not you, Remembrancer*"; and it was then that Pietro realized that Athoth rather than the First Citizen was speaking directly to him without words.

"Are you—?"

"Yes, I reside once again within the First Citizen." Athoth said, speaking with Guiliano de Medici's lips.

"And what of the First Citizen? Is he...dead?"

Athoth/Guiliano de Medici smiled, but it was an expression of sadness. "No, he is just absent. I can only hope that my presence will help him recover himself...and that it will be soon."

Relieved, Pietro asked, "And you?"

"I will do what I can...what I must during this respite from Belias' devices, for your friend Lucian will not be able to contain him for very long."

"*O mio Deo*," Pietro said, recalling with horror what Lucian had done. "He has given up his soul, his—"

"Perhaps, perhaps not, Athoth said. "But we must use well the time he has gained us."

"To do what?"

"To regain what Belias has taken."

"Regain Florence?"

"We must certainly gather enough strength to contain Belias' forces, which he will gather when he returns, and return he will; but that is the least of it. There is something else that must be done."

"What more can be done?"

The First Citizen looked grim, and Pietro was sure that his appearance of slack fatigue was not only the result of Valentine's bodily torment, but was also an expression of Athoth's state of mind.

"If we are to have any hope of defeating the demiurge, we must help to balance the scales in our favor. We must release the souls Belias has taken... *all* the souls he has taken."

"And how would you propose we do that?"

"You and I, remembrancer, must follow your companion Lucian into Belias' heaven."

Pietro shivered at the thought.

"Belias is the designated keeper of the souls," Athoth continued, "because the demiurge would never allow Himself proximity to their taint."

"Taint...?"

"You—none of you—can completely separate yourselves from this," and Athoth/Guiliano pinched Pietro's flesh.

"Then you plan to release the First Citizen."

"I have not imprisoned him," Athoth said. "He is trapped in his own grief. He must release himself."

"And if he does not...if he cannot?"

"If he does not; and I vacate his heart and lungs and pneuma, he will remain inert. Like the soulless ones Valentine appropriated to maintain and enlarge his army."

"Well, *I* will watch over him," Pietro said, defiance in his thoughts if not in his voice; and then he corrected himself, as if the absent, sleeping soul that was Guiliano de Medici, First Citizen of the city and country of Florence could hear him, "I will watch over...*you*, Ser Guiliano."

"*That's commendable, but* I *need you*," Athoth said, silently speaking directly to Pietro, mind to mind, soul to soul as he gazed at him through the First Citizen's sightless eyes.

"What could you, an aeon, an angel of fury, possibly need *me* for?"

"*As a disguise…and to strengthen Gabriel's soul, which is what enabled your companion Lucian to overcome Belias.*"

"It was Gabriel's seal—the serpent—that overcame Belias," Pietro insisted.

"*The serpent, the tablet, they are one and the same, as are you and Lucian—*"

"I am *not* Lucian!" Pietro interrupted; and he realized and regretted his impudence and misplaced familiarity as soon as the words escaped him: gasping in pain, he cried out for forgiveness as Athoth's anger, or rather deadly disappointment, scalded him like steam; indeed, heat radiated throughout the room, immediately evaporating the residue of melting ice on walls, ceiling, and floor.

"*—for you and Lucian are one and the same in that you both contain the angel's sapphire soul,*" continued the aeon as if his rebuke was immediately forgotten. "*I myself gouged Lucian's serpent out of Gabriel's sapphire tablet, and did not the angel transform* your *very flesh and bones into stone? Into the tablet? Into his soul?*"

"Yes, aeon, but how could I disguise *you?*" Pietro asked, contrite.

"*By cloaking me in Gabriel's soul; perhaps Belias will not be able to discern the incremental addition.*"

Guiliano suddenly staggered backwards, and as if in imitation, so did Pietro.

Pietro felt a familiar burden, as Athoth passed into him as easily as a sharp knife into flesh. He also regained his connection with Lucian, which was now a conduit of hopelessness and darkness. Although the First Citizen could hardly stand now that Athoth had vacated his body, he turned to Pietro and nodded. Naked, burned, and flensed, his hair matted with blood and perspiration, his penis as shriveled and puckered as a child's, he looked less than a man, much less a ruler. And yet…

"It is I, Guiliano, young ser. I will not easily forget the god that dwelled inside me."

"Not a god, First Citizen," Pietro said, "but a perfect spirit." He felt Athoth's mirth: satin and needles rubbing inside him.

"Yes, Remembrancer," Guiliano said, his voice gaining strength, "he instructed me merely by his presence"; and then the First Citizen dropped to his knees as if in supplication.

"No, please, ser," Pietro said.

"*It is not meant for you, self-important fool,*" Athoth said. "*It is physical exhaustion, grief, and the submission that attends revelation.*"

Pietro's face burned in humiliation.

There was a knock at the door.

Acting quickly, Pietro helped the First Citizen to a cushioned chair; then he located a yellowed surplice hanging from a peg near the long-unused alter and wrapped the soiled and dusty gown around the citizen king. Guiliano nodded in appreciation and, looking to the door, said, "Enter."

But even as the First Citizen spoke, Athoth said to Pietro: "*It is time, remembrancer.*" The aeon was a sea of calm inside Pietro: fear and desire were submerged as they traversed the eternity between Urbino and Belias' dark, cratered heaven; and in that instant, Pietro thought...asked, "*And if we do not succeed, what then of the daughter of light?*" In the suffocating darkness, in the dead-cold darkness, Athoth replied, "*Her fate—the fate of us all—lies with your friends.*"

A world away the dwarf Achille Bentivogli and Elisabetta da Montefeltro—Duchess of Urbino, wife and consort of the murdered ruler Guidobaldo—found Guiliano de Medici, First Citizen of Florence, on his knees praying in the corpse-strewn yet empty torture chamber known as the Chapel of Absolution.

TWENTY-THREE
The Secrets of Shadows

When the miasmas of Lethe

  Flow like pneuma through her veins,

Then will she forget

  The meaning of all her pain...

—Prudentius, *Que Divinationem*

Fascination is a conjuration produced and maintained by the conjurer and sent out like igneous rays from open eyes to deceive the hearts, minds, and souls of those to whom it is directed.

—Giordano Bruno, *Concordia Magiaque*

"Welcome home, *filiæ lucis. We have awaited you for a thousand years...*"

Isabella kneeled before the fleshy pope and kissed his sapphire ring; but as she did so, the pope smiled at Louisa, who was not sure whether to kneel, bow, or stand her place. Then the pope grasped Isabella's hand firmly in his, and pulling her upright before him as if she weighed no more than a purse, said, "We should be kneeling before you, keeper of the flints from the Holy Sepulcher"—he turned his gaze back to Louisa—"and especially you, daughter of light."

How could he know about the flints? Louisa thought, bowing her head. *Could the archbishop be alive...could he be* here? *Or...could it be possible that the church* was *in thrall to the dark aeon Belias?*

As soon as the pope had spoken, his entire retinue knelt; all except for the theurgist, who genuflected but kept his place beside his master. "My physician, diviner, and most trusted councilor Magister Gian Dei will attend to your immediate needs, both spiritual and of this world," continued the pope, directing himself to Louisa, "and I, of course, as your humble servant, will be at your beck and call."

Louisa could not help but sense the irony and the slightest note of sarcasm in his voice, yet it did not matter because for the first time since she had left her home, since she had sailed through the crack in the sky, she felt...safe. In that dizzying instant, wrapped as she was in a nimbus of light and adoration—the exception being the imagined glint of avarice and trickery in the pope's slightly protuberant eyes—she attributed its cause to some thaumaturgy of Doctor Dei; that followed by a cold stab of guilt, for could it not be, rather, should it not be, that she had indeed come home, "come to the Lord" as the Reverend John Williams Jones always used to say when he preached to the Virginia Regulars?

"Welcome home," Doctor Dei said to Louisa, as if he had indeed read her mind. He smiled at Isabella, who grasped and squeezed Louisa's hand as if she, too, was disconcerted—somehow frightened—by this sudden onset of comfort and calm, and continued: "Now let us expose ourselves no longer to the crowds and canals, for danger can lurk in even the brightest light." The pope nodded in agreement. He waved to his worshippers who were crying "*Borgia vive! Vive Alexander, Venetiae beata manet!*" from roofs, balconies, boats, and the well-guarded streets and squares and led the daughters of light into the sudden cool shadows of the arcade, then through the Rio della Canonica and up a secret staircase into the well-guarded magnificence of his private apartments.

"We shall talk later," said the pope, stopping before a curtained doorway. One of his Swiss guard parted the draperies, while another unlocked the carved and inlaid door. Louisa glimpsed an ornamented golden ceiling and a wedge of a vibrantly colored painting in the erotic Florentine style of Botticelli. "Doctor Dei will settle you so that you may accustom yourselves to your new home." With a bow and a nod, he disappeared into the yellow glow of the candlelit rooms; and the theurgist guided Louisa and Isabella through a maze of tapestried corridors to their suite, which overwhelmed with its ornately carved and gilded ceilings decorated with friezes of Mercury and Minerva, Janus and Juno, Apollo and Aphrodite, Ares and Athena, and the deities of the day and the night: Hemera and Nyx. Statues seemed to loiter like ghosts behind candle-lit archways; high, narrow windows now dark would suffuse the rooms tomorrow with roseate light; and the stucco walls were covered with fine paintings depicting the Madonna and Child, angels frolicking in the meadows of heaven, and the resurrection of the Virgin in the temple. But it was a small diptych describing the trials and tribulations of Sophia and the flight of the daughter of light that caught Louisa's attention. Feeling suddenly dizzy, she sat down on a cushioned cassone.

"Yes, I thought that Albegreno's little painting might give you pleasure," Dei said, running his finger around its golden frame. "But, of course, I can see that you and your companion are so very tired." He smiled at Isabella who stood before him and looked confused. "You will find your bedrooms at the far end of the hallway," he said to Louisa. "Everything has been provided. Nuns will soon attend to your bath and will call you both to a late supper. I look forward to seeing you then." He bowed and took his leave, and after the door shut, there was another sound: that of a key turning in the lock. Whispering voices, then hollow quiet. As Louisa stood up to test whether they were indeed prisoners in this gallery of treasures, Isabella asked, "What did the theurgist say to you?"

"What do you mean? You heard him as well as I."

"But he spoke in a foreign tongue," Isabella said, looking at her curiously. "Was it your native tongue?"

Surprised, Louisa said, "Why, yes, of course. He spoke to me in a stilted way, but in English."

"And you did not think that strange?"

Louisa nodded. "Somehow it just seemed…natural."

"I think I need to rest," Isabella said, yawning. "But I also wish to stay right here, to savor every precious moment. Can you, too, feel the…holiness of this place? I feel that we are closer to God here than—" She looked up at the ceiling, as if it were itself one of the lower heavens. Then she turned back to Louisa and said, "Yet I can't help but feel that something…something is terribly wrong. We are *not* home. We are—" Then she folded her hands as if she had forgotten what she had been trying to say. Although she made no move to sit down or proceed to the bedroom, she repeated, "I'm very tired, Louisa."

Louisa nodded. She did not feel benumbed; tired, yes, but clear, comfortable, comforted. But why? And then she remembered the archbishop, remembered how she had cried out in pain when he had grasped her hand, burning her, and she remembered his words: *"I burned a path back to your soul to help you remember. Your soul remembers, even if you forget."* She pressed her thumb against the glassy pebbly seal that he had burned into her palm in the catacombs and remembered. She whispered *"Serpens sum."*

I am the serpent.

She remembered being captured by Belias, remembered his attack upon Athoth on the airship, remembered shattering his vines as if she were breaking crystal, and she whispered, *"Deuoraui arbustum."*

And I devour the vine.

Louisa had penetrated the theurgist's glamour. She sensed the intensities of darkness and light pulsing inside her. She trembled and shivered in the previously unfelt chill and menace of this place. She had regained herself, and now everything beautiful and sumptuous around her took on a new cast; but even as she gained clarity, even as she started to remember who she was—*what* she was—she felt herself wrapped in crystal calm once again, embraced and defeated, numbed and brought to heel by the unnatural glamour that infiltrated this place. She stood beside the door, desperately trying to recapture herself, trying to plumb her memories, but Doctor Dei's cantrip—or the overwhelming perfume and presence of the Lord of Hosts—was too strong; and Louisa was hopelessly lost in reverie or daydream, lost in an epiphany or a spell that confounded time. Or, perhaps, she was simply experiencing the honest and innocent bliss of being close to the machinations of the divine.

Suddenly the atmosphere in the room began to shift and clear.

Louisa could not tell whether a few moments or a few hours had passed, but *something* had disturbed the soul-numbing glamour. She could hear the faint yet comprehensible words of men in the corridor: Swiss guards speaking Germanic. But she drew her ear away from the door when she heard a scream, followed by shouting and the chaotic stomping of boots.

"Louisa, what is it?" Isabella asked, now alert and animated.

"I heard a scream," Louisa said, motioning to Isabella to wait.

The guards on the other side of the door held their positions. One of them called out and in turn received a response from the other end of the hall. "*Valentine ist tot.*"

"A scream...?" Isabella asked impatiently. "Who—?"

"I think it was the Holy Father," Louisa said, still listening at the door. "His son is dead. Valentine." But even as she spoke, she felt her palm grow hot. Once again she pressed her thumb against its glassy seal. She sensed her serpent self, her true soul, the soul of a thousand reincarnations. And she knew that she—Louisa Mary Morgan of Bartonsville, Virginia—was the last of those reincarnations. Just so could she sense the faint presence of the archbishop. She was certain he was here, here in the papal palace. Just as she was sure that the pope's son wasn't dead.

But he soon would be...

Pope Alexander VI had sequestered himself in his private chapel to grieve and stoke his anger and hatred of all things Florentine, especially the traitorous aeon Athoth and Pico Della Mirandola's servant and apprentice, the young Jew Lucian ben-Hananiah: they had both killed—or, rather, would kill—his son, and he was starving for revenge. His theurgist Gian Dei had compounded a preparation of opium tincture, crushed pearls, musk, nutmeg, ambergris, and saffron to calm the restive pontiff; but Alexander had the constitution of a bear. He had also consumed enough sugared hippocras to put any three men into coma. With only a crimson robe draped over his shoulders, he sat half-naked on a throne that had once belonged to the Patriarch of Rome. Behind him, illuminated by soft afternoon light, was a huge canvas by Carpaccio depicting the pope with a court of angels in attendance. "Don't stare at my balls," he said to his theurgist who stood patiently before him.

Dei nodded and bowed, but did not kneel: he had only knelt before the Borgia pope once, and that was when he was granted absolution. "What is your wish, Holiness?"

Alexander stared at him, his agony and rage controlled yet apparent in his expression. "If you had told me about my son's fate earlier, I could have—"

The theurgist stood where he was, not moving, waiting for the pope to continue; and when he didn't, Dei said, "I told you the moment I knew, Holiness."

"You told me on your way back from escorting the daughters of light to their rooms!"

"That was when I knew, Holiness."

"So you've said, theurgist, but I don't believe you." The pope sighed, his bulbous face seemed closed, his eyes unseeing: now revealing he was certainly drunk. "No man can walk and gaze into a skrying crystal at the same time, not even you." When Dei did not respond, the pope said, "Well…?"

"But I am here because I can, Holiness. I am here because I *can* double myself, which is how I protect you."

"Protect me?" the pope shouted.

"Was I not the one who told you of your archbishop's treachery?" Dei asked; and then continuing, his voice controlled, his affect patience itself: "I've explained how my shadow works, Holiness. But even so, even together, we can only do so much. Your pain is also my own."

"No, Gian," Alexander said softly. "My pain is mine alone."

"Then allow me to exorcise it, Rodrigo. Allow me to sponge it away."

The pope started when he heard his true baptismal name spoken, then settled back and smiled. "No, my devious thaumaturge; it is enough that your glamour extends throughout my palace. I will not put myself under your power now, especially now. It was in fact just for times such as this that I insisted you bind the fire demon Azâzêl. I did that to protect myself from…you."

"You have never needed—and will never need to be protected from me, Holiness. I offer you a temporary balm of forgetfulness, the same strong anodyne that prevents the daughter of light from recovering her memory before she is prepared for true revelation…the same anodyne that protects *you* from any premature evil she may—"

The pope waved his hand, commanding silence. "Invoke the demon."

The theurgist nodded reluctantly and closed his eyes; and as he generated a true image of Azâzêl in his mind's eye, so did the demon simultaneously appear in fleshy guise before the pope. Although its presence was as a stunted, wizened man, the demon exuded sexuality and a concentrated power. The small adamantine horns protruding from his forehead were so dark that they could be mistaken for declivities rather than extrusions; his green velvet gown was a brocade of intricately branching vines.

Ignoring Dei, Azâzêl bowed and said, "How might I ease your terrible pain, Holiness?"

"It is your place to respond, not initiate," Dei said.

Azâzêl acknowledged the theurgist with a solemn, exaggerated bow.

"Abominable creature, tell me of my son Valentine," said the pope.

"He is being murdered as we speak, Holy Father."

The pope glanced at Dei angrily. "And can that be changed, creature?"

"My name is Azâzêl, Holy Father. Is this my reward for revealing the secrets of the world which were prepared in the heavens? To be called—"

"Answer him, demon!" Dei said.

Azâzêl nodded insolently and said, "His flesh is mortified, Holy Father. Ah, but you're asking if time and circumstance can be undone."

"Yes, Azâzêl, that's exactly what I'm asking you."

"Time can be twisted and shifted, beguiled as it were," said the demon. "But that is certainly not an undertaking for the likes of mortals." Azâzêl bowed to the theurgist, then continued addressing the pope. "It is even beyond the capabilities of lesser spiritual beings…beings such as myself and all the various lesser angels. You would have to solicit the services of an aeon, or an archangel at the least."

"And such a being could bring my son back to life?"

"The dead cannot be so easily resurrected, Holy Father. Were circumstance or time hindered, then your son would be alive: he would never have died… and you would not be here grieving and praying for his resurrection."

"I am not praying for his resurrection, demon Azâzêl," the pope said, his face now hard, his surging hope repressed, controlled. "I am seeking a solution. Are you here then to tell me it is beyond your power to solve this… problem?

"No, Holiness, but if I compact with you, there must be fair quid pro quo."

"That would depend on my son. His life for—what do you seek, demon?"

"To be completely free and never to be called upon again by you or by anyone you claim." The demon turned to Dei and smiled.

"I think there is another more felicitous solution," Dei said, staring down the demon.

"Yes, theurgist, I'm listening."

"Holiness, we do have an aeon to whom we may beg a favor, and would it not be better to have an obligation to heaven than to free this loathsome demon who has gained intelligence of us?"

"And you could summon this aeon?" asked the pope.

"One does not summon an aeon, Your Holiness." The pope gestured impatiently, and Dei continued: "But we could invoke his name and pray for an incarnation."

The pope nodded, then said to Azâzêl, "You seem suddenly merry."

The demon bowed so low that he might have been directing his words to the inlaid floor: "I could never be merry in the presence of such grief as yours, Holy One; but might I suggest you ask your thaumaturge for the name of the aeon he intends to…summon."

"Shall I cast you back into the abyss from whence you came?" Dei asked the demon. "It is only by the largess of—"

"What aeon *do* you allude to?" the pope asked, now even more impatient with his theurgist.

"Belias," answered Dei, and then, directing himself to the demon, "our Lord's eighth authority who reigns in darkness."

Azâzêl simply shook his head.

"Speak, demon," said the pope.

"The dark aeon cannot help you for he is himself held captive…held captive, in fact, by the Jew who killed your son, Holiness."

"Do you believe we can be so easily deceived by such nonsense?" Dei asked.

The demon shrugged and said, "The Holy Father asked me what I know to be true, and I've told him."

"How could such a thing happen?" asked the pope.

"Like the daughter of light, the Jew is a reincarnated and as yet unrealized power," Azâzêl said. "Albeit a significantly lesser one. He used the serpent seal gifted to him by the angel Gabriel to capture Belias' soul; and he was aided in this endeavor by the traitorous aeon Athoth."

"I did not skry any such thing," Dei said.

"No," said Azâzêl, "but *I* did." He turned back to the pope. "Your theurgist did not ask for my council; and it was not my place to give it, even though my vision penetrates deeper."

"How could such energies be hidden?" Dei asked himself, but his thought was unguarded and the demon responded:

"While the Jew swallowed Belias' soul, Athoth gathered his weakened vines—his discarnate limbs—and twisted them to shift time around itself and hide their theft from heaven's eyes." Although the demon answered Dei's unspoken question, he directed himself to the pope.

"So you claim to perceive what is hidden from heaven itself?" Dei said. "Is that what you would have us believe?"

"If I could see with heaven's eyes, I would not be beholden to *you*, Magister," the demon said, resisting the theurgist's binding power. His voice had the timbre of an echo rather than breath. "It is because I can see through the darkness that you released me from the abyss and summon me now."

"I summoned you because the Holy Father—"

Overwhelmed with impatience, the pope banged his fists against the marble lions that served as armrests. "*Chiudi il culo!*"

Shut the fuck up!

Both theurgist and demon bowed their heads and fell silent.

"Demon Azâzêl, contrive to bring back my son, and I will grant your reward," said the pope.

Azâzêl nodded.

"Well, then, what is your plan?"

"I will need Magister Dei to facilitate or, at the very least, not interfere with my strategy."

"I shall have his word on that." The pope waited for his theurgist's acknowledgement, then said, "Now stop burning daylight and tell me what you propose, demon."

"It must be done quickly and with stealth," said the demon, "but you must kill the daughter of light, murder her just as the filthy Jew and his renegade aeon killed your son."

"Holiness—!" pleaded Dei as he tried to control the resisting demon.

The pope ignored him and addressed the demon coolly. "You would have me murder God's messenger, she who is to bring the end of days and open the gates of heaven to His elect?"

"Pretty words and untested promises which will not bring your son Valentine back," said the demon.

"This I cannot do!" said the pope. "And why...why should I even consider perpetrating such an abomination?"

"Because her soul, which is the soul of an aeon, can be manipulated by *me* to accomplish what you seek, can be manipulated to strangle time just enough to squeeze away the death of your son...and all memory of its"—the demon made a generous motion with his hands—"having ever happened." The shadow of a smile passed over the demon's face. "Because it would not have *ever* happened."

"Allow me to send him back to hell now, Holiness," Dei said, desperately trying to regain his hold over Azâzêl, even as he felt the deadly release of the demon's power. "How can you even contemplate—"

Confident enough now to interrupt his master, the demon said, "Holiness, you are simply releasing her soul...or I should say collecting it. You are not killing an aeon, for she is not yet an aeon. She is merely an envelope that contains the soul. But should she awaken to who she is, should she become her true self, then your son is lost forever."

"I cannot—could not—commit such as offense against God."

"You cannot destroy her soul, Holiness. You will not be destroying the daughter of light. You will, in fact, be fulfilling God's plan."

"By destroying his messenger?"

"By postponing the end of days and the time of darkness."

"Holiness," said Dei, pleading, "such an act could only *obstruct* God's will. The demon means to prevent the destruction of Satan and all the fallen angels he commands. What is he but a creature of darkness?"

"Why would I wish to save the very entities which imprisoned me?" asked the demon, addressing himself to the pope. "My loyalty is to you who have released me," the demon said, lying, keeping to the pretence that Jehovah was God and not the demiurge and that Satan was free and not imprisoned in the icy realms of Belias. "I have no wish to return to the abyss, and I certainly have no wish to preserve those who would confine me."

Determined to take matters into his own hands, whatever the consequences, Dei began an invocation that would expel the demon; but the pope commanded Azâzêl to prevent it. Dei felt his throat constrict. He began to gag on his own tongue. He could not draw breath. In desperation, he tried to make the sign of dismissal; but could not move his arms: the demon had become more powerful than the conjuror.

"Enough," the pope said to the demon. "I do not wish to lose my theurgist... at least just yet"; and then to Dei: "Would you presume to disobey me again?"

Dei shook his head while he strained to draw breath.

"You would do well to remember that if I decide to do something, it *is* God's will," the pope said to Dei.

Dei nodded. Struggling, he said, "You might ask the creature just how long he intends to retain the power of the daughter's soul...long enough, perhaps, to overthrow the very church, which you, Holiness, embody?"

But the pope did not seem to hear him.

"Make it so," he said to the demon, "and if my theurgist fails you, then kill him." With that, the pope instantly fell asleep.

PARTITION SEVEN
The Dark Companions

'Trismegistus, tell me, then, what happens after the Great Darkness.'

'Not even scripture can see past that, Rheginus.'

'But how can that be, Trismegistus? Even aeons can see through time.'

'Would you believe scripture to be composed by aeons?

'If not aeons, then who, Trismegistus?'

'Many believe scripture to be dictated directly by the Invisible One or by the favored aeons who serve his lights. But many also liken our sacred words to golden soot, the golden soot of dreams and epiphanies: the dreams and epiphanies of the chosen.'

'That smacks of blasphemy, Trismegistus.'

'Truth often does, Rheginus.'

'Tell me, then, Trismegistus, what do you believe?'

'I believe that we—we who have the shame of being the offspring of the demiurge—must content ourselves with the golden soot of hopeful dreams and epiphanies, Rheginus.'

—*Excerpt from the Seventh Discourse 22,34-37*

TWENTY-FOUR
Flints and Daggers

The flowing Lethean waters
Now steal through every vein,
Yet still she can remember
The meaning of her pain.

—Prudentius, *"After Sleep"*

Be careful not to change yourself from manipulator into
the tool of phantasms.

—Giordano Bruno, *De Magia*

Beneath the papal palace, in one of the tombs called wells by the prison guards because of the canal water that flowed into them through grates no larger than a hand span, the magus and archbishop of Florence Francesco Salviati slept fitfully. He lay curled up on a trestle that served both as bed and cupboard. Filthy water rose and subsided beneath him, gurgling and soughing and splashing as it passed through the gratings that provided the only light. Although this cell was larger than some of the others in this subterranean prison, the sweating ceiling was so low that, had he been awake, he could reach up and touch it with his hand. Cold water dripped onto his face, but with no effect: for the archbishop was already submerged, submerged in a lucid dream that removed him from the claustrophobic confines of his cell, a dream that chilled him even as it gave him an inchoate, irrational hope. He dreamed that he was holding a transparent crystal dagger with which he could free himself, but was this freedom a presentiment of his death and removal from the cares of his flesh? Or was it something else? As he questioned himself, the dagger fell from his hand, fell like droplets of rain, and transformed itself into clear water, which swirled like oil around his legs and then swallowed him entire. But, no, it was not water: it was an infinitely deep ocean of living, animate sapphire concentrated into a perfect geometrical object...and floating in its transparent depths were other perfect objects: the seven flints from the Holy Sepulcher.

The archbishop awakened with a start and reflexively ran his tongue over the flinty surface of a false tooth, which was indeed the smallest of the holy flints he had rescued from the chapel of the burning church in Florence: he had shaped and chiseled it before jamming it into his gap-toothed gum, which had wept tears of blood before accepting it.

He intoned a cantrip to ease the lingering pain of a leg that was badly twisted and a shoulder dislocated when he had fallen from the airship. Both his arms and legs had been entangled in his rope ladder, which was caught by the outstretched branches of a tall cypress tree near the monastery of San Michelle...and it was there, there on the Isle of the Dead that the good monks of San Michelle found him, cared for him, and betrayed him.

The pain became barely noticeable after a few moments: his arm a phantom limb, his chest, stomach, and back a distant ache. I'm getting too old for this, he thought as he contemplated a huge water rat eyeing him from the corner of the tomb. He held at the ready a makeshift cudgel hidden by a former prisoner and wondered when the pope's theurgist would interrogate and torture him again. This time he would no doubt be lowered onto the *culla di Guida*, the Judas Cradle, a device which was no more than a stool with a fecal smeared iron pyramid affixed to the top; but the archbishop could bear pain as well as his torturer; it would simply be an ignominious and humiliating death. Nevertheless the archbishop was not sanguine: Gian Dei just might penetrate his psychological inner sanctum, the manifold mental barricades and buttresses that protected his thoughts and memories; and if that happened, then the pope's sorcerer would suck out the archbishop's life and knowledge just as easily as Belias' vines swallowed souls.

If need be, he could club himself. He caressed the cudgel on his lap and positioned himself to drop easily and directly into the water; and then, to calculate the most efficacious angle, he directed the cudgel toward his head several times.

But suicide is a mortal sin.

He smiled at the idea of an old *assassino* having compunctions about self-murder. He gazed into the mephitic water rising and falling below him and listened to the muted screams of the prisoners in other cells.

And patiently, ever so patiently, he waited...

Mother Arcangela Dolabella, prioress of the convent of San Zaccaria and the former mistress of Gian Dei, then known as Jack Day, was indeed received by the theurgist in the papal palace; but not quite in the manner she had anticipated.

First she was searched on the Foscari Porch in a small room beside the *Scala dei Giganti* by two seemingly dazed, sloe-eyed guards under the watchful eye of the demon Azâzêl, who had retained the form of a stunted wizened man dressed in green velvet; neither did he try to disguise his adamantine horns. At Azâzêl's direction, the guards tore open her habit, and the demon snatched the tablet she had secured under her breasts; but to her surprise the demon screamed in agony when he grasped it. He dropped it immediately; and then, squeezing his burned hand as if to quell the pain, he looked up at the Prioress, who had betrayed herself with the slightest hint of a smile. "You came to betray your lover. You came to carry this piece of slippery carrion"— he glanced at the tablet—"into God's house."

"God's house? You horrid little distortion of a man."

The demon seemed surprised that the Prioress was able to speak to him like that.

Mother Dolabella felt her throat constricting, but she managed to continue: "A fire demon speaking of God's house? You filthy perversion of—"

She gagged. She could not breathe, could not swallow.

"Croak like a frog, mother of whores," Azâzêl said softly. "Think now, have you just taken your last breath? Do you wish to live, or shall I just think you dead right now?" In jest he asked the guards for their opinion; but they could have no opinion, for they'd been emptied of their souls for more days than they might have counted.

Mother Dolabella stumbled forward, her hands around her neck, as if she could pull away the invisible hands strangling her...as if she could squeeze out the invisible fist pushing deep into her throat.

"Ah, I think that if these doughty soldiers could think as I do, they would have some little compassion for the old and the weak," said the demon, releasing his hold on the Prioress.

The prioress took a deep, wheezing breath.

"Now, isn't that better?" asked Azâzêl, as if he were speaking to a child. "And just to prove the boundlessness of my compassion, I'm going to deliver you to the man you thought to betray." Now it was his turn to smile. He nodded to one of the guards to pick up the tablet and told the other to take this "*pote de Cristo*" to the pope's theurgist.

Her vision distorted by tears, the prioress could still not stop coughing as one of the guards—a toothless wreck of perhaps twenty years with a pocked face and strong boney hands—dragged her through a doorway and down a flight of filth-slippery stone steps, led her down one flight then another into the subterranean tombs, into the sewers of the palace. She did her best to keep upright as they sloshed through canal water, and then, the turn of a key, the rasping click of a lock, and she felt herself pushed into a tiny dark cell. Another click, the swashing sounds of the guard leaving as he spoke to himself in singsong, "Where, where, where, where are you, lost, dear, lost, lost", his voice soft and plaintive; and as Arcangela Dolabella kneeled in cool, stinking water, she coughed, gasped for breath, and felt strong hands lifting her, lifting her onto a pallet.

"You don't recognize me, do you...Cecilia?"

The voice sounded muffled, as if it were no more than a thought in her head. Nevertheless she stiffened upon hearing her old name, a name she had buried along with many other ancient, womb-tearing memories.

Wet and shivering, the prioress looked at the man who was so very close to her. She could smell his acrid perspiration, a perfume that galvanized those very memories of love and anger and loss; but try as she might, she could not really *see* him. *Perhaps it's just the lack of light, or the corrupt humours that have clouded my eyes. But, no, that could not be...* "I could never forget you," she whispered.

"Nor could I forget you, and I am pleased that you remembered what I had taught you so very long ago."

"I hadn't forgotten," the prioress said, "but that filthy demon easily pierced my veil. He is powerful, more powerful than—"

"But you did not forfeit your thoughts to him, and you protected yourself from his vaporous enchantment almost as well as I could..."

As he spoke, his face and form suddenly resolved, and the prioress could see what the Angevin theurgist Gian Dei had become: an old man, his once pale and freckled face now lined, his fair skin turned to parchment; but his eyes, his eyes were still as deep-set and as piercingly blue as when he was forty and virile.

He smiled sadly as he looked at his old lover.

He could still see into her.

"I did not expect to find you in...*here*," she said.

He looked around the cell and laughed softly. "Neither did I."

"What happened?"

"I had what you might call a disagreement with the pope and my demon."

"Your demon?"

"He did not *belong* to me," Dei said. "I merely invoked him upon His Holiness's order."

"His name?"

"I would not repeat it here."

She nodded. "And your disagreement?"

"The pope ordered me to acquiesce to the murder of the daughter of light."

"*O Lux Deus noster*, how could he—even he—consider such a thing?"

Dei explained.

With a lump in her throat she asked, "And the daughter of light, is she…?"

The theurgist shrugged and asked, "Do you remember my familiar, my sometimes fleshy shadow?"

"Yes," she said impatiently. "It was as I recall one of your many perversions."

"Indeed, I would not argue with God's sister, but be that as it may, the demon has taken it from me as easily as a nipple from a child."

"And…?"

"The shadow was my eyes and ears and the locus of what little strength and power I possessed."

The prioress made the sign of the snake over her breast.

"And *that*," Dei said, "has always been at the heart of *our* disagreement. However, I still have some residue of strength. The demon couldn't take everything, for my soul—my shadow—is like these motes of dust that drift in the air. Some little of it is still left." He waved his hand. "And yes, the daughter of light lives. But for how long, I cannot say."

"Can you help her?"

"You mean can I help you."

The prioress did not reply.

"Did you think that by changing your name from Cecilia to Arcangela I would not know who you are and where you were?" asked Dei. "Did you not have at least some curiosity to see me once again?"

"I saw you, Jack."

"But you could not abide what I've become, is that it?"

"You became what you desired."

"I desired to serve my church."

"And *this* pope?"

"*The* pope."

The prioress nodded.

"I've always loved you, Cecilia, but I couldn't—and can't—abide your heretical beliefs."

"Yet you did not unmask me."

"It *had* occurred to me," Dei said. "Many times." Then after a beat, he continued: "You have, no doubt, heard the rumors about me. Do you believe them…?"

As he was in earnest the prioress said softly, "No, Jack. You are many things, but I do not believe you murdered your poor wife and daughters."

He nodded in thanks.

After the moment had passed, she said, "But I would not disabuse anyone of their beliefs, Jack, for you *are* a dangerous, cruel, narrow-sighted man."

"Yet you expect me to go against everything I hold sacred to help you."

"No, I expect you to prevent an atrocity against God."

"Yours or mine?" Dei asked, smiling sadly at his old lover. But you've lost the tablet to the demon...lost your gift for the archbishop. Do you know that he is here in the tombs, too, although I must confess I have tortured him almost to his death."

"Why...? He is one of your own."

"No, Cecilia, he is one of *your* own; but if he can see past his pain and his loathing of me, then perhaps, just perhaps..." He reached into a pile of what seemed to be garbage: bits and pieces he had salvaged from the ebbing and flowing canal water: a lump of charcoal would serve as a pen, a piece of bloodstained cloth would suffice in lieu of parchment. He wrote a note in his slanted, almost feminine script and then made a low whistling sound.

A huge water rat swam up to the trestle where Dei sat.

"*Santa Madre di Dio*," Mother Dolabella said, backing away from the evil-smelling creature.

"Hush," Dei said to her as he held the cloth out to the rat, which grasped it delicately between its teeth and then, holding it above water, swam through an enlarged opening, which had once housed a grill.

"What can you hope to gain by using that abomination to—?"

"Patience, Cecilia. Patience."

Five minutes, ten minutes, an hour, and as the light waned and the water turned black, the rat returned, its eyes glints of sapphire; and it disgorged something dark and slippery into Dei's waiting hand.

"What is it?" asked the prioress.

Dei nodded as he dried the shard that had the rough shape of a tooth and then scratched the ivory hued patina away with his fingernail. "It is one of the flints stolen from the Holy Sepulture." Musing, he continued, "So your archbishop held something back from the companion of the daughter of light...and from Athoth himself. Well," he said to the prioress, "shall we take a chance?"

"What do you mean?"

And with that Dei raised the flint to his mouth and breathed on it until it shimmered and wavered and became transparent. As the prioress watched, the flint also seemed to increase in size and change shape until it resembled a small, yet deadly dagger.

Suddenly frightened for Dei, she tried to push the dagger away from his face; but too late: it silently exploded. Dei's face, rapturous, was bathed in its sharp white light. He stood up so quickly that his feet splashed water all over the prioress. Then he invoked the demon, which appeared before him. Azâzêl's look of perplexity turned immediately to anger, then abject fear, as Dei whispered an incantation and with one quick motion passed his hand through the demon, slicing him apart like meat.

Mother Dolabella thought she saw something in the theurgist's hand, something sharp and crystalline; but then she gagged as the demon, burning without flames, was reduced to a foully acrid and suffocating miasma that filled the cell and settled upon the canal water as black scum.

"Jack," she cried as Dei fell gasping upon the pallet. She supported him as best she could, cradling him in her arms.

"I can only pray that the archbishop's flint has not been ill used," he said; and summoning what little strength he had left, he willed the cell locks to open. "That will let the lion out of the cage," he whispered.

"You know about the lion in the tablet?"

"I meant Salviati, the archbishop, but, yes, I know about the lion and the tablet. Those contained in the tablet are now free." He winced, his face expressing terror and revulsion. "But I am not."

"What do you mean?"

He looked down into the water. "There, it still retains substance. Quickly, pick up the flint and do to me what I did to the demon."

The prioress could see something reflective in the foul water: the flint... the miniature transparent dagger.

"No, I cannot!"

"The demon has sent my double, my shadow, to murder the daughter of light. You must stop it by—"

But it was indeed too late, for even as Dei rested in the prioress's arms, he became nothing more than the sweet sour odor Mother Dolabella remembered from all those years ago.

He left the prioress with only a whisper:

"You must stop her. You must sabotage the keeper of the flints..."

Isabella Sabatini, the keeper of the flints, lay beside Louisa Mary Morgan, the daughter of light, and looked up through the parted bed canopy and curtains at the vaulted, pale blue ceiling decorated with gold leaf and richly painted friezes. On the walls, wan light shimmered through small, glass circlets geometrically set beside and atop each other in domed and circular casings; and candles guttered in sconces. Quietly, so as not to disturb Louisa—who was snoring softly, exhausted from trying to overcome the invisible, numbing miasmas: the glamour that brought false comfort, peace, and a conviction that this place was filled with God's holiness—Isabella heeded the soft voice that had awakened her.

The voice that whispered to her, whispered to her alone.

Was it the voice of God commanding?

Was it the voice of an aeon, an angel?

Or, perhaps, yes, that was it…it was the voice of the archbishop, the very one who had helped her and Louisa through their ordeals in the catacombs and in the airship. Hadn't he saved them? And now he was here, must be here in the pope's palace, the very center of the church. It is God's will, she thought. God had saved him, just as he had saved her and Louisa.

Isabella hesitated, for Louisa—turning and groaning in the bed, twisting the satin sheets around her like winding cloth—was talking in her sleep. What was she saying? Isabella could just make out:

"*Hoc non…*"

"*est…*"

Turning over, pulling the covers around her as if she were cold.

"*sanctus locus.*"

"No, Louisa," Isabella whispered, "this place *is* holy." She backed away toward the sitting room. Even in her sleep, she would argue with me. This place *is* holy! She repeated "*Locus est hic sanctus*" as if it were an incantation or a psalm. Isabella had enough proof: her feelings, her instincts, the ongoing moment by moment epiphanies, the absolute certainty that she had finally, finally found God's truth. Right here, right now, in this holy place, she was bathed in bliss. She was a flower opening to holiness, reveling in the light that could not be seen but only felt; yet even here, even now, she felt a poignant sadness for her beloved cousin Pico Della Mirandola and all those he influenced with his poisonous heretical ideas.

Jehovah is God…and his archbishop is calling me.

"It's not the archbishop," Louisa mumbled in her sleep; but Isabella didn't hear her. Instead, she heard a voice which was like a thought in her head.

"*Walk toward the Hall of the Scudo, that's right, and I'll—*"

Isabella felt a chill when the archbishop's voice suddenly ceased, as if swallowed. The atmosphere of certainty, holiness, and calm was immediately transformed into one of dread, darkness, and twisted hatred. It was as if she could see truly, pierce the glamour, the falsity; but then the break was mended, and a blissful calm once again flowed around her like water in a hot spring. She forgot Louisa who was trying to break the shackles of her dream coma.

"*There you are,*" said a voice; but was the voice a consequence of breath? Was it inside or outside her head? She looked for the archbishop in the tapestry covered corridor, but all she could glimpse was a shadow…the shadow that had once belonged to Gian Dei, the pope's theurgist.

Freed, the archbishop Francesco Salviati made his way to the cell the prioress Arcangela Dolabella had shared with Gian Dei. The prioress offered the blade shaped flint she had retrieved from the scummy water to Salviati. It was no longer smooth and crystalline. "You are the last person I would expect to be handing a holy object."

Salviati smiled, his face shadowed, as he accepted the flint.

"It is as warm and"—she paused—"enervating as—"

"As the sapphire tablet?" asked the archbishop. He gazed at the flint, which looked to be the essence of *materia*, the opposite of the aetheric, as if he were trying to penetrate time and event…which he was. "Certain objects such as this and the sapphire tablet are attributes of the divine. They are pathways to power, lures to demons and angels; but we, fleshy beings, cannot long withstand their presence. They steal our souls as do Belias' vines, albeit more slowly." He looked up at the prioress, first accusingly, and then his face softened. "You did not use the flint to destroy the theurgist, as he asked, did you?"

"I could not. I would not know how, I—" Her old eyes were filled with tears. Humiliated, she turned away from the archbishop.

"Well, holy sister, I fear that you have given Dei to the demon."

"But Jack destroyed the demon."

"Not entirely. The demon reached into your theurgist's—"

"He's not—he wasn't *my* theurgist," the prioress said, spitting, defending.

"The demon poisoned Dei's shadow, the familiar he created out of his own pneuma. By killing Dei when he asked you would have destroyed his shadow and saved the daughter of light." The prioress' reaction was a plosive exhalation. After a beat she asked, "What then can be done, *Amplitudo Vestra*? Can she still be saved?"

The archbishop closed his eyes, concentrating.

"I must leave. Now!" He bent low and backed out of the cell.

"What can I do to help?" asked the prioress.

"Return to your convent."

"The tablet…you *must* find the tablet."

But the archbishop had already disappeared into the darkness.

TWENTY-FIVE

Assaults and Barricades

Oh, unhallowed guardians of darkness, have you dispatched your myrmidons to barricade your doors and prevent the companions of Gabriel from entering your sites?

—Bohuslav Hasištejnský z Lobkovic, *Assault On Erebus, Canto XX*

Learn this from the fox and the lion: the lion does not defend himself against traps; the fox does not defend himself against wolves. Thus one must be a fox to identify traps and a lion to frighten off wolves.

—Niccoló Machiavelli, *The Prince*

The archbishop found the soulless guard who had escorted him to his cell: the same guard who had later escorted the prioress. The guard stood in his way, watching him, yet showing neither surprise nor belligerence. His eyes as guileless as a cow's.

"Your master is the demon, is he not?" asked the archbishop.

The guard curled his long fingers around the hilt of his sword, then released them, curl and release, curl and release—a nervous tic—and intoned, "Lost, dear, lost, lost."

"What have you lost?"

"It's lost, dear," said the guard.

"Your demon is lost, too," said the archbishop. "Lost forever. As dead as an immaterial spirit can be."

The guard lowered himself into a fighting stance, legs apart; but did not draw his sword. "I must obey man-who-is-not-man. I obey him, Azâzêl, I must obey Azâzêl."

"Azâzêl is no longer your master."

"He is lost, too, dear?" he asked, trying to think something through, then blinking his eyes when he failed.

"Yes, Azâzêl is lost forever," answered the archbishop. "Lost...just like your poor soul."

With that the guard started wailing, "Where, where, where, where are you, lost, dear, lost, lost." As he spoke, the guard moved toward the archbishop, who stepped backward: he had learned from experience that those who had lost their souls seemed to gain in return a brute, almost mechanical strength; and, of course, they felt no pain, like the fabled *Hashshashins* in the East.

"Perhaps, perhaps it can be found," the archbishop said, lying. "Your soul."

The guard stopped, confounded.

"But only if you help me," continued the archbishop.

"Then you, you are the man-who-is-not-man?"

After pausing to weigh up the dangers of his reply, the archbishop said, "Yes, if you like."

"And you will find my dear, my lost, my...?"

"Yes, but as I told you, I need your help. I need to know the location of the tablet. Azâzêl couldn't touch it, but you...you could, couldn't you? You or one of the other guards could touch it, hold it. Move it." When the guard's only response was a blink of his eyes, the archbishop moved his hands before his chest to indicate a rectangle. "Blue...like your eyes. Blue...blue. Think. Can you remember?" It is entirely possible that he never saw it, mused the archbishop, perhaps I should—

"Man-who-is-not-man. Gave it to me to give to Hell."

"You mean Azâzêl," the archbishop asked, testing.

"Man-who-is..." The guard's voice trailed off.

"So Azâzêl gave *you* the tablet, the sapphire tablet?"

The guard gave an exaggerated nod.

"And you gave it to Hell?"

Another nod.

"What do you mean, gave it to Hell? Tell me exactly."

The guard seemed conflicted, angry, and stepped forward, then backward. He smacked his toothless gums, then said, "Gave it to Hell, to...darkness just like man-who-is-not-man showed me."

The archbishop risked touching the guard's wrist, hoping to gain some sense of his mind, hoping to burn and communicate as he had with the daughter of light; but it was like touching rough sandstone, *materia* without the precious infusion of soul and pneuma. But, no, there *was* something; he sensed, glimpsed something shaped like a doorway; indeed, a doorway that led into the dark, cold realm of Hell...Belias' realm of ice.

"Why would Azâzêl order you to give the tablet to...Hell?" the archbishop asked.

The guard shook his head, then looking belligerent, said, "Now find my dear, find it, dear. Man-who-is-not-man said the tablet the power was cold dangerous don't give the power to the daughter, no, no, don't do that, man-who-is-not-man said, he said give it back to the dark where it can't hurt man-who-is-not-man, can only—"

"Can only what?"

The guard shook his head again, then unsheathed his sword. "Now find my dear, you promised dear."

The archbishop calculated his best escape route and asked, "Yes, we will find your dear, we will indeed; but first you must tell me what you saw in the tablet."

"In the blue almost night which sent into the dark?"

"Yes."

The guard moved toward the archbishop, his face now hard and threatening. "Eyes," he said. "Eyes big and big yellow like a cat now find my dear you promised, tablet is blue your blood is red, give me back or you are—"

Dead?

But the archbishop disappeared—or rather stepped deftly into shadow, then slipped through a narrow passage that led to narrow stairs, which, in turn, led to the bloodstained Sufferer's Staircase and the Floor of the Loggias—and the guard grasped empty air, his face reflecting a faint, shallow expression of surprise before returning to its natural state of slack oblivion.

The lion leaped out of the sapphire tablet and slipped on the icy surface of a world forever dark and cold. When it finally came to a stop and gained its footing, it sniffed the crystal air, shivered, and turned back to the tablet, which was a bright rent, a doorway standing like a cryolite cenotaph in the silvery monochrome darkness of Belias' cratered heaven. The lion watched Mirandola and the nun Maria Theresa da Rieti step onto the stony, slippery surface of this heaven of night and shadow. Watched the doorway narrow, then close.

"Where *are* we?" Mirandola asked, turning, looking around, trying to get his bearings and quell his panic. His breath was icy, silvered; and, like the lion, he too shivered. He gazed into the lion's eyes, as if he were looking into the tablet itself, but saw nothing but yellow shadows, fear (his own?), and curiosity.

"Help me find the sapphire tablet," Maria Theresa whispered just loud enough to be heard. She was on her knees, crawling along the ice. "It must be here; it can't have disappeared." And then she said, "Magister, here. It *is* here. Help me dig it out. It is…under the ice." She looked up at Mirandola, a quizzical expression on her face, then back to the tablet, which was almost invisible in the darkness: it appeared as a matte shadow against the inverted blackness of the ice.

Mirandola struck at the ice with his dagger, sending shards flying into the silvery darkness. After a few moments he stopped and said, "No, it's buried too deep under this ice, if, indeed, that's what it is."

"I'm sure it's the tablet," Maria Theresa said.

"No, I meant the ice." He placed his open hand against the ice, then quickly pulled back. "Cold, yet…" He shook his head. "It must be permeable. Or perhaps it isn't material at all. Perhaps it's pure aether, perhaps it's—" He leaned closer to the ice, staring into it, ignoring the numbing ache in his hands and knees, which were in contact with the surface. He had glimpsed *something* in the tablet, but the striations in the ice obscured it. He lowered his head, trying to get a better view. His eyes burned from the cold, ice crystals formed in his nose: he could not remain long in that position. His warm breath fogged the ice, and then he gasped and stood up, slipping, as he did so, almost falling backward.

"What? What did you see?" asked Maria Theresa.

"I can't—I can't be sure, but this place, it belongs to the dark aeon."

"Belias?"

"Yes, and I saw"—he shook his head—"or I think I saw my apprentice Lucian wrestling with him. Wrestling with his vines. Wrestling to the death."

So many vines…

Lucian…

"How could your apprentice be here…and why are *we* here when we should be in the palace?"

Mirandola shook his head distractedly. "He is in dire trouble, but I couldn't determine whether he was holding fast to Belias, or whether he was trapped in Belias' embrace." But how could Lucian have the strength to hold onto an aeon? he asked himself. There must be more which I cannot discern. He knelt over the tablet once again, braving the numbing cold to try to gaze through the haziness of the ice; but the image—or presentiment, if, indeed, that's what it was—had passed; he could see nothing but glace swirls; but he could feel a tremor in the ice, which groaned as if crying for release. Would it try to pull itself apart or thrust its great mass upward?

"Did you feel *that*?" he asked Maria Theresa.

"We must retrieve the tablet," Maria Theresa said, insistent. Although she indeed felt something shift, she ignored his question. "We have to get back to the palace. We must help the daughter of light. That was the purpose of all of this."

"And what would you propose I do?" Mirandola asked, digging at the ice again. "I cannot free it."

"Perhaps your apprentice can."

"I fear that even if he enlisted the aid of Gabriel himself, he would remain enchained."

"Well, whether that be true or not, we must do *something*."

Mirandola laughed reflexively, more a bark of fear. She's right, he thought. Somehow, we must try to help Lucian; but before he could stand up, another tremor cracked through the ice, creating crystalline shatter-webs, turning it opaque.

Maria Theresa slipped, regained her balance, and said, "Magister... someone approaches."

Could it be? Mirandola asked himself, disbelieving his eyes, which discerned a phantom stepping out of the frozen darkness.

"*Pietro...?*"

Holding the blade shaped flint tightly but carefully in his hand, the archbishop made his way out of the pope's subterranean prison. He hurried through back-corridors and tunnels, through pantries and saltcellars and the many dark secret passageways that were built into walls. He passed through the long and narrow Trionfo Hall, where the polychrome shields and arms of disposed doges hung on the walls as reminders of the victories of the church over the state, and thus entered the pope's private precincts. Guards were everywhere, but the archbishop passed through the galleries and torch-lit hallways without notice or molestation. The guards seemed vacant, as if they were all blinded by a spell; and, indeed, the very air was heavy, for the castle had been blighted, blasted, and beghosted by the lingering shadow of the late Gian Dei. The shadow that the demon Azâzêl had enslaved and programmed for murder.

The archbishop was trying to reach the daughter of light before Dei's shadow; but the flint—the same flint that had cleaved the demon apart and sent it into oblivion—was attracted to its own lodestones: the six flints that Isabella Sabatini carried in her blood, viscera, and pneuma.

The flint subtly directed him to the dimly lit, gold ornamented Hall of the

Scudo where Isabella was waiting for him.

But Dei's shadow was also trying to reach Isabella.

If it was to destroy the daughter of light, it needed to augment its powers. As the shadow could not hope to gain the power that inhered in the sapphire tablet (which Azâzêl had so foolishly and precipitously cast into darkness), it sought to steal the power invested in the flints of the Holy Sepulcher.

"It *is* you, Your Reverence," Isabella called to the archbishop just as he reached the Hall of the *Scudo*. She stood in the center of the high-ceilinged and windowed room, which appeared to be submerged in soft, watery light: the day's last long rays. Candles in sconces cast bright circles of light, revealing the silvery motes of dust that danced furiously inside the golden aureoles. "I heard the voices of angels directing me here to find you, and yet it was no dream, for here you are, *Miracolo*."

She smiled at him; and in the flickering candle-light, her curly hair was like a dark halo framing her pale, beautiful face. Then sensing another presence she turned to Dei's shadow, which seemed to materialize out of her own pale shadow. "And you...why you are here, too, Magister Dei," she said, suddenly frightened.

"Step away from there, Isabella," shouted the archbishop as he lunged toward her. "Back away!" but too late, for Dei's shadow was already upon her, stepping into her, possessing her, wearing her like clothes. She let out a strangled cry; and then suddenly, with preternaturally enhanced agility, she turned upon the onrushing archbishop, wresting the flint from his hand and slashing it deftly across his throat.

Francesco Salviati's arterial blood spurted upon her white satin gown.

Almost instantly the numbing chill of death eased his pain, terror, intentions, and desire. He mouthed a last apology to the aeon Athoth, the aeon whom he had failed, the aeon who had given him his penultimate epiphany.

Although the archbishop had expected to fall into light, his eyes closed upon darkness as Isabella, now hollowed out and owned by what had once been the familiar of the magus Gian Dei, made her way quickly back to the apartments she shared with her mistress, the daughter of light.

"**C**an it really be you, Pietro?" Mirandola asked the figure approaching him and Maria Theresa.

"Yes, Maestro, it is me," Pietro said, stepping carefully over the frozen ridges of shallow craters that shimmered like satin in the glassy darkness of Hell; he nodded to Mirandola's companion, as if he knew who she was.

Behind him, in the far distance, silvery mountain peaks disappeared into a starless, stygian sky.

"No, Pietro," Mirandola said, accusing. "It cannot be."

Pietro smiled deferentially at his old master and said, "Truly, it is I who speaks to you, Maestro. Just now the aeon who inhabits me listens."

"Aeon?" asked Maria Theresa.

Pietro bowed, but his smile was not his own. "*I am also known as Athoth, little sister. You dreamed of me when you escaped the burning convent.*"

"I can't remember—", but as she spoke Pietro/Athoth touched her cheek; and she felt suddenly faint and also angry, for she felt the invasive connection: the aeon pierced her thoughts, memories, beliefs, and humiliations, lighting all her dark corners with a gentle, yet scouring persistence; and as she pulled away from him, she felt his pity overwhelming her, felt his frightening aspect, comprehending that he was as large and extensive as the icy ground upon which she stood and the black heavens above her; and she suddenly remembered what had been hidden in her dream. She kneeled before him, asked for forgiveness, and said, "Yes, *angelus*, I remember."

The ground suddenly shivered and pitched, and Mirandola—catching his balance—could hear a thunderous cracking as ice sheets parted. Tiny veins also radiated outward from the ice directly below him. Athoth/Pietro motioned him to step aside and, kneeling over the area where the sapphire tablet was buried, pushed his hand through the ice as if it were nothing but still water. He pulled out the tablet, snapped it in two as Lucian had once done to a similar wafer of pure sapphire, and, handing half of it to Maria Theresa, said, "Here is what you are looking for, little sister."

She held the tablet against her chest, feeling its familiar warmth and a concomitant enervating weakness. "But why did you—?"

"*I—we—cannot remain here with you,*" the aeon said, turning back to Mirandola. "*We have made our choice, and now you, both of you, must make yours.*"

"And what choice have you made?" Mirandola asked, hearing Athoth's words inside his head as well as seeing Pietro's lips move.

"We seek Lucian, who, as you know, is here," Pietro said: his face no longer looked boyish; his expression was one of sadness, perhaps resignation. "And while we try to help him restrain and perhaps even subdue Belias—"

"I will help you!" Mirandola said, interrupting. "If the presentiment I saw earlier is true, there is no time to waste."

"*There is time,*" said Athoth, "*for we are isolated, hidden in time, or what you might think of as time. But you, and you*"—nodding to Maria Theresa—"*have different destinies spread before you.*" Again, an expression of deep sadness passed across Pietro's face, the face that Athoth was just now wearing.

"Can you *see* what will happen?" asked Maria Theresa. "Do you know whether—"

"*Do you wish to help the daughter of light?*"

"Why, yes, of course I do."

"*Then go and find her. Now!*"

"How?"

"*Just as you tried to do before.*"

Maria Theresa seemed puzzled for an instant, then, nodding, she placed her half of the sapphire tablet on the ice. "And what am I to do?" she asked the aeon.

"*Find the daughter of light. Help her.*"

"But...how?"

The aeon turned away from her, and Maria Theresa gasped at the loss of his attention. But then she heard the shadowy whisper of a voice inside her head, an echo, a distant entreaty.

"*Help me, help me, Holy Mother.*"

Could that even be meant for me? she asked herself, then nodding to herself in acceptance, she stepped onto and into the tablet lying before her: it was as small as a hand span and as large as a doorway. But she was not to leave alone, for to Mirandola's surprise, the lion leaped into the tablet after her.

And even as Mirandola grasped his half of the tablet and prayed for Maria Theresa to have a safe destiny, he could not help but feel an even greater pang of loss for the lion whose senses he had shared...whose eyes he had peered through.

"*And you, Magister,*" asked Athoth, breaking through Mirandola's reverie by asking the same question he had once asked Lucian and Pietro, "*are you willing to die? Are you prepared to lose both your celestial soul and your terrestrial body, with no hope of redemption or deliverance?*"

Mirandola turned to his beautiful, blue-eyed, club-footed young apprentice, and even though he sensed the presence of a being as old as eternity, he said, "For what cause would you ask such a thing of me? To set upon Belias? Have I not already told you that I—"

Athoth's displeasure flashed in Pietro's blue eyes; and Mirandola gasped, trying to catch his breath. When breath returned once again, he genuflected and said, "Forgive my impertinence, Angelus. Please accept my apology. I don't know what came over me."

"*I speak to you now, Maestro.*"

"Is it you...Pietro?"

"Yes, Maestro."

"How can you contain such...such power, such...largeness?"

Pietro smiled grimly. "You hold such largeness in your hands," he said, indicating Mirandola's tablet. "But are you prepared to use it, Maestro?"

"What would you have me do?"

"It is not what *I* would have you do. It is what you must *choose* to do."

"And that would be?"

"*To descend into the abyss of souls—*" answered the aeon; and Mirandola heard those words as a terrible, irresistible music: a plangent Kyrie of necessity and conviction. And before the theurgist could respond, the aeon continued "*—and release them.*" Mirandola looked upon the face of his young apprentice and listened to Athoth's plan.

The distant ringing of bells: the voice of the aeon.

The soft clap of a death knell...or perhaps of redemption.

"*Do you understand, Magister, that you—like ourselves—may be confined here for eternity...?*" asked Athoth. "*Think carefully.*"

"Do you agree, Maestro...?" asked Pietro; his face, no longer young, reflected his profound sadness. The theurgist nodded and bade goodbye to the last aeon and the last mortal he would ever expect to see. Setting the tablet before him, he disappeared into its sapphire depths.

"*O, Domine, mittas lucem tuam, que me ducant.*"

Oh, my Lord, please send your light to lead me.

And for an instant, as if in answer to his prayer, Mirandola once again looked through the eyes of the lion: as he fell into the deepest and darkest crevasse of Belias' frozen hell, a mountain inverted, he glimpsed flickering, candlelit images which were now a world—an eternity—away.

The prioress Arcangela Dolabella had no intention of returning to her convent.

She left the subterranean prison cell moments after the archbishop, yet would reach the apartments of the daughter of light even before Isabella, for she had memorized the floor plans of the papal palace: generations of nuns had contributed the puzzle pieces, the myriad bits of secret information; and she had created her own mnemonic, her own palace of memory, a mental map that contained every secret passage, closet, room, tunnel, and hidden corridor in the residence. She didn't need light to navigate, for her mnemonic acted as an overlay lighting her way; and had the archbishop given her a moment to question him about his intentions instead of disappearing like a cheap stage magician, she could have directed him along the quickest route to whatever his destination.

No matter now, she thought.

He would do whatever he must; but she...she would direct herself to the daughter of light. Old woman she may be, and certainly helpless against the demonomagic of Gian Dei's purloined shadow, but she could move quickly—and invisibly, as Dei had taught her all those years ago—and if she could reach the daughter of light before the shadow, then perhaps, just perhaps...

The prioress found an audit ingeniously concealed behind a convex cistern wall. She worked its locking mechanism until a faux wall opened, revealing a secret lifting device built for the last pope from specifications found in a stolen copy of al-Muradi's *Book of Secrets*. Once she stepped into the narrow, confined space before her—once she stepped onto a creaking wooden platform, the audit groaned back into position. Now she was trapped between four closely set walls. Using all her weight and strength, she pulled on the plumbed pulley ropes that disappeared into the darkness above her. Pulled herself upward. One level click two levels click; and as the platform juddered to a stop, she could feel a slight but welcome breeze, a wafting of stale air.

It was pitch dark; not even a crack of light was visible.

Before her was a secret tunnel that led to the pope's apartments...and the guest accommodation where the daughter of light was quartered.

The prioress listened for voices or movement. Satisfied that all was clear, she walked quickly. Walked as if she could see through the darkness.

Rats scurried before her, and she imagined she could smell the acrid talcum of desiccated corpses: no doubt rodents or birds. It should be about here, she thought, feeling for the indentations of a panel, then manipulating the release mechanism.

Her eyes blinked in the soft light streaming through the small glass circlets under the vaulted ceiling, and the false glamour that permeated the palace—the miasmas that she had been resisting with cantrips taught to her by Gian Dei—by her lover Jack Day— so very long ago—seemed markedly stronger here in the bedchamber of the daughter of light. But so was the awakening power and reincarnated presence of the aeon Sophia, which inhered in the young woman who was born Louisa Mary Morgan.

"I can see you, I can hear you, Holy Mother, but I can't wake up," called a voice, just above a whisper, from behind the canopied curtains of a bed. "Help me, help me, Holy Mother." And then the voice continued—"Oh, dear, where am I, lost, lost in"—then stopped midsentence.

The prioress felt a chill feather up her spine, as she was reminded of the soulless guard. "How could you know me...see me?" she asked, moving tentatively closer to the curtained bed until she was close enough to open the woven tapestries that were hung from iron rods and served as bed curtains. "*Fiat voluntas Dei*," she whispered, parting the curtains. She blinked, as if she had just looked into the pure, burning light of the sun; and for a blinding, vertiginous instant, she felt that she had fallen from a precipice: a precipice so high that had she had time to think and pray, she might relive her entire life before she would be broken on whatever reefs lay hidden far below. Yet physically the daughter of light appeared small and vulnerable to Mother Dolabella's cataract-clouded eyes. Her curly red hair was spread like a mantle over the pillows that supported her head. A dimple appeared and reappeared on the side of her face: a slight muscle contraction synchronized with the beat of her heart. She wore a thin *camisa* sleeping gown, and the prioress could see her breasts rising and falling with the slow rhythm of deep sleep.

The daughter of light turned toward the prioress as if she were indeed waking up; but her eyes were closed: she was seeing the old woman through the eyes of dream. "I'm learning who I was...am"—she shuddered, her eyes opening, then closing—"and will be." After a beat, she said in a barely audible voice, "I'm waking to myself, but I cannot...cannot awaken to—", and, turning away from the prioress, whispered, "You must leave now, Holy Mother, you must—" She sighed and said, "Oh, sapphire one, oh, Gabriel, have you lost yourself in those who have taken your parts? Have you lost yourself in *materia*? Are you the doorway, are you the—?"

"You must awaken, little daughter," the prioress said, trying to wake her up, shaking her gently, then more vigorously. "We must leave this place now. I know the way. You must escape—" Suddenly the atmosphere thickened... darkened; and the prioress turned just as Isabella entered the room, her blood-spattered chemise wet with the archbishop's blood.

The daughter of light spoke to Isabella from her dream; and Isabella, in an instant of recognition, resisted the shadowy force that animated her. She tried to speak, but choked; and then—once more under the shadow's control— she approached the daughter of light, who now opened her snake-green eyes. The prioress tried to step between them; Isabella simply threw her across the room and attacked the daughter of light directly, slashing her throat with the archbishop's blood-crusted flint, just as she had slashed the archbishop. But even though her eyes were now open, even as blood jetted toward the golden ceiling and she shook and shivered in her death throes, the daughter of light seemed to be looking across the room: the prioress, paralyzed with shock and sudden grief, imagined that she was looking directly at her, perhaps trying to reveal something heretofore masked and vital.

But the prioress was wrong, for she could not see that the daughter of light was just now gazing blindly into the depths of one of Gabriel's sapphire tablets.

An instant later, however, the prioress saw something that stopped her heart.

And then she heard a voice speaking to her...a whisper inside her head.

"Bring me the tablet..."

PARTITION EIGHT

Sophia

'But surely you saw past that, Trismegistus.'

'Past what, Rheginus?'

'The Great Darkness.'

'I am no aeon to see through time. To see past scripture.'

'But your dream, Trismegistus, your golden dream. Was that not given to you as epiphany? You, who have been chosen?'

'Blasphemy, Rheginus! It was simply a dream, a broken memory of the night. Divulging it to you, however, was also blasphemy, may He Who Sees All forgive us both.'

'But, Trismegistus, your dream had the texture of truth, both bright and terrible.'

'As do the Gospels of the demiurge, Rheginus.'

—*Excerpt from the Eighth Discourse 57, 19-34*

'How then, Rheginus, would you have me indulge such fancies?'

'By telling me of the resurrection of the daughter of light, Trismegistus.'

'I dreamed of her death.'

'But what of resurrection?'

'I cannot tell you that, Rheginus.'

'Pray, why not, Trismegistus?'

'Because I also dreamed that my heart stopped and my eyes went blind.'

—*Excerpt from the Eighth Discourse 58, 1-11*

TWENTY-SIX

Awakenings

When therefore the mind is separated, and departeth from the earthly body, presently it puts on its fiery coat, which it could not do having to dwell in an earthly body.
—*The Divine Pymander of Hermes Trismegistus*

And in its power hath it made itself ready, so that it may take your lights which are in you, and ye may become dark; and its power hath brought it to pass, so that it may take your power from you and ye go to ground.
—*The Second Book of Pistis Sophia, 79,4*

And so did the theurgist Pico Della Mirandola fall into the black pit of the aeon Belias' heaven, a region so dark, so emptied of substance that it was heavy—dense as it were—with absence. It was bereft of latitude, longitude, width, and perspective; and all that was available for the falling theurgist to perceive was infinite, agonizing depth: he had no proprioceptive sense of descent, no sensation of plunging or sinking. There was no sound, no declension, just the ever-swallowing darkness.

Frozen with terror, Mirandola tried to scream. He opened his mouth to expel the horror twisting inside him, but there was no air in his lungs to expel. No air to breathe. No life, except what he retained in that frozen instant when he had stepped through the sapphire portal. He held the sapphire tablet with both hands, held the thin crystalline wafer of Gabriel's warmth and soul against his chest; but he could not move it, could not shift muscle and bone to push it before him, to force himself back into it, to escape…possibly escape this frozen waste entirely.

The aeon Athoth had known that he was consigning Mirandola to this eternity. That was why he extracted that pledge: "*Are you willing to die? Are you prepared to lose both your celestial soul and your terrestrial body, with no hope of redemption or deliverance?"*

And yet...and yet within this frozen hell, this frozen instant, Mirandola could *imagine* movement, could reconstruct the idea of his mouth opening to scream, could deduce the tearing sounds of inhalation and exhalation. He could close his eyes or, rather, commemorate how he had once been able to do so; and it was thus that he graduated from abject fear to an agony of grief and despair, and then to a more exquisite hell: that of thought without extremity, without emotion or the warming fires that attend lucid recollection. For now memory was but myriad sequences of numbers, and all the frozen instants of his life were simply algorithms that ended here.

One two three four hundred thousand million quadrillion seconds minutes years decades centuries millennia to think cold, barren thoughts.

Endless thoughts.

Could there be an end? he asked himself as he grew into numbers past counting, numbers whose cognate were years, years passing, years crawling so slowly that they confounded all motion and meaning as he, now timeless and fleshless as an equation, fell suspended into the ever-deepening abyss of trapped souls.

It took an eternity to focus his thoughts through the tablet, but focus them he did. He had become a calculation calculating; and he, or the number—the fractions of time that had been Pico Della Mirandola—gazed inwardly at the distant glowing constellations of souls below: the souls he could release and lead through the sapphire sky of the tablet only if Belias could be contained...

Only if the daughter of light could awaken to her true self.

As the theurgist Pico Della Mirandola fell into eternity, into the abyss of souls, Pietro Neroni and the aeon Athoth journeyed across Belias' empty, crystalline wastes.

In a sense Pietro and Athoth were stepping over or passing through the dark aeon's volcanic, thundering body, for Belias and his world—his dark heaven—were the same, each a glittering reflection of the other, a reflection of a reflection, a reflection nested in itself; and if one wished to visualize these moments as Pietro experienced them, one might imagine Athoth, the beautiful aeon Athoth and his club-footed companion Pietro simply walking together. Around them was a darkness so deep and sharp and soul-destroying that the surrounding mountains and cratered ice sheets were simply chiaroscuro contrasts of the same tenebrous void. As Pietro moved through this negative terrain, he imagined that he was looking into (or through) a crystal gazing globe that had been crazed with glittering cracks, so that the darkness within appeared as shards of black, their various changing shapes defined only by slight differences of darkness and edgings of silver.

The darkness was palpable, tactile, numbing; and Pietro experienced a cold yet distant grief as he tried to remember his tender feelings (love?) for the beautiful Isabella as he visualized her heart shaped, freckled face and dark curly hair; and he remembered, yes, he remembered when she had caught him gazing into Maestro Mirandola's gazing globe, which was now part of his soul and viscera; remembered her calling him a heretic in the catacombs of Florence...remembered his prediction that she would betray all her companions.

"*You were right,*" Athoth said.

"About what?"

"*About your inamorata Isabella.*"

"She was never my lover," Pietro said, stung.

"*Only because she wouldn't have you.*"

"You are as cold as...as this place."

Pietro braced himself, but there was no chastising response, only: "*Perhaps I am not so different from Belias,*" Athoth said. "*And you might find that neither are you: an unintended consequence of being in Hell. It freezes the pain of memory and regret.*"

"Tell me, then, what I was right about, angel?" Pietro asked, ignoring what he could not yet bear to hear.

"*That Isabella would betray us.*"

Pietro was about to speak; but all around them the ground shook, cracked, was thrust upward to the deafening sound of crashing thunder; and he fell backward, sprawling onto the ice. He slid onto the lip of a small yet deep crater.

Athoth waited for him to get up.

"*The quakes are increasing. Lucian won't be able to contain Belias,*" Athoth said, matter-of-factly. "*He becomes stronger while Lucian becomes weaker.*" The aeon's eyes were closed, as if he were watching distant events with the blind sight of a heavenly spirit; and his head was cocked, as if he were listening to distant voices. "*The eruptions will become worse.*" Then after a beat he continued, "*But you will find your legs, remembrancer.*"

Pietro recovered himself and planting one foot firmly beside the other, asked, "How...how has Isabella betrayed us?"

"*By murdering the daughter of light.*"

Pietro felt as if he were slipping, falling, again.

"Then...it is over. All has been lost."

"*Perhaps it is...perhaps it isn't.*"

"Well, which is it?" After an instant, he politely added, *"Angelus."*

"That depends on our companions who have passed through the tablet... and on us."

"Then we must hurry."

The aeon's smile was a fleeting sensation of warmth and sadness. *"Yes, remembrancer, we must hurry..."*

And so they made their way across ice fields, through glacé passes and up slopes and braes and craigs and slippery escarpments toward a towering crown of ice that stood between sky-piercing mountain walls to the north. But direction, like time, was merely a mnemonic in the minds of aeons such as Athoth and Belias. In an instant or all the time it would take to approach eternity, they climbed to the crest of the crown; and as they climbed, the world of darkness shivered and quaked around them. Shards of ice rained down from the emptiness above like arrows shot from a thousand longbows: shafts that appeared to Pietro's mind's eye as scratchings of silver dropping out of a starless night.

Below them now was an enormous pit, an adamantine amphitheatre built to contain cities of titans, behemoths, and leviathans; and if one could imagine light enfolded in darkness to reveal shape and movement, it was here. Pietro was staring into negative space, as architecturally beautiful, as intricate as Mazelli's mezzotint engravings of the City of God. Here upon a silver-shot platform which overlooked a cratered structure that was a palace or a country of unnatural extrusions and concretions...here were echoing sounds and frantic movements, here were uncountable snapping, sharp-edged vines, a boiling mass swirling around the aeon Belias, so thick and slippery that they could have been mistaken for some twisting Lernaean hydra, squeezing and crushing its pray in the sunless depths of the sea.

And the prey was Lucian and his sapphire snake, Gabriel's living seal, his soul; and as the vines strangled Lucian, so did Lucian's lone sapphire scaled serpent strangle the dark aeon. The serpent radiated its own warmth, its own light. Inside the gigantic bowl of darkness, golden light; but wan, shriveled, for as Belias gained power and Lucian lost, so did the serpent's natural radiance decay into a thin, curling diffraction no brighter than the last embers in a cold, soot-blackened hearth.

"Too late, too late."

Lucian's thoughts were a whisper inside Pietro's head. The connection was but momentarily reestablished. Pietro called out to Lucian, his voice deadened by the weight of empty darkness. Athoth also answered Lucian's call, his warning, but there was no response.

Lucian was silent.

The serpent's life flickered, flickering out, overcome by vines and darkness and Belias' will; and as Athoth carried Pietro down into the nest of vines that protected Belias and tore at the souls of Lucian and the serpent that had endured within and without him, the ice walls of the amphitheater cracked and fell crashing after them. Belias' ice fields and mountains shook and divided, as if they were all part of an iceberg the size of a universe, an iceberg that was tilting, shifting, slipping into a sea of nothingness.

In that ice storm of an instant, or eternity, Athoth and Pietro stood with Lucian against Belias. They did not speak, for language was now redundant. There was nothing ahead but the task at hand: to repulse Belias' vines, which would weaken them with every passing, every soul draining attack; but there would always be more, a plenum, a world, a universe of vines.

An eternity of vines.

Memory evaporated, leaving only the frozen reality of endless confrontation

There would be no escape for Lucian, for Pietro, for Athoth.

Or for Belias...

The old prioress looked like a crumpled doll thrown against the bedroom wall. Across the dimly-lit room, the dying daughter of light seemed to be staring at her through parted, blood-runneled bed curtains.

Beside the bed stood Isabella Sabatini, her back to the prioress, the flint she had used to stab the daughter of light still in her hand; and as the prioress watched, a dark miasma, a particulate cloud that was Gian Dei's shadow, escaped from Isabella, steamed around her, and assumed the shape of its former master. It was almost invisible in the shifting, dust-swirling light, and the prioress strained to see it...in fact, she could not entirely believe what she was seeing: holding the six flints that Isabella had carried within her like aetheric souls, the shadowy presence plucked the seventh bloodied flint from her hand. For an instant the shadowy presence seemed to shiver with power; then it reached for the daughter of light...reached out to smother and overwhelm her soul before it could fully awaken to itself: the enormously powerful and dangerous soul of the Queen of Heaven and mother of the demiurge, the soul of Sophia, which still dwelled within the flesh of the dying daughter of light.

"O, *Deus, Deus*, what has happened?" Isabella cried wretchedly, now that she was released from the shadow's possession. "What have I done?"

But the prioress was hearing another voice, a voice that spoke directly to her without sound, without breath... It was a whisper inside her head.

It was the daughter of light calling to her.

"*Bring me the tablet...*"

The prioress tried to get up, to stand, to help somehow; but only seconds had passed, and her shocked attention was diverted by a doorway, a rectangle of sapphire, which had appeared beside her. At first she thought the wall itself had split open; but when the huge beast that had accompanied the theurgist Mirandola leaped through the sapphire doorway into the room, followed by the young nun Maria Theresa, she understood and reached for the sapphire tablet which had now resolved itself into an object on the floor, it's top edge resting against the wall.

In that instant, in that shielded disconnected instant when the prioress picked up the tablet, she once again heard the daughter of light. Heard her thoughts.

"*Bring me the tablet…*"

Saw through her dying eyes.

And was privileged to witness the onset of her transformation, her epiphany.

Events and processes that were occurring simultaneously now seemed stretched and isolated, for as she held the tablet, so was she also connected to the angel Gabriel, to this sliver of his soul. As the lion leapt toward the shadow of Gian Dei, the prioress heard the silent words the daughter of light directed toward the tablet, toward Gabriel.

"*Oh, sapphire one, so you are the doorway. Angelus Gabriel…I am ready, I am—*"

She saw the lion clawing at the shadow…

Saw Sister Maria Theresa attack Isabella.

And without volition, without realization, the prioress was on her feet. Holding the tablet like a shield across her chest with her left arm (for her right was broken, inert), she limped across the room in great pain while crying out to Maria Theresa, "No, no, it's not her fault, it's the—"

Too late, for Maria Theresa had expertly broken Isabella's neck; and just then the lion, which was but an arm's length away from the young nun, roared in agony and, as if suddenly and completely eaten by acid, dissolved into something wet and gray, which splashed onto the beautifully patterned parquet floor like gruel dropped from a basin. Realizing her mistake in attacking Isabella instead of the shadowy form, which she could now clearly discern, Maria Theresa tried to interpose herself between the shadow and the still quivering body of the daughter of light. The shadow simply wiped her away as if she were composed of cobwebs instead of blood and bone, and the nun dissolved and spattered like dirty wet snow upon the body of the daughter of light even as the prioress reached out to her.

Reached out to the inanimate daughter of light.

The prioress lowered herself into the shadowy miasma, pressed the sapphire tablet against the daughter of light, and died, died as the daughter of light took her last breath and disappeared into the tablet: just as she had done once before in the Pope's airship. The tablet stretched around her like a cloak; and the last image that the prioress' old eyes registered was the blinding, reawakened soul of the aeon Sophia. It was the embodiment of light: pure and bright and panoptic. It was an unfolding explosion that incinerated souls and matter alike, that rivaled the insinuating power of her misbegotten offspring, the demiurge.

The shadow that was but a draught away from swallowing the aeon's very being became nothing, was eliminated now and before, as Sophia scoured her past and present impediments; and as she did so, the prioress—whose heart had stopped, whose eyes were burning with light, whose soul was lifted into the whiteness that turned her flesh to swirling dust—heard snatches of conversation, words of fire and tangible presence, words that were themselves worlds and universes.

Heard Sophia speaking to her son the demiurge.

The blind creator.

Jehovah.

"*No, my son, my love, my befouled, blinded spawn,*" Sophia whispered as softly as a thunderclap creating and destroying worlds, her words and irradiating thoughts carrying the poignant sadness and weariness of millennia. "*You have not won.*"

"*And neither have you, Pistis Sophia,*" said the demiurge, his words like music, like a breeze suffused with summer scents.

"*I cannot conquer you, my love, my terrible sin. I can only stand in your way and wait…*"

Like the sound of a thousand pens scratching on parchment, he asked, "*And what would you wait for, Mother of Monsters?*"

"*Why for you, my creation, for you…*"

POSTLUDE

After the Cataclysm

'A waken, Trismegistus, awaken.'

'Rheginus, what is the matter? Why do you disturb me at such an early hour?'

'Because, Trismegistus, I feared you were dead.'

'Could you not hear my breath, Rheginus? Could you not see the rising and falling of my chest?'

'No, I could not, Trismegistus. Now, please, tell me what I have said that makes you smile?'

'Perhaps you were right, my young friend. Perhaps I was dead.'

'How could that be, Trismegistus, for you are here and alive?'

'But that was then, Rheginus. And this is now.'

—*Excerpt from the Last Discourse 1,1-27*

TWENTY-SEVEN
The Scales of Circumstance

That with their weight they make the balances
To crack beneath them.

—Dante Alighieri, *The Divine Comedy, Canto XXIII*

Now it is time, time to return home.

—Giordano Bruno, *Gli Eroici Furori*

In that instant, in that eternity when the daughter of light perished and the reincarnated soul of Sophia, the aeon of aeons, the queen of the aeons, awakened to restrain the demiurge and block his plans for annihilating all that was, is, and would be...in that instant the theurgist Pico Della Mirandola stopped falling. He hung suspended—a suspended number in a recursive equation, a thought ever thinking and rethinking, his life past, present, and future focused through sapphire prisms—and watched constellations of souls rising toward him. They grew in brightness as they spun, uncountable lives in uncountable times and dimensions: all on their way upward, rising out of Belias' cavern of souls, escaping to other dark and sunlit places.

All on their way to living fleshy recipients while Mirandola hung suspended in darkness.

And as the theurgist inhaled and exhaled the journeying souls, he dreamed in loops and fractals. He concentrated and calculated and questioned all that was left to him.

"*And what of me...?*

"*And what of Lucian and Pietro and Athoth?*"

But no amount of concentration, no amount of calculation, could break the bonds that held any of them.

"**Y**ou *must* allow me to take you to safety, my queen." The duchess Elisabetta da Montefeltre had been kneeling and praying before receiving the dwarf Achille into her private chapel. Now she stood before a window and gazed out at the town and its sunset blushed hills.

"Guidobaldo used to called this room his *alta quieta*, his lofty quiet," she said. "Did you know that? He gave it to me as a wedding present. It was his favorite room, his retreat."

"Yes, *Duchessa*," Achille said, his heart quickening as he nervously watched her from a respectable distance. She was as fragile as porcelain, and as dark as the man who had killed her husband was blond. Although her face was inclined away from him, it didn't matter, for he had memorized it: her high, unlined forehead; her eyes sad and heavy-lidded; her nose sharp and wide-nostrilled, as if she had just smelled a delicious perfume or sweet dessert; her mouth, naturally rouged and slightly puckered. "It delighted him to see the pleasure this *studiolo* gave you."

"He was generosity itself," she said softly, still distant, still gazing out the window. "And this room still contains him. Can you not sense it?"

Then she took a step backward, grimaced, and made the sign of protection over her heart. Achille could not see what she saw; but he could well imagine, for the sounds of murder and mayhem penetrated the thick castle walls. Although Baldassare's Florentine soldiers had taken back Urbino in the battle that had already become known as "The Midnight Execution", more than a few renegade soldiers, peasants, ruffians, idlers, and mountebanks were still looting and killing anyone who might seem conveniently unfamiliar.

"We must leave, *Duchessa*," Achille insisted. "The First Citizen has offered us his protection." Elisabetta closed the shutters on the offending window and sat down in her favorite chair, indicating Achille to take the stool opposite her.

"Guiliano de Medici was kind enough to visit me. I know that he and his men are leaving." She closed her eyes, tented her hands under her chin, and said, "I would suppose you will now tell me that the Borgia bastard's ten thousand papal troops have already left *Pian del Monte* and will soon be in Urbino."

Achille leaned toward her and said, "Yes, *Duchessa*. I would tell you exactly that. I would also tell you that the duke, may God bless his eternal soul, had ordered me to deliver you to your sister in Mantua, should circumstances demand. And the First Citizen has agreed to do that very thing. You must allow him to preserve your life and honor the cherished memory of *Duca Guidobaldo.*"

"Should circumstances demand," Elisabetta said, repeating what Achille had said as if she were savoring the words. "But I cannot leave my home, Achille, and I certainly cannot leave my husband."

"I don't quite understand what you mean, *Duchessa*, but I can tell you that all is readied: your servants have taken care of everything."

"Certainly not on my order," Elisabetta said, her face stony.

"Forgive me, *Duchessa*, but we have tried not to intrude upon your grief."

She nodded, as if she was impatient. "You were my husband's theurgist, were you not?"

"I was just one of his many household servants and advisors, Madonna."

"I know you were much more than that," she said. "I know you would wish me to leave, but I cannot leave him, Achille."

"But he is...dead, *Duchessa*."

"And so shall I be, if you will help me."

The dwarf stood up, accidentally kicking over the stool. He bowed, apologized, and said, "No, Madonna, no, I cannot. I would not. Surely Duca Guidobaldo would not want you to destroy your soul by committing such a sin."

"Pick up the stool and sit down." Then, looking into his eyes as if Achille were her lover rather than her servant, she said, "It is the only thing I will ever ask you...out of love."

Achille could feel his face burning as if scorched with an iron.

"You know what I intimate," she said. "You have made your feelings for me quite clear over the years you have served your master."

"But *Duchessa*, I never—"

She smiled sadly, a smile that only Leonardo—or memory—could capture, and said, "Prepare a draught for me...and I shall go to my sleep and my husband in your arms."

"No, *Duchessa*, please, I cannot—"

The sounds of church bells cut him off.

Bells ringing, pealing, near and far, clanging from every church and tower high and low.

"What could that be?" asked Elisabetta, distracted. "You'd think it was the Jubilee."

They looked out the great window that overlooked the *Cortile d'Onore*, which was defined by graceful stone arches, looked out at the town's descending streets and alleys and the piazzas, all crowded with soldiers and townspeople, peasants, traders, priests, monks, and acolytes. All were looking up at the sky still glowing with twilight; and from the darkening heavens stars seemed to fall, constellations of stars descending, myriad pinpricks of light, light spinning, spiraling, drifting like spores carried by summer winds, each intensity a soul attracted to its mortal lodestone; and the air was filled with warmth and fire; and the crowds grew as those who had lost their souls and still lived were found and restored.

The bells stopped ringing.

Sudden silence, silence and awe—

Which was punctuated but once by a distant roaring.

"What is that?" Elisabetta asked, dazed, her eyes filled with light.

"I don't know," Achille said, experiencing sight and sound as if in a dream. "But it sounds like...a lion."

L ouisa Mary Morgan stood on the deck of a barge being towed by her father's ship , which had been commissioned to transfer a fully-inflated twenty-four foot diameter hydrogen balloon from the Richmond Gas Works to General Langdon at Chuffin's Bluff. Beside her was her friend: the young aeronaut Lawrence Dunean of the Balloon Corps of the Confederate States of America. She could not help but notice how handsome he looked in his yellow-gray uniform with blue silk shoulder straps; neither could he help but notice how pretty she looked in her muslin cap and floral print calico dress. And when the field batteries of the Union army, which were positioned on the far bank of the James River, fired a thunderous volley, immediately answered by a 24-pounder howitzer mounted on the deck of her father's paddle-wheeler, he put his arm protectively around her shoulder and said, "It will be all right, child. The Yanks will stop shooting now. It's all over."

She looked at all the activity across the muddy banks. The Union soldiers were already getting drunk, dancing with each other and with the camp whores, shouting and singing as if they had never ever aimed a gun at a rebellionist man, woman, or child. "Does this mean that the war is really over?" she asked.

He smiled and nodded.

"But we...we didn't win."

"Neither did they. That's the point."

But the bluebelly bastards killed my mother, she said to herself.

"General Longstreet says it's being called an extended truce," he continued. "The Yanks are calling it the Union Armistice, whatever the hell that means." Then he motioned toward the paddle-wheeler and said, "Your Daddy's waving to you."

Louisa waved back at her father; and when his attention was taken up once again by the Union officers who had come aboard, she asked, "So what's going to happen to the balloon?"

"Well," said Major Dunean, "me and my corpsmen are going to take it up and back to Richmond for the celebrations."

"Can I come along with you?"

"No, child, *you're* going with your Daddy, who's supposed to be taking some of the wounded soldiers back to Richmond. So I expect we'll be seeing each other there…if, of course, your Daddy approves."

Louisa smiled modestly and thought, *I'm sure he'll approve.*

But instead of experiencing an urgent flood of joy and satisfaction (for she was sure she was in love with him), she felt bereft and unnerved: it was as if the deafening cannonade had started again…as if it was the very sound of grief; and she just wanted to close her eyes and put her hands over her ears. She whispered "Mommy" and looked up at the guileless blue sky. *That's what I heard: the sky cracking, breaking*; and, indeed, for an instant she imagined that she could see an ugly crack dividing God's heaven into two perfect sapphire hemispheres.

"Louisa?" asked Major Dunean, concerned. "Did you say something."

She turned to him and smiled sadly. "No, Lawrence, I was just thinking of my mother and…" Her voice trailed off. She looked up at the sky once again, but saw only a few streamers of pure white cirrus below its opaque surface.

"Your pain will lessen with time."

She nodded, listening to the silent cannonade inside her head and feeling an overwhelming sadness and sense of loss, as if she had left something—or someone—behind.